Praise for #1 *New York Times* bestselling author

NORA ROBERTS

"You can't bottle wish fulfillment, but Nora Roberts certainly knows how to put it on the page."

—*New York Times*

"Nora Roberts is among the best."

—*Washington Post*

"Her stories have fueled the dreams of twenty-five million readers."

—*Entertainment Weekly*

"When Roberts puts her expert fingers on the pulse of romance, legions of fans feel the heartbeat."

—*Publishers Weekly*

"America's favorite writer."

—*New Yorker*

"Roberts…is at the top of h̶e̶r̶

—*People* magazine

Dear Reader,

The Stars of Mithra miniseries by the incomparable master of romantic suspense Nora Roberts revolves around strong heroines and the priceless gems that are destined to bring them lasting, passionate love. We began with *Hidden Star*, which we were delighted to feature in the recent volume *Midnight Shadows*. Here we wrap up the trilogy with the final two books in the miniseries!

The adventure continues in *Captive Star*, when cynical bounty hunter Jack Dakota goes after bail jumper M.J. O'Leary, only to discover that she's innocent—and they've both been set up. Now, handcuffed together, they must go on the run from a pair of hired killers after the giant blue gem hidden in M.J.'s purse.

Secret Star is a fitting conclusion to this captivating miniseries. Lieutenant Seth Buchanan is shocked when a murder victim turns up—alive—at the crime scene where she supposedly died. Grace Fontaine is keeping deadly secrets, but with a killer at large, she'll have to start talking.

We don't want to give anything away, but we will say this: you're in for the ride of your life—and that's after one of the best openings ever.

Enjoy!

The Editors

Silhouette Books

NORA ROBERTS

SECRET GETAWAY

Includes *Captive Star* & *Secret Star*

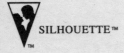 SILHOUETTE™

Recycling programs for this product may not exist in your area.

Secret Getaway

ISBN-13: 978-1-335-42599-7

Copyright © 2022 by Harlequin Enterprises ULC

Captive Star
First published in 1997. This edition published in 2022.
Copyright © 1997 by Nora Roberts

Secret Star
First published in 1998. This edition published in 2022.
Copyright © 1998 by Nora Roberts

For questions and comments about the quality of this book, please contact us at CustomerService@Harlequin.com.

Silhouette
22 Adelaide St. West, 41st Floor
Toronto, Ontario M5H 4E3, Canada
www.Harlequin.com

Printed in U.S.A.

CONTENTS

CAPTIVE STAR

To independent women

Chapter 1

He'd have killed for a beer. A big, frosty mug filled with some dark import that would go down smoother than a woman's first kiss. A beer in some nice, dim, cool bar, with a ball game on the tube and a few other stool-sitters who had an interest in the game gathered around.

While he staked out the woman's apartment, Jack Dakota passed the time fantasizing about it.

The foamy head, the yeasty smell, the first gulping swallow to beat the heat and slake the thirst. Then the slow savoring, sip by sip, that assured a man all would be right with the world if only politicians and lawyers would debate the inevitable conflicts over a cold one at a local pub while a batter faced a count of three and two.

It was a bit early for drinking, at just past one in the

afternoon, but the heat was so huge, so intense and the cooler full of canned sodas just didn't have quite the same punch as a cold, foamy beer.

His ancient Oldsmobile didn't run to amenities like air-conditioning. In fact, its amenities were pathetically few, except for the pricey, earsplitting stereo he'd installed in the peeling faux-leather dash. The stereo was worth about double the blue book on the car, but a man had to have music. When he was on the road, he enjoyed turning it up to scream and belting them out with the Beatles or the Stones.

The muscle-flexing V-8 engine under the dented gutter-gray hood was tuned as meticulously as a Swiss watch, and got Jack where he wanted to go, fast. Just now the engine was at rest, and as a concession to the quiet neighborhood in northwest Washington, D.C., he had the CD player on murmur while he hummed along with Bonnie Raitt.

She was one of his rare bows to music after 1975.

Jack often thought he'd been born out of his own time. He figured he'd have made a pretty good knight. A black one. He liked the straightforward philosophy of might for right. He'd have stood with Arthur, he mused, tapping his fingers on the steering wheel. But he'd have handled Camelot's business his own way. Rules complicated things.

He'd have enjoyed riding the West, too. Hunting down desperadoes without all the nonsense of paperwork. Just track 'em down and bring 'em in.

Dead or alive.

These days, the bad guys hired a lawyer, or the state gave them one, and the courts ended up apologizing to them for the inconvenience.

We're terribly sorry, sir. Just because you raped, robbed and murdered is no excuse for infringing on your time and civil rights.

It was a sad state of affairs.

And it was one of the reasons Jack Dakota hadn't gone into police work, though he'd toyed with the idea during his early twenties. Justice meant something to him, always had. But he didn't see much justice in rules and regulations.

Which was why, at thirty, Jack Dakota was a bounty hunter.

You still hunted down the bad guys, but you worked your own hours and got paid for a job and didn't answer to a lot of bureaucratic garbage.

There were still rules, but a smart man knew how to work around them. Jack had always been smart.

He had the papers on his current quarry in his pocket. Ralph Finkleman had called him at eight that morning with the tag. Now, Ralph was a worrier and an optimist—a combination, Jack thought, that must be a job requirement for a bail bondsman. Personally, Jack could never understand the concept of lending money to complete strangers—strangers who, since they needed bond, had already proved themselves unreliable.

But there was money in it, and money was enough motivation for most anything, he supposed.

Jack had just come back from tracing a skip to North Carolina, and had made Ralph pitifully grateful when he hauled in the dumb-as-a-post country boy who'd tried to make his fortune robbing convenience stores. Ralph had put up the bond—claimed he'd figured the kid was too stupid to run.

Jack could have told him, straight off, that the kid was too stupid *not* to run.

But he wasn't being paid to offer advice.

Jack had planned to relax for a few days, maybe take in a few games at Camden Yards, pick one of his female acquaintances to help him enjoy spending his fee. He'd nearly turned Ralph down, but the guy had been so whiny, so full of pleas, he didn't have the heart.

So he'd gone into First Stop Bail Bonds and picked up the paperwork on one M. J. O'Leary, who'd apparently decided against having her day in court to explain why she shot her married boyfriend.

Jack figured she was dumb as a post, as well. A good-looking woman—and from her photo and description, she qualified—with a few working brain cells could manipulate a judge and jury over something as minor as plugging an adulterous accountant.

It wasn't like she'd killed the poor bastard.

It was a cream-puff job, which didn't explain why Ralph had been so jumpy. He'd stuttered more than usual, and his eyes had danced all over the cramped, dusty office.

But Jack wasn't interested in analyzing Ralph. He wanted to wrap up the job quickly, get that beer and start enjoying his fee.

The extra money from this quick one meant he could snatch up that first edition of *Don Quixote* he'd been coveting, so he'd tolerate sweating in the car for a few hours.

He didn't look like a man who hunted up rare books or enjoyed philosophical debates on the nature of man. He wore his sun-streaked brown hair pulled back in a stubby ponytail—which was more a testament to his distrust of barbers than a fashion statement, though the sleek look enhanced his long, narrow face, with its slashing cheekbones and hollows. Over the shallow dent in his chin, his mouth was full and firm, and looked poetic when it wasn't curled in a sneer.

His eyes were razor-edged gray that could soften to smoke at the sight of the yellowing pages of a first-edition Dante, or darken with pleasure at a glimpse of a pretty woman in a thin summer dress. His brows were arched, with a faintly demonic touch accented by the white scar that ran diagonally through the left and was the result of a tangle with a jackknife wielded by a murderer in the second who hadn't wanted Jack to collect his fee.

Jack had collected the fee, and the skip had sported a broken arm and a nose that would never be the same unless the state sprang for rhinoplasty.

Which wouldn't have surprised Jack a bit.

There were other scars. His long, rangy body had the marks of a warrior, and there were women who liked to coo over them.

Jack didn't mind.

He stretched out his yard-long legs, cracked the tightness out of his shoulders and debated popping the top on another soft drink and pretending it was a beer.

When the MG zipped by, top down, radio blasting, he shook his head. Dumb as a post, he thought—though he admired her taste in music. The car jibed with his paperwork, and the quick glimpse of the woman as she'd flown by confirmed it. The short red hair that had been blowing in the breeze was a dead giveaway.

It was ironic, he thought as he watched her unfold herself out of the little car she'd parked in front of him, that a woman who looked like that should be so pathetically stupid.

He wouldn't have called her easy on the eyes. There didn't look to be anything easy about her. She was a tall one—and he did have a weakness for long-legged, dangerous women. Her narrow teenage-boy hips were hugged by a pair of faded jeans that were white at the stress points and ripped at the knee. The T-shirt tucked into the jeans was plain white cotton, and her small, unhampered breasts pressed nicely against the soft fabric.

She hauled a bag out of the car, and Jack received a interesting view of a firm female bottom in tight denim. Grinning to himself, he patted a hand on his heart. Small wonder some slob had cheated on his wife for this one.

She had a face as angular as her body. Though it was milkmaid-pale, to go with the flaming cap of hair, there was nothing of the maid about it. Pointed chin and pointed cheekbones combined to create a tough, sexy face tilted off center by a lush, sensual mouth.

She was wearing dark wraparound shades, but he knew her eyes were green from the paperwork. He wondered if they'd be like moss or emeralds.

With an enormous shoulder bag hitched on one shoulder, a grocery bag cocked on her hip, she started toward him and the apartment building. He let himself sigh once over her loose-limbed, ground-eating stride.

He sure did go for leggy women.

He got out of the car and strolled after her. He didn't figure she'd be much trouble. She might scratch and bite a bit, but she didn't look like the kind who'd dissolve into pleading tears.

He really hated when that happened.

His game plan was simple. He could have taken her outside, but he hated public displays when there were other choices. So he'd push himself into her apartment, explain the situation, then take her in.

She didn't look like she had a care in the world, Jack noted as he stepped into the building behind her. Did she really figure the cops wouldn't check out the homes of her friends and associates? And driving her own car to shop for groceries. It was amazing she hadn't already been picked up.

But then, the cops had enough to do without scrambling after a woman who'd had a spat with her lover.

He hoped her pal who lived in the apartment wasn't home. He'd kept the windows under surveillance for the best part of an hour, and he'd seen no movement. He'd heard no sound when he took a lazy walk under the open third-floor windows, and he'd wandered inside to listen at the door.

But you could never be too sure.

Since she turned away from the elevator, toward the stairs, so did he. She never glanced back, making him figure she was either supremely confident or had a lot on her mind.

He closed the distance between them, flashed a smile at her. "Want a hand with that?"

The dark glasses turned, leveled on his face. Her lips didn't curve in the slightest. "No. I've got it."

"Okay, but I'm going a couple flights up. Visiting my aunt. Haven't seen her in—damn—two years. Just blew into town this morning. Forgot how hot it got in D.C."

The glasses turned away again. "It's not the heat," she said, her voice dry as dust, "it's the humidity."

He chuckled at that, recognizing sarcasm and annoyance. "Yeah, that's what they say. I've been in Wisconsin the past few years. Grew up here, though, but I'd forgotten... Here let me give you a hand."

It was a smooth move, easing in as she shifted the bag to slip her key into the lock of the apartment door. Equally smooth, she blocked with her shoulder, pushed the door open. "I've got it," she repeated, and started to kick the door shut in his face.

He slid in like a snake, took a firm hold on her arm. "Ms. O'Leary—" It was all he got out before her elbow cracked into his chin. He swore, blinked his vision clear and dodged the kick to the groin. But it had been close enough to have him swiftly changing his approach.

Explanations could damn well wait.

He grabbed her, and she turned in his arms, stomped down hard enough on his foot to have stars springing into his head. And that was before she backfisted him in the face.

Her bag of groceries had gone flying, and she delivered each blow with a quick expulsion of breath. Initially he blocked her blows, which wasn't an easy matter. She was obviously trained for combat—a little detail Ralph had omitted.

When she went into a fighting crouch, so did he.

"This isn't going to do you any good." He hated thinking he was going to have to deck her—maybe on that sexy pointed chin. "I'm going to take you in, and I'd rather do it without messing you up."

Her answer was a swift flying kick to his midsection he wished he'd been able to admire from a distance. But he was too busy crashing into a table.

Damn, she was good.

He expected her to bolt for the door, and was up on the balls of his feet quickly to block her. But she merely circled him, eyes hidden behind the dark glasses, mouth curled in a grimace.

"Come on, then," she taunted him. "Nobody tries to mug me on my own turf and walks away."

"I'm not a mugger." He kicked away a trio of firm, ripe peaches that had spilled out of her bag. "I'm a skip tracer, and you're busted." He held up a hand, signaling peace, and, hoping her gaze had flickered there, moved in fast, hooked a foot under her leg and sent her sprawling on her butt.

He tackled her, and might have appreciated the long, economical lines of her body pressed beneath him, but her knee had better aim than her initial kick. His eyes rolled, his breath hissed, as the pain only a man understands radiated in sick waves. But he hung on.

He had the advantage now, and she knew it. Vertical, she was fast, and her reach was nearly as long as his and the odds were more balanced. But in a wrestling match, he outweighed her and outmuscled her. It infuriated her enough to have her resorting to dirty tactics. She fixed her teeth in his shoulders like a bear trap, felt the adrenaline and satisfaction rush through her as he howled.

They rolled, limbs tangling, hands grappling, and crashed into the coffee table. A wide blue bowl filled with chocolate drops shattered on the floor. A shard pierced his undamaged shoulder and made him swear again. She landed a blow to the side of his head, another to his kidneys.

She was just beginning to think she could take him, after all, when he flipped her over. She landed with a jarring smack, and before she could suck in breath, he had her hands locked behind her back and was sitting on her.

The fact that his breath was coming in pants was very little satisfaction. And for the first time, she was seriously afraid.

"Don't know why the hell you shot the guy, when you could've just beat the hell out of him," Jack muttered. He reached into his back pocket for his cuffs, swore again when he came up empty. They'd popped out during the match.

He simply rode her out as she bucked, and caught his breath. He hadn't had a fight of this magnitude with a female since he hunted down Big Betsy. And she'd been two hundred pounds of sheer muscle.

"Look, it's only going to be harder on you this way. Why don't you just go quietly, before we bust up any more of your friend's apartment?"

"You're crushing me, you jerk," she said between her teeth. "And this is my apartment. You try to rape me, and I'll twist your pride clean off and hand it to you. There won't be enough left of you for the cops to scrape off their shoes."

"I don't force women, sugar. Just because some accountant couldn't keep his hands off you doesn't mean I can't. And the cops aren't interested in me. They want you."

She blew out a breath, tried to suck another in, but he was crushing her lungs. "I don't know what the hell you're talking about."

He pulled the papers out of his pocket, shoved them in front of her face. "M. J. O'Leary, assault with a deadly, malicious wounding, and blah-blah. Ralph's real disappointed in you, sugar. He's a trusting man and didn't expect a nice woman like you to try to skip out on the ten-K bond."

"This is a crock." She could see her name and some downtown address on what appeared to be some kind of arrest warrant. "You've got the wrong person. I didn't post bail for anything. I haven't been arrested, and I live here. Idiot cops," she muttered, and tried to buck him off again. "Call in to your sergeant, or whatever. Straighten this out. And when you do, I'm suing."

"Nice try. And I suppose you've never heard of George MacDonald."

"No, I haven't."

"Then it was really rude of you to shoot him." He eased up just enough to flip her faceup, then caught both of her hands at the wrist. She'd lost her glasses, he noted, and her eyes were neither moss nor emerald, he decided—they were dark shady-river green. And, just now, full of fury. "Look, you want to have a hot affair with your accountant, sister, it's no skin off my nose. You want to shoot him, I don't particularly care. But you skip bond, and it ticks me off."

She could breathe slightly easier now, but his hands were like steel bands at her wrists. "My accountant's name is Holly Bergman, and we haven't had a hot affair. I haven't shot anyone, and I haven't *skipped* bond because I haven't *posted* bond. I want to see your ID, ace."

He thought it took a lot of nerve to make demands in her current position. "My name's Dakota, Jack Dakota. I'm a skip tracer."

Her eyes narrowed as they skimmed over his face. She thought he looked like something out of the gritty side of a Western. A cold-eyed gunslinger, a tough-talking gambler. Or...

"A bounty hunter. Well, there's no bounty here, jerk." It wasn't rape, and it wasn't a mugging. The fear that had iced her heart thawed into fresh temper. "You son of a bitch. You break in here, tear up my things, ruin twenty bucks' worth of produce, and all because you can't follow the right trail? Your butt's in a sling, I promise you. When I'm done, you won't be able to trace your own name with a stencil. You won't—" She broke off when he stuck a photo in her face.

It was her face, and the photograph might have been taken yesterday.

"Got a twin, O'Leary? One who drives a '68 MG, license plate SLAINTE, and is currently shacked up with some guy named Bailey James."

"Bailey's a woman," she murmured, staring at her own face while new worries raced in her head. Was this about Bailey, about what Bailey had sent her? What kind of trouble could her friend be in? "And this isn't her apartment, it's mine. I don't have a twin." She looked up into his eyes again. "What's going on? Is Bailey all right? Where's Bailey?"

Under his clamped hands, her pulse had spiked. She was struggling again, with a fresh and vicious energy he knew was brought on by fear. And he was dead certain it wasn't fear for herself.

"I don't know anything about this Bailey except this address is listed under her name on the paperwork."

But he was beginning to smell something, and he didn't like it. He was no longer thinking M. J. O'Leary was dumb as a post. A woman with any brains wouldn't have left herself with so many avenues to be tracked if she was on the run.

Ralph, Jack mused, frowning down into M.J.'s face. Why were you so jumpy this morning?

"If you're being straight with me, we can confirm it quick enough. Maybe it was a clerical mix-up." But he didn't think so. No indeed. And there was an itching at the base of his spine. "Listen," he began, just as the door broke open and the giant roared in.

"You were supposed to bring her out," the giant said, and waved an impressive .357 Magnum. "You're talking too much. He's waiting."

Jack didn't have much time to decide how to play it. The big man was a stranger to him, but he recognized the type. It looked like all bulk and no brains, with the huge bullet head, small eyes and massive shoulders. The gun was big as a cannon and looked like a toy in the ham-size hands.

"Sorry." He gave M.J.'s wrist a quick squeeze, hoping she'd understand it as a sign of reassurance and remain still and quiet. "I was having a little trouble here."

"Just a woman. You were supposed to just bring the woman out."

"Yeah, I was working on it." Jack tried a friendly smile. "Ralph send you to back me up?"

"Come on, up. Up now. We're going."

"Sure. No problem. You won't need the gun now. I've got her under control." But the gun continued to point, its barrel as wide as Montana, at his head.

"Just her." And the giant smiled, floppy lips peeling back over huge teeth. "We don't need you now."

"Fine. I guess you want the paperwork." For lack of anything better, Jack snagged a can of tomato sauce on his way up and winged it. It made a satisfactory crunching sound on the big man's nose. Ducking, Jack rushed forward like a battering ram. It felt a great deal like beating his head against a brick wall, but the force took them both tumbling backward and over a ladder-back chair.

The gun went off, putting a fist-size hole in the ceiling before it flew across the room.

She thought about running. She could have been out of the door and away before either of them untangled. But she thought about Bailey, about what she had weighing down her shoulder bag. About the mess she'd somehow stepped in. And was too mad to run.

She went for the gun and ended up falling backward as Jack flew into her. She cushioned his fall, and he was up fast, springing into the air and landing a double-footed kick in the big man's midsection.

Nice form, M.J. thought, and scrambled to her own feet. She snagged her shoulder bag, spun it over her head and cracked it hard over the sleek, bullet-shaped head.

He went down hard on the sofa, snapping the springs.

"You're wrecking my place!" she shouted, and smacked Jack in the side, simply because she could reach him.

"Sue me."

He dodged a fist the size of a steamship and went in low. Pain sang through every bone as his opponent slammed him into a wall. Pictures fell, glass shattering on the floor. Through his blurred vision he saw the woman charge, a redheaded fireball that flew up and latched like a plague of wasps on the man's enormous back. She used her fists, pounding the sides of his face as he spun wildly and struggled to grab her.

"Hold him still!" Jack shouted. "Damn it, just hold him for a minute!"

Spotting an opening, he grabbed what was left of a table leg and rushed in. He checked his first swing as the duo spun like a mad two-headed top. If he followed through, he might have cracked the back of M.J.'s head open like a melon.

"I said hold him still!"

"You want me to paint a bull's-eye on his face while I'm at it?" With a guttural snarl, she hooked her arms around the man's throat, clamped her thighs like a vise around his wide steel beam of a torso and screamed, "Hit him, for God's sake. Stop dancing around and hit him."

Jack cocked back like a batter with two strikes already on his record and swung full out. The table leg splintered like a toothpick, blood gushed like water in a fountain. M.J. had just enough time to jump clear as the man toppled like a redwood.

She stayed on her hands and knees a minute, gasping for air. "What's going on? What the hell's going on?"

"No time to worry about it." Self-preservation on his mind, Jack grabbed her hand, hauled her to her feet. "This type doesn't usually travel alone. Let's go."

"Go?" She snagged the strap of her purse as he pulled her toward the door. "Where?"

"Away. He's going to be mean when he wakes up, and if he's got a friend, we're not going to be so lucky next time."

"Lucky, my butt." But she was running with him,

driven by a pure instinct that matched Jack's. "You son of a bitch. You come busting into my place, push me around, wreck my home, nearly get me shot."

"I saved your butt."

"I saved *yours!*" She shouted it at him, cursing viciously as they thudded down the stairs. "And when I get a minute to catch my breath, I'm going to take you apart, piece by piece."

They rounded the landing and nearly ran over one of her neighbors. The woman, with helmet hair and bunny slippers, cowered, back against the wall, hands pressed to her deeply rouged cheeks.

"M.J., what in the world—? Were those gunshots?"

"Mrs. Weathers—"

"No time." Jack all but jerked her off her feet as he headed down the next flight.

"Don't you shout at me, you jerk. I'm making you pay for every grape that got smashed, every lamp, every—"

"Yeah, yeah, I get the picture. Where's the back door?" When M.J. pointed down the corridor, he gave a nod and they both slid outside, then around the corner of the building. Screened by some bushes in the front, Jack darted a gaze up and down the street. There was a windowless van less than half a block down, and a small, chicken-faced man in a bad suit dancing beside it. "Stay low," Jack ordered, thankful he'd parked right out front as they ran down the walkway and he all but threw M.J. into the front seat of his car.

"My God, what the hell is this?" She shoved at the can she'd sat on, kicked at the wrappers littering the floor, then joined them when Jack put a hand behind her head and shoved.

"Low!" he repeated in a snarl, and gunned the engine. The faint ping told him the man with the chicken face was using the silenced automatic he'd pulled out.

Jack's car screamed away from the curb, and he two-wheeled it around the corner and shot down the street like a rocket. Tossed like eggs in a broken carton, M.J. rapped her head on the dash, cursed, and struggled to balance herself as Jack maneuvered the huge boat of a car down side streets.

"What the hell are you doing?"

"Saving your butt again, sugar." His eyes flicked to the rearview as he took a hard, tire-squealing right turn. A couple of kids riding bikes on the sidewalk lifted their fists and cheered the maneuver. In instant reaction, Jack flashed a grin.

"Slow this junk heap down." M.J. had to crawl back onto the seat and clutch the chicken stick for balance. "And let me out before you run over some kid walking his dog."

"I'm not going to run over anybody, and you're staying put." He spared her a quick glance. "In case you didn't notice, the guy with the van was shooting at us. And as soon as I make sure we've lost him and find someplace quiet to hole up, you're going to tell me what the hell's going on."

"I don't know what's going on."

He shot her a look. "That's bull."

Because he was sure it was, he took a chance. He swung to the curb again, reached under his seat and came up with spare cuffs. Before she could do more than blink, he had her locked by the wrist to the door handle. No way was she skipping out on him until he knew why he'd just been tossed around by a three-hundred-pound gorilla.

To block out her shouting, and her increasingly imaginative threats and curses, Jack turned up his stereo and drowned her out.

Chapter 2

At the very first opportunity, she was going to kill him. Brutally, M.J. decided. Mercilessly. Two hours before this, she'd been happy, free, wandering around the grocery store like any normal person on a Saturday, squeezing tomatoes. True, she'd been weighed down with curiosity about what she carried in the bottom of her purse, but she'd been sure Bailey had a good reason— and a logical explanation—for sending it to her.

Bailey James always had good reasons and logical explanations for everything. That was only one of the aspects about her that M.J. loved.

But now she was worried—worried that the package Bailey had shipped to her by courier the day before was not only at the bottom of her purse, but also at the bottom of her current situation.

She preferred blaming Jack Dakota.

He'd pushed his way into her apartment and attacked her. Okay, so maybe she'd attacked first, but it was a natural reaction when some jerk tried to muscle you. At least it was M.J.'s natural reaction. She was an ace student in the school of punch first, ask questions later.

It was humiliating that he'd been able to take her down. She had a lot of notches on her fifth-degree black belt, and she didn't like to lose a match.

But she'd pay him back for that later.

All she knew for certain was that he seemed to be at the root of it all. Because of him, her apartment was wrecked, her things tossed every which way. Now they'd gone, leaving the front door open, the lock broken. She didn't form close attachments to things, but that wasn't the point. They were *her* things, and thanks to him, she was going to have to waste time shopping for replacements.

Which was almost as bad as having some gun-wielding punk the size of Texas busting down her door, having to run for her life from her own home, and being shot at.

But all of that, all of it, paled next to one infuriating fact—she was handcuffed to the door handle of an Oldsmobile.

Jack Dakota had to die for that.

Who the hell was he? she asked herself. Bounty hunter, excellent hand-to-hand fighter, slob—she added as she pushed candy wrappers and paper cups around with her foot—and nerveless driver. Under different circumstances, she'd have been impressed by the way he handled the tank of a car, swinging it around curves, screaming around corners, whipping it through yellow lights and zipping onto the Washington Beltway like the leader in a Grand Prix event.

If he'd walked into her bar, she'd have looked twice, she admitted grudgingly. Running a pub in a major city meant more than being able to mix drinks and work the books. It meant being able to size people up quickly, tell the troublemakers from the lonely hearts. And know how to deal with both.

She'd have tagged him as a tough customer. It was in his face. A damn good face, all in all, hard and handsome. Yeah, she'd have looked twice, M.J. thought, teeth gritted, as she looked out the window of the speeding car. Pretty boys didn't interest her much. She preferred a man who looked as though he'd lived, crossed a few lines and would cross a few more.

Jack Dakota fit that bill. She'd gotten a good close look into those eyes—granite gray—and knew that he wasn't one to let a few rules get in his way.

Just what would a man like him do if he knew she was carrying a king's ransom in her battered leather purse?

Damn it, Bailey. Damn it. M.J. fisted her free hand and tapped it restlessly on her knee. Why did you send me the diamond, and where are the other two?

She cursed herself as well, for not going directly to Bailey's door after she came home from closing M.J.'s the night before. But she'd been tired, and she'd figured Bailey was sound asleep. And as her friend was the steadiest, most practical person M.J. knew, she'd simply decided to wait for what she was certain would be a very practical, sensible reason.

Stupid, she told herself now. Why had she assumed Bailey had sent the stone to her simply because she

knew M.J. would be home in the middle of the day
and around to receive the package? Why had she assumed the rock was a fake, a copy, even though the
note that accompanied it asked M.J. to keep it with
her at all times?

Because Bailey just wasn't the kind of woman to
ship off a blue diamond worth more than a million
with no warnings or explanations. She was a gemologist, dedicated, brilliant, and patient as Job. How else
could she continue to work for the creeps who mas-
queraded as her family?

M.J.'s mouth tightened as she thought of Bailey's
stepbrothers. The Salvini twins had always treated
Bailey as though she were an inconvenience, something they were stuck with because their father had
left her a percentage of the business in his will. And,
blindly loyal to family, Bailey had always found ex-
cuses for them.

Now M.J. wondered if they were part of the reason.
Had they tried to pull something? She wouldn't put it
past them, no indeed. But it was hard to believe Timothy and Thomas Salvini would be stupid enough to
try something fancy with the Three Stars of Mithra.

That was what Bailey had called them, and she'd
had a dreamy look in her eyes. Three priceless blue
diamonds, in a golden triangle that had once been held
in the open hands of a statue of the god Mithra, and
now property of the Smithsonian. Salvini, with Bailey's reputation behind it, was to assess, verify and
appraise the stones.

What if the creeps had gotten it into their heads to
keep them?

No, it was too wild, M.J. decided. Better to believe

this whole mess was some sort of mix-up, a mistaken identity tangle.

Much better to concentrate on how she would repay Jack Dakota for ruining her afternoon off.

"You are a dead man." She said it calmly, relishing the words.

"Yeah, well, everybody dies sooner or later." He was heading south on 95, and he was grateful she'd stopped swearing at him long enough to let him think.

"It's going to be sooner in your case, Jack. Lots sooner." The traffic was thick, thanks to the Fourth of July holiday weekend, but it was fast.

How humiliating would it be, she wondered, to stick her head out the window and scream for help? Mortifying, she supposed, but she might have tried it if she'd believed it would work. Better if they could just run into one of the inexplicable traffic snags that stopped cars dead for miles.

Where the hell were the road crews and the rubberneckers who loved them when she needed them?

Seeing nothing but clear sailing for miles, she told herself to deal with Jack "The Idiot" Dakota herself. "If you want to live to see another sunrise, pull this excuse for a car over, uncuff me and let me go."

"Go where?" He flicked his eyes from the road long enough to glance at her. "Back to your apartment?"

"That's my problem, not yours."

"Not anymore, sister. I take it personal, real personal, when someone shoots at me. Since you seem to be the reason why, I'll be keeping you for a while."

If they hadn't been doing seventy, she'd have punched him. Instead, she rattled her chain. "Take these damn things off me."

"Nope."

A muscle twitched in her jaw. "You've stepped in it now, Dakota. We're in Virginia. Kidnapping, crossing state lines. That's federal."

"You came with me," he pointed out. "Now you're staying with me until I get this figured out." The doors rattled ominously as he whipped around an eighteen-wheeler. "And you should be grateful."

"Oh, I should be grateful. You broke into my apartment, knocked me around, busted up my things and have me cuffed to a door handle."

"That's right. If I hadn't, you'd probably be lying in that apartment right now, with a bullet in your head."

"They came after you, ace, not me."

"I don't think so. My debts are paid, I'm not fooling around with anyone's wife, and I haven't pissed anyone off lately. Except for you. Nobody's got a reason to send muscle after me. You, on the other hand..." He skimmed his gaze over her face again. "Somebody wants you, sugar."

"Thousands do," she said, stretched out her long legs as she shifted toward him.

"I'll bet." He didn't give in to the impulse to look at those legs—he just thought about them. "But other than the brainless idiots you'd kick in the heart, you've got someone real interested. Interested enough to set me up, and take me out with you. Ralph, you bastard."

He shoved aside a copy of *The Grapes of Wrath* and a torn T-shirt and snagged his car phone. Steering one-handed, he punched in numbers, then hooked the receiver under his chin.

"Ralph, you bastard," he repeated when the phone was answered.

"D-D-Dakota? That you? You track d-d-down that skip?"

"When I figure my way clear of this, I'm coming for you."

"What—what're you talking about? You find her? Look, it's a straight trace, Jack. I g-g-gave you a plum. Just a c-c-couple's hours' work for full f-f-fee."

"You're stuttering more than usual, Ralph. That won't be a problem after I knock your teeth down your throat. Who wants the woman?"

"Look, I—I—I got problems here. I gotta close early. It's the holiday weekend. I got p-p-personal problems."

"There's no place you can hide. Why the phony paperwork? Why'd you set me up?"

"I got p-p-problems. Big p-p-problems."

"I'm your big problem right now." He tapped the brakes, swung around a convertible and hit the fast lane. "If whoever's pushing your buttons is trying to trace this, I'm in my car, just tooling around." He thought for a moment, then added, "And I've got the woman."

"Jack, listen to me. L-l-listen. Tell me where you are, dump her and d-d-drive away. J-j-just drive. Stay out of it. I wouldn'ta tagged you for the job, 'cept I knew you could handle yourself. Now I'm telling you, stash her somewhere, give me the l-l-location and drive away. Far away. You don't want this."

"Who wants her, Ralph?"

"You don't n-n-need to know. You d-d-don't want to know. Just d-d-do it. I'll throw in five large. A b-b-bonus."

"Five large?" Jack's brows lifted. When Ralph

parted with an extra nickel, it was big. "Make it ten and tell me who wants her, and we may deal."

It pleased him that M.J. protested that with a flurry of curses and threats. It added substance to the bluff.

"T-t-ten!" Ralph squeaked it, stuttered for a full ten seconds. "Okay, okay, ten grand, but no names, and b-b-believe me, Jack, I'm saving your life here. Just t-t-tell me where you're going to stash her."

Smiling grimly, Jack made a pithy and anatomically impossible suggestion, then disconnected.

"Well, sugar, your hide's now worth ten thousand to me. We're going to find a nice, quiet spot so you can tell me why I shouldn't collect."

He zipped off an exit, did a quick turnaround and headed back north.

Her mouth was dry. She wanted to believe it was from shouting, but there was fear clawing at her throat. "Where are you going?"

"Just covering my tracks. They wouldn't get much of a trace on a cellular, but it doesn't hurt to be cautious."

"You're taking me back?"

He didn't look at her, and didn't grin. Though the waver of nerves in her voice pleased him. If she was scared enough, she'd talk. "Ten thousand's a hefty incentive, sugar. Let's see if you can convince me you're worth more alive."

He knew just what he was looking for. He trolled the secondary roads, skimming through the holiday traffic. He'd forgotten it was the Fourth of July weekend. Which was just as well, he thought, as it didn't look like there were going to be a lot of opportunities to kick back with that cold beer and watch any fireworks.

Unless they came from the woman beside him.

She was a firecracker, all right. She had to be afraid by now, but she was holding her own. He was grateful for that. There was nothing more irritating than a whiner. But scared or not, he was certain she'd try to take a chunk out of him at the first opportunity.

He didn't intend to give her one.

With any luck, once they were settled, he'd have the full story out of her within a couple hours.

Then maybe he'd help her out of her jam. For a fee, that is. It could be a small one because at this point he was ticked and figured he had a vested interest in dealing with whoever had set him on her.

Whoever it was, they'd gone to a great deal of trouble. But they hadn't picked their goons very well. He could figure the scam well enough. Once he captured his quarry and had her secured and in his car, the men in the van would have run them off the road. He'd have figured it to be the action of a competing bounty hunter, and though he wouldn't have given up his fee without a fight, he'd have been outnumbered and outgunned.

Skip tracers didn't go crying to the cops when a competitor snatched their bounty.

The goons might have let him off with a few bruises, maybe a minor concussion. But the way that mountain of a man had been waving his cannon in M.J.'s apartment, Jack thought it was far more likely that he'd have sported a brand-new hole in some vital part of his body.

Because the mountain had been an moron.

So at this point he was on the run with an angry woman, a little over three hundred in cash and a quarter tank of gas.

He intended to know why.

He spotted what he was after north of Leesburg, Virginia. The tourists and holiday travelers, unless they were very down on their luck, would give a dilapidated dump like the Kountry Klub Motel a wide berth. But the low-slung building with the paint peeling on the green doors and the pitted parking lot met Jack's requirements perfectly.

He pulled to the farthest end of the lot, away from the huddle of rusted cars near the check-in, and cut the engine.

"Is this where you bring all your dates, Dakota?"

He smiled at her, a quick flash of teeth that was unexpectedly charming. "Only first class for you, sugar."

He knew just what she was thinking. The minute he cut her loose, she'd be all over him like spandex. And if she could get out of the car, she'd be sprinting toward the check-in as fast as those mile-long legs would carry her.

"I don't expect you to believe me." He said it casually as he leaned over to unlock the cuff from the door handle. "But I'm not going to enjoy this."

She was braced. He could feel her body tense to spring. He had to be quick, and he had to be rough. She'd no more than hissed out a breath before he had her hands secured and locked behind her. She sucked in air just as he clamped a hand over her mouth.

She bucked and rolled, tried to bring up her legs to kick, but he pinned her on the seat, flipped her face-down. He was out of breath by the time he'd tied the bandanna over her mouth.

"I lied." Panting, he rubbed the fresh bruise where

her elbow had connected with his ribs. "Maybe I enjoyed that a little."

He used the torn T-shirt to tie her legs, tried not to appreciate overmuch the length and shape of them. But, hell, he was only human. Once he had her trussed up like a turkey, he looped the slack of the handcuffs around the gearshift, then wound up the windows.

"Hot as hell, isn't it?" he said conversationally. "Well, I won't be long." He locked the car and walked away whistling.

It took her a moment to regain her balance. She was scared, she realized. Really, bone-deep scared, and she couldn't remember if she'd ever felt this kind of mind-numbing panic before. She was trembling, and had to stop. It wouldn't help her out of this fix.

Once, when she'd just opened her pub, she'd been closing down late at night. She'd been alone when the man came in and demanded money. She'd been scared then, too, terrified by the wild look in his eyes that shouted drugs. So she'd handed over the till, just as the cops recommended.

Then she'd handed him the fat end of the Louisville Slugger she had behind the bar.

She'd been scared, but she'd dealt with it.

She would deal with this, too.

The gag tasted of man and infuriated her. She couldn't push or wiggle or slide it out, so she gave up on it and concentrated on freeing the loop of the cuffs. If she could free her hands from the gearshift, she could fold herself up, bend her legs through her arms and get some mobility.

She was agile, she told herself. She was strong and she was smart. Oh, God, she was scared. She moaned and whimpered in frustration. The handcuffs might as well have been cemented to the gearshift.

If she could only see, twist herself around so that she could see what she was doing. She struggled, all but dislocating her shoulder, until she managed to flip around. Sweat seemed to boil over her, dripped into her eyes as she yanked at the steel.

She stopped herself, closed her eyes and got her breath back. She used her shaking fingers to probe, to trace along the steel, slide over the smooth length of the gearshift. Keeping them closed, she visualized what she was doing, carefully, slowly, shifting her hands until she felt steel begin to slide. Her shoulders screamed as she forced them into an unnatural position, but she bit down on the gag and twisted.

She felt something give, hoped it wasn't a joint, then collapsed in an exhausted, sweaty heap as the cuffs slipped off the stick.

"Damn, you're good," Jack commented as he wrenched open the door. He dragged her out and tossed her over his shoulder. "Another five minutes, you might have pulled it off." He carried her into a room at the end of the concrete block. He'd already unlocked the door, and he'd paused for a minute to observe, and admire, her struggles before he came back to the car.

Now he dumped her on the bed. Because her adrenaline was back and she was fighting him, he simply lay her flat on her back, letting her bounce until she was worn-out.

And he enjoyed that, too. He wasn't proud of it, he thought, but he enjoyed it. The woman had incredible energy and staying power. If they'd met under different circumstances, he imagined they could have torn up those cheap motel sheets like maniacs and parted as friends.

As it was, he was going to have a hard time not imagining her naked.

Maybe he lay on her, smelled her, just a little longer than necessary. He wasn't a saint, was he? he asked himself grimly as he unlocked one of her hands and secured the cuff to the iron headboard.

He rose, ran a hand through his hair. "You're making this tougher than necessary for both of us," he told her, as she murdered him with a scalding look out of hot green eyes. He was out of breath and knew he couldn't blame it entirely on the last, minor skirmish. That tight little bottom of hers pressing against his crotch had left him uncomfortably aroused.

And he didn't want to be.

Turning from her, he switched on the TV, let the volume boom out. M.J. had already ripped the gag away with her free hand and was hissing like a snake. "You can scream all you want now," he told her as he took out a small knife and sliced through the phone cord. "The three rooms down from here are vacant, so nobody's going to hear you." Then he grinned. "Besides, I put it around at check-in that we're on our honeymoon, so even if they hear, they're not going to bother us. Be back in a minute."

He went out, shutting the door behind him.

M.J. closed her eyes again. Dear God, what was going on with her? For a moment, for just one insane moment, when he pressed her into the mattress with his body, she'd felt weak and hot. With lust.

It was sick, sick, sick.

But just for that one insane moment, she'd imagined being stripped and taken, being ravaged, having his mouth on her. His hands on her.

More, she'd wanted it.

She shuddered now, praying it was just some sort of weird reaction to shock.

She wasn't a woman who shied away from good, healthy, hot sex. But she didn't give herself to strangers, to men who knocked her down, tied her up and tossed her into bed in some cheap motel.

And he'd been aroused. She hadn't been so stupid, or so dazed with shock, that she was unaware of his reaction. Hell, the man had been wrapped around her, hadn't he? But he'd backed off.

She struggled to even her breathing. He wasn't going to rape her. He didn't want sex. He wanted— God only knew.

Don't feel, she ordered herself. Just think. Just clear your mind and think.

Slowly, she opened her eyes, took a survey of the room.

It was, in a word, hideous.

Obviously, some misguided soul had thought that using an eye-searing combo of orange and blue would turn the cheaply furnished, cramped little room into the exotic.

He couldn't have been more wrong.

The drapes were as thin as paper, and looked to be of about the same consistency. But he'd pulled them closed over the narrow front window, so the room was deep in shadow.

The television blared out a poorly dubbed Hercules movie on its rickety gray pedestal. The single dresser was ringed with interlinking watermarks. There was a metal box beside the bed. For a couple of bucks in quarters, she could treat herself to dancing fingers. Whoopee.

The yellow glass ashtray on the night table was chipped, and didn't look heavy enough to make an effective weapon. Even over the din of Hercules, she could hear the roaring sputter of an air-conditioning unit that was doing absolutely nothing to cool the room.

The print near a narrow door she assumed was to the bathroom was a garish reproduction of a country landscape in autumn, complete with screaming red barn and stupid-faced cows.

Reaching over, she tested the bedside lamp. It was bright blue glass, with a dingy and yellowing shade, but it had some heft. It might come in handy.

She heard the rattle of the key and set it down again, stared at the door.

He came in with a small red-and-white cooler and dropped it on the dresser. Her heart thumped when she saw her purse slung over his shoulder, but he tossed it on the floor by the bed so casually that she relaxed again.

The diamond was still safe, she thought. And so was the can of Mace, the can opener and the roll of nickels she habitually carried as weapons.

"Nothing I like better than a really bad movie," he commented, and paused to watch Hercules battle several fierce-looking warriors sporting pelts and bad teeth. "I always wonder where they come up with the dialogue. You know, was it really that bad when it was scripted in Lithuanian or whatever, or does it just lose it in the translation?"

With a shrug, he walked over, lifted the top on the cooler and took out two soft drinks.

"I figure you're thirsty." He walked to her, offered a can. "And you're not the type to cut off your nose." His assessment was proved correct when she grabbed the can and drank deeply. "This place doesn't run to room service," he continued. "But there's a diner down the road, so we won't go hungry. You want something now?"

She eyed him over the top of the can. "No."

"Fine." He sat on the side of the bed, settled himself and smiled at her. "Let's talk."

"Kiss my butt."

He blew out a breath. "It's an attractive offer, sugar, but I've been trying not to think along those lines." He gave her thigh a friendly pat. "Now, the way I see it, we're both in a jam here, and you've got the key. Once you tell me who's after you and why, I'll deal with it."

The worst of her thirst was abated, so she sipped slowly. Her voice dripped sarcasm. "*You'll* deal with it?"

"Yeah. Consider me your champion-at-arms. Like good old Herc there." He stabbed a thumb at the set behind him. "You tell me about it, then I'll go take care of the bad guys. Then I'll bill you. And if the offer about kissing your butt's still open, I'll take you up on that, too."

"Let's see." She leaned her head back, kept her eyes level on his. "What was it you told your pal Ralph to do? Oh, yeah." She peeled her lips back in a snarl and repeated it.

He only shook his head. "Is that any way to talk

to the guy who kept you from getting a bullet in the brain?"

"*I* kept *you* from getting a bullet in the brain, pal, though I have serious doubts he'd have been able to hit it, as it's clearly so small. And you pay me back by manhandling me, tying me up, gagging me, and dumping me in some cheap rent-by-the-hour motel."

"I'm assured this is a family establishment," he said dryly. God, she was a pistol, he thought. Spitting at him despite his advantage, daring him to take her on, though she didn't have a hope of winning the game. And sexy as bloody hell in tight jeans and a wrinkled shirt.

"Think about this," he said. "That brainless giant said something about me taking too long, talking too much, which leads me to believe they were listening from the van. They must have had surveillance equipment, and he got antsy. Otherwise, if you'd gone along with me like a good girl, they'd have pulled us over somewhere along the line and taken you. They didn't want direct involvement, or witnesses."

"You'd be a witness," she corrected.

"Nothing to sweat over. I'd have been ticked off about having another bounty hunter snatch my job, but people in my line of work don't go running to the cops. I'd have lost my fee, considered my day wasted, maybe bitched to Ralph. That's the way they'd figure it, anyway. And Ralph would have probably passed me some fluff job to keep me happy."

His eyes changed, went hard again. Knife-edged gray ice. "Somebody's got their foot on his throat. I want to know who."

"I couldn't say. I don't know your friend Ralph—"

"Former friend."

"I don't know the gorilla who broke my door, and I don't know you." She was pleased her voice was calm, without a single hitch or quiver. "Now, if you'll let me go, I'll report all this to the police."

His lips twitched. "That's the first time you've mentioned the cops, sugar. And you're bluffing. You don't want them in on this. That's another question."

He was right about that. She didn't want the police, not until she'd talked to Bailey and knew what was going on. But she shrugged, glanced toward the phone he'd put out of commission. "You could call my bluff if you hadn't wrecked the phone."

"You wouldn't call the cops, but whoever you called might have their phone tapped. I didn't go through all the trouble to find us these plush out-of-the-way surroundings to get traced."

He leaned over, took her chin in his hand. "Who would you call, M.J.?"

She kept her eyes steady, fighting to ignore the heat of his fingers, the texture of his skin against hers. "My lover." She spit the words out. "He'd take you apart limb by limb. He'd rip out your heart, then show it to you while it was still beating."

He smiled, eased a little closer. He just couldn't resist. "What's his name?"

Her mind was blank, totally, completely, foolishly blank. She stared into those slate-gray eyes a moment, then shook his hand away. "Hank. He'll break you in half and toss you to the dogs when he finds out you've messed with me."

He chuckled, infuriated her. "You may have a lover, sugar. You may have a dozen. But you don't have one named Hank. Took you too long. Okay, you don't want to spill it and rely on me to work us out of this, we'll go another route."

He rose, leaned over. He heard her quickly indrawn breath when he reached down for her purse. Without a word, he dumped the contents on the bed. He'd already removed the weapons. "You ever use that can opener for more than popping a beer?" he asked her.

"How dare you! How dare you go through my things!"

"Oh, I think this is small potatoes after what we've been through together." He picked up the velvet pouch, slid the stone into his hand, where it flashed like fire, despite its lowly surroundings.

He admired it, as he had been unable to in the car, when he searched her bag. It was deeply, brilliantly blue, big as a baby's fist and cut to shoot blue flame. He felt a tug as it lay nestled in his hand, an odd need to protect it. Almost as inexplicable, he thought, as his odd need to protect this prickly, ungrateful woman.

"So." He sat, tossing the stone up, catching it. "Tell me about this, M.J. Just where did you get your hands on a blue diamond big enough to choke a cat?"

Chapter 3

Options whirled through her mind. The simplest, and the most satisfying, she thought, was to make him feel like a fool.

"Are you crazy?" She rolled her eyes and scoffed. "Yeah, that's a diamond, all right, a big blue one. I carry a green one in my glove compartment, and a pretty red one in my other purse. I spend all the profits from my pub on diamonds. It's a weakness."

He studied her, idly tossing the stone, catching it. She looked annoyed, he decided. Amused and cocky. "So what is it?"

"A paperweight, for God's sake."

He waited a beat. "You carry a paperweight in your purse."

Hell. "It was a gift." She said it primly, her nose in the air.

"Yeah, from Hank the Hunk, no doubt." He rose, casually pushed through the rest of the contents he'd dumped out. "Let's see, other than the blackjack—"

"It was a roll of nickels," she corrected.

"Same effect. Mace, a can opener I doubt you cart around to pop Bud bottles, we've got an electronic organizer, a wallet with more photos than cash—"

"I don't appreciate you rifling my personal belongings."

"Sue me. A bottle of designer water, six pens, four pencils. Some eyeliner, matches, keys, two pair of sunglasses, a paperback copy of Sue Grafton's latest—good book, by the way, I won't tell you the ending—a candy bar..." He tossed it to her. "In case you're hungry. A flip phone." He tucked that in his back pocket. "About three dollars in loose change, a weather radio and a box of condoms." He lifted a brow. "Unopened. But then, you never know."

Heat, a combination of mortification and fury, crawled up her neck. "Pervert."

"I'd say you're a woman who believes in being prepared. So why not carry a paperweight around with you? You might run into a stack of paper that needs anchoring. Happens all the time."

He made a couple of swipes to gather and dump the items scattered on the bed back into her bag, then tossed it aside. "I won't ask what kind of fool you take me for, because I've already got that picture." Moving to the mirror over the dresser, he scraped the stone diagonally across the glass. It left a long, thin scratch.

"They just don't make motel mirrors like they used to," he commented, then came back and sat on the bed beside her. "Now, back to my original question.

What are you doing with a blue diamond big enough to choke a cat?"

When she said nothing, he vised her chin in his hand, jerked her face to his. "Listen, sister, I could truss you up again, leave you here and walk away with your million-dollar paperweight. That's door number one. I can kick back, watch the movie and wait you out, because sooner or later you'll tell me what I want to know. That's door number two. Behind door number three, you tell me now why you're carrying a stone that could buy a small island in the West Indies and we start figuring out how to get us both out of this jam."

She didn't flinch, she didn't blink. He had to admire the sheer nerve. Because he did, he waited patiently while she studied him out of those deep green cat-tilted eyes.

"Why haven't you taken door number one already?"

"Because I don't like having some gorilla try to break me in half, I don't like getting shot at, and I don't like being hosed by some skinny woman with an attitude." He leaned closer, until they were nose-to-nose. "I've got debts to pay on this one, sugar. And you're the first stop."

She grabbed his wrist with her free hand, shoved. "Threats aren't going to cut it with me, Dakota."

"No?" He shifted gears smoothly. His hand came back to her face, but lightly now, a skim of knuckles along a cheekbone that had her blinking in shock before her eyes narrowed. "You want a different approach?"

His fingers trailed down her throat, down the center of her body and back, before sliding around to cup her neck. His mouth hovered, one hot breath away from hers.

"Don't even think about it," she warned.

"Too late." His lips curved, and his eyes stared straight into hers. "I've been thinking about it ever since you swaggered up the apartment steps in front of me."

No, he'd been thinking about it, he realized, since Ralph shoved her photo at him. But he'd consider that later.

He skimmed his mouth over hers, drew back fractionally. He'd expected her to cringe away or fight. God knew he was ruthlessly pushing all those female fear buttons. It was deplorable, but he'd consider that later, as well. He just wanted the pressure to work, to get her to spill before they both got killed. And if he got a little twisted pleasure out of the whole thing, well, hell, he had his flaws.

But she didn't fight and she didn't cringe. She didn't move a muscle, just kept those goddess-green eyes lasered on his. A dark, primitive thrill rippled down to his loins.

What was one more sin on his back, he thought, and, clamping his hand on her free one, he took a long, deep gulp of her.

It was all heat, primitive as tribal drums. No thought, no reason, all instinct. That surprisingly lush mouth gave under his, so he dived deeper. A rumble of pure male triumph sounded in his throat as he moved into her, plunging his tongue between those full, inviting lips, sinking into that long, tough body, fisting his hand in that cap of flame-colored hair.

His mind shut off like a shattered lamp. He forgot it was a con, a ploy to intimidate, forgot he was a civilized man. Forgot she was a job, a puzzle, a stranger. And knew only that she was his for the taking.

His hand closed greedily over her breast, his thumb and forefinger tugging at the nipple that pressed hard against the thin cotton of her shirt. She moved under him, arched to him. And the blood pounded like thunder in his brain.

She moved fast, all but twisting his ear from his head while her teeth clamped down like a bear trap on his bottom lip.

He yelped, jerked back, and, certain she would saw off a chunk of him, pinched her chin hard until she let him loose. He pressed the back of his hand to his throbbing lip, scowled at the blood he saw on it when he took it away.

"Damn it."

"Pig." She was vibrating now, scrambling to her knees on the bed to take another swipe at him, swearing when her reach fell short. "Pervert."

He spared her one murderous look, then turned on his heel. The bathroom door slammed shut behind him. She heard water running. And, closing her eyes, she sank back and let the shudders come.

My God, dear God, she thought, pressing a hand to her face. She'd lost her mind.

Had she fought him? No. Had she been filled with outrage, with disgust? No.

She'd enjoyed it.

She rocked herself, berated herself, and damned Jack Dakota to hell.

She'd let him kiss her. There was no pretending otherwise. She'd stared into those dangerous gray eyes, felt the zip of an electric current when that cocky mouth brushed over hers.

And she'd wanted him.

Her muscles had gone lax, her breasts had tingled, and her blood had begun to swim. She'd let him kiss her without a murmur of protest. She'd kissed him back, without a thought for the consequences.

M. J. O'Leary, she thought, wincing, tough gal, who prided herself on always being in control, who could flip a two-hundred-pound man onto his back and have her foot on his throat in a heartbeat—confident, kick-butt M.J.—had melted into a puddle of mindless lust.

And he'd tied her up, he'd gagged her, he had her handcuffed to a bed in some cheap motel. Wanting him even for an instant made her as much of a pervert as he was.

Thank God she'd snapped out of it. It didn't matter that bone-deep fear of her feelings had been the motivation for stopping him. The fact was, she had stopped him—and she knew she'd been an instant away from letting him do whatever he wanted to do.

She was very much afraid that if she'd had both hands free, she would have flipped him onto his back. Then ripped off his clothes.

It was the shock, she told herself. Even a woman who prided herself on being able to handle anything that came her way was entitled to go a little loopy with shock under certain circumstances.

Now she had to put this aberration behind her and figure out what to do.

The facts were few, but they were clear. She had to contact Bailey. Whatever her friend's purpose in sending the stone, Bailey couldn't have had any idea just how dangerous the act would be. She'd had her reasons, M.J. was sure, and she thought it was likely to have been one of Bailey's rare acts of impulse and defiance.

She didn't intend for Bailey to pay the price for it.

What had Bailey done with the other two stones? Did she have them, or... Oh God.

She dropped back weakly on the bricklike pillow. She would have sent one to Grace. It had to be. It was logical, and Bailey was nothing if not logical. There'd been three stones, and she'd sent one to M.J. So it followed that she'd kept one, and sent the other to the only other person in the world she'd trust with such a responsibility.

Grace Fontaine. The three of them had been close as sisters since college. Bailey, quiet, studious and serious. Grace, rich, stunning and wild. They'd roomed together for four years at Radcliffe and stayed close since. Bailey moving into the family business, M.J. following tradition and opening her own bar, and Grace doing whatever she could to shock her wealthy, conservative and disapproving relatives.

If one of them was in trouble, they were all in trouble. She had to warn them.

She would have to escape from Jack Dakota. Or she'd have to use him.

But how much, she asked herself, did she dare trust him?

In the bathroom, Jack studied his mutilated lip in the mirror. He'd probably have a scar. Well, he admitted, he deserved it. He *had* been a pig and a pervert.

Not that she was entirely innocent, either, lying there on the bed with that just-try-it-buster look in her eyes.

And hadn't she pressed that long, tight body to his, opened that soft, sexy mouth, arched those neat, narrow hips?

Pig. He scrubbed his hands over his face. What choice had he given her?

Dropping his hands, he looked at himself in the mirror, looked dead-on, and admitted he hadn't wanted to give her a choice.

He'd just wanted her.

Well, he wasn't an animal. He could control himself, he could think, he could reason. And that was just what he was going to do.

He'd probably have a scar, he thought again, grimly, as he touched a fingertip gingerly to his swollen lip. Just let that be a lesson to you, Dakota. He jerked his head in a nod at the reflection in the spotty mirror. If you can't trust yourself, you sure as hell can't trust her.

When he came out, she was frowning at the hideous drapes on the window. He glared at her. She glared back. Saying nothing, he sat in the single ratty chair, crossed his feet at the ankles and tuned into the movie.

Hercules was over. He'd probably triumphed. In his place was a Japanese science-fiction flick with an incredibly poorly produced monster lizard who was currently smashing a high-speed train. Hordes of extras were screaming in terror.

They watched awhile, as the military came rushing in with large guns that had virtually no effect on the giant mutant lizard. A small man in a combat helmet was devoured. His chickenhearted comrades ran for their lives.

M.J. found the candy bar from her purse that Jack had tossed her earlier, broke off a chunk and ate it contemplatively as the lizard king from outer space lumbered toward Tokyo to wreak reptilian havoc.

"Can I have my water?" she asked in scrupulously polite tones.

He got up, fetched it out of her bag, handed it over.

"Thanks." She took one long sip, waited until he'd settled again. "What's your fee?" she demanded.

He took another soda out of his cooler. Wished it was a beer. "For?"

"What you do." She shrugged. "Say I had skipped out on bail. What do you get for bringing me back?"

"Depends. Why?"

She rolled her eyes. "Depends on what?"

"On how much bail you'd skipped out on."

She was silent for a moment as she considered. The lizard demolished a tall building with many innocent occupants. "What was it I was supposed to have done?"

"Shot your lover—the accountant. I believe his name was Hank."

"Very funny." She broke off another hunk of chocolate and, when Jack held out a hand, reluctantly shared. "How much were you going to get for me?"

"More than you're worth."

Now she sighed. "I'm going to make you a deal, Jack, but I'm a businesswoman, and I don't make them blind. What's your fee?"

Interesting, he thought, and drummed his fingers on the arm of the chair. "For you, sugar, considering what you're carrying in that suitcase you call a purse, adding in what Ralph offered me to turn you over to the goons?" He thought it over. "A hundred large."

She didn't bat an eye. "I appreciate you trying to lighten the situation with an attempt at wry humor. A hundred K for a man who can't even take out a single hired thug by himself is laughable—"

"Who said I couldn't take him out?" His pride leaped up and bit him. "I *did* take him out, sugar. Him and his cannon, and you haven't bothered to thank me for it."

"Oh, excuse me. It must have slipped my mind while I was being dragged around and handcuffed. How rude. And you didn't take him out, I did. But regardless," she continued, holding up her free hand like a traffic cop, "now that we've had our little joke, let's try to be serious. I'll give you a thousand to work with me on this."

"A thousand?" He flashed that quick, dangerous grin. "Sister, there isn't enough money in the world to tempt me to work with you. But for a hundred K, I'll get you out of the jam you're in."

"In the first place—" she drew up her legs, sat lotusstyle "—I'm not your sister, and I'm not your sugar. If you have to refer to me, use my name."

"You don't have a name, you have initials."

"In the second place," she said, ignoring him, "if a man like you got his hands on a hundred thousand, he'd just lose it in Vegas or pour it down some stripper's cleavage. Since I don't intend for that to happen to my money, I'm offering you a thousand." She smiled at him. "With that, you can have yourself a nice weekend at the beach with a keg of imported beer."

"It's considerate of you to look out for my welfare, but you're not really in the position to negotiate terms here. You want help, it'll cost you."

She didn't know if she wanted his help. The fact was, she wasn't at all sure why she was wrangling with him over a fee. Under the circumstances, she felt she could promise him any amount without any obligation to pay up if and when the time came.

But it was the principle of the thing.

"Five thousand—and you follow orders."

"Seventy-five, and I don't ever follow orders."

"Five." She set her teeth. "Take it or leave it."

"I'll leave it." Casually he picked up the stone again, held it up, studied it. "And take this with me." He rose, patted his back pocket. "And maybe I'll call the cops on your fancy little phone after I'm clear."

She fisted her fingers, flexed them. She didn't want to involve the police, not until she'd contacted Bailey. Nor could she risk him following through on his threat to simply take the stone.

"Fifty thousand." She bit the words off like raw meat. "That's all I'll be able to come up with. Most everything I've got's tied up in my business."

He cocked a brow. "The finder's fee on this little bauble's got to be worth more than fifty."

"I didn't steal the damn thing. It doesn't belong to me. It's—" She broke off, clamped her mouth shut.

He started to sit on the edge of the bed again, remembered what had happened before, and chose the arm of the chair. "Who does it belong to, M.J.?"

"I'm not spilling my guts to you. For all I know you're as big a creep as the one who broke down my door. You could be a thief, a murderer."

He cocked that scarred eyebrow. "Which is why I've robbed and murdered you."

"The day's young."

"Let me point out the obvious. I'm the only one around."

"That doesn't inspire confidence." She brooded a

moment. How far did she dare use him? she wondered. And how much did she dare tell him?

"If you want my help," he said, as if reading her mind, "then I need facts, details and names."

"I'm not giving you names." She shook her head slowly. "That's out until I talk to the other people involved. And as for facts and details, I don't have many."

"Give me what you do have."

She studied him again. No, she didn't trust him, not nearly as far as she could throw him. If she ever got the opportunity. But she had to start somewhere. "Unlock me."

He shook his head. "Let's just leave things as they are for the moment." But he rose, walked over and shut off the television. "Where'd you get the stone, M.J.?"

She hesitated another instant. Trust wasn't the issue, she decided. He might help, if in no other way than just by providing her with a sounding board. "A friend sent it to me. Overnight courier. I just got it yesterday."

"Where did it come from?"

"Originally from Asia Minor, I believe." She shrugged off his hiss of annoyance. "I'm not telling you where it was sent from, but I will tell you there had to be a good reason. My friend's too honest to steal a handshake. All I know is it was sent, with a note that said for me to keep it with me at all times, and not to tell anyone until my friend had a chance to explain."

Abruptly she pressed a hand to her stomach and the arrogance died out of her voice. "My friend's in trouble. It's got to be terrible trouble. I have to call."

"No calls."

"Look, Jack—"

"No calls," he repeated. "Whoever's after you might

be after your pal. His phone could be tapped, which would lead them back to you. Which leads them to me, so no calls. Now how did your honest friend happen to get his hands on a blue diamond that makes the Hope look like a prize in a box of Cracker Jack?"

"In a perfectly legitimate manner." Stalling, she combed her fingers through her hair. He thought her friend was male—why not leave it that way?

"Look, I'm not getting into all of that. All I'm going to tell you is he was supposed to have his hands on it. Look, let me tell you about the stone. It's one of three. At one time they were part of an altar set up to an ancient Roman god. Mithraism was one of the major religions of the Roman Empire—"

"The Three Stars of Mithra," he murmured, and had her eyeing him first in shock, then with suspicion.

"How do you know about the Three Stars?"

"I read about them in the dentist's office," he murmured. Now, when he picked up the stone, it wasn't simply with admiration, it was with awe. "It was supposed to be a myth. The Three Stars, set in the golden triangle and held in the hands of the god of light."

"It's not a myth," M.J. told him. "The Smithsonian acquired the Stars through a contact in Europe just a couple months ago. My friend said the museum wanted to keep the acquisition quiet until the diamonds were verified."

"And assessed," he thought aloud. "Insured and under tight security."

"They were supposed to be under security," M.J. told him, and he answered with a soft laugh.

"Doesn't look like it worked, does it? The diamonds represent love, knowledge and generosity." His eyes narrowed as he contemplated the ancient stone. "I wonder which this one is?"

"I couldn't say." She continued to stare at him, fascinated. He'd gone from tough guy to scholar in the blink of an eye. "But apparently you know as much about it as I do."

"I know about Mithraism," he said easily. "It predates and parallels Christianity. Mankind's always looked for a kind and just god." His shoulders moved as he turned the stone in his hand. "Mankind doesn't always get what it wants. And I know the legend of the Three Stars. It was said the god held the triangle for centuries, and holding it tended the world. Then it was lost, or looted, or sank with Atlantis."

For his own pleasure, he switched on the lamp, watched the stone explode with power in the dingy light. "More likely it just ended up in the treasure room of some corrupt Roman procurer." He traced the facets with his thumbs. "It's something people would kill for. Or die for," he murmured. "Some legends have it in Cleopatra's tomb, others have Merlin casing it in crystal and holding it in trust until Arthur's return. Others say the god himself hurled them into the sky and wept at man's ignorance. But the smart money was that they'd simply been stolen and separated."

He looked up, over the stone and into her eyes. "Worth a fortune singly, and within the triangle, worth immortality."

Yes, she could admit he fascinated her, the way that deep, all-man voice had cooled into professorial tones. And the way he stroked the gleaming diamond as a man might stroke a woman's gleaming flesh.

But she shook her head over the last statement. "You don't believe that."

"No, but that's the legend, isn't it? Whoever holds the triangle, with the Stars in place, gains the power of the god, and his immortality. But not necessarily his compassion. People have killed for less. A hell of a lot less."

He set the stone on the table between them, where it glowed with quiet fire. It had all changed now, he realized. The stakes had just flown sky-high, and the odds mirrored them.

"You're in a hell of a spot, M.J. Whoever's after this won't think twice about taking your head with it." He rubbed his chin, his fingers dancing over the shallow dimple. "And my head's awfully damn close to yours just now."

He couldn't believe how poor his luck was. His own mistake, he told himself as he calmed himself with Mozart and Moët. Because he tried to keep his distance from events, he'd had to count on others to handle his business.

Incompetents, one and all, he thought, and soothed himself by stroking the pelt of a sable coat that had once graced the shoulder of Czarina Alexandra.

To think he'd enjoyed the irony of having a bounty hunter track down the annoying Ms. O'Leary. It would have been simpler to have her snatched from her apartment or place of business. But he'd preferred finesse and, again, the distance.

The bounty hunter would have been blamed for her abduction, and her death. Such men were violent by nature, unpredictable. The police would have closed the case with little thought or effort.

Now she was on the run, and most certainly had the stone in her possession.

She would turn up, he thought, taking slow, even breaths. She would certainly contact her friends before too much longer. He'd been assured they were admirably loyal to each other.

He was a man who appreciated loyalty.

And when Ms. O'Leary attempted to contact her friends—one who had vanished, the other out of reach—he would have her.

And the stone.

With her, he had no doubt he would acquire the other two stars.

After all, he thought with a pleasant smile. Bailey James was reputed to be a good friend, a compassionate and intelligent woman. Intelligent enough, he mused, to have uncovered her stepbrothers' attempt to copy the Stars, smart enough to thwart them before they had made good on delivery.

Well, that, too, would be dealt with.

He was sure Bailey would be loyal to her friend, compassionate enough to put her friend first. And her loyalty and compassion would deliver the stones to him without much more delay.

In exchange for the life of M. J. O'Leary.

He had spent many years of his life in search of the Three Stars. He had invested much of his great wealth. And had taken many lives. Now they were almost in his hands. So close, he thought, so very close, his fingers tingled with anticipation.

And when he held them, fit them into the triangle,

set them on the altar he'd had built for them, he would have the ultimate power. Immortality.

Then, of course, he would kill the women.

A fitting sacrifice, he reflected, to a god.

Chapter 4

He'd left her alone. Now she had to consider the matter of trust. Should she believe he'd just go out, pick up food and come back? He hadn't trusted her to stay, M.J. mused, rattling the handcuffs.

And she had to admit he'd gauged her well. She'd have been out the door like a shot. Not because she was afraid of him. She'd considered all the facts, all her instincts, and she no longer believed he'd hurt her. He would have done so already.

She'd seen the way he dealt with the gorilla who broke in her door. True, he'd had his hands full, but he'd handled himself with speed, strength, and an admirable streak of mean.

It galled to admit it, but she knew he'd held back when he tangled with her. Not that it excused him trussing her up and tossing her in some cheap motel room, but if she was going to be fair-minded, she had to say he could have done considerable damage to her during their quick, sweaty bout if he'd wanted to.

And all he'd really bruised was her pride.

He had a brain—which had surprised her. That was, she supposed, a generalizing-from-a-first-impression mistake she'd fallen into because of his looks, and that sheer in-your-face physicality. But in addition to the street smarts she would have expected from his type, it appeared Jack Dakota had an intellect. A good one.

And she didn't believe he did his reading in the dentist's office. A guy didn't read about ancient religions while he was waiting to have his teeth cleaned. So, she had to conclude there was more to him than she'd originally assumed. All she had to do was decide whether that was an advantage, or a disadvantage.

Now that she'd calmed down a little, she was certain that he wasn't going to push himself on her sexually, either. She'd have given odds that little interlude had shaken him as much as it had shaken her. It had been, she was sure, a misstep on his part. Intimidate the woman, flex the testosterone, and she'll tell you whatever you want to know.

It hadn't worked. All it had done was make them both itchy.

Damn, the man could kiss.

But she was getting off track, she reminded herself, and scowled at the ridiculous movie he'd left blaring on the television.

No, she wasn't afraid of him, but she was afraid of the situation. Which meant she didn't want to sit here on her butt and do nothing. Action was her style.

Whether the action was wise or not wasn't the point. The doing was.

Shifting to her knees, she peered at the handcuffs, turning her wrist this way and that, flexing her hand as if she were an escape artist preparing to launch into her latest trick.

She tested the rungs on the headboard and found them distressingly firm.

They didn't make cheap hotels like they used to, she thought with a sigh. And wished for a hairpin, a nail file, a hammer.

All she found in the sticky drawer of the nightstand was a torn phone book and a linty wedge of hard candy.

He'd taken her purse with him, and though she knew she wouldn't find that hairpin, nail file or hammer inside, she still resented the lack of it.

She could scream, of course. She could shout down the roof, and endure the humiliation if someone actually paid any attention to the sounds of distress.

And that wouldn't get her out of the cuffs, unless someone called a locksmith. Or the cops.

She took a deep breath, struggled for the right avenue of escape. She was sick with worry for Bailey and Grace, desperate to reassure herself that they were both well.

If she did go to the police, what kind of trouble would Bailey be in? She had, technically, taken possession of a fortune. Would the authorities be understanding, or would they slap Bailey in a cell?

That, M.J. wouldn't risk. Not yet. Not as long as she felt it was remotely possible to even the odds. And to do that, she had to know what the hell she was up against.

Which again meant getting out of the room.

She was considering gnawing at the headboard with her teeth when Jack unlocked the door. He flashed a quick smile at her, one that told her he had her thoughts pegged.

"Honey, I'm home."

"You're a laugh riot, Dakota. My sides are aching."

"You make quite a picture cuffed to that bed, M.J." He set down two white take-out bags. "A lesser man would be toying with impure notions right about now."

It was her turn to smile, wickedly. "You already did. And you'll probably have a scar on your bottom lip."

"Yeah." He rubbed his thumb gingerly over the wound. It still stung. "I'd say I deserved it, but you were cooperating initially."

That stung, too. The truth often did. "You go right on thinking that, Jack." She all but purred it. "I'm sure an ego like yours requires regular delusions."

"Sugar, I know a delusion from a lip lock. But we've got more important things to do than discuss your attraction for me." Pleased with that last sally, he reached into one of the bags. "Burgers."

The smell hit her like a fist, right in the empty stomach. Her mouth watered. "So are we going to hole up here like a couple of escaped convicts—" she rattled her chain for emphasis "—and eat greasy food?"

"You bet." He handed her a burger and took out an order of fries designed to clog the arteries and improve the mood. "I think better when I'm eating."

Companionably, he stretched out beside her, back against the headboard, legs extended, food on his lap. "We've got us a serious problem here."

"If *we've* got us a serious problem here, why am I the only one with handcuffs?"

He loved the sarcastic edge in her voice, and he wondered what was wrong with him. "Because you'd have done something stupid if I hadn't left you secured. I'm looking out for my investment." He gestured with the rest of his burger. "And that's you, sugar."

"I can look out for myself. And if I'm hiring you, then you should be taking orders. The first order is unlock these damn things."

"I'll get to it, once we set up the ground rules." He popped open a paper package of salt, dribbled it on the fries. "I've been thinking."

"Well, then." She munched bitterly on an overcooked burger between two slices of slightly stale bun. "Why am I worried? You've been thinking."

"You've got a sarcastic mouth. But I like that about you." He handed her a tiny paper napkin. "You got ketchup on your chin. Now, somebody put the pressure on Ralph—enough that Ralph falsified official paperwork and put my butt in a sling. He wouldn't have done it for money—not that Ralph doesn't like money," Jack continued. "But he wouldn't risk his license, or risk me coming after him, for a few bucks. So he was saving his skin."

"And since Ralph is a pillar of the community, no doubt, this narrows down the list?"

"It means it was somebody with punch, somebody who wasn't afraid old Ralph would tip me off or go to the cops. Somebody who wanted you taken out. Who knows you've got the rock?"

"Nobody, except the person who sent it to me." She frowned at her burger. "And possibly one other."

"If more than one person knows a secret, it isn't a

secret. How did your friend get the diamond, M.J.? You can't keep dancing around the data here."

"I'll tell you after I clear it with my friend. I have to make a phone call."

"No calls."

"You called Ralph," she pointed out.

"I took a chance, and we were mobile. You're not making any calls until I know the score. The diamond was shipped just yesterday," he mused. "They tagged you fast."

"Which means they tagged my friend." Her stomach turned over. "Jack, please. I have to call. I have to know."

The emotion choking her voice both weakened and annoyed him. He stared into her eyes. "How much does he mean to you?"

She started to correct him, then just shook her head. "Everything. No one in the world means more to me."

"Lucky guy."

It wasn't the response she'd wanted or expected. Fueled by frustration and fears, she grabbed his shirt. "What the hell's wrong with you? Someone tried to kill us. How can we just sit here?"

"That's just why we're sitting here. We let them chase their tails awhile. Your friend's on his own for now. And since I can't picture you falling for some jerk who can't handle himself, he should be fine."

"You don't understand anything." She sat back, dragged her fingers through her hair. "God, this is a mess. I should be getting ready to go in to work now, and instead I'm stuck here with you. I'm supposed to be behind the stick tonight."

"You tend bar?" He lifted a brow. "I thought you owned the place."

"That's right, I own the place." It was a source of pride. "I like tending bar. You have a problem with that?"

"Nope." Since the topic had distracted her, he followed it. "Are you any good?"

"Nobody complains."

"How'd you get into the business?" When she eyed him owlishly, he shrugged. "Come on, a little conversation over a meal can't hurt. We got time to kill."

That wasn't all she wanted to kill, but the rest would have to wait. "I'm a fourth-generation pub owner. My great-grandfather ran his own public house in Dublin. My grandfather immigrated to New York and worked behind the stick in his own pub. He passed it to my father when he moved to Florida. I practically grew up behind the bar."

"What part of New York?"

"West Side, Seventy-ninth and Columbus."

"O'Leary's." The grin came quick and close to dreamy. "Lots of dark wood and lots of brass. Live Irish music on Saturday nights. And they build the finest Guinness this side of the Atlantic."

She eyed him again, intrigued despite herself. "You've been there?"

"I downed many a pint in O'Leary's. That would have been ten years ago, more or less." He'd been in college then, he remembered. Working his way through courses in law and literature and trying to make up his mind who the devil he was. "I was up there tracing a skip about three years ago. Stopped in. Nothing had changed, not even the scars on that old pine bar."

It made her sentimental—couldn't be helped. "Nothing changes at O'Leary's."

"I swear the same two guys were sitting on the same stools at the end of the bar—smoking cigars, reading the *Racing Form* and drinking Irish."

"Callahan and O'Neal." It made her smile. "They'll die on those stools."

"And your father. Pat O'Leary. Son of a bitch." Steeped in the haze of memory, he shut his eyes. "That big, wide Irish face and wiry shock of red hair, with a voice straight out of a Cagney movie."

"Yeah, that's Pop," she murmured, only more sentimental.

"You know, when I walked in—it had been at least six years since I'd walked out—your father grinned at me. 'How are you this evening, college boy?' he said to me, and took a pint glass and starting building my beer."

"You went to college?"

His hazy pleasure dimmed considerably at the shock in her voice. He opened one eye. "So?"

"So, you don't look like the college type." She shrugged and went back to her burger. "I build a damn good Guinness myself. Could use one now."

"Me too. Maybe later. So this friend of yours, how long have you known him?"

"My friend and I go back to our own college days. There's no one I trust more, if that's what you're getting at."

"Maybe you ought to rethink it. Just consider," he said when her eyes fired. "The Three Stars are a big temptation, for anyone. So maybe he was tempted, maybe he got in over his head."

"No, it doesn't play like that, but I think someone else might have, and if my friend found out about it…" She pressed her lips together. "If you wanted to protect those stones, to make certain they weren't stolen, didn't fall as a group into the wrong hands, what would you do?"

"It isn't a matter of what I'd do," he pointed out, "but what he'd do."

"Separate them," M.J. said. "Pass them on to people you could trust without question. People who would go to the wall for you, because you'd do the same for them. Without question."

"Absolute trust, absolute loyalty?" He balled his napkin, two-pointed it into the waste can. "I can't buy it."

"Then I'm sorry for you," she murmured. "Because you can't buy it. It just is. Don't you have anyone who'd go to the wall for you, Jack?"

"No. And there's no one I'd go to the wall for." For the first time in his life, it bothered him to realize it. He scooted down, closed his eyes. "I'm taking a nap."

"You're taking a what?"

"A nap. You'd be smart to do the same."

"How can you possibly sleep at a time like this?"

"Because I'm tired." His voice was edgy. "And because I don't think I'm going to get much sleep once we get started. We've got a couple hours before sundown."

"And what happens at sundown?"

"It gets dark," he said, and tuned her out.

She couldn't believe it. The man had shut down like a machine switched off—like a hypnotist's subject at the snap of a finger. Like a… She scowled when she ran out of analogies.

At least he didn't snore.

Well, this was just fine, she fumed. This was just dandy. What was she supposed to do while he had his little lie-me-down?

M.J. nibbled on the last of her fries, frowned at the TV screen, where the giant lizard was just meeting his violent end. The cable channel had promised more where that came from on its Marathon Monsters and Heroes Holiday Weekend Festival.

Oh, goody.

She lay in the darkened room, considering her options. And, considering, fell asleep.

And, sleeping, dreamed of monsters and heroes and a blue diamond that pulsed like a living heart.

Jack woke wrapped in female. He smelled her first, a tang, just a little sharp, of lemony soap. Clean, fresh and simple.

He heard her—the slow, even, relaxed breathing. Felt the quiet intimacy of shared sleep. His blood began to stir even before he felt her.

Long, limber limbs. A shapely yard of leg was tossed over his own. One well-toned arm, with skin as smooth as new cream, was flung over his chest. Her head was settled companionably on his shoulder.

M.J. was a cuddler, he realized, and smiled to himself. Who'd have thought it? Before he could talk himself out of it, he lifted a hand, brushed it lightly over her tousled cap of hair. Bright silk, he mused. It was quite a contrast to all that angled toughness.

She sure had style. His kind of style, he decided, and wondered what direction they might have taken if he just walked into her pub one night and put some moves on her.

She'd have kicked him out on his butt, he thought, and grinned. What a woman.

It was too bad, too damn bad, that he didn't have time to try out those moves. Because he really wanted another taste of her.

And because he did, he slid out from under her, stood and stretched out the kinks while she shifted and tried to find comfort. She rolled onto her back and flung her free hand over her head.

The restless animal inside him stirred.

He grabbed it in a choke hold and reminded himself that he was, occasionally, a civilized man. Civilized men didn't climb onto a sleeping woman and dive in.

But they could think about it.

Since it would be safer all around to think about it at a distance, he went into the bathroom, splashed cold water on his face and considered his next move.

In dreams, she was holding the stone in her hand, wondering at it, as streams of sunlight danced through the canopy of trees. Instead of penetrating the stone, the rays bounced off, creating a flashing whirl of beauty that stung the eyes and burned the soul.

It was hers to hold, if not to keep. The answers were there, secreted inside, if only she knew where to look.

From somewhere came the growl of a beast, low and feral. She turned toward it, rather than away, the stone protected in the fist of her hand, her other raised to defend.

Something moved slyly in the brush, hidden, waiting, searching. Hunting.

Then he was there, astride a massive black horse. At his side was a sword of dull silver, its width a thick slab of violence. His gray eyes were granite-hard, and as dangerous as any beast that slunk over the ground. He held a hand down to her, and there was challenge in that slow smile.

Danger ahead. Danger behind.

She stepped forward, clasped hands with him and let him pull her up on the gleaming black horse. The horse reared high, trumpeted. When they rode, they rode fast. The blood beating in her head had nothing to do with fear, and everything to do with triumph.

She came awake with her heart pounding and her blood high. She was in the dim, cramped motel room, with Jack shaking her shoulder roughly.

"What? What?"

"Nap's over." He considered kissing her awake, risking her fist in his face. But it would be too distracting. "We've got places to go."

"Where?" She struggled to shake off sleep, and the silky remnants of the dream.

"To visit a friend." He unlocked the cuffs from the headboard, snapped them on his own wrist, linking M.J. to him.

"You have a friend?"

"Ah, she's awake now." He pulled her outside, into a misty dusk that still pulsed with heat. "Get in and slide over," he instructed when he opened the driver's side door.

She was still groggy enough that she obeyed without question. But by the time he'd started the engine, her wits were back. "Look, Jack, these handcuffs have got to go."

"I don't know, I kind of like them this way. Did you ever see that movie with Tony Curtis and Sidney Poitier? Great flick."

"We're not escaped cons running for a train here, Dakota. If we're going to have a business relationship, there has to be an element of trust."

"Sugar, you don't trust me any more than I trust you." He steered out of the pitted lot, kept to the speed limit. "Look at it this way." He lifted his hand, causing hers to jerk. "We're both in the same boat. And I could have just left you back there."

She drummed her fingers on her knee. "Why didn't you?"

"I thought about it," he admitted. "I could move faster without you along. But I'd rather keep my eye on you. And if things go wrong and I can't get back, I'd hate for you to have to explain why you're cuffed to the bed of a cheap motel."

"Damn considerate of you."

"I thought so. Though it's your fault I'm flying blind. It'd be easier if you'd fill in the blanks."

"Think of it as a challenge."

"Oh, I do. It, and you." He slanted her a look. "What's this guy got, M.J.? This *friend* of yours you'd risk so much for?"

She looked out her window, thought of Bailey. Then pushed the thought aside. Worry for Bailey only brought the fear back, and fear clouded the mind and made it sluggish.

"You wouldn't understand love, would you, Jack?" Her voice was quiet, without its usual edge, and her gaze passed over his face in a slow search. "The kind that doesn't ask questions, doesn't require favors or have limits."

"No." Inside the emptiness her words brought him curled an edgy fist of envy. "I'd say if you don't ask questions or have limits, you're a fool."

"And you're no fool."

"Under the circumstances, you should be grateful I'm not. I'll get you out of this, M.J. Then you'll owe me fifty thousand."

"You know your priorities," she said with a sneer.

"Yeah, money smooths out a lot of bumps on the road. And I say before you pay me off we end up in bed again. Only this time it won't be to take a nap."

She turned toward him fully, and ignored the quick pulse of excitement in her gut. "Dakota, the only way I'll end up in the sack with you is if you handcuff me again."

There was that smile, slow, insolent, damnably attractive. "Well, that would be interesting, wouldn't it?"

Wanting to make time, he swung onto the interstate, headed north. And he promised himself that not only would he get her into bed, but she wouldn't think of another man when he did.

"You're heading back to D.C."

"That's right. We've got some business there." In the glare of oncoming headlights, his face was grim.

He took a roundabout route, circling, cruising past his objective, winding his way back, until he was satisfied none of the cars parked on the block were occupied.

There was pedestrian traffic, as well. He'd sized

it up by his second pass. Deals were being made, he mused. And that kind of business kept people moving.

"Nice neighborhood," she commented, watching a drunk stumble out of a liquor store with a brown paper sack. "Just charming. Yours?"

"Ralph's. We're only a couple blocks from the courthouse." He cruised past a prostitute who was well off the usual stroll and pulled around the corner. "He likes the location."

It was an area, she knew, that even the most fearless cabbies preferred to avoid. An area where life was often worth less than the spit on the sidewalk, and those who valued theirs locked their doors tight before sundown and waited for morning.

Here, the graffiti smeared on the crumbling buildings wasn't an art form. It was a threat.

She heard someone swearing viciously, then the sound of breaking glass. "A man of taste and refinement, your friend Ralph."

"Former friend." He took her hand, obliging her to slide across the seat when he climbed out.

"That you, Dakota? That you?" A man slipped out of the shadows of a doorway. His eyes were fire red and skittish as a whipped dog's. He ran the back of his hand over his mouth as he shambled forward in battered high-tops and an overcoat that had to be stifling in the midsummer heat.

"Yeah, Freddie. How's it going?"

"Been better. Been better, Jack, you know?" His eyes passed over M.J., then moved on. "Been better," he said again.

"Yeah, I know." Jack reached in his front pocket

for the bills he'd already placed there. "You could use a hot meal."

"A hot meal." Freddie stared at the bills, moistened his lips. "Sure could do with a hot meal, all right."

"You seen Ralph?"

"Ain't." Freddie's shaky fingers reached for the money, clamped on. He blinked up when Jack continued to hold the bills. "Ain't," he repeated. "Musta closed up early. It's a holiday, the Fourth of July. Damn kids been setting off firecrackers already. Can't tell them from gunshots. Damn kids."

"When's the last time you saw Ralph?"

"I dunno. Yesterday?" He looked at Jack for approval. "Yesterday, probably. I've been here awhile, but I ain't seen him. And his place is locked up."

"Have you seen anybody else who doesn't belong here?"

"Her." Freddie pointed at M.J. and smiled. "She don't."

"Besides her."

"Nope. Nobody." The voice went whiny. "I sure been better, Jack, you know."

"Yeah." Without bothering to sigh, Jack turned the money loose. "Get lost, Freddie."

"Yeah, okay." And he hurried down the street, around the corner.

"He's not going to buy food," M.J. murmured. "You know what he's going to buy with that."

"You can't save the world. Sometimes you can't even save a little piece of it. But maybe he won't mug anybody tonight, or get himself shot trying to." Jack shrugged. "He's been dead since the first time he picked up a needle. Nothing I can do about it."

"Then why do you feel so lousy about it?" She lifted a brow when he looked down at her. "It's all over your face, Dakota."

"He used to have a family" was all he said by way of an answer. "Let's go." He led her up the street, then ducked down the side of a building. To her surprise, he unlocked the cuffs. "You've got more sense than to take off in this neighborhood." He smiled. "And I've got your rock locked in the trunk of my car."

"On a street like this, you'll be lucky if your car's still there when you get back around."

"They know my car. Nobody'll mess with it." Then he turned—whirled, really—and made her jolt as he slammed two vicious kicks into a dull gray door.

She heard wood splinter, and pursed her lips in appreciation as the door gave way on the third try. "Nice job."

"Thanks. And if Ralph didn't get cute and change the code, we're in business." He stepped inside, scanned an alarm box beside the broken door. With quick fingers he stabbed numbers.

"How do you know his code?"

"I make it my business to know things. Move aside." With a strength she had to admire, he hauled the broken door up, muscled it back into place. "Ralph should have gone for steel. Too cheap."

He flicked on the lights, scanned the tiny space that was crammed with file boxes and smelled of must. M.J. watched a mouse scamper out of sight.

"Charming. I'm very impressed with your associates so far, Dakota. Would this be his secretary's year off?"

"Ralph doesn't have a secretary, either. He's a big believer in low overhead. Office is through here."

"I can't wait." Wary of rodents and anything else with more than two legs, she watched her step as she followed him. "This is what they call nighttime breaking and entering, isn't it?"

"Cops have a name for everything." He paused with his hand on a doorknob, glanced over his shoulder. "If you wanted someone who'd knock politely on the front door, you wouldn't be with me."

She lifted her arm, rattled the dangling handcuffs. "Remember these?"

He only shook his head. "You wouldn't be with me," he repeated, and opened the door.

She sucked in her breath, but it was the only sound she made. Later, he would remember that and appreciate her grit and her control. The backwash of light from the anteroom spilled into the closet-size office.

Gunmetal-gray file cabinets, scarred and dented, lined two walls. Papers spilled out of the open drawers, littered the floor, fluttered on the desk under the breeze of a whining electric fan.

Blood was everywhere.

The smell of it roiled in her stomach, had her clamping her teeth and swallowing hard. But her voice was steady enough when she spoke.

"That would be Ralph?"

Chapter 5

It had been a messy job, Jack thought. If it had been pros, they hadn't bothered to be quick or neat. But then, there'd been no reason for either. Ralph was still tied to the chair.

Or what was left of him was.

"You can wait in the back," Jack told her.

"I don't think so." She wasn't a stranger to violence. A girl didn't grow up in a bar and not see blood spilled from time to time.

But she'd never seen anything like this. As realistic as she considered herself, she hadn't really believed it was possible for one human being to inflict this kind of horror on another.

She kept her eyes on the wall, but stepped in beside him. "What do you think they were after?"

"The same thing I am. Anything that leads back

to whoever used Ralph to set us up. Stupid son of a bitch." His voice softened all at once, with what could only have been termed regret. "Why didn't he run?"

"Maybe he didn't have the chance." Her stomach was settling, but she continued to take small, shallow breaths. "We have to call the police."

"Sure, we'll call 911, then we'll wait and explain ourselves. From the inside of a cell." Crouching down, he began shuffling through papers.

"Jack, for God's sake, the man's been murdered."

"He won't be any less dead if we call the cops, will he? Never could figure out Ralph's filing system."

"Haven't you got any feelings at all? You knew him."

"I haven't got time for feelings." And since they were trying to surface, his voice was rough as sand. "Think about it, sugar. Whoever did this to him would love to play the same game with you. Take a good look, and ask yourself if that's how you want to end up."

He waited a moment, then accepted her silence as understanding. "Now you can go in the back room and save your sensibilities, or you can help me sort through this mess."

When she turned, he assumed she'd walk away. That she might keep on walking, no matter the neighborhood. But she stopped at a file cabinet, grabbed a handful of papers. "What am I looking for?"

"Anything."

"That narrows it down. And why should there be anything left? They've already been here."

"He'd keep a backup somewhere." Jack hissed at the snowfall of papers. "Why the hell didn't he use a computer like a normal person?"

Rising, he went to the desk, wrenched out a drawer. He searched it, turning it over, checking the underside, the back, then tossing it aside and yanking out another. On the third try, he found a false back.

His quick grunt of approval had M.J. turning, watching him take out a penknife and pry at wood. Giving up her own search, she walked to him. By tacit agreement with him, she gripped the loosened edge and tugged while he worked the knife around. Wood splintered from wood.

"It's practically cemented on," Jack muttered. "And recently."

"How do you know it's recent?"

"It's clean. No dust, no grime. Watch your fingers. Here, you take the knife. Let me…" They switched jobs. He skinned his knuckles, swore, and continued to peel the wood back. All at once it popped free.

Jack took the knife again, cut through the tape affixing a key to the back of the drawer. "Storage locker," he muttered. "I wonder what Ralph has tucked away."

"Bus station? Train station? Airport?" M.J. leaned closer to study the key. "It doesn't have a name, just a number."

"I'd go with one of the first two. Ralph didn't like to fly, and the airport's a trek from here."

"That still leaves a lot of locks on a lot of boxes," she reminded him.

"We'll track it down."

"Do you know how many storage lockers there must be in the metropolitan area?"

He turned the key between his fingers and smiled thinly. "We only need one." He took her hand, and before she realized his intent, he'd cuffed them together again.

"Oh, for God's sake, Jack."

"Just covering my bases. Come on, we've got work to do."

At the first bus station, he'd grudgingly removed the cuffs before dragging M.J. into a phone booth, and making an anonymous call to the police to report the murder. Then he carefully wiped down the phone. "If they've got caller ID," he told her, "they'll track down where the call was made."

"And I take it your prints are on file."

He flashed a grin. "Just a little disagreement over pool in my misspent youth. Fifty dollars and time served."

Because he'd shifted, she was backed into the corner of the booth, pressed to the wall by his body. "It's a little crowded in here."

"I noticed." He lifted a hand, skimmed back the hair at her temple. "You did all right back there. A lot of women would have gotten hysterical."

"I don't get hysterical."

"No, you don't. So give me a break here, will you?" He tipped her face up, lowered his head. "Just for a minute." And he closed his mouth over hers.

She could have resisted. She meant to. But it was an easy kiss, with need just a whispering note. It was almost friendly, could have been friendly, if not for the press of his body to hers, and the heat rising from it.

And an easy, almost friendly kiss shouldn't have made her want to cling, to hold on and hold tight. She compromised by fisting a hand on his back, not holding but not protesting.

If her lips softened under his, warmed and parted, it was only for a moment. It meant nothing. Could mean nothing.

"I want you." He murmured the words against her mouth, then again when his lips pressed to her throat. "This is a hell of a time for it, a hell of a place. But I want you, M.J. I'm having a hard time getting past that."

"I don't go to bed with strangers."

"Who's asking you to?" He lifted his head, met her eyes. "We've got each other figured, don't we? And you're not the kind of woman who needs fussy dates or fancy words."

"Maybe not." The fire he'd kindled inside her was still smoldering. "Maybe I haven't figured out what I need."

"Then think about it." He backed off, then took her hand and pulled her out of the booth. "We'll check the lockers. Maybe we'll get lucky."

They didn't. Not in that terminal or in the next two. It was nearly one in the morning before he pocketed the key.

"I want a drink."

She let out a breath, rolled her shoulders. After twelve hours in a waking nightmare, she could see his point. "I wouldn't turn one down. You buying?"

"Why not?"

He steered clear of any of the places where he might be recognized and chose instead a dingy little dive not far from Union Station.

"Good thing I've had my shots." M.J. wrinkled her

nose at the sticky, stamp-size table and checked the chair before she sat.

"It was either this or a fern bar. We can check out Union Station when we've had a break. Two of what you've got on tap," he told the waitress, and cracked a peanut.

"I don't know how places like this stay in business." With a critical eye, M.J. studied the atmosphere. Smoke-choked air, a generally stale smell, sticky floor littered with peanut shells, cigarette butts and worse. "A few gallons of disinfectant, some decent lighting, and this joint would turn up one full notch."

"I don't think the clientele cares." He glanced toward the surly-faced man at the bar, and the weary-eyed working girl who was casing him. "Some people just come into a bar to engage in the serious business of drinking until they're drunk enough to forget why they came into the bar to begin with."

She acknowledged his comment with a nod. "That's the type I don't want in my place. You get them from time to time, but they rarely come back. They're not looking for conversation and music or a companionable drink with a pal. That's what I serve at my place."

"Like father, like daughter."

"You could say that." M.J.'s eyes narrowed in disapproval as the waitress slammed down their mugs. Beer sloshed over the tops. "She wouldn't last five minutes at M.J.'s."

"Rude barmaids have their own charm." Jack picked up his beer and sipped gratefully. "I meant what I said earlier." He grinned when her gaze narrowed on his. "About that, too, but I meant how you handled yourself. It was a tough room, M.J., for anybody."

"It was a first for me." She cleared her throat, drank. "You?"

"Yeah, and I don't mind saying I hope it's my last. Ralph was a jerk, but he didn't deserve that. I'd have to say whoever did that to him enjoyed his work. You've got some real bad people interested in you."

"It looks that way." And those same people, she thought, would be interested in Bailey and Grace. "How long do you figure it'll take to find the lock that fits that key?"

"No telling. Knowing Ralph, he wouldn't go too far afield. He hid the key in his office, not his apartment, so odds are the box is close."

But if it wasn't, it could be hours, even days, before they found it. She wasn't willing to wait that long. She took another gulp of beer. "I need the restroom." When he narrowed his eyes, she smirked. "Want to come with me?"

He studied her a moment, then moved his shoulders. "Make it fast."

She didn't rush toward the back, but her mind was racing. Ten minutes, she calculated. That was all she needed, to get out, get to the phone booth she'd seen outside and get through to Bailey.

She closed the door of the ladies' room at her back, scanned the woman in black spandex primping in the mirror, then grinned at the small casement window set high in the wall.

"Hey, give me a leg up."

The woman perfected a second coat of bloodred lipstick. "A what?"

"Come on, be a pal." M.J. hooked a hand on the narrow sill. "Give me a boost, will you?"

Taking her maddening time, the woman slid the top back on her tube of lipstick. "Bad date?"

"The worst."

"I know the feeling." She tottered over on ice-pick heels. "Do you really think you can squeeze through that? You're skinny, but it'll be a tight fit."

"I'll make it."

The woman shrugged, exuded a puff of too-sweet designer-knockoff perfume and cupped her hands. "Whatever you say."

M.J. bounced a foot in the makeshift stirrup, then boosted herself up until she had her arms hooked on the sill. A quick wriggle and she was chest-high. "Just another little push."

"No problem." Getting into the spirit, the woman set both hands on M.J.'s bottom and shoved. "Sorry," she said when M.J. cracked her head on the window and swore.

"It's okay. Thanks." She wiggled, grunted, twisted and forced herself through the opening. Head, then shoulders. Taking a quick breath, trying not to imagine herself remaining corked in the window, she muscled her way through with only a quick rip of denim.

"Good for you, honey."

M.J. stayed on her hands and knees long enough to shoot her assistant a quick grin. Then she was off and running. She dug in her pocket as she went for the quarter habitually carried there.

She could hear her mother's voice. *Never leave the house without money for a phone call in your pocket. You never know when you'll need it.*

"Thanks, Ma," she murmured, and reached the

phone booth at a dead run. "Be there, be there," she whispered, plugging in the coin, stabbing numbers.

She heard Bailey's calm, cool voice answer on the second ring and swore as she recognized the recorded message.

"Where are you, where are you?" She clamped down on panic, took a breath. "Bailey, listen up," she began, the instant after the beep. "I don't know what the hell's going on, but we're in trouble. Don't stay there, he may come back. I'm in a phone booth outside some dive near—"

"Damn idiot." Jack reached in, grabbed her arm.

"Hands off, you son of a bitch. Bailey—" But he'd already disconnected her. Using the confines of the booth to his advantage, he twisted her around and clamped the cuffs on so that her arms were secured. Then he simply lifted her up and tossed her over his shoulder.

He let her rant, let her kick, and had her dumped back into the car before a single Good Samaritan could take interest. Her threats and promises bounced off him as he peeled away from the curb and shot down side streets.

"So much for trust." And where there wasn't trust, he thought, there had to be proof. Cautious, he doubled back, scouting the area until he found a narrow alley half a block from the phone booth. He backed in, shut off the lights and engine.

Reaching over, he vised a hand around the back of her neck, pulled her face close. "You want to see where your phone call would have gotten us? Just sit tight."

"Take your hands off me."

"At the moment, having my hands on you is the least of my concerns. Just be quiet. And wait for it."

When his grip loosened, she jerked back. "Wait for what?"

"It shouldn't take much longer." And, brooding into the dark, he watched the street.

It took less than five minutes. By his count, a little more than fifteen since her call. The van crept up to the curb. Two men got out.

"Recognize them?"

Of course she did. She'd seen them only that morning. One of them had broken in her door. The other had shot at her. With a quick tremor of reaction, she shut her eyes. They'd traced the call from Bailey's line, she realized. Traced it quickly and efficiently.

And if Jack hadn't moved fast, they might very well have snapped her up just as quickly, just as efficiently.

The smaller of the two went into the bar while the other stood by the phone booth, scanning the street, one hand resting under his suit jacket.

"He'll pass the bartender a couple of bucks to see if you were in there, if you were alone, how long ago you left. They won't hang around long. They'll find out you're still with me, so they'll be looking for the car. We won't be able to use it anymore around here tonight."

She said nothing as the second man came back out, joined the first. They appeared to discuss something, argue briefly, and then they climbed back in the van. This time it didn't creep down the street, it rocketed.

She remained silent for another moment, continued to stare straight ahead. "You were right," she said at length. "I'm sorry."

"Excuse me? I'm not sure I heard that."

"You were right." She had to swallow when she found herself distressingly close to tears. "I'm sorry."

Hearing the tears in her voice only heightened his temper. "Save it," he snapped, and started the engine. "Next time you want to commit suicide, just make sure I'm out of range."

"I needed to try. I couldn't not try. I thought you were overreacting, or just pushing my buttons. I was wrong. How many times do you want me to say it?"

"I haven't decided. If you start sniveling, I'm really going to get ticked."

"I don't snivel." But she wanted to. The tears were burning her throat. It cost nearly as much to swallow them as it would have to let them free.

She worked on calming herself as he drove out of the city and headed down a deserted back road in Virginia. The city lights giving way to comforting dark.

"No one's following us," she said.

"That's because I'm good, not because you're not stupid."

"Get off my back."

"If I'd sat in there another five minutes waiting for you, I could be as dead as Ralph right now. So consider yourself lucky I don't just dump you on the side of the road and take myself off to Mexico."

"Why don't you?"

"I've got an investment." He caught the look, the glimmer of wet eyes, and ground his teeth. "Don't look at me like that. It really makes me mad."

Swearing, he swerved to the shoulder. Yanking the key from his pocket, he unlocked her hands, then slammed out of the car to pace.

Why the hell was he tangled up with this woman? he asked himself. Why hadn't he cut himself loose? Why wasn't he cutting loose right now? Mexico wasn't such a bad place. He could get himself a nice spot on the beach, soak up the sun and wait for all this to blow over.

Nothing was stopping him.

Then she got out of the car, spoke quietly. "My friend's in trouble."

"I don't give a damn about your friend." He whirled toward her. "I give a damn about me. And maybe I give one about you, though God knows why, because you've been nothing but grief ever since I watched you swagger up those apartment steps."

"I'll sleep with you."

That cut his minor tirade off in midstream. "What?"

She squared her shoulders. "I'll sleep with you. I'll do whatever you want, if you help me."

He stared at her, at the way the moonlight showered over her hair, at the way her eyes continued to glisten. And wanted her mindlessly.

But not in a barter.

"Oh, that's nice." Bitterness spewed through his voice. "That's great. I don't even have to tie you to the damn railroad tracks." He stepped toward her, grabbed her by the arms and shook. "What the hell do you take me for?"

"I don't know."

"I don't use women," he said between his teeth. "And when I take one to bed, it's a two-way street. So thanks for the offer, but I'm not interested in the supreme sacrifice."

He let her go, started back to the car. Fury had him

turning back. "Do you think your friend would appreciate the gesture if he found out you'd slept with me to help him?"

She took a deep, steadying breath. The depth of his sense of insult had gone farther toward gaining her trust than any promise or oath could have. "No. It wouldn't stop me, but no."

She stepped toward him, stopping only when they were within an arm span. "My friend's name is Bailey James. She's a gemologist."

He recognized the name from the doctored paperwork. But the pronoun was the most vital piece of information to him. "She?"

"Yes, she. We went to college together, we roomed together. One of the reasons I located in D.C. was because of Bailey, and Grace. She was our other roommate. They're the closest friends I have, ever have had. I'm afraid for them, and I need your help."

"Bailey's the one who sent you the stone?"

"Yes, and she wouldn't have done it without good reason. I think she may have sent the third one to Grace. It would be Bailey's kind of logic. She does a lot of consulting work for the Smithsonian."

Suddenly tired, M.J. rubbed her gritty eyes. "I haven't seen her since Wednesday evening. We were supposed to get together tonight at the pub. I put a note under her door to check the time with her. I work a lot of nights, she works days, so even though we live right across the hall from each other, we pass a lot of notes under the door. And lately, since she got the job working on the Three Stars for the Smithsonian, she's been putting in a lot of overtime. I didn't think anything of it when I didn't see her for a couple days."

"And Friday you got the package."

"Yes. I called her at work right away, but I only got the service. They'd closed until Tuesday. I'd forgotten she'd told me they were closing down for the long weekend, but that she'd probably work through it. I went by, but the place was locked up. I called Grace, got her machine. By that time, I was annoyed with both of them. I figured I just was going to have to assume Bailey had her reasons and would let me know. So I went to work. I just went on to work."

"There's no use beating yourself up about that. You didn't have much choice."

"I have a key to her place. I could have used it. We've got this privacy arrangement, which is why we pass notes. I didn't use the key out of habit." She shuddered out a breath. "But she didn't answer the phone now, when I called from outside that bar, and it was two o'clock in the morning. Bailey's arrow-straight, she's not out at 2:00 a.m., but she didn't answer the phone. And I'm afraid... What they did to that man... I'm afraid for her."

He put his hands on her shoulders, and this time they were gentle. "There's only one thing to do." Because he thought she might need it, he pressed a kiss to her brow. "We'll check it out."

She let out her breath on a shuddering sigh. "Thanks."

"But this time you have to trust me."

"This time I will."

He opened the door, waited for her to get in. "The other friend you were talking about, the he?"

She pushed her hair back, looked up. "There is no he."

So he leaned down, captured her mouth with his in one long, searing kiss. "There's going to be."

He took a chance, went back to Union Station first. They'd be looking for his car, true enough, but he was banking on the moldy gray of the Olds, with its scarred vinyl top, blending in.

And he intended to be quick.

Bus and train stations were all very much the same in the middle of the night, he thought. The people curled in chairs or stretched out in blankets weren't all waiting for transportation. Some of them just had nowhere else to go.

"Keep moving," he told M.J. "And keep sharp. I don't want to get cornered in here."

She wondered, as she matched her pace to his, why such places smelled of despair in the early hours. There was none of the excitement, the bustle, the anticipation of goings and comings, so evident during the daylight hours. Those who traveled at night, or looked for a dry corner to sleep, were usually running low on hope.

"You said we were going to check on Bailey."

"Soon as I'm done with this." He headed straight for the storage lockers, did a quick scan. "Sometimes you just get lucky," he murmured, and, matching numbers, slid the key into a lock.

M.J. leaned over his shoulders. "What's in there?"

"Stop breathing down my neck and I'll see. Backup copies of your paperwork," he said, and handed them to her. "Souvenir for you."

"Gee, thanks. I'm really going to want a memento of our little vacation jaunt." But she stuffed them in her bag after a cursory glance. Her interest perked up when Jack drew out a small notebook covered in fake black leather. "That looks more promising."

"Where's his running money?" Jack wondered, deeply disappointed not to find any cash when he swiped his hand around the locker a last time. "He'd have kept some ready in here if he had to catch a train fast."

"Maybe he'd already taken it out."

He opened his mouth to disagree, then shut it again. "Yeah, you've got a point. Could be he wanted to have it on him if he wanted to make a fast exit." Brows knit, he flipped through the book. "Names, numbers."

"Addresses? Phone numbers?" she asked, craning her neck to try to see.

"No. Amounts, dates. Payoffs," he decided. "Looks to me like Ralph was running a little blackmail racket on the side."

"Salt of the earth, your friend Ralph."

"Former friend," Jack said automatically, before he remembered it was literally true. "Very former," he murmured. "If this got out, he'd have lost more than his business. He'd have been doing time in a cell."

"Do you think someone decided to blackmail the blackmailer?"

"Follows. And not everybody puts the arm on for money." He shook his head. According to the figures, Ralph had made more than a decent income with his sideline. "Sometimes they go for blood."

"What good does this do us?" M.J. demanded.

"Not a hell of a lot." He tucked the book into his back pocket, scanned the terminal again. "But someone Ralph was squeezing squeezed back. Or, more likely, someone who knew about Ralph's little moonlighting project saved the information until it became useful."

"Then killed him," M.J. added as her stomach tightened. "Whoever did isn't just connected with that little book, or Ralph. They're connected to Bailey through the stones. I have to find her."

"Next stop," he said, and took her hand in his.

Chapter 6

M.J. understood the risk, and prepared herself to make no arguments whatever about Jack's instructions. She'd ask no questions. This was his area of expertise, after all, and she needed a pro.

That vow lasted less than thirty minutes.

"Why are you just driving around?" she demanded. "You should have turned left back at the corner. Did you forget how to get there?"

"No, I didn't forget how to get there. I don't forget how to get anywhere."

She rolled her eyes in his direction. "Well, if you've got a map in your head, you've just taken a wrong turn."

"No, I didn't."

Men, she thought on a huff of breath. "I'm telling

you—I live here. The apartment's three blocks that way."

He'd told himself he'd be patient with her. She was under a lot of stress, they'd both put in a long, rough day.

His good intentions fled to the place M.J.'s vow had gone.

"I know where you live," he snapped. "I had your place staked out for two hours while you were out shopping."

"I wasn't shopping. I was buying, and that's entirely different. And you still haven't answered my very simple question."

"Do you ever shut up?"

"Are you ever anything but rude?"

He braked at a light, drummed his fingers on the wheel. "You want to know why I'm driving around, I'll tell you why I'm driving around. Because there are two guys with guns in a van looking for us, specifically in this car, and if they happen to be in the area, I'd just as soon see them before they see us. And the reason for that is, I'd prefer not being shot tonight. Is that clear enough?"

She folded her arms over her chest. "Why didn't you just say so in the first place?"

His answer was a mutter as he turned again. He drove sedately for a half block, then pulled over to the curb, shut off the engine.

"Why are you stopping here? We're still blocks away. Look, Jack, if your testosterone's low and you're lost, I won't hold it against you. I can—"

"I'm not lost." He put both hands in his hair, and

was tempted to pull. "I never get lost. I know what I'm doing." He reached over, popped open the glove box.

"Well, then, why—"

"We're going on foot," he told her, and grabbed a pencil-beam flashlight and a .38. He made sure she saw the gun and took his time checking the clip. She barely blinked at it.

"That doesn't make any sense. If we have to—"

"We're doing this my way."

"Oh, big surprise. I'm simply asking—"

"I'm tired of answering, *really* tired of answering." But he sighed out a breath. "We're going to cut down this street, then between those two yards, around the building on the next block, then through to the back of the apartment. We're going on foot because we'll be tougher to spot if they've got your building staked out."

She thought it over, considered the angles, then nodded. "Well, that makes sense."

"Thanks, thanks a lot." He grabbed her purse and, while she stuttered out a shocked protest, emptied her wallet of cash.

"Just what the hell do you think you're doing? That's my money." She snatched back her empty wallet as he stuffed bills in his pocket, then goggled as he plucked out the diamond and pushed it in after the bills. "Give me that. Are you out of your mind?"

She made a grab for him. Jack simply shoved her back against the seat, held her in place and, risking another bloody lip, crushed his mouth to hers. She wriggled, muttered what he assumed were oaths, popped her fist against his ribs. Then she decided to cooperate.

And her cooperation, hot, avid, was a great deal more difficult to resist than her protests. He lost himself in her for a moment, experienced the shock of being helpless to do otherwise.

It was like the first time. Consuming. The thought circled in his mind that he'd been waiting all his life to find his mouth pressed to hers.

Just that simple. Just that terrifying.

The fist she'd struck him with relaxed, and her open fingers slid around, up his back, hooked possessively over his shoulder. Mine, she thought.

Just that easy. Just that staggering.

When he shifted back, they stared at each other in the dim light, two strong-minded people who'd just had their worlds tilt under them. Her hand was still gripped on his shoulder, and his on hers.

"Why'd you do that?" she managed.

"It was mostly to shut you up." His hand skimmed up her shoulder, into her hair. "It changed."

Very slowly, she nodded. "Yes, it did."

He had a strong urge to drag her into the backseat and play teenager. The idea nearly made him smile. "I can't think about this now."

"No, me either."

The hand in her hair moved and, in a surprisingly sweet gesture took hers, laced fingers with hers. "We're going to do more than think about it later."

"Yeah." Her lips curved a little. "I guess we are."

"Let's go. No, don't take the purse." When she opened her mouth to argue, he simply tugged it away from her, tossed it into the back. "M.J., that thing weighs a ton. We may have to move fast. I'm taking the cash, and the stone, because they might make the car, or we may not get back to it."

"All right." She got out, waited for him on the sidewalk. Glanced briefly at the gun he secured in a shoulder holster. "I know this is risky. I have to do it, Jack."

He took her hand again. "Then let's do it."

They followed the route he'd mapped out, slipped between yards, a dog barking halfheartedly at them. The moon was out, a bright beacon that both guided their path and spotlighted them.

He had a moment to intensely wish he'd had her change out of the white T-shirt. It glowed in the dark like a lit-up flag. But she moved well, with quiet, long strides. He already knew she could run if necessary. He had to be satisfied with that.

"You have to do what I tell you," he began, keeping his voice low as he surveyed the back of her building. "I know that goes against the grain for you, but you'll have to swallow it. If I tell you to move, you move. If I tell you to run, you run. No questions, no arguments."

"I'm not stupid. I just like to know the reasons."

"This time you just do what you're told, and we'll discuss my reasoning later."

She struggled to fall into step. "Her car's here," she told him quietly. "The little white compact."

"Okay, so maybe she's home." Or, he thought, she hasn't been able to drive. But he didn't think that was what M.J. needed to hear. "We'll go in the side, through the fire door, work our way around to the stairs. No noise, M.J., no conversation."

"Okay."

Her eyes were already on Bailey's windows as they hurried toward the side door. The windows were dark, the curtains drawn. Bailey left her curtains open, was all she could think. Bailey liked to look out the windows and rarely shut out her view.

They slipped inside like shadows and, with Jack a half step in the lead, walked quietly to the steps. The security light beamed, lighting the hall and stairs. Jack glanced out the front door, keeping well to the side. If anyone was watching, he mused, they'd be spotted easily going into the light.

It was a chance they'd have to take.

As they moved up the stairs, he listened for any sound, any movement. It was so late it was early. The building slept. There wasn't even the murmur of a late-night TV behind any of the doors they passed on the second floor.

When they reached the third, M.J. made her first sound, just a quickly indrawn breath, instantly muffled. There was police tape over her door.

"Your neighbor with the bunny slippers called the cops," Jack murmured. "Odds are they're looking for you, too." He held out a hand. "Key?"

She turned, kept her eyes on Bailey's door as she dug into her pocket, handed it to him. He gestured her back toward the steps to give her room to run away, unsheathed his gun, then unlocked the door.

Keeping low, he used his light to scan, saw no movement. Holding a hand up to keep M.J. in place, he stepped inside. What he'd seen had already decided him that no one was there, but he wanted to check the bedroom, the kitchen, before M.J. joined him.

He'd taken the first steps when her gasp, unmuffled this time, had him turning. "Stay back," he ordered. "Stay quiet."

"Oh, God. Bailey." She shot toward the bedroom, leaping over ripped cushions, overturned chairs like a hurdler coming off the mark.

He reached the door a step ahead, shoved her roughly out of the way. "Hold it together, damn it," He hissed, then opened the door. "She's not here," he said a moment later. "Go close the front door, lock it."

On legs that trembled, she crossed back, taking a winding path through the destruction of the living room. She closed the door, locked it, then leaned back weakly.

"What have they done to her, Jack? Oh, God, what have they done to her?"

"Sit down. Let me look."

She squeezed her eyes tight, fought for control. Images flitted through her head. Her and Grace sitting in the shade of a boulder while Bailey gleefully hunted rocks. The three of them giggling like fools late at night over a jug of wine. Bailey, a wave of blond hair falling into her face soberly contemplating a pair of Italian shoes in a store display.

"I'll help," she said, and let out a whoosh of breath. "I can help."

Yeah, he thought, watching the way her spine stiffened, her shoulders squared, she probably could. "Okay, you've got to keep it quiet, and keep it quick. We can't risk the lights, or much time."

He skimmed the beam over the room. Contents of drawers and closets had been tossed and scattered. A few breakables smashed. The cushions, the mattress, even the back of chairs, had been slashed so that stuffing poured out in an avalanche of destruction.

"You're not going to be able to tell if anything's missing in all this mess." He surveyed the surface damage and calculated that the woman had gone in for tchotchkes in a big way. "But I can tell you, I don't think your friend was here when this went on."

M.J. pressed a hand to her heart, as though to hold in hope. "Why?"

"This wasn't a struggle, M.J. It was a search, a quick, messy and mostly quiet one. I'd say we have a pretty good idea what they were looking for. Whether they found it or not—"

"She'd have it with her," M.J. said quickly. "Her note was very clear that I should keep the stone with me. She'd have kept it with her."

"If that's true, then odds are she still has it. She wasn't here," he repeated, scanning the light into the living room. "She didn't put up a fight here, she wasn't hurt here. There's no blood."

Her knees wobbled again. "No blood." And she pressed a hand to her mouth to cut off the little sob of relief. "Okay. She's okay. She went underground, the same way we did."

"If she's as smart as you say she is, that's just what she'd do."

"She's smart enough to run if she had to run." It helped to look at the tumbled room with a more careful eye. "She doesn't have her car, so she's on foot or using public transportation." And M.J.'s heart sank at the thought of it. "She doesn't know the streets, Jack. She doesn't know the ropes. Bailey's brilliant, but she's naive. She trusts too easily, likes to believe the best in people. She's sweet," M.J. added, on a little shudder.

"She must have picked up something from you." He appreciated the fact that she could smile at that, even a little. "Let's just take a quick look through this stuff, see if anything pops out. Check her clothes—you could probably tell if she'd packed things."

"She has a travel kit, fully stocked. She'd never go anywhere without it." Buffered by that simple, everyday fact, M.J. headed into the bath to check the narrow linen closet.

Even there, items had been pulled out, the shelves stripped, bottles opened and emptied. But she found the kit itself, opened and empty on the floor, recognized several of its contents—the travel toothbrush, the fold-up hairbrush, the travel-size shampoos and soaps.

"It's here." She stepped into the bedroom, did her best to inventory clothes. "I don't think she took anything. There's a suit missing. It's fairly new, so I remember. A neat little blue silk. She might be wearing it. Hell, shoes and bags, I don't know. She collects them like stamps."

"She keep a stash anywhere?"

Insulted, she jerked up her head. "Bailey doesn't do drugs."

"Not drugs." Patience, he told himself, and cast his eyes at the ceiling. "You sure have an opinion of me, sugar. Money, cash."

"Oh." She rose from her crouch. "Sorry. Yeah, she keeps some cash." It bothered her a little, but she led him into the kitchen. "Boy, is she going to hate seeing this. She really likes things ordered. It's kind of an obsession with her. And her kitchen." She kicked some cans, coated with the flour and sugar and coffee that had been dumped out of canisters. "You'd be hard-pressed to find a crumb in the toaster."

"I'd say we've all got bigger problems than housekeeping."

"Right." She bent down, retrieved a soup can. "It's one of those fake safe things," she explained, and twisted off the top. "She didn't take her emergency money, either." And there was relief in that. "She probably hasn't even been back here since— Hey!" She jerked the can back, but he'd already scooped out the cash. "Put that back."

"Listen, we can't risk using plastic, so we need money. Cash money." He stuck a comfortingly thick wad of it in his pocket. "You can pay her back."

"I can? You took it."

"Details," he muttered, grabbing her hand. "Let's go. There's nothing here, and we're pushing our luck."

"I could leave her a note, in case she comes back. Stop dragging me."

"She may not be the only one who comes back." He yanked her through the door and kept tugging until they were heading down the stairs.

"I've got to see about Grace."

"One friend at a time, M.J. We're getting out of Dodge for a while."

"I could call her, on my phone, or your cellular. Jack, if Bailey and I are in the middle of this, Grace is, too."

"Travel as a pack, do you?"

"So?" She hurried toward the side door with him, fueled by fresh worry. "I have to contact her. She has a place in Potomac. I don't think she's there. I think she's up at her country place, but—"

"Quiet." He eased open the door, scanned the quiet side lot, the sleeping neighborhood. It had been smooth and easy so far. Smooth and easy made him edgy. "Keep it down until we're clear, will you? God, you've got a mouth."

She snarled with it as he pulled her outside and started eating up the ground. "I don't see what the problem is. Whoever was looking for Bailey and the diamond have been and gone."

"Doesn't mean they won't come back." He caught the glint of moonlight off the chrome of the van just as it squealed into the lot. "Sometimes I hate being right. Go!" he shouted, shoving her ahead of him.

He whirled to protect her back, tried a quick prayer that they hadn't been spotted. And decided God was busy at the moment, when the van doors burst open. The gun was in his hand, the first shot fired, before he spun around and sprinted after her.

He hoped the single shot would give his pursuers something to consider. "I said go!" he snapped out when he all but mowed her down.

"I heard a shot. I thought—"

"Don't think. Run." He grabbed her hand to be certain she did, and was grateful she had no problem keeping pace.

They stormed between the yards, and this time the dog took a keener interest, sending up a wild din that carried for blocks. Moonlight flowed in front of them. Though he heard no footsteps pounding in pursuit, Jack didn't break stride as they whipped around the side of a building, turned the corner.

He took time to scan the street, then hit the ground running. "In" was all he said as he sprinted to the driver's side.

He needn't have bothered with the order. M.J. was already wrenching open the door and diving onto the seat. "They didn't come after us," she panted. "That's bad. They should have come after us."

"You catch on." He flicked the key, hit the gas and shot out from the curb just as the van screamed around the corner. "Grab on to something."

Though she wouldn't have believed it possible, he spun the big car into a fast U-turn, riding two wheels over the opposing curb. His bumper kissed lightly off the fender of a sedan, and then he was screaming down the quiet suburban street at sixty.

He took the first turn with the van three lengths behind. "You know how to use a gun?"

M.J. picked it up off the seat. "Yeah."

"Let's hope you don't have to. Get your seat belt on, if you can manage it," he suggested as he jerked the Olds around another corner. M.J.'s elbow rapped against the dash. "And don't point that thing in this direction."

"I know how to handle a gun." Teeth set, she braced herself and watched through the rear window. "Just drive. They're closing in."

Jack flicked his gaze into the rearview, measured the distance from the oncoming headlights. "Not this time," he promised.

He wound through the streets like a snake, tapping the brake, flooring the gas, whipping the wheel so that his tires whined. The challenge of it, the speed, the insanity, had him grinning.

"I like to do this to music." And he switched the radio up to blare.

"You're crazy." But she found herself grinning madly back at him. "They want to kill us."

"People in hell want snow cones." He hit a four-lane and pushed the car to eighty. "This tank might not look like much, but she moves."

"So does that van. You're not shaking them."

"I haven't gotten started." He skimmed his gaze fast, left, right, then plowed recklessly through a red light. Traffic was sparse, even as they zipped toward downtown. "That's the trouble with D.C.," he commented. "No nightlife. Politicians and ambassadors."

"It has dignity."

"Yeah, right." He wrestled the car around a curve at fifty, and began to travel the rabbit warren of narrow back streets and circles. He heard the ping of metal against metal as a bullet hit his rear fender.

"Now they're getting nasty."

"I think they're trying to shoot out the tires."

"I just bought these babies."

Old or new, she thought, if a bullet hit rubber, the game was over. M.J. took a deep breath, held it, then popped out the window to her waist and fired.

"Are you crazy?" His heart jumped into his throat and nearly had him crashing into a lamppost. "Get your head back in here before you get it blown off."

Grim-eyed, too wired to be afraid, she fired again. "Two can play." With the third shot, she hit a headlight. The shattering glass pumped her adrenaline. It hardly mattered that she'd been aiming at the windshield. "I hit them."

With a mindless snarl, Jack grabbed the seat of her jeans and dragged her in. For the first time in his life, his hands trembled on the wheel of his car. "Who do you think you are, Bonnie Parker?"

"They backed off."

"No, they didn't. I'm outrunning them. Just let me handle this, will you?"

He twisted his way back to the four-lane, careened

straight across, shooting over the median with a bone-rattling series of bumps. Sparks spewed out like stars as steel skidded on concrete. With a skill M.J. admired, he wrestled the car into a wide arc, then headed north.

"They're trying it." She twisted in the seat, poked her head out the window again, despite Jack's steady swearing. "I don't think they're gonna—" She hooted at the sound of crunching metal. "They're backing up, heading north on the southbound."

"I can see. I don't need a damn play-by-play. Get back in here. Strap in this time."

He hit the on-ramp for the Beltway at sixty. And had gained just enough time, he calculated, to make it work. He barreled off at the first exit and headed into Maryland.

"You lost them." She crawled over and gave him an enthusiastic smack on the cheek. "You're good, Dakota."

"Damn right." He was also shaky. The moment he felt he could afford it, he pulled to the shoulder and wiped her grin away by grabbing her shoulders and giving her a hard, teeth-rattling shake. "Don't you ever do anything so stupid again. You're lucky you didn't fall out of the window, or get your head shot off."

"Cut it out, Jack." Her hand was already fisting. "I mean it." Then she went limp as he hauled her against him and held tight. His face was buried in her hair, his heart was pounding. "Hey." Baffled, moved, she patted his back. "I was just pulling my weight."

"Don't." His mouth found hers in a desperate kiss. "Just don't." And as abruptly as he'd grabbed her, he shoved her away. "You've gotten to me," he muttered, furious at the emotions storming through him. "Just shut up." His head whipped around when she opened her mouth. "Just shut up. I don't want to talk about it."

"Fine." Her own stomach was trembling. As if the fate of the world depended on it, she meticulously buckled her seat belt as he pulled back onto the road. "I'd really like to call my friend Grace."

His hands were tensed on the wheel, but he kept his voice even. "We can't risk it now. We don't know what kind of equipment they've got in that van, and they're too close yet. We'll see what we can manage tomorrow."

Knowing she'd have to settle for that, she rubbed her restless hands on her knees. "Jack, I know what you risked going to Bailey's to try to ease my mind. I appreciate it."

"Just part of the service."

"Is it?"

He glanced over, met her eyes. "Hell, no. I said I don't want to talk about it."

"I'm not talking about it." She wasn't sure she knew how, or what to do about these unexpected feelings swimming through her. "I'm thanking you."

"Then you're welcome. Look, I'm heading back to the Bates Motel. Which are you more—hungry or tired?"

That, at least, didn't take any thought. "Hungry."

"Good, so am I."

She had a lot of considering to do, M.J. decided. Her friend was missing, she had a priceless blue diamond in her possession—or in Jack's pocket—and she'd been chased, shot at and handcuffed.

Added to that, she was very much afraid she was

falling for some tough-eyed, swaggering bounty hunter who drove like a maniac and kissed like a dream.

A hot, sweaty dream.

And she knew barely more of him than his name.

It made no sense, and though she enjoyed being reckless in some areas, her heart wasn't one of them. She'd always kept a firm hand there, and it was frightening to feel that grip slipping over a man she'd literally rammed into only the day before.

She wasn't a romantic woman, or a fanciful one. But she was an honest woman. Honest enough to admit that whatever danger she was facing from the outside, she was facing danger just as great, just as real, from her own heart.

He was trembling with fury. Incompetence. It was unacceptable to find himself surrounded by utter incompetence. It was true he'd had to hire the men quickly, and with only the thinnest of recommendations, but their failure to execute one small task, to deal with one woman, was simply outrageous.

He had no doubt he could have dealt with her handily himself, if he could have risked the exposure.

Now, with the moon set and the stars fading, he stood on the terrace, calming his soul with a glass of wine the color of new blood.

It was partly his fault, he conceded. Certainly, he should have checked more carefully into the matter of Jack Dakota. But time had been of the essence, and he had assumed the fool of a bail bondsman was capable of following the orders to assign someone just competent enough to take her, and wise enough to turn her over.

Apparently, Jack Dakota wasn't a wise man, but a stubborn one. And the woman was infuriatingly lucky. M. J. O'Leary. Well, perhaps she had the luck of the Irish, but luck could change.

He would see to that.

Just as he would see to Bailey James. She would have to surface eventually. He'd be ready. And Grace Fontaine... Pity.

Well, he would find the third stone, as well.

He would have all of them. And a heavy price would be paid by all who had tried to stop him.

His fingers snapped the fragile stem. Glass tinkled on the stone. Wine splattered and pooled. Grimly he smiled down, watched the red liquid seek the cracks.

More than blood would be spilled, he promised himself.

And soon.

Chapter 7

They settled in the little all-night diner just down from the motel. Coffee, strong enough to walk on, came first, served by a sleepy-eyed waitress wearing a cotton-candy-pink uniform and a plastic name tag that declared her Midge.

M.J. shifted in the booth, catching her jeans on the torn vinyl of the seat, perused the hand-typed menu under its plastic coating, then propped an elbow on the scarred surface of the coffee-stained linoleum that covered their table.

A very ancient country-and-western tune was twanging away on the juke, and the air was redolent of the thick odor of frying grease.

Aesthetics weren't served there, but breakfast was. Twenty-four hours a day.

"That's almost too perfect," M.J. commented after

she ordered a whopping breakfast, including a short stack, eggs over and a rasher of bacon. "She even looks like a Midge—hardworking, competent and friendly. I always wondered if people grew into their names or vice versa. Like Bailey—cool, studious, smart. Or Grace, elegant, feminine and generous."

Jack rubbed a hand over the stubble on his chin. "So what's M.J. stand for?"

"Nothing."

He cocked a brow. "Sure it does. Mary Jo, Melissa Jane, Margaret Joan, what?"

She sipped her coffee. "It's just initials. And that's been made legal, too."

His lips curved. "I'll get you drunk and you'll spill it."

"Dakota, I come from a long line of Irish pub owners. Getting me drunk is beyond your capabilities."

"We'll have to check that out—maybe in your place. Dark wood?" he asked with a half smile. "Lots of brass. Irish music, live on weekends?"

"Yep. And not a fern in sight."

"Now we're talking. And seeing as you own it, you can buy the first round as soon as we're clear."

"It's a date." She picked up her cup again. "And, boy, am I looking forward to it."

"What, we're not having fun yet?"

She eased back as the waitress set their heaping plates on the table. "Thanks." Then picked up a fork and dug in. "It's had its moments," she told him. "Can I see Ralph's book?"

"What for?"

"So I can admire its handsome plastic binding," she said sweetly.

"Sure, why not?" He lifted his hips, drew it out and tossed it on the table. As she flipped through the pages, he sampled his eggs. "See anyone you know?"

It was the cocky tone of his voice that made her delighted to be able to glance up at him, smile and say, "Actually, I do."

"What?" He would have snatched the book back if she hadn't held it out of reach. "Who?"

"T. Salvini. That's got to be one of Bailey's stepbrothers."

"No kidding?"

"No kidding. There's a five and three zeros after his name. Just think. Tim or Tom did business with Ralph. You did business with Ralph, now I'm—in a loose manner of speaking—doing business with you." Those dark-river-green eyes shifted up, met his. "Small world, right, Jack?"

"From where I'm sitting," he agreed.

"Here's another payment, about five K. Looks like the bill came in on the eighteenth of the month—goes four, no, five months back." Thoughtfully she tapped the book on the edge of the table. "Now I wonder what one, or both, of the creeps did that was worth twenty-five thousand to keep Ralph quiet about it."

"People do things all the time they want kept quiet—and they pay for it, one way or another."

She angled her head. "You're a real student of human nature, aren't you, Dakota? And a cynic, as well."

"Life's a cynical journey. Well, we've got one solid connection back to Ralph. Maybe we'll pay the creeps a visit soon."

"They're businessmen," she pointed out. "Slimy,

from my viewpoint, but murder's a big jump. I can't see it."

"Sometimes it's a much smaller step than you'd think." He took the book back, pocketed it again. "On that cynical journey."

"I can see them cooking the books," she said speculatively. "Timothy has a gambling problem—meaning he likes to play and tends to lose."

"Is that so? Well, Ralph had a lot of connections when it came to, let's say, games of chance. That's a link that slides neat onto the chain."

"So Ralph finds out the creep's playing deep, maybe skimming the till to keep from getting his legs broken, and he puts the pressure on."

"It might work. And Salvini whines to somebody who's got more muscle—somebody who wants the Stars." He moved his shoulders and decided to give it a chance to brew. "In any case, that wasn't bad work, sugar."

"It was great work," she corrected.

"I'll cop to good. And you looked pretty natural with your hips hanging out the car window, shooting at a speeding van." He drowned his pancakes in syrup. "Even if it did stop my heart. If you ever decide to change careers, you'd make a passable skip tracer."

"Really?" She wasn't sure if she should be complimented or worried by the assessment. She decided to be flattered. "I don't think I could spend my life on the hunt—or being hunted." She shook enough salt on her eggs to make Jack—a sodium fan—wince. "How do you? Why do you?"

"How's your blood pressure?"

"Hmm?"

"Never mind. I figure you go with your strengths. I'm good at tracking, backtracking, then figuring out the steps people are planning to take. And I like the hunt." He grinned wolfishly. "I love the hunt. Doesn't matter what size the prey is, as long as you bring them down."

"Crime's crime?"

"Not exactly. That's a cop attitude. But if you've got the right point of view, it's just as satisfying to snag some deadbeat father running from back child support as it is to bag a guy who shot his business partner. You can bring down both if you get to know your quarry. Mostly they're stupid—they've got habits they don't break."

"Such as?"

"A guy dips into the till where he works. He gets caught, charged, then he jumps bail. Odds are he's got friends, relatives, a lover. It won't take long before he asks somebody for help. Most people aren't loners. They think they are, but they're not. Something always pulls them back. They'll make a call, a visit. Leave a paper trail. Take you."

Surprised, she frowned. "I hadn't done anything."

"That's not the issue. You're a smart woman, a self-starter, but you wouldn't have gone far, you wouldn't have gone long without calling your friends." He scooped up eggs, smiled at her. "In fact, that's just what you did."

"And what about you? Who would you call?"

"Nobody." His smile faded. He continued to eat as the waitress topped off their coffee.

"No family?"

"No." He picked up a slice of bacon, snapped it in

two. "My father took off when I was twelve. My mother handled it by hating the world. I had an older brother, signed with the army the day he hit eighteen. He decided not to come back. I haven't heard from him in ten, twelve years. Once I got into college, my mother figured her job was done and hit the road. You could say we don't keep in touch."

"I'm sorry."

He jerked his shoulder against the sympathy, irritated with himself for telling her. He didn't talk family. Ever. With anyone.

"You haven't seen your family in all these years," she continued, unable to prevent herself from probing just a bit. "You don't know where they are—they don't know where you are?"

"We weren't what you'd call close, and we didn't spend enough time together to be considered dysfunctional."

"But still—"

"I always figured it was in the blood," he said, cutting her off. "Some people just don't stay put."

All right, she thought, his family was out of the conversation. It was a tender spot, even if he didn't realize it. "What about you, Jack? How long have you stayed put?"

"That's part of the appeal of the job. You never know where it's going to take you."

"That's not what I meant." She searched his face. "But you knew that."

"I never had any reason to stay." Her hand rested on the table, an inch from his. He was tempted to take it, just hold it. That worried him. "I know people, a lot of people. But I don't have friends—not the way you do with Bailey and Grace. A lot of us go through life without that, M.J."

"I know. But do you want to?"

"I never gave it a hell of a lot of thought." He rubbed both hands over his face. "God, I must be tired. Philosophizing over breakfast in the Twilight Diner at five in the morning."

She glanced out the window at the lightening sky to the east, the all-but-empty road. "'And down the long and silent street, the dawn—'"

"'With silver-sandaled feet, crept like a frightened girl.'" Finishing the quote, he shrugged. She was goggling at him.

"How do you know that? Just what did you take in college?"

"Whatever appealed to me."

Now she grinned, propped her elbows on the table. "Me too. I drove my counselors crazy. I can't tell you how many times I was told I had no focus."

"But you can quote Oscar Wilde at 5:00 a.m. You can shoot a .38, drop-kick your average man, you eat like a trucker, understand ancient Roman gods, and I bet you mix a hell of a boilermaker."

"The best in town. So here we are, Jack, a couple of people most would say are overeducated for their career choices, drinking coffee at an ungodly hour of the morning, while a couple of guys in a van with one headlight hunt for us and the pretty rock you've got in your pocket. It's the Fourth of July, we've known each other less than twenty-four hours under very possibly the worst of circumstances, and the person who brought us together is dead as Moses."

She pushed her plate aside. "What do we do now?"

He took bills out of his pocket, tossed them on the table. "We go to bed."

The motel room was still tacky, cramped and dim. The thin flowered spread was still mussed where they had stretched out on it hours before.

Only hours, she thought. It felt like days. A lifetime. More than a lifetime. It felt as if she'd known him forever, she realized as she watched him empty his pocket onto the dresser, that he'd been a vital part of her forever.

If that wasn't enough, maybe the wanting was. Maybe wanting like this was the best thing to hold on to when your world had gone insane. There was nothing and no one left to trust but him.

Why should she say no? Why should she turn away from comfort, from passion? From life?

Why should she turn away from him, when every instinct told her he needed those things as much as she did?

He turned, and waited. He could have seduced her. He had no doubt of it. She was running on sheer nerves now, whether she knew it or not. So she was vulnerable, and needy, and he was there.

Sometimes that alone was enough.

He could have seduced her, would have, if it hadn't been important. If she hadn't been so inexplicably and vitally important. Sex would have been a relief, a release, a basic physical act between two free-willed adults.

And that should have been all he wanted.

But he wanted more.

He stayed where he was, beside the dresser, as she stood at the foot of the bed.

"I've got something to say," he began.

"Okay."

"I'm in this with you until it's over because that's the way I want it. I finish what I start. So I don't want anything that comes from gratitude or obligation."

If her heart hadn't been jumping, she might have smiled. "I see. So if I suggested you sleep in the bathtub, that wouldn't be a problem?"

He eased a hip onto the dresser. "It'd be your problem. If that's what you want, you can sleep in the bathtub."

"Well, you never claimed to be a gentleman."

"No, but I'll keep my hands off you."

She angled her head, studied him. He looked dangerous, plenty dangerous, she decided as her pulse quickened. The dark stubble, the wild mane of hair, those hard gray eyes so intense in that tough, rawboned face.

He thought he was giving her a choice.

She wondered if either of them was fool enough to believe she had one.

So her smile was slow, arrogant. She kept her eyes on his as she reached down, tugged her T-shirt out of her jeans. She watched his gaze flick down to her hands, follow them up as she pulled the shirt over her head, tossed it aside.

"I'd like to see you try," she murmured, and unsnapped her jeans. He straightened on legs gone watery when she began to lower the zipper.

"I want to do that."

With heat already tingling in her fingertips, she let her hands fall to her sides. "Help yourself."

Her shoulders were long, fascinating curves. Her breasts were pale and small and would cup easily in a man's palm. But for now, he looked only at her face.

He took his time, tried to, crossing to her, catching the metal tab between his thumb and finger, drawing it slowly down. And his eyes were on hers when he slid his hand past the parted denim and cupped her.

Felt her, hot, naked. Felt her tremble, quick, deep.

"I had a feeling."

She let out a careful breath, drew in another through lungs that had become stuffed with cotton. "I didn't get to my laundry this week."

"Good." He eased the denim down another inch, slid his hands around her bottom. "You're built for speed, M.J. That's good, because this isn't going to be slow. I don't think I could manage slow right now." He yanked her against him, arousal to arousal. "You're just going to have to keep up."

Her eyes glinted into his, her chin angled in a dare. "I haven't had any trouble keeping up with you so far."

"So far," he agreed, and ripped a gasp from her when he lifted her off her feet and clamped his hungry mouth to her breast.

The shock was stunning, glorious, an electric sizzle that snapped through her blood and slapped her heartbeat into overdrive. She let her head fall back and wrapped her legs tight around his waist to let him feed. The scrape of his beard against her skin, the nip of teeth, the slide of his tongue—each a separate, staggering thrill.

And each separate, staggering thrill tore through her system and left her quivering for more.

The fall to the bed—a reckless dive from a cliff. The grip of his hands on hers—another link in the chain. His mouth, desperate on hers—a demand with only one answer.

She pulled at his shirt, rolled with him until he was free of it and they were both bare to the waist. And found the muscles and bones and scars of a warrior's body. The heat of flesh on flesh raged through her like a firestorm.

Her hands and mouth were no less impatient than his. Her needs no less brutal.

With something between an oath and a prayer, he flipped her over, dragging at her jeans. His mouth busily scorched a path down her body as he worked the snug denim off. Desire was blinding him with hammer blows that stole the breath and battered the senses. No hunger had ever been so acute, so edgy and keen, as this for her. He only knew if he didn't have her, all of her, he'd die from the wanting.

Those long naked limbs, the energy pulsing in every pore, those harsh, panting gasps of her breath, had the blood searing through his veins to burn his heart. Wild for her, he yanked her hips high and used his mouth on her.

The climax screamed through her, one long, hot wave with jagged edges that had her sobbing out in shock and delight. Her nails scraped heedlessly down his back, then up again until they were buried in his thick mane of gold-tipped hair. She let him destroy her, welcomed it. And, with her body still shuddering from the onslaught, wrestled him onto his back to tear at the rest of his clothes.

She felt his heart thud, could all but hear it. Their flesh, slick with sweat, slid smoothly as they grappled. His fingers found her, pierced her, drove her past desperation. If speech had been possible, she would have begged.

Rather than beg, she clamped her thighs around him, and took him inside, fast and deep.

His fingers dug hard into her hips when she closed over him. His breath was gone; his heart stopped. For an instant, with her raised above him, her head thrown back, his hands sliding sinuously up her body, he was helpless.

Hers.

Then she began to move, piston-quick, riding him ruthlessly in a wild race. Her breath was sobbing, her hands were clutched in her hair. In some part of his brain he realized that she, too, was helpless.

His.

He reared up, his mouth greedy on her breast, on her throat, wherever he could draw in the taste of her while they moved together in a merciless, driving rhythm.

Then he wrapped his arms around her, pressed his lips to her heart, groaning out her name as they shattered each other.

They stayed clutched, joined, shuddering. Time was lost to him. He felt her grip slacken, her hands slide weakly down his back, and brushed a kiss over her shoulder. He lay back, drawing her with him so that she was sprawled over his chest.

He stroked a hand over her hair and murmured, "It's been an interesting day."

She managed a weak chuckle. "All in all." They were sticky, exhausted, and quite possibly insane, she thought. Certainly, it was insane to feel this happy, this perfect, when everything around you was wrecked.

She could have told him she'd never been intimate with a man so quickly. Or that she'd never felt so in tune, so close to anyone, as with him.

But there didn't seem to be a point. What was happening to them was simply happening. Opening her eyes, she studied the stone resting atop the scarred dresser. Did it glow? she wondered. Or was it simply a trick of the light of the room?

What power did it have, really, beyond material wealth? It was just carbon, after all, with some elements mixed in to give it that rare, rich color. It grew in the earth, was of the earth, and had once been taken, by human hands, from it.

And had once been held in the hands of a god.

The second stone was knowledge, she thought, and closed her eyes. Perhaps some things were known only to the heart.

"You need to sleep," Jack said quietly. The tone of his voice made her wonder where his mind had wandered.

"Maybe." She rolled off him, stretched out on her stomach across the width of the bed. "My body's tired, but I can't shut off my head." She chuckled again. "Or I can't now that I'm able to think again. Making love with you is a regular brain drain."

"That's a hell of a compliment." He sat up, running a hand over her shoulder, down her back, then stopping short at the subtle curve of her bottom. Intrigued, he narrowed his eyes, leaned closer. Then grinned. "Nice tattoo, sugar."

She smiled into the hot, rumpled bedspread. "Thanks. I like it." She winced when he switched on the bedside lamp. "Hey! Lights out."

"Just want a clear look." Amused, he rubbed his thumb over the colorful figure on her butt. "A griffin."

"Good eye."

"Symbol of strength—and vigilance."

She turned her head, cocked it so that she could see his face. "You know the oddest things, Jack. But yeah, that's why I chose it. Grace got this inspiration about the three of us getting tattoos to celebrate graduation. We took a weekend in New York and each got our little butt picture."

Her smile slid away as thoughts of her friends weighed on her heart. "It was a hell of a weekend. We made Bailey go first, so she wouldn't chicken out. She picked a unicorn. That's so like her. Oh, God."

"Come on, turn it off." He was mortally afraid she might weep. "As far as we know, she's fine. No use borrowing trouble," he continued, kneading the muscles of her back. "We've got plenty of our own. In a couple hours, we'll clean up, go out and cruise around, try to call Grace."

"Okay." She pulled in the emotion, tucked it into a corner. "Maybe—"

"Did you run track in college?"

"Huh?"

The sudden change of subject accomplished just what he'd wanted it to. It distracted her from worry. "Did you run track? You've got the build for it, and the speed."

"Yeah, actually, I was a miler. I never liked relays. I'm not much of a team player."

"A miler, huh?" He rolled her over and, smiling, traced a fingertip over the curve of her breast. "You gotta have endurance."

Her brows lifted into her choppy bangs. "That's true."

"Stamina." He straddled her.

"Absolutely."

He lowered his head, toyed with her lips. "And you have to know how to pace yourself, so you've got wind for that final kick."

"You bet."

"That's handy." He bit her earlobe. "Because I'm planning on pacing myself this time. You know the saying, M.J.? The one about slow and steady winning the race?"

"I think I've heard of it."

"Why don't we test it out?" he suggested, and captured her mouth with his.

This time she slept, as he'd hoped she would. Face-down again, he mused, studying her, crossways over the bed. He stroked her hair. He couldn't seem to touch her enough, and couldn't remember ever having this need to touch before. Just a brush on the shoulder, the link of fingers.

He was afraid it was ridiculously sentimental, and was grateful she was asleep.

A man with a reputation for being tough and cynical didn't care to be observed mooning like a puppy over a sleeping woman.

He wanted to make love with her again. That, at

least, was understandable. To lose himself in sex—the hot, sweaty kind, or the slow and sweet kind.

She'd turn to him, he knew, if he asked. He could wake her now, arouse her before her mind cleared. She'd open for him, take him in, ride with him.

But she needed to sleep.

There were shadows under her eyes—those dark, witchy green eyes. And when the flush of passion faded from her skin, her cheeks had been pale with fatigue. Sharp-boned cheeks, defined by a curve of silky skin.

He pressed his fingers to his eyes. Listen to him, he thought. The next thing he knew, he'd be composing odes or something equally mortifying.

So he nudged her over, made himself comfortable. He'd sleep for an hour, he thought, setting his internal clock. Then they would step back into reality.

He closed his eyes, shut down.

M.J. woke to the sound of rain. It reminded her of lazy mornings, summer showers. Snuggling into the pillow, shifting from dream to dream.

She did so now, sliding back into sleep.

The horse leaped over the narrow stream, where shallow water flashed blue. Her heart leaped with it, and she clutched the man tighter. Smelled leather and sweat.

Around them, buttes rose like pale soldiers into a sky fired by a huge white sun. The heat was immense.

He was in black, but it wasn't her knight. The face was the same—Jack's face—but it was shadowed under a wide-brimmed black hat. A gun belt rode low on his hips, instead of a silver sword.

The empty land stretched before them, wide as the

sea, with waves of rocks, sharp-edged as honed knives. One misstep, and the ground would be stained with their blood.

But he rode fearlessly on, and she felt nothing but the power and excitement of the speed.

When he reined in, turned in the saddle, she poured herself into his arms, met those hard, demanding lips eagerly with her own.

She offered him the stone that beat with light and a fire as blue as the hottest flame.

"It belongs with the others. Love needs knowledge, and both need generosity."

He took it from her, secured it in the pocket over his heart. "One finds the other. Both find the third." His eyes lit. "And you belong to me."

In the shadow of a rock, the snake uncoiled, hissed out its warning. Struck.

M.J. shot up in bed, a scream strangled in her throat. Both hands pressed to her racing heart. She swayed, still caught in the dream fall.

The snake, she thought with a shudder. A snake with the eyes of a man.

Lord. She concentrated on steadying her breathing, controlling the tremors, and wondered why her dreams were suddenly so clear, so real and so odd.

Rather than stretch out again, she found a T-shirt—Jack's—and slipped it on. Her mind was still fuzzy, so it took her a moment to realize it wasn't rain she was hearing, but the shower.

And that alone—knowing he was just on the other side of the door—chased away the last remnants of fear.

She might be a woman whose pride was based on

being able to handle herself in any situation. But she'd never faced one quite like this. It helped to know there was someone who would stand with her.

And he would. She smiled and rubbed the sleep out of her eyes. He wouldn't back down, he wouldn't turn away. He would stick. And he would face with her whatever beasts were in the brush, whatever snakes there were in the shadows.

She rose, raking both hands through her hair, just as the bathroom door opened.

He stepped out, a billow of steam following. A dingy white towel was hooked at his waist, and his body still gleamed with droplets of water. His hair was slick and wet to his shoulders, gold glinting through rich brown.

He had yet to shave.

She stood, heavy-eyed, tousled from sleep, wearing nothing but his wrinkled T-shirt, tattered at the hem that skimmed her thighs.

For a moment, neither of them could do more than stare.

It was there, as real and alive in the tatty little room as the two of them. And it gleamed as bright, as vital, as the stone that had brought them to this point.

Jack shook his head as if coming out of a dream—perhaps one as vivid and unnerving as the one M.J. had awakened from. His eyes went dark with annoyance.

"This is stupid."

If she'd had pockets, her hands would have been in them. Instead, she folded her arms and frowned back at him. "Yeah, it is."

"I wasn't looking for this."

"You think I was?"

He might have smiled at the insulted tone of her

voice, but he was too busy scowling, and trying desperately to backpedal from what had just hit him square in the heart. "It was just a damn job."

"Nobody's asking you to make it any different."

Eyes narrowed, he took a step forward, challenge in every movement. "Well, it is different."

"Yeah." She lowered her hands to her sides, lifted her chin. "So what are you going to do about it?"

"I'll figure it out." He paced to the dresser, picked up the stone, set it down again. "I thought it was just the circumstances, but it's not." He turned, studied her face. "It would have happened, anyway."

Her heartbeat was slowing, thickening. "Feels like that to me."

"Okay." He nodded, planted his feet. "You say it first."

"Uh-uh." For the first time since he'd opened the door, her lips twitched. "You."

"Damn it." He dragged a hand through his dripping hair, felt a hundred times a fool. "Okay, okay," he muttered, though she was waiting silently, patiently. Nerves drummed under his skin, his muscles coiled like wires, but he looked her dead in the eye.

"I love you."

Her response was a burst of laughter that had him clamping his teeth until a muscle jerked in his jaw. "If you think you're going to play me for a sucker on this, sugar, think again."

"Sorry." She snorted back another laugh. "You just looked so pained and ticked off. The romance of it's still pittering around in my heart."

"What, do you want me to sing it?"

"Maybe later." She laughed again, the delighted

sound rolling out of her and filling the room. "Right now I'll let you off the hook. I love you right back. Is that better?"

The ice in his stomach thawed, then heated into a warm glow. "You could try to be more serious about it. I don't think it's a laughing matter."

"Look at us." She pressed a hand to her mouth and sat down on the foot of the bed. "If this isn't a laughing matter, I don't know what is."

She had him there. In fact, he realized, she had him, period. Now his lips curved, with determination. "Okay, sugar, I'm just going to have to wipe that smirk off your face."

"Let's see if a big tough guy like you can manage it."

She was grinning like a fool when he shoved her back on the bed and rolled on top of her.

Chapter 8

She had to learn to defer to him on certain matters, M.J. told herself. That was compromise, that was relationship. The fact was, he had more experience in situations like the one they were in than she did. She was a reasonable person, she thought, one who could take instruction and advice.

Like hell she was.

"Come on, Jack, do I have to wait till you drive to Outer Mongolia to make one stupid phone call?"

He flipped her a look. He'd been driving for exactly ten minutes. He was surprised she'd waited that long to complain. She was worried, he reminded himself. The past twenty-four hours had been rough on her. He was going to be reasonable.

In a pig's eye.

"You use that phone before I say, and I'll toss it out the window."

She drummed her fingers on the little pocket phone in her hand. "Just answer me this. How is anybody going to trace us through this portable? We're out in the middle of nowhere."

"We're less than an hour outside of D.C., city girl. And you'd be surprised what can be traced."

Okay, maybe he wasn't exactly sure himself if it could be done. But he thought it was possible. If her friend's phone was tapped, and whoever was after them had the technology, it seemed possible that the frequency of her flip phone could be a trail of sorts.

He didn't want to leave a trail.

"How?"

He'd been afraid she'd ask. "Look, that thing's essentially a radio, right?"

"Yeah, so?"

"Radios have frequencies. You tune in on a frequency, don't you?" It was the best he could do, and it was a relief to see her purse her lips and consider it. "Plus, I want to put some distance between where we are and where we're staying. If it was the FBI on our tails, I'd want them chasing in circles."

"What would the FBI want with us?"

"It's an example." He didn't beat his head on the steering wheel, but he wanted to. "Just deal with it, M.J. Just deal with it."

She was trying to, trying to remind herself that it had only been a day, after all. One single day.

But her life had changed in that single day.

"At least you could tell me where we're going."

"I'm taking 15, north toward Pennsylvania."

"Pennsylvania?"

"Then you can make your call. After, we'll head

southeast, toward Baltimore." He flicked her another glance. "If the Os are in town, we can take in a game."

"You want to go to a ball game?"

"Hey, it's the Fourth of July. Ball games, beer, parades and fireworks. Some things are sacred."

"I'm a Yankee fan."

"You would be. But the point is, a ballpark's a good place to lose ourselves for a couple hours—and a good place for a meet if you're able to contact Grace."

"Grace at a baseball game?" She snorted. "Right."

"It's a good cover," he began, then frowned. "Your friend has something against the national pastime?"

"Sports aren't exactly Grace's milieu. Now, a nice, rousing fashion show, or maybe a thrilling opera."

It was his turn to snort. "And you're friends?"

"Hey, I've been known to go to the opera."

"In chains?"

She had to laugh. "Practically. Yeah, we're friends." She let out a sigh. "I guess it's hard, surface-wise, to see why. The scholar, the Mick and the princess. But we just clicked."

"Tell me about them. Start with Bailey, since this starts with Bailey."

"All right." She drew a deep breath, watched the scenery roll by. Little snatches of country, thick with trees and hills that rolled. "She's lovely, has this fragile look about her. Blonde, brown-eyed, with rose-petal skin. She has a weakness for pretty things, silly, pretty things, like elephants. She collects them. I gave her one carved out of soapstone for her birthday last month."

Remembering how normal it had all been, how simple, had her pressing her lips together. "She likes old movies, especially the film noir type, and she can be a little dreamy at times. But she's very focused. Of the three of us back in college, she was the only one who knew exactly what she wanted and worked toward it."

He liked the sound of Bailey, Jack thought. "And what did she want?"

"Gemology. She's fascinated by rocks, stones. Not just jewel types. We keep talking about the three of us going to Paris for a couple weeks, but last year we ended up in Arizona, rockhounding. She was happy as a pig in slop. And she's had a lot of unhappiness in her life. Her father died when she was a kid. He was an antique dealer—so that's another of her weaknesses, beautiful old things. Anyway, she adored her dad. Her mother tried to hold the business together, but it must have been rough. They lived up in Connecticut. You can still hear New England in her voice. It's classy."

She lapsed into silence a moment, struggling to push back the worry. "Her mother married again a few years later, sold the business, relocated in D.C. Bailey was fond of the guy. He treated her well, got her interested in gems—that was his area—sent her to college. Her mother died when she was in college—a car accident. It was a rough time for Bailey. Her stepfather died a couple years later."

"It's tough, losing people right and left."

"Yeah." She glanced at Jack, thought of him losing father, brother, mother. Perhaps never really having them to lose. "I've really never lost anyone."

He understood where her mind had gone, and he shrugged. "You get through. You go on. Didn't Bailey?"

"Yeah, but it scarred her. It's got to scar a person, Jack."

"People live with scars."

He wouldn't discuss it, she realized, and turned back to the scenery. "Her stepfather left her a percentage of the business. Which didn't sit well with the creeps."

"Ah, yeah, the creeps."

"Thomas and Timothy Salvini—they're twins, by the way, mirror images. Slick-looking characters in expensive suits, with hundred-dollar haircuts."

"That's one reason to dislike them," Jack noted. "But it's not your main one."

"Nope. I never liked their attitudes—toward Bailey, and women in general. It's easiest to say Bailey considered them family from the get-go, and the sentiment wasn't returned. Timothy was particularly rough on her. I get the impression they mostly ignored her before their old man died, and then went ballistic when she inherited part of Salvini in the will."

"And what's Salvini?"

"That's their name, and the name of the gem business. They design, buy, sell gems and jewelry out of a fancy place in Chevy Chase."

"Salvini... Can't say I've heard of it, but then I don't buy a lot of baubles."

"They sell some awesome glitters—especially the ones Bailey designs. And they do consultant work for estates, museums. That's primarily Bailey's forte, too. Though she loves design work."

"If Bailey does design work and consulting, what do the creeps do?"

"Thomas handles the business end—accounts, sales, takes a lot of trips to check out sources for gems. Timothy works in the lab when it suits him, and likes to stride around the showroom looking important."

Restless, she reached out to fiddle with the buttons of his stereo and had her fingers slapped. "Hands off."

"Touchy about your toys, aren't you?" she muttered. "Well, anyway, it's a pretty posh little firm, old established rep. It was her contacts at the Smithsonian that copped them the job with the Three Stars. She was dancing on the ceiling when it came through, couldn't wait to get her hands on them, put them under one of those machines she uses. The somethingmeters, and whattayascopes she uses in their lab."

"So she was verifying authenticity, assessing value."

"You got it. She was dying for us to see them, so Grace and I went in last week. That was the first time I'd laid eyes on them—but they seemed almost familiar. Spectacular, almost unreal, yet familiar. I suppose it's because Bailey'd described them to us." She rolled her shoulders to toss off the sensation, and the memory of the dreams. "You've seen the one, touched it. It's magnificent. But to see the three of them, together, it just stops your heart."

"Sounds to me as though they stopped someone's conscience. If Bailey's as honest as you say—"

M.J. interrupted him. "She is."

"Then we'll have to check out the stepbrothers."

Her brows shot up. "Would they actually have the nerve to try to steal the Three Stars?" she wondered. "Could that be why Ralph was blackmailing one of them, rather than the gambling?"

"No."

"Well, why not?" Then she shook her head, answering her own question. "Couldn't be—the payments started months ago, and they'd just recently got the contract."

"There you go."

She brooded over it a moment longer. "But maybe they were planning to steal the Stars. If they were trying to pull a fast one, got away with it, it would destroy their business...the business their father slaved a lifetime to build," she added slowly. "And that would destroy Bailey. Even the thought of it. She'd do almost anything to prevent that from happening."

"Like ship off the stones to the two people in the world she felt she could trust without question."

"Yeah—and face down her stepbrothers. Alone." Fear was a claw in her throat. "Jack."

"Stay logical." His voice snapped to combat the waver in hers. "If they're involved in this—and I'd say it fits—it means they've got a client, a buyer. And they need all three Stars. She's safe as long as they don't. She's safe as long as we're out of reach."

"They'd be desperate. They could be holding her somewhere. They might have hurt her."

"Hurt's a long way from dead. They'd need her alive, M.J., until they round up all three. And from the rundown you've just given me, your pal may have a fragile side, and she may be naive, but she's not a chump."

"No, she's not." Steadying herself, M.J. looked at the phone in her lap. The call, she realized, wasn't just a risk for herself, but a risk for all of them. "If you want to drive to New York before I use this, it's okay with me."

He reached out, squeezed a hand over hers. "We're not going to Yankee Stadium, no matter how much you beg."

"I don't just owe you for me now. I should have realized it before. I owe you for Bailey, and for Grace. I've put them in your hands, Jack."

He drew his hand away, clamped it on the wheel. "Don't get sloppy on me, sugar. It pisses me off."

"I love you."

His heart did a long, slow circle in his chest, made him sigh. "Hell. I guess you want me to say it again, now."

"I guess I do."

"I love you. What's the M.J. stand for?"

It made her smile, as he'd hoped it would. "Look, Jack, wild sex and declarations of love are one thing. But I haven't known you long enough for that one."

"Martha Jane. I really think it's Martha Jane."

She made a rude buzzing sound. "Wrong. And that puts you out of this round, sir, better luck next time."

There'd be a birth certificate somewhere, he mused. He knew how to hunt. "Okay, tell me about Grace."

"Grace is a complicated woman. She's utterly, unbelievably beautiful. That's not an exaggeration. I've seen grown men turn into stuttering fools after one flash of her baby blues."

"I'm looking forward to meeting her."

"You'll probably swallow your tongue, but that's all right, I'm not the jealous sort. And it's kind of a kick to watch guys go into instant meltdown around Grace. You flipped through the pictures in my wallet when you searched my purse, didn't you?"

"Yeah, I took a look."

"There's a couple of me with Grace and Bailey in there."

He skimmed his mind back, focused in. And didn't want to tell her he'd barely noted the blonde or the brunette. The redhead had taken most of his attention. "The brunette—wearing a big silly hat in one of them."

"Yeah, that was on our rockhounding trip last year. We had a tourist snap it. Anyway, she's gorgeous, and she grew up privileged. And orphaned. She lost her folks young and lived with an aunt. The Fontaines are filthy rich."

"Fontaine…Fontaine…" His mind circled. "As in Fontaine Department Stores?"

"Right the first time. They're rich, stuffy, snotty snobs. Grace enjoys shocking them. She was expected to do her stint at Radcliffe, do the obligatory tour of Europe, and land the appropriate rich, stuffy, snotty snob husband. She's done everything but cooperate, and since she's got mountains of money of her own, she doesn't really give two damns what her family thinks."

She paused, considered. "I don't think she'd give two damns if she was flat broke, either. Money doesn't drive Grace. She enjoys it, spends it lavishly, but she doesn't respect it."

"People who work for their money respect it."

"She's not a do-nothing trust-funder." M.J. said, immediately defensive. "She just doesn't care if people see her that way. She does a lot of charity work—quietly. That's private. She's one of the most generous people I know. And she's loyal. She's also contrary and moody. She'll take off for days at a time when the whim strikes her. Just go. It might be Rome—or it might be Duluth. She just has to go. She has a place up in western Maryland—I guess you'd call it a country home, but it's small and sweet. Lots of land, very isolated. No phone, no neighbors. I think she was going there this weekend."

She shut her eyes, tried to image. "I don't know if I could find the place. I've only been up there once, and Bailey did the driving. Once I get out of the city, all those country roads look the same. It's in the mountains, near some state forest."

"It might be worth checking out. We'll see. Would she go to her family if there was trouble?"

"The last place."

"How about a man?"

"Why would you depend on something you could twist into knots with a smile? No, there's no man she'd go to."

He thought about that one awhile, then blinked, remembered and grinned. "Grace Fontaine—the Ivy League Miss April. It was the hat in the wallet shot that threw me off. I'd never forget that…face."

"Really?" Voice dry as dirt, she shifted to look at him over the top of her sunglasses. "Do you spend a lot of your time drooling over centerfolds, Dakota?"

"I did over Miss April," he admitted cheerfully, and rubbed a hand over his heart. "My God, you're pals with Miss April."

"Her name's Grace, and she posed for that years ago, when we were in college. She did it to needle her family."

"Thank the Lord. I think I still have that issue somewhere. I'm going to have to take a much closer look now. What a body," he remembered, fondly. "Women built like that are a gift to mankind."

"Perhaps you'd like to pull over, and we'll have a moment of silence."

He looked over, kept right on grinning. "Gee, M.J.,

your eyes are greener. And you said you weren't the jealous sort."

"I'm not." Normally. "It's a matter of dignity. You're having some revolting, prurient fantasy about my best friend."

"It's not revolting, I promise. Prurient, maybe, but not revolting." He took the punch on the arm without complaint. "But it's you I love, sugar."

"Shut up."

"Do you think she'll sign the picture for me? Maybe right across the—"

"I'm warning you."

Fun was fun, he thought, but a man could push his luck. In more ways than one. He turned off 15, headed east.

"Wait, I thought we were going up to P.A. to call."

"You just said Grace had a place in western Maryland. It wouldn't be smart to head in that general direction just now. Change of plans. We head in toward Baltimore first. Go ahead and make the call. I think we've said our last goodbye to our little motel paradise." He smiled patted her hand. "Don't worry, sugar, we'll find another."

"It couldn't possibly be the same. I hope," she added, and dialed hurriedly. "It's ringing."

"Keep it short, don't say where you are. Just tell her to go to a public phone, public place, and call you back."

"I—" She swore. "It's her machine. I was afraid of this." She tapped her fist impatiently against her knees as Grace's recorded voice flowed through the receiver. "Grace, pick up, damn it. It's urgent. If you check in for messages, don't go home. Don't go to the house.

Get to a public phone and call my portable. We're in trouble, serious trouble."

"Wrap it up, M.J."

"Oh, God. Grace, be careful. Call me." She disconnected with a little catch of breath. "She's up in the mountains—or she got a wild hair and decided to fly to London for the Fourth. Or she's on the beach in the West Indies. Or...they've already found her."

"Doesn't sound like a lady who's easy to track. I'm leaning toward your first choice." He cut off on the interstate, headed north. "We're going to circle around a little, then stop and fill up the tank. And buy a map. Let's see if we can jog some of your memory and find Grace's mountain hideaway."

The prospect settled her nerves. "Thanks."

"Isolated, huh?"

"It's stuck in the middle of the woods, and the woods are stuck in the middle of nowhere."

"Hmm. I don't suppose she walks around naked up there." He chuckled when she hit him. "Just a thought."

They found a gas station, and a map. In a truck stop just off the interstate, they stopped for lunch. With the map spread out over the table, they got down to business.

"Well, there's only, like, a half a dozen state forests in western Maryland," Jack commented, and forked up some of his meat-loaf special. "Any one of them ring a bell?"

"What's the difference? They're all trees."

"A real urbanite, aren't you?"

She shrugged, bit into her ham sandwich. "Aren't you?"

"Guess so. I never could understand why people want to live in the woods, or in the hills. I mean, where do they eat?"

"At home."

They looked at each other, shook their heads. "Most every night, too," he agreed. "And where do they go for fun, for a little after-work relaxation? On the patio. That's a scary thought."

"No people, no traffic, no restaurants or movie theaters. No life."

"I'm with you. Obviously our pal Grace isn't."

"*My* pal," she said with an arched brow. "She likes solitude. She gardens."

"What, like tomatoes?"

"Yeah, and flowers. The time we went up, she'd been grubbing in the dirt, planting—I don't know, petunias or something. I like flowers, but all you have to do is buy them. Nobody says you have to grow them. There were deer in the woods. That was pretty cool," she remembered. "Bailey got into the whole business. It was okay for a couple days, but she doesn't even have a television up there."

"That's barbaric."

"You bet. She just listens to CDs and communes with nature or whatever. There's a little store—had to be at least four miles away. You can get bread and milk or sixpenny nails. It looked like something out of Mayberry, except that's in the South. There was a bank, I think, and a post office."

"What was the name of the town?"

"I don't know. Dogpatch?"

"Funny. Try to imagine the route, just more or less. You'd have headed up 270."

"Yeah, and then onto 70 near, what is it? Frederick. I zoned out some. Think I even slept. It's an endless drive."

"You had pit stops," he prompted her. "Girls don't take road trips without plenty of pit stops."

"Is that a slam?"

"No, it's a fact. Where'd you stop—what did you do?"

"Somewhere off 70. I was hungry. I wanted fast food."

She shut her eyes, tried to bring it back.

You're still eating like a teenager, M.J.

So?

Why don't we try a salad for a change?

Because a day without fries is a sad and wasted day.

It made her smile, remembering now how Bailey had rolled her eyes, laughed, then given in.

"Oh, wait. We grabbed a quick lunch, but then she saw this sign for antiques. Big antique barnlike place. She went orgasmic, had to check it out. It was off the interstate, had a silly country-type name. Ah…" She strained for it. "Rabbit Hutch, Chicken Coop. No, no, with water. Trout Stream. Beaver Creek!" she remembered. "We stopped to antique at this huge flea market or whatever it's called at Beaver Creek. She'd have spent the weekend there if I hadn't dragged her out. She bought this old bowl and pitcher for Grace—like a housewarming gift. I bought her a rocking chair for her porch. We had a hell of a time loading it in Bailey's car."

"Okay." With a nod, he folded the map. "We'll finish eating, then head toward Beaver Creek. Take it from there."

Later, when they stood in the parking lot of the antique mart, M.J. sipped a soft drink out of a can. She'd done the same on the trip with Bailey, and she hoped it would somehow jog her memory.

"I know we got back on 70. Bailey was chattering away about some glassware—Depression glass. She was going to come back and buy the place out. There was some table she wanted, too, and she was irritated she hadn't snapped it up and had it shipped. I won the tune toss."

"The what?"

"The tune toss. Bailey likes classical. You know, Beethoven. Whenever we drive, we flip a coin to see who gets to pick the tunes. I won, so we went for Aerosmith—my version of longhair."

"I think we're made for each other. It's getting scary." He leaned down, nipped her mouth with his. "What was she wearing?"

"What is this sudden obsession with how my friends dress?"

"Just bring it all back. Complete the picture. The more details, the clearer it should be."

"Oh, I get it." Mollified, she pursed her lips and studied the sky. "Slacks, sort of beige. Bailey shies away from bold colors. Grace is always giving her grief about it. A silk blouse, tailored, sort of pink and pale. She had on these great earrings. She'd made them. Big chunks of rose quartz. I tried them on while she was driving. They didn't suit me."

"Pink wouldn't, not with that hair."

"That's a myth. Redheads can wear pink. We got off the interstate onto a western route. I can't remember the number, Jack. Bailey had it in her head. It was written down, but she didn't need me to navigate."

He consulted the map. "68 heads west out of Hagerstown. Let's see if it looks familiar."

"I know it was another couple hours from here," she said as she climbed back in. "I could drive for a while."

"No, you couldn't."

She skimmed her gaze over the car, noting that the back door was hooked shut with wire. "This heap is hardly something to be proprietary about, Jack."

His jaw set. The heap had, until recently, been his one true love. "There's more chance of you remembering if we stick with the plan."

"Fine." She stretched out her legs as he turned out of the parking lot. "Do you ever think about a paint job?"

"The car has character just the way it is. And it's what's under the hood that counts, not a shiny surface."

"What's under the hood," she said, then glanced at the stereo system. "And in the dash. I bet that toy set you back four grand."

"I like music. What about that Tinkertoy you drive?"

"My MG is a classic."

"It's a kiddie car. You must have to fold up your legs just to get behind the wheel."

"At least when I parallel-park, it's not like docking a steamship in port."

"Pay attention to the road, will you?"

"I am." She offered him the rest of her soft drink. "I know it looks like it, but you don't actually live in this car, do you?"

"When I have to. Otherwise, I've got a place on Mass Avenue. A couple of rooms."

Dusty furniture, he thought now. Mountains of

books, but no real soul. No roots, nothing he couldn't leave behind without a second thought.

Just like his life had been, up to the day before.

What the hell was he doing with her? he thought abruptly. There was nothing behind him that could remotely be called a foundation. Nothing to build on. Nothing to offer.

She had family, friends, a business she'd forged herself. What did they have in common, other than the situation they were in, similar tastes in music and a preference for city life?

And the fact that he was in love with her.

He glanced over at her. She was concentrating now, he noted. Leaning forward in the seat, frowning out the window as she tried to pick out landmarks.

She wasn't beautiful, he thought. He might have been blind in love, but he would never have termed her by so simple a term. That odd, foxy face caught the eye—certainly the male eye. It was sexy, unique, with the contrast of planes and angles and the curve of that overlush mouth.

Her body was built for speed and movement, rather than for fantasy. Yet he'd lost himself in it, in her.

He knew he'd turned a corner when he met her, but hadn't a clue where the road would lead either of them.

"This is the road." She turned, beamed at him, and stopped his heart. "I'm sure of it."

He bumped up the speed to sixty-five. As long as one of them was sure, he thought.

Chapter 9

The road cut straight through the mountain. M.J. supposed it was some sort of nifty feat of engineering, but it made her uneasy. Particularly all the signs warning of falling rock and those high, jagged walls of cliffs on either side of them.

Muggers she could understand, anticipate, but who, she wondered, could anticipate Mother Nature? What was to stop her from having a minor tantrum and perhaps heaving down a couple of boulders at the car? And since it was big enough to sleep eight, it was a dandy target.

M.J. kept a wary eye out of the side window, willing the rocks to stay put until they were through the pass.

Ahead, mountains rose and rolled, lushly green with summer. Heat and humidity merged to make the air thick as syrup. Tires hummed along the highway.

Occasionally she would see houses behind the road-side trees, glimpses only, as if they were hiding from prying eyes. She wondered about them, those tucked-away houses, undoubtedly with neat yards guarded by yapping dogs, decorated with gardens and swing sets, accented with decks and patios for grills and red-wood chairs.

It was one way to live, she supposed. But you had to tend that garden, mow that lawn.

She'd never lived in a house. Apartments had always suited her lifestyle. To some, she supposed, an apartment would seem like a box tucked with other boxes within a box. But she'd always been satisfied with her own space, with the camaraderie of being part of the hive.

Why would you need a lawn and a swing set unless you had kids?

She felt a quick little jitter in her stomach at the idea. Had she actually ever thought about having children before? Rocking a baby, watching it grow, tying shoes and wiping noses.

It was Grace who was soft on children, she thought. Not that she herself didn't like them. She had a platoon of cousins who seemed bent on populating the world, and M.J. had spent many an hour on a visit home cooing over a new baby, playing on the floor with a toddler or pitching a ball to a fledgling Little Leaguer.

She didn't imagine it was quite the same when the child was yours. What did it feel like, she mused, to have your own baby rest its head on your shoulder and yawn, or to have a shaky-legged toddler lift its arms up to you to be held?

And what in God's name was she doing thinking

about children at a time like this? Weary, she slipped her fingers under her shaded glasses, pressed them to her eyes.

Then slid a considering glance at Jack's profile. What, she wondered, did he think about kids?

Incredibly, she felt heat rising to her cheeks, and turned her face back to the window quickly. Idiot, she told herself. You've known the guy an instant, and you're starting to think of diapers and booties.

That, she thought grimly, was just what happened to a woman when she got herself tied up over some man. She went soft all over, particularly in the head.

Then she let out a shout that surprised them both. "There! That's the exit! That's where we got off. I'm sure of it."

"Next time just shoot me," Jack suggested as he swung the car into the right lane. "It's bound to be less of a shock than a heart attack."

"Sorry."

He eased off the exit, giving her time to orient herself as they came to a two-lane road.

"Left," she said after a moment. "I'm almost sure we went left."

"Okay, I need to gas up this hog, anyway." He headed for the closest service station and pulled up next to the pumps. "What was on your mind back there, M.J.?"

"On my mind?"

"You went away for a while."

The fact that he'd been able to tell disconcerted her. She shifted in the seat, shrugged her shoulders. "I was just concentrating, that's all."

"No, you weren't." He cupped a hand under her

chin, turned her face to his. "That's exactly what you weren't doing." He rubbed his thumb over her lips. "Don't worry. We'll find your friends. They're going to be all right."

She nodded, felt a wash of shame. Grace and Bailey should have been on her mind, and instead she'd been daydreaming over babies like some lovesick idiot. "Grace will be at the house. All we have to do is find it."

"Hold that thought." He leaned forward, touched his lips to hers. "And go buy me a candy bar."

"You've got all the dough."

"Oh, yeah." He got out, reached into his front pocket and pulled out a handful of bills. "Splurge," he suggested, "and buy yourself one, too."

"Gee, thanks, Daddy."

He grinned as she walked away, long legs striding, narrow hips twitching under snug denim. Hell of a package, he mused as he slipped the nozzle into the gas tank. He wasn't going to question the twist of fate that had dropped her into his life, and into his heart.

But he wondered how long it would be before she did. People didn't stay in his life for long—they came and went. It had been that way for so long, he'd stopped expecting it to be different. Maybe he'd stopped wanting it to be.

Still, he knew that if she decided to take a walk, he'd never get over it. So he'd have to make sure she didn't take a walk.

Feeding the greedy tank of the Olds, he watched her come back out, cross to the soft-drink machine. And he wasn't the only one watching, Jack noted. The teenager fueling the rusting pickup at the next pump had an eye on her, too.

Can't blame you, buddy, Jack thought. She's a picture, all right. Maybe you'll grow up lucky and find yourself a woman half as perfect for you.

And blessing his luck, Jack screwed the cap back on his tank, then strolled over to her. She had her hands full of candy and soft drinks when he yanked her against him and covered her mouth in a long, smoldering, brain-draining kiss.

Her breath whooshed out when he released her. "What was that for?"

"Because I can," he said simply, and all but swaggered in to pay his tab.

M.J. shook her head, noted that the teenager was gawking and had overfilled his tank. "I wouldn't light a match, pal," she said as she passed him and climbed into the car.

When Jack joined her, she went with impulse, plunging her hands into his hair and pulling him against her to kiss him in kind.

"That's because I can, too."

"Yeah." He was pretty sure he felt smoke coming out of his ears. "We're a hell of a pair." It took him a moment to clear the lust from his mind and remember how to turn the key.

Both thrilled and amused by his reaction, she held out a chocolate bar. "Candy?"

He grunted, took it, bit in. "Watch the road," he told her. "Try to find something familiar."

"I know we weren't on this road very long," she began. "We turned off and did a lot of snaking around on back roads. Like I said, Bailey had it all in her head.

Bailey!" As the idea slammed into her, she pressed her hands to her mouth.

"What is it?"

"I kept asking myself where she would go. If she was in trouble, if she was running, where would she go?" Eyes alight, she whirled to face him. "And the answer is right there. She knows how to get to Grace's place. She loved it there. She'd feel safe there."

"It's a possibility," he agreed.

"No, no, she'd go to one of us for sure." She shook her head fiercely, desperately. "And she couldn't get to me. That means she headed up here, maybe took a bus or a train as far as she could, rented a car." Her heart lightened at the certainty of it. "Yes, it's logical, and just like her. They're both there, up in the woods, sitting there figuring out what to do next and worrying about me."

And so was he worrying about her. She was putting all her hope into a long shot, but he didn't have the heart to say it. "If they are," he said cautiously, "we still have to find them. Think back, try to remember."

"Okay." With new enthusiasm, she scanned the scenery. "It was spring," she mused. "It was pretty. Stuff was blooming—dogwoods, I guess, and that yellow bush that's almost a neon color. And something Bailey called redbuds. There was a garden place," she remembered suddenly. "A whatchamacallit, nursery. Bailey wanted to stop and buy Grace a bush or something. And I said we should get there first and see what she already had."

"So we look for a nursery."

"It had a dopey name." She closed her eyes a moment, struggled to bring it back. "Corny. It was right on the road, and it was packed. That's one of the reasons I didn't want to stop. It would have taken forever. Buds 'N' Blooms." She smacked her hands together as she remembered. "We made a right a mile or so beyond it."

"There you go." He took her hand, lifted it to his mouth to kiss. And had them both frowning at the gesture. He'd never kissed a woman's hand before in his entire life.

Inside M.J.'s stomach, butterflies sprang to life. Clearing her throat, she laid her hand on her lap. "Well, ah… Anyway, Grace and Bailey went back to the plant place. I stayed at her house. Those two get a big bang out of shopping. For anything. I figured they'd buy out the store—which they almost did. They came back loaded with those plastic trays of flowers, and flowers in pots, and a couple of bushes. Grace keeps a pickup at her place. I can imagine what they'd write in the *Post*'s style section about Grace Fontaine driving a pickup truck."

"Would she care?"

"She'd laugh. But she keeps this place to herself. The relatives—that's what she calls her family, the relatives—don't even know about it."

"I'd say that's to our favor. The less people who know about it, the better." His lips curved as he noted a sign. "There's your garden spot, sugar. Business is pretty good, even this late in the year."

Delight zinged through her as she spotted the line of cars and trucks pulled to the side of the road, the crowds of people wandering around tables covered with flowers. "I bet they're having a holiday sale. Ten percent off any red, white or blue posies."

"God bless America. About a mile, you said?"

"Yeah, and it was a right. I'm sure of that."

"Don't you like flowers?"

"Huh?" Distracted, she glanced at him. "Sure, they're okay. I like ones that smell. You know, like those things, those carnations. They don't smell like sissies, and they don't wimp out on you after a couple days, either."

He chuckled. "Muscle flowers. Is this the turn?"

"No...I don't think so. A little farther." Leaning forward, she tapped her fingers on the dash. "This is it, coming up. I'm almost sure."

He downshifted, bore right. The road rose and curved. Beside it fences were being slowly smothered by honeysuckle, and behind them cows grazed.

"I think this is right." She gnawed on her lip. "All the damn roads back here look the same. Fields and rocks and trees. How do people find where they're going?"

"Did you stay on this road?"

"No, she turned again." Right or left? M.J. asked herself. Right or left? "We kept heading deeper into the boonies, and climbing. Maybe here."

He slowed, let her consider. The crossroads was narrow, cornered on one side by a stone house. A dog napped in the yard under the shade of a dying maple. Concrete ducks paddled over the grass.

"This could be it, to the left. I'm sorry, Jack, it's hazy."

"Look, we've got a full tank of gas and plenty of daylight. Don't sweat it."

He took the left, cruised along the curving road that climbed and dipped. The houses were spread out now, and the fields were crammed with corn high as a man's waist. Where fields stopped, woods took over, growing thick and green, arching their limbs over the road so that it was a shady tunnel for the car to thread through.

They came to the rise of a hill, and the world opened up. A dramatic and sudden spread of green mountains, and land that rolled beneath them.

"Yes. Bailey almost wrecked the car when we topped this hill. If it is this hill," she added. "I think that's part of the state forest. She was dazzled by it. But we turned off again. One of these little roads that winds through the trees."

"You're doing fine. Tell me which one you want to try."

"At this point, your guess is as good as mine." She felt helpless, stupid. "It just looks different now. The trees are all thick. They just had that green haze on them when we came through."

"We'll give this one a shot," he decided, and, flipping a mental coin, turned right.

It took only ten minutes for them to admit they were lost, and another ten to find their way out and onto a main road. They drove through a small town M.J. had no recollection of, then backtracked.

After an hour of wandering, M.J. felt her patience fraying. "How can you stay so calm?" she asked him. "I swear we've fumbled along every excuse for a road within fifty miles. Every street, lane and cow path. I'm going crazy."

"My line of work takes patience. I ever tell you about tracking down Big Bill Bristol?"

She shifted in her seat, certain she'd never feel sensation in her bottom again. "No, you never told me about tracking down Big Bill Bristol. Are you going to make this up?"

"Don't have to." To give them both a breather, he swung off the road. There was a small pulloff beside what he supposed could be called a swimming hole. Trees overhung dark water and let little splashes of sun hit the surface and bounce back. "Big Bill was up on assault. Lost his temper over a hand of seven-card stud and tried to feed the pot to his opponent. That was after he broke his nose and knocked the guy out. Big Bill is about six-five, two-eighty, and has hands the size of Minneapolis. He doesn't like to lose. I know this for a fact, as I have spent the occasional evening playing games of chance with Big Bill."

M.J. smiled winningly. "Gosh, Jack, I just can't wait to meet your friends."

Recognizing sarcasm when it was aimed at him, he merely slanted her a look. "In any case, Ralph fronted his bond, but Big Bill found out about a floating game in Jersey and didn't want to miss out. The law frowns, not only on floating games, but on bail-jumping, and his bail was revoked. Bill was on the skip list."

"And you went after him."

"Well, I did." Jack rubbed his chin, thought fleetingly about shaving. "It should have been cut-and-dried. Find the game, remind Bill he had to have his day in court, bring him back. But it seemed Bill had won large quantities of money in Jersey, and had moved on to another game. I should add that Bill is big, but not in the brain department. And he was on a hot streak, moving from game to game, state to state."

"With Jack Dakota, bounty hunter, hot on his trail."

"On his trail, anyway. A lot of it his back trail. If

the jerk had planned to lose me, he couldn't have done a better job. I crisscrossed the Northeast, hit every game."

"How much did you lose?"

"Not enough to talk about." He answered her grin. "I got into Pittsburgh about midnight. I knew there was a game, but I couldn't bribe or threaten the location out of anyone. I'd been on Bill's trail for four days, living out of my car and playing poker with guys named Bats and Fast Charlie. I was tired, dirty, down to my last hundred in cash. I walked into a bar."

"Of course you did."

"I'm telling the story," he said, tugging her hair. "Picked it at random, no thought, no plan. And guess who was in the back room, holding a pair of bullets and bumping the pot?"

"Let's see… Could it have been…Big Bill Bristol?"

"In the flesh. Patience and logic had gotten me to Pittsburgh, but it was instinct that had me walking into that game."

"How'd you get him to go back with you?"

"There I had a choice. I considered hitting him over the head with a chair. But more than likely that would have just annoyed him. I thought about appealing to his good nature, reminding him he owed Ralph. But he was still on that hot streak, and wouldn't have given a damn. So I had a drink, joined the game. After a couple of hours, I explained the situation to Bill, and appealed to him on his own level. One cut of the cards. I draw high, he comes back with me, no hassle. He draws high, I walk away."

"And you drew high?"

"Yeah, I did." He scratched his chin again. "Of

course, I'd palmed an ace, but like I said, brains weren't Big Bill's strong suit."

"You cheated?"

"Sure. It was the clearest route through the situation, and everybody ended up happy."

"Except Big Bill."

"No, him, too. He'd had a nice run, had enough of the ready to pay off the guy whose skull he'd cracked. Charges dropped. No sweat."

She cocked her head. "And what would you have done if he'd decided to not go back with you peacefully?"

"I'd have broken the chair over his head, and hoped to live through it."

"Quite a life you lead, Jack."

"I like it. And the moral of the story is, you just keep looking, follow logic. And when logic peters out, you go with instinct." So saying, he reached into his pocket, drew out the stone. "The second stone is knowledge." His eyes met hers. "What do you know, M.J.?"

"I don't understand."

"You know your friends. You know them better than I know Big Bill, or anyone else, for that matter." He could come to envy her that, he realized. And would think on it more closely later. "They're part of what you were, who you are, and, I guess, who you will be."

Her chest went tight. "You're getting philosophical on me, Dakota."

"Sometimes that works, too. Trust your instincts, M.J." He took her hand, closed it over the stone. "Trust what you know."

Her nerves were suddenly on the surface of her skin,

chilling it. "You expect me to use this thing like some sort of compass? Divining rod?"

"You feel that, don't you?" It was a shock to him as well, but his hands stayed steady, his eyes remained on hers. "It's all but breathing. You know the thing about myths? If you reach down deep enough inside them, you pull out truth. The second stone is knowledge." He shifted back, put his hands on the wheel. "Which way do you want to go?"

She was cold, shudderingly cold. Yet the stone was like a sun burning in her hand. "West." She heard herself say it, knew it was odd for a city woman to use the direction, rather than simply right or left. "This is crazy."

"We left sanity behind yesterday. No use trying to find that back trail. Just tell me which way you want to go. Which way feels right."

So she held the stone gripped in her hand and directed him through the winding roads sided with trees and outcroppings of rock. Along a meandering stream that trickled low from lack of rain, past a little brown house so close that its door all but opened into the road.

"On the right," M.J. said, through a throat dust-dry and tight as a drum. "You have to watch for it. We passed it, had to double back. Her lane's narrow, just a cut through the woods. You can barely see it. She doesn't have a mailbox. She goes into town and picks it up when she's here. There." her hand trembled a bit as she pointed. "Just there."

He turned in. The lane was indeed narrow. Branches skimmed and scraped along the sides of the car as he drove slowly up, over gravel, around a curve that was sheltered by more trees.

And there, in the center of the lane, still as a stone statue, stood a deer with a pelt that glowed dark gold in the flash of sun.

It should be a white hind, Jack thought foolishly. A white hind is the symbol of a quest.

The doe watched the lumbering approach, her head up, her eyes wide and fixed. Then, with a flick of the tail, a quick spin of that gorgeous body, she leaped into the trees on thin, graceful legs. And was gone with barely a rustle.

The house was exactly as M.J. remembered. Tucked back on the hill, above a small, bubbling creek, it was a neat two stories that blended into the backdrop of woods. It was wood and glass, simple lines, with a long front porch painted a bold blue. Two white rockers sat on it, along with copper pots overflowing with trailing flowers.

"She's been busy," M.J. murmured, scanning the gardens. Flowers bloomed everywhere, wildly, as if unplanned. The flow of colors and shapes tumbled down the hill like a river. Wide wooden steps cut through the color, meandered to the left, then marched down to the lane.

"At the house in Potomac she hired a professional landscaper. She knew just what she wanted, but she had someone else do it. Here, she wanted to do everything herself."

"It looks like a fairy tale." He shifted, uncomfortable with his own impressions. He wasn't exactly up on his fairy tales. "You know what I mean."

"Yeah."

A shiny blue pickup truck was parked at the end of the lane. But there was no sign of the car Grace would have driven to her country home. No dusty rental car announcing Bailey's presence.

They've just gone to the store, M.J. told herself. They'll be back any minute.

She wouldn't believe they'd come this far, found the house, and not found Grace and Bailey.

The minute Jack pulled up beside the truck, she was out and dashing toward the house.

"Hold it." He gripped her arm, skidded her to a halt. "Let's get the lay of the land here." Gently he uncurled her fingers, took the stone. When it was tucked back in his pocket, he took her hand. "You said she leaves the truck here?"

"Yes. She drives a Mercedes convertible, or a little Beemer."

"Your pal has three rides?"

"Grace rarely owns one of anything. She claims she doesn't know what she's going to be in the mood for."

"There's a back door?"

"Yeah, one out the kitchen, and another on the side." She gestured to the right, fought to ignore the weight pressing against her chest. "It leads onto a little patio and into the woods."

"Let's look around first."

There was a gardening shed, neatly filled with tools, a lawn mower, rakes and shovels. Where the lawn gave way, stepping-stones had been set, with springy moss growing between. More flowers—a raised bed with blooms and greenery spilling over the dark wall, and the cliff behind growing with ivy.

A hummingbird hovered at a bright red feeder, its iridescent wings blurred with speed. It darted off like a bullet at their approach, its whirl the only sound.

He spotted no broken windows or other signs of forced entry as they circled around the back, passed an herb garden fragrant with scents of rosemary and mint. Brass wind chimes hung silently near the rear door. Not a leaf stirred.

"It's creepy." She rubbed her arm. "Skulking around like this."

"Let's just skulk another minute."

They came around the far side with the little patio. There, a glass table, a padded chaise, more flowers in concrete troughs and clay pots. Just beyond was a small pond with young ornamental grasses.

"That's new." M.J. paused to study. "She didn't have that before. She talked about it, though. It looks fresh."

"I'd say your pal's done some planting this week. You think there's a plant or flower in existence she's missed?"

"Probably not." But M.J.'s smile was weak as they came back around to the front. "I want to go in, Jack. I have to go in."

"Let's take a look." He climbed the porch steps, found the front door locked. "She got a hidey-hole for a key?"

"No." Despite the miserable heat, she rubbed her hands over her chilled arms. Too quiet, was all she could think. It was much too quiet. "She used to keep an extra for the Potomac house, in this flowerpot outside the door, but her cousin Melissa found it and made herself at home while Grace was in Milan. Really ticked her off."

He crouched, examined the locks. "She's got good ones. Simpler to break a window."

"You're not breaking one of her windows."

He sighed, rose. "I was afraid you'd say that. Okay, we do it the hard way."

While she frowned, he went back to his car, popped the trunk. Inside, it was loaded with tools, clothes, books, water jugs and paperwork. He pushed around, selected what he needed.

"Does she have an alarm system?"

"No. Not that I know of, anyway." M.J. studied the leather pouch. "What are you going to do?"

"Pop the locks. It may take a while, I'm rusty." But he rubbed his hands together, anticipating the challenge. "You could go around, check the other doors and windows, just in case she left something unlocked."

"If she locked one, she locked them all. But okay."

She circled around again, pausing at each window, tugging, then peering in. By the time she'd made a complete circuit, Jack was on the second lock.

Intrigued, she watched him finesse it. It was cooler here than in the city, but the heat was still nasty. Sweat dampened his shirt, gleamed on his throat.

"Can you teach me to do that?" she asked him.

"Ssh!" He wiped his hands on his jeans, took a firmer hold on his pick. "Got it." He stood, swiped an arm over his brow. "Cold shower," he murmured. "Cold beer. I'll kiss your pal's feet if she's got both."

"Grace doesn't drink beer." But M.J. was pushing in the door ahead of him.

The living area was homey, tidy but still lived-in, with its wide striped sofa, the deep chairs that picked up the rich blue tones. In the brick fireplace, a lush green fern rose out of a brass spittoon.

M.J. moved quickly through the rooms, over wide-planked chestnut floors and Berber rugs, into the sunny kitchen, with its forest green counters and white tiles, through to the cozy parlor Grace had turned into a library.

The house seemed to echo around her, as she raced upstairs, looked in the bedrooms, the baths.

Grace's gleaming brass bed was tidily made, the handmade lace spread she'd purchased in Ireland accented with rich dots of colorful pillows. A book on gardening lay on the nightstand.

The bathroom was empty, the ivory shell of the sink scrubbed clean and shining in its powder blue counter. Towels were neatly folded on the shelves on a tall wicker stand.

Knowing it was useless, she looked in the bedroom closet. It was ridiculously full and ruthlessly organized.

"They're not here, M.J." Jack touched her shoulder, but she jerked away.

"I can see that, can't I?" Her voice snapped out, broke like a rigid twig. "But Grace was here. She was just here. I can still smell her." She closed her eyes, drew in the air. "Her perfume. It hasn't faded yet. That's her scent. Some fragrance tycoon who fell for her had it designed for her. I can smell her in here."

"Okay." He caught the scent himself, classy sex with wild undertones. "Maybe she ran into town for supplies, or took a drive."

"No." She walked away from him, toward the window as she spoke. "She wouldn't have locked the house up for that. She always says how lovely it is not to worry about locking up out here. She only does when she closes the place up and heads somewhere else. Bailey isn't here. Grace isn't here, and she's not planning on coming back for a while. We've missed her."

"Back to Potomac?"

She shook her head. The tightness in her chest was unbearable, as if greedy hands were squeezing her heart and lungs. "Not likely. She'd avoid the city on the Fourth. Too much traffic, too many tourists. That's why I was sure she'd stay through until tomorrow at least. She could be anywhere."

"Which means she'll surface somewhere." He started toward her, caught the gleam on her cheek and stopped dead, like a man who'd run face-first into a glass wall. "What are you doing? Are you crying?" It was an accusation, delivered in a voice edged with abject terror.

M.J. merely wrapped her arms over her chest and hugged her elbows. All the excitement, the tension, the frustration, of the search fell away into sheer despair.

The house was empty.

"I want you to stop that. Right now. I mean it. Sniveling isn't going to do you any good." And it certainly wasn't going to do him any good. It terrified him, left him feeling stupid, clumsy and annoyed.

"Just leave me alone," she said, and her voice broke on a muffled sob. "Just go away."

"That's just what I'm going to do. You keep that up, and I'm walking. I mean it. I'm not standing around and watching you blubber. Get a grip on yourself. Haven't you got any pride?"

At the moment, pride was low on her list. Giving up, she pressed her brow to the window glass and let the tears fall.

"I'm walking, M.J." He snarled at her and turned for the door. "I'm getting a drink and a shower. So when you've got yourself in order, we'll figure out what to do next."

"Then go. Just go."

He made it as far as the threshold, then, swearing ripely, whirled back. "I don't need this," he muttered.

He hadn't a clue how to handle a woman's tears, particularly those from a strong woman who was obviously at the end of her endurance. He cursed her again as he turned her into his arms, folded her into them. He continued to swear at her as he picked her up, sat with her in a wide-backed chair.

He rocked and cursed and stroked.

"Get it over with, then." Kissed her temple. "Please. You're killing me."

"I'm afraid." Her breath hitched as she turned her face into his shoulder. His strong, broad shoulder. "I'm so tired and afraid."

"I know." He kissed her hair, held her closer. "I know."

"I couldn't stand for anything to happen to them. I just can't bear it."

"Don't." He tightened his grip, as if he could strangle off those hot, terrifying tears. But his mouth skimmed up her cheek, found hers, and was tender. "It's going to be all right. Everything's going to be all right." He brushed at her tears clumsily with his thumbs. "I promise."

Eyes brimming, she stared into his. "I was just so sure they'd be here."

"I know." He brushed the hair back from her face. "You've got a right to break down. I don't know anyone else who'd have made it this far without a blowout. But don't cry anymore, M.J. It rips me up."

"I hate to cry." She sniffled, knuckled tears away.

"I'm glad to hear it." He took her hands, kissed them both this time, without that moment of surprise. "Think about this. She was here today, maybe as little as an hour ago. She's tidied up, locked up. Which means she was just fine when she left."

She let out an unsteady breath, drew in another. "You're right. I'm not thinking straight."

"That's because you need a break. A decent meal, a little rest."

"Yeah." But she laid her head against his shoulder again. "Can we just sit here for a little while. Just sit like this?"

"Sure." It was easy to wrap his arms around her, hold her close. And just sit.

Chapter 10

He told her it didn't make sense to drive back to the city, fight the traffic generated by fireworks fans. Not when they had a perfectly good place to stay the night.

The fact was, he thought, if she'd broken down once, she could easily do so again. And a decent meal, along with a decent night's sleep, might shore up some holes in her composure.

In any case, they'd been in the car for more than five hours that day already, after little more than an hour's sleep. Driving straight back was bound to make them both feel as though the effort to find Grace's house had been wasted.

And he wanted time to work on a plan that was beginning to form in his mind.

"Take a shower," he told her. "Borrow a shirt or something from your pal. You'll feel better."

"It couldn't hurt." She managed a smile. "I thought you wanted a shower? Don't you want to conserve water?"

"Well…" It was tempting. He could envision himself getting under a cool spray with her, lathering up—lathering her up—and letting nature take its very interesting course.

And it also occurred to him that she hadn't had five full minutes of privacy in hours. It was about all he had the power to give her at the moment.

"I'm going to hunt up a drink. See if your friend has some cans around here I can open." He kissed the tip of her nose affectionately. "Go ahead and get started without me."

"Okay, you can hunt me up a drink while you're at it, but you're not going to find any beer in the fridge. And God knows what she's got in cans around here."

M.J. headed for the bath, stopped, turned. "Jack? Thanks for letting me get it out."

He tucked his hands in his pockets. Her eyes, those exotically tilted cat's eyes, were still swollen from weeping, and her cheeks were pale with fatigue. "I guess you needed to."

"I did, and you didn't make me feel like too much of a jerk. So thanks," she said again, and stepped into the bath.

She stripped gratefully, peeling cotton and denim away from her clammy, overheated skin. The simple style Grace had chosen for the rest of the house didn't follow through to the master bath. This was pure self-indulgence.

The tiles were soft blue and misty green, so that it was like stepping into a cool seaside glade. The tub was an oversize lake of white, fueled with water jets and framed by a wide lip where more ferns grew lushly in biscuit-toned pots.

The acre of counter boasted a cutout for a vanity stool and held a brass makeup mirror. Overhead was a garden of tulip-shaped lights of frosted glass. Doors holding linens and sheet-size towels were mirrored, tossing the room back and giving the illusion of enormous, luxurious space.

Though M.J. briefly considered the tub, and the bubbling jets, she stepped instead toward the wavy glass block of the shower enclosure. Her showerheads were set in three sides at varying levels. With a need for pampering, M.J. turned them all on full, then, after one enormous sigh, helped herself to some of Grace's pricey soap and shampoo.

And the fragrance made her weepy again. It was so Grace.

But she refused to cry, already regretted her earlier tears. They helped nothing. Practicalities did, she reminded herself. A shower, a meal, a respite from activity for a brief time, would all serve to clear the brain. Undoubtedly, she needed a few hours' sleep to recharge. It wasn't just the crying jag that made her feel woozy and weak, she imagined.

Something had to be done, some move had to be made, and quickly. To make it, she needed to be sharp and to be ready.

It hardly mattered that it hadn't been much more than a day that had passed. Every hour she lived through without being able to contact either Bailey or Grace was one short, tense lifetime.

Things had to be settled, her world had to be set

right again. And then she would have to face whatever was happening, and whatever would happen, between her and Jack.

She was in love with him, there was no doubt of that. The speed with which she'd fallen only increased the intensity of the emotion. She'd never felt for any man what she felt for him—this emotion that cut clean through the bone. And melded with the feeling of passion, which she could have dismissed, was a sense of absolute trust, an odd and deep affection, a prideful respect, and the certainty that she could pass the years of her life with him—if not in harmony, in contentment.

She understood him, she realized as she held her face under the highest spray. She doubted he knew that, but it was absolutely true. She understood his loneliness, his scarred-over pain, and his pride in his own skills.

He had kindness and cynicism, patience and impulse. He had a questing intellect, a touch of the poet—and more than a touch of the nonconformist. He lived his own way, making his own rules and breaking them when he chose.

She would have wanted no less in a life partner.

And that was what worried her. Finding herself thinking of marriage, permanence and making a family with a man who so obviously ran from all three, and had run from them most of his life.

But perhaps, since those concepts had bloomed so recently in her, she could nip them in the bud. She had a business of her own, a life of her own. Wanting Jack to be a part of that didn't have to change the basic order of things.

She hoped.

She switched off the showerheads, toweled off and, because it was there, slathered on some of Grace's silky body cream. And felt nearly human again. Rubbing a towel over her hair, she padded naked into the bedroom to raid the closet.

At least in the country Grace's choice of attire ran toward the simple. M.J. slipped on a short-sleeved shirt of minute white-and-blue checks and found a pair of cotton shorts in the bureau. They bagged a little. Grace was still built like the centerfold she'd once been, and M.J. had no hips to speak of. They also ran short, as M.J. had several inches more leg than her friend.

But they were cool, and when she slid them on she stopped feeling like a woman who'd been living in her clothes for two days.

She started to toss the towel aside, then rolled her eyes when she thought of how Grace would react to that. Fastidiously she went back to the bath and draped it over the shower. Then, in bare feet, her hair still damp and curling around her face, she went in search of Jack.

"I not only started without you," she said when she found him in the kitchen, "I finished without you. You're slow, Dakota."

Still frowning at the small jar in his hand, he turned. "All I found was..." And trailed off, staggered.

He'd told himself she wasn't beautiful, and that was true. But she was striking. The impact of her slammed into him anew, those sharp, sexy looks, the long, long legs set off by tiny blue shorts. She had her thumbs tucked in the front pockets of them, a half-cocked grin on her face, and her hair was dark and damp and curling foolishly over her ears.

His mouth simply watered.

"You clean up good, sugar."

"It's hard not to, in that fancy shower of Grace's. Wait till you get a load of it." She angled her head as a nice flush of heat began to work up from her toes. "I don't know why you're looking at me like that, Jack. You've seen me naked."

"Yeah. Maybe I've got a weakness for long women in little shorts." He lifted a brow. "Did you borrow any of her underwear?"

"No. Some things even close friends don't share. Men and underwear being the top two."

He set the jar down. "In that case—"

She shot a hand up, slapped in on his chest. "I don't think so, pal. You don't exactly smell like roses at the moment. And besides, I'm hungry."

"The woman gets cleaned up, she gets picky." But he ran a hand over his chin again, reminded himself to get his shaving kit out of the trunk this time. "There's not a hell of a lot to choose from around here. She's got fancy French bubbly in the fridge, more fancy French wine in a rack in the closet over there. Some crackers in tins, some pasta in glass jars. I found some tomato paste, which I guess is embryonic spaghetti sauce."

"Does that mean one of us has to cook?"

"I'm afraid it does."

They considered each other for ten full seconds.

"Okay," he decided. "We flip for it."

"Fair enough. Heads, you cook," she said as he dug out a quarter. "Tails, I cook. Either way, I have a feeling we'll be looking for her antacid."

She hissed when the quarter turned up tails. "Isn't

there anything else? Something we can just eat out of a can or jar?"

"You cook," he said, but held out a jar. "And there's fish eggs."

She blew out a breath as she studied the jar of beluga. "You don't like caviar?"

"Give me a trout, fry it up, and that's dandy. What the hell do I want to eat eggs that some fish has laid?" But he tossed her the jar. "Help yourself. I'll go clean up while you do something with that tomato paste."

"You probably won't like it," she said darkly, but dug out a pan as he wandered off.

Thirty minutes later, he wandered in again. His hair was slicked back, his face clean-shaven. The smells coming from the simmering pan weren't half-bad, he decided. The kitchen door was open, and there was M.J., sitting out on the patio, cramming a caviar-loaded cracker in her mouth.

"Not too bad," she said over it when she saw him. "You just pretend it's something else, then wash it down with this." She sipped champagne, shrugged. "Grace goes for this stuff. Always did. It was the way she was raised."

"Environment can twist a person," he agreed, then opened his mouth and let M.J. ram a cracker in. He grimaced, snagged her glass and downed it. "A hot dog and a nice dark beer."

She sighed, perfectly in tune with him. "Yeah, well, beggars can't be choosers, pal. It's nice out here. Cooled off some. But you know the trouble? You just can't hear anything. No traffic, no voices, no movement. It kind of creeps me out."

"People that live in places like this don't really like

being around other people." He was hungry enough to load up a cracker for himself. "You and me, M.J., we're social animals. We're at our best in a crowded room."

"Yeah, that's why I work the pub most nights. I like the busy hours." She brooded, looking off to where the sun was sinking fast behind the trees. "Tonight would be slow. Sunday, holiday. Everybody'll be wondering where I am. I've got a good head waitress, though. She'll handle it."

She shifted restlessly, reached for her glass. "I guess the cops have gone by, talked to her and my bartenders, some of the regulars. They'll be worried."

"It won't take much longer." He'd been working on refining his plan, looking for the pitfalls. "Your pub'll run a few days without you. You take vacations, right?"

"A couple weeks here and there."

"It's supposed to be Paris next."

She was surprised he remembered. "That's the plan. Have you ever been there?"

"No, have you?"

"Nope. We went to Ireland when I was a kid, and my father got all misty-eyed and sentimental. He grew up on the West Side of Manhattan, but you'd have thought he'd been born and bred in Dublin and had been wrenched away by Gypsies. Other than that, I've never been out of the States."

"I've been up to Canada, down to Mexico, but I've never flown over the ocean." He smiled and took the glass from her again. "I think your sauce is burning, sugar."

She swore, shot up and scrambled inside. While she muttered, he eyed the level of the bottle. Normally he wouldn't have recommended alcohol as a tranquilizer, but these were desperate times. He'd seen that misery come into her eyes when he mentioned Paris—and reminded her of her friends.

For a few hours, for this one night, he was going to make her forget.

"I caught it in time," she told him, dragging her hair back as she stepped out again. "And I put on the water for the pasta. I don't know how long that sauce is supposed to cook—probably for three days, but we're eating it rare."

He grinned, handed her the glass he'd just topped off. "Fine with me. There was another bottle of this chilling, right?"

"Yeah, I get it for her by the case. My distributor just loves it." She knocked some back, chuckled into the exquisite bubbles. "I can imagine what my customers would say if I put Brother Dom on the menu."

"I'm getting used to it." He rose, skimmed a hand over her hair. "I'm going to put some music on. Too damn quiet around here."

"Good idea." With a considering look, she glanced over her shoulder. "You know, I think Grace said they have, like, bears and things up here."

He looked dubiously into the woods. "Guess I'll get my gun, too."

He got more than that. To her surprise, he brought candles into the kitchen, turned the stereo on low and found a station that played blues. He stuck a pink flower that more or less resembled a carnation to him behind her ear.

"Yeah, I guess redheads can wear pink," he decided after a smiling study. "You look cute."

Blowing her hair out of her eyes, she drained the pasta. "What's this? A romantic streak?"

"I've got one I keep in reserve." And while her hands were full, he leaned in and nuzzled the back of her neck. "Does that bother you?"

"No." She angled her head, enjoying the leaping thrill up her spine. "But to complete the mood, you're going to have to eat this and pretend it's good." She frowned a little when he retrieved another bottle of champagne from the refrigerator. "Do you know what that costs a bottle, ace? Even wholesale?"

"Beggars can't be choosers," he reminded her, and popped the cork.

As meals went, they'd both had better—and worse. The pasta was only slightly overdone, the sauce was bland but inoffensive. And, being ravenous, they dipped into second helpings without complaint.

He made certain he steered the conversation away from anything that worried her.

"Probably should have used some of those herbs she's got growing out there," M.J. considered. "But I don't know what's what."

"It's fine." He took her hand, pressed a kiss to the palm, and made her blink. "How are you feeling?"

"Better." She picked up her glass. "Full."

Nerves? Funny, he thought, she hadn't shown nerves when he handcuffed her, or when he drove like a madman through the streets of Washington with potential killers on their tail.

But nuzzle her hand and she looked edgy as a virgin bride on her wedding night. He wondered just how much more nervous he could make her.

"I like looking at you," he murmured.

She sipped hastily, set the glass down, picked it up again. "You've been looking at me for two days."

"Not in candlelight." He filled her glass again. "It puts fire in your hair. In your eyes. Star fire." He smiled slowly, held the glass out to her. "What's that line? 'Fair as a star, when only one is shining in the sky.'"

"Yeah." She gulped wine, felt it fizz in her throat. "I think that's it."

"You're the only one, M.J." He pushed the plates aside so that he could nibble on her fingers. "Your hand's trembling."

"It is not." Her heart was, but she tugged her hand free, just in case he was right. She drank again, then narrowed her eyes. "Are you trying to get me drunk, Dakota?"

His smile was slow, confident. "Relaxed. And you were relaxed, M.J. Before I started to seduce you."

A hot ball of need lodged in the pit of her stomach. "Is that what you call it?"

"You're ripe for seducing." He turned her hand over, grazed his teeth over the inside of her wrist. "Your head's swimming with wine, your pulse is unsteady. If you were to stand right now, your legs would be weak."

She didn't have to stand for them to be weak. Even sitting, her knees were shaking. "I don't need to be seduced. You know that."

"What I know is that I'm going to enjoy it. I want you trembling, and weak, and mine."

She was afraid she already was, and pulled back, unnerved. "This is silly. If you want to go to bed—"

"We'll get there. Eventually." He rose, drew her to her feet, then slid his hands in one long, possessive stroke down the sides of her body. Then back up. "You're worried about what I can do to you."

"You don't worry me."

"Yes, I do." He eased her against him, kept his mouth hovering over hers a moment, then lowered it to nip lightly at her jaw. "Just now I worry you a lot."

Her breath was thick, unsteady. "Cook a man one meal and he gets delusions of grandeur." And when he chuckled, his breath warm on her cheek, she shivered. "Kiss me, Jack." Her mouth turned, seeking his. "Just kiss me."

"You're not afraid of the fire." He evaded her lips, heard her moan as his mouth skimmed her throat. "But the warmth unnerves you. You can have both." His lips brushed hers, retreated. "Tonight, we'll have both. There won't be any choice."

The wine was swimming in her head, just as he'd said. In sparkling circles. She was trembling, just as he'd said. In quick, helpless quivers.

And she was weak, just as he'd said.

Even as she strained for the fire, the flash danced out of her reach. There was only the warmth, enervating, sweet, drugging. Her breath caught, then released in a rush when he lifted her.

"Why are you doing this?"

"Because you need it," he murmured. "And so do I."

He heated her skin with nibbling kisses as he carried her from the room. Filled his head with the scent that was foreign to both of them and only added to the mystery.

The house was dark, empty, with the silvery shower of moonlight guiding his path up the steps. He laid her on the bed, covered her with his body. And finally, finally, lowered his mouth to hers.

Her limbs went weak as the kiss drained her, sent her floating. She struggled once, tried to find level ground. But he deepened the kiss so slowly, so cleverly, so tenderly, she simply slid into the velvet trap he'd already laid for her.

She murmured his name, heard the echo of it whisper through her head. And surrendered.

He felt the change, that soft and complete yielding. The gift of it was powerfully arousing, sent dark ripples of delight dancing through his blood. Even as his desire quickened, his mouth slipped down to gently explore the pulse that beat so hard and thick in the hollow of her throat.

"Let go," he said quietly. "Just let go of everything, and let me take you."

His hands were gentle on her, skimming and tracing those curves and angles. This, he thought, makes her sigh. And that makes her moan. As if their time were endless, he tutored himself in the pleasures of her. The strong curve of her shoulder, the long muscles of her thigh, the surprisingly fragile line of her throat.

He undressed her slowly, pressing his lips to the hands that reached for him until they went limp again.

He left her nothing to hold on to but trust. Gave her nothing to experience but pleasure. Tenderness destroyed her, until her world was whittled down to the slowly rising storm inside her own body.

The fire was there, that flash of lightning and outrageous heat, the whip of wind and roll of power. But he held it off with clever hands and patient mouth, easing her along the path he'd chosen for them.

He turned her over, and those hands stroked the muscles in her shoulders and turned them to liquid. That mouth traced kisses down her spine and made her quake even as her mind went misty.

She could hear the rustle of the sheets as he moved over her, hear the whisper of his promises, feel the warm glow of promises kept.

And from outside, in the deepening night, came the long haunting call of an owl.

No part of her body was ignored. No aspect of seduction forgotten. She lay helpless beneath him, open to any demand. And when demand finally came, her moan was long, throaty, the response of her body instant and full.

He buried his face between her breasts, fighting back the urge to rush, now that he'd brought her so luxuriously to the peak.

"I want more of you," he murmured. "I want all of you. I want everything."

He closed his mouth over her breast until she moved under him again, until her breath was nothing but feverish little pants. When her voice broke on his name, he slipped inside her, filled her slowly.

Teetering on a new brink, she arched toward him. Her eyes locked on his as they linked hands. There was only his face in the moonlight, dark eyes, firm mouth, the rich flow of hair threaded with gold.

Swept by a rushing tide of love, she smiled up at him. "Take more of me." She felt his fingers tremble in hers. "Take all of me." Saw the flash that was both triumph and need in his eyes. "Take everything."

The fire reached out for both of them.

* * *

While she slept, he held her close against him and worked out the final points of his plan. It had as much chance of working, he'd decided, as it did of blowing up in his face.

Even odds weren't such a bad deal.

He'd have risked much worse for her, much more to prevent those tears from slipping down her cheeks again. He'd waited thirty years to fall, which, he concluded, was why he'd fallen so hard, and so fast.

Unless he wanted to take the more mystical route and believe it was all simply fated—the timing, the stone, M.J. Either way, he'd come to the same place. She was the first and only person he'd ever loved, and there was nothing he wouldn't do to protect her.

Even if it meant breaking her trust.

If this was the last time he'd lie beside her, he could hardly complain. She'd given him more in two days than he'd had in his entire life.

She loved him, and that answered all the questions.

As Jack lay in the deep country dark, contemplating his life, wondering about his future, another sat in a room washed with light. His day had been full, and now he was weary. But his mind wouldn't shut off, and he couldn't afford the fatigue.

He had watched fireworks streak across the sky. He had smiled, conversed, sipped fine wine. But all the while the rage had eaten at him, like a cancer.

Now, he was blessedly alone, in the room that soothed his soul. He feasted his eyes on the Renoir. Such lovely, subtle colors, he mused. Such exquisite brush strokes. And only he would ever look upon its magnificence.

There, the puzzle box of a Chinese emperor. Glossy with lacquer, a red dragon streaking over it and into a black sky. Priceless, full of secrets. And only he had the key.

Here, a ruby ring that had once graced the royal finger of Louis XIV. He slipped it on his pinkie, turned the stone toward the light and watched it shoot fire. From the king's hand to his, he thought. With a few detours along the way, but it was where it belonged now.

Usually such things brought him a deep, exquisite pleasure.

But not tonight.

Some had been punished, he thought. Some were beyond punishment. Yet it wasn't enough.

His treasure room was filled with the stunning, the unique, the ancient. Yet it wasn't enough.

The Three Stars were the only thing that would satisfy him. He would trade every treasure he owned for them. For with them, he would need nothing else.

The fools believed they understood them. Believed they could control them. And elude him. They were meant for him, of course. Their power was always meant for him.

And the loss of them was like ground glass in his throat.

He rose, ripping the ruby from his finger and flinging it across the room like a child tossing a broken toy. He would have them back. He was sure of it. But a sacrifice must be made. To the god, he thought with a slow smile. Of course, a sacrifice to the god.

In blood.

He left the room, leaving the lights burning. And most of his sanity behind.

Chapter 11

Jack considered leaving a note. When she woke, she'd be alone. At first, she'd probably assume he'd gone out to find that little store she'd spoken of, to buy some food.

She'd be impatient, a little annoyed. After an hour or so, she might worry that he'd gotten himself lost on the back roads.

But it wouldn't take her long to realize he was gone.

As he walked quietly down the stairs, just as dawn broke, he imagined her first reaction would be anger. She'd storm through the house, cursing him, threatening him. She'd probably kick something.

He was almost sorry to miss it.

She might even hate him for a while, he thought. But she'd be safe here. That was what mattered most.

He stepped outside, into the quiet mist of morning

that shrouded the trees and hazed the sky. A few birds were up with him, stretching their vocal cords. Grace's flowers perfumed the air like a fantasy, and there was dew on the grass. He saw a deer, likely the same doe that had been on the lane the day before, standing at the edge of the woods.

They studied each other a moment, each both interested in and wary of the alien species. Then, dismissing him, she moved with hardly a sound along the verge of the trees, until she was slowly swallowed by them.

He glanced back at the house where he'd left M.J. sleeping. If everything went as he hoped, he'd be back for her by nightfall. It would take some doing, he knew, but he had to believe he'd convince her—eventually—that he'd acted for the best. And if her feelings were hurt, well, hurt feelings weren't terminal.

Again, he considered leaving a note—something short and to the point. But he decided against it. She'd figure it out for herself quickly enough. She was a sharp woman.

His woman, he thought as he slipped behind the wheel of the car. Whatever happened to him in the course of this day, she would be safe.

A soldier prepared for battle, a knight armed for the charge, he steeled himself to leave his lady and ride off into the mist. Such was his mood when he turned the key and the engine responded with a dull click.

His mood deflated like a sail emptied of wind.

Terrific, great, just what he needed. He swung out of the car, resisted slamming the door, and rounded the hood. Muttering oaths, he popped it, stuck his head under.

"Lose something, ace?"

Slowly he withdrew his head from under the hood. She was standing on the porch, legs spread, hands fisted on her hips, venom in her eyes. It had taken only a glance to see that his distributor cap was missing. He didn't even need to look at her to conclude that she'd nailed him.

But he was cool. He'd faced down worse than one angry woman in his checkered career. "Looks that way. You're up early, M.J."

"So are you, Jack."

"I was hungry." He flashed a smile—and kept his distance. "I thought I'd hunt up some breakfast."

She cocked a brow. "Got your club in the car?"

"My club?"

"That's what Neanderthals do, don't they? Get their club and go off into the woods to bash a bear for meat."

As she came down the steps toward him, he kept the smile plastered to his face, leaned back on the fender. "I had something a little more civilized in mind. Something like bacon and eggs."

"Oh? And where are you going to find bacon and eggs around here at dawn?"

She had him there. "Ah...I thought I could, you know, find a farmer and—" The breath whooshed out of his lungs as her fist plunged into his belly.

"Don't you lie to me. Do I look stupid?"

He coughed, got his breath back and managed to straighten. "No. Listen—"

"Did you think I couldn't tell what was going on last night? The way you made love to me? Did you think you'd soften me up so I wouldn't know that was a big goodbye scene? You bastard!" She swung again, but this time he ducked, so she missed his jaw by inches.

Now his own temper began to climb. He'd never treated a woman with such care as he'd treated her with in the night, and now she was tossing it back in his face. "What did you do, sneak down here in the middle of the night and sabotage my ride?"

He saw the answer to that in the thin, satisfied smile that spread on her face. "Oh, that's nice. Real nice. Trusting."

"How dare you talk about trust! You were going to leave me here."

"Yeah, that's right. Now where's the distributor cap?" He took her by the arms, firmly, before she could take another shot at him. "Where is it?"

"Where do you think you're going? What sort of idiotic plan have you mapped out in that tiny, feeble brain of yours?"

"I'm going to take care of business," he said grimly. "I'll come back for you when I'm done."

"Come back for me? What am I, a pet?" She jerked, but didn't manage to free herself until she'd hammered her heel onto his instep. "You're going back to the city, aren't you? You're going looking for trouble."

His fury was such that he wondered only briefly how many bones in his foot she might have broken. "I know what I'm doing. It's what I do. And what you're going to do is give me the cap, then you're going to wait."

"The hell I am. We started this together, and we finish it together."

"No." He swung her around until her back was pressed into the car. "I'm not taking any chances with you."

"Since when are you in charge? I take my own chances. Get your hands off me."

"No." He leaned in, cuffing her hands with his. "For once in your life, you're going to do what you're told. You're going to stay here. I can move faster without you, and I'll be damned if I'm going to be distracted worrying about you."

"Nobody's asking you to worry about me. Just what are you planning to do?"

"I've wasted enough time letting them chase me. It's time to flush them out, on my turf, my terms."

"You're going after those two maniacs in the van?" Her heart lodged in her throat and was ruthlessly swallowed. "Fine. Good idea. I'm going with you."

"You're staying here. They haven't found this place, and it doesn't look like they're going to. You'll be safe." He lifted her to her toes, shook her. "M.J., I can't risk you. You're everything that matters to me. I love you."

"And I'm supposed to sit here, like some helpless female, and risk you?"

"Exactly."

"You arrogant jerk. What am I supposed to do if you get yourself killed? In case you've forgotten, this is my problem, my deal. You're the one who's along for the ride, and you're not going anywhere without me."

"You'll be in my way."

"That's bull. I've held my own through this thing. I'm going, Jack, and unless you want to ride your thumb back to D.C., that's the deal."

He jerked away, snarling. Then whirled to pace. He considered cuffing her inside the house. It would be an ugly struggle—he could almost have looked forward to that aspect of it—and he'd win. But if things went wrong, he couldn't know how long it would be before someone found her.

No, he couldn't leave her alone and handcuffed in some isolated house in the boondocks.

He could lie. Agree to her terms, then ditch her. She wouldn't be easy to shake, but it was an option. Or he could try a different tack altogether.

He turned, smiled winningly. "Okay, sugar, I'll come clean. I've had enough."

"Have you?"

"It was fun. It was educational. But it's getting tedious. Even the fifty thousand you promised me just isn't worth risking my neck for. So I figured I'd cruise up north for a few weeks, wait for things to blow over." He gave a careless shrug as she stared at him. "Things were getting a little heavy between you and me. That's not my style. So I figured I'd take off, avoid the obligatory scene. If I were you, I'd call the cops, turn over the stone, and chalk it all up to one of your more interesting holiday weekends."

"You're dumping me," she said, in a small voice that made him feel like sludge.

"Let's say I'm just moving on. A guy's got to look out for number one."

"All the things you said to me…"

"Hey, sugar, we're both free agents. We both know the score. Tell you what. I'll drop you off at the nearest town, give you a few bucks for transpo."

In answer, she staggered toward the porch, every step a slice through his heart. When she collapsed, buried her face in her hands, he wished himself in hell.

She'll be safe, he reminded himself. All that mattered was that she'd be—

Laughing her guts out. He gaped as she threw back her head and roared with laughter. Her arms were clutched around her stomach, not in defense against heartbreak, but to keep herself from shaking apart with mirth.

"Oh, you idiot," she managed. "Did you really think I was going to fall for that?" She could hardly get the words out between great gusts of laughter. The darker his expression, the wilder her glee. "Now, I guess, I'm supposed to tearfully hand over the distributor cap and let you leave me off somewhere to nurse my shattered heart." She wiped her streaming eyes. "You're so in love with me, Dakota, you can't think straight."

He was thinking straight enough, he determined. He wondered how she'd like it if he closed his hands over that throat of hers and gave it a nice, loving squeeze.

"I could get over it," he muttered.

"No, you couldn't. It's hit you right between the eyes, and I know the feeling. We're stuck with each other, Jack. There's no getting past it for either of us." She breathed deep, rubbed a hand over her aching ribs. "I ought to kick your butt for trying this, but it was too stupid. And too sweet."

He jammed his hands in his pockets. It was the "sweet" that made him feel most foolish. Outmaneuvering her hadn't worked, he considered. Temper and threats hadn't made a dent, and lies had only amused her.

So he would try the truth, he decided. Simple, unvarnished. And he would plead with it.

"Okay, you got me." He walked over, sat beside her, took her hand. "I've never told anyone I loved them before," he began. "I never loved anyone. Not a woman, not family, not a friend."

"Jack." Swamped with emotion, she brushed the hair from his brow. "You just never had a chance to."

"Doesn't matter." He said it fiercely, his fingers tightening on hers. "I meant what I said last night. There's only you, M.J."

He pressed the back of her hand to his lips, held it there a moment. "You wouldn't understand that, not really. You've had other people in your life, important people."

"Yes." Touched, she leaned over, kissed his cheek. "There are people I love. Maybe there's not only you, Jack. But there is you. And what I feel for you is different than anything I've felt before, for anyone."

He stared down at their hands a moment. They fit so well, didn't they? he noticed. Just slid together, as if they'd been waiting for the match. "I've done things my own way for a long time," he continued. "I've avoided complications that I wasn't interested in. It's been easy to evade attachments. Until you."

He looked into her eyes as he touched a hand to her cheek. "You cried yesterday, over those other people you love. It cut me off at the knees. And when I was holding you, and you were crying, I knew I'd do anything for you. Let me do this."

"You planned to leave me here because I cried?"

"Because when you did I finally realized just what your friends mean to you, and how much you'd been holding it in. I need to help you. And them."

She looked away from him for a moment. It wouldn't do either of them any good if she wept again. And his words, and the quiet and deep emotion that flowed behind them, had touched her in a new part of her heart. "I already love you, Jack." She let out a long sigh. "Now, I'm close to adoring you."

"Then you'll stay."

"No." She cupped his face as irritation raced over it. "But I'm not mad at you anymore."

"Great." He pushed off the steps to pace again. "Haven't you heard anything I've said? I can't risk you. I couldn't handle it if anything happened to you."

"But I'm supposed to handle it if something happens to you? It doesn't work that way, Jack." She rose and faced him. "Not for me. What you feel for me, I feel for you. We're in this together. Equal ground." She held up a hand before he could speak. "And you're not going to say something lame about you being a man and me being a woman."

Actually, it had been very close to coming out of his mouth. "A lot of good it would do me."

"Then it's settled." She angled her head. "And let me add something here, just in case you've got a bright idea about ditching me along the way. If you try it, I'll go to the nearest phone and call the cops. I'll tell them you kidnapped me, molested me. I'll give them your description, a description of what you call a car, and your tag number. You'll be trying to explain yourself to Sheriff Bubba and his team before you get twenty miles."

His eyes kindled. "You would, wouldn't you?"

"Damn straight. And I'll make it good, so good they'll probably mess up your pretty face before they toss you in a cell. Now, do we know where we stand?"

"Yeah." He pushed impotently against the corner

she'd boxed him into. "We know where we stand. You cover your angles, sugar."

"You can count on that." She walked toward him, laid her hands on his tensed shoulders. "And you can count on me, Jack. I'm sticking with you." Expecting no response, she touched her lips to his. And got none. "I won't walk out on you," she murmured, and saw the flicker of understanding in his eyes. "And I won't let you down." She brushed her lips over his again. "I won't go away and leave you."

She saw too much, he realized. More, perhaps, than he'd seen himself. "This isn't about me."

"Yes, it is. No one's stuck with you, but I will. No one loved you enough, but I do." She skimmed her hands up his shoulders until they framed his face. "That makes all this about us. I'm going to be there for you, even when you try to play hero and shake me loose."

He was losing, and knew it. "You could start being there tomorrow."

"I'm already there. Now, are you going to kiss me, or not?"

"Maybe."

Her lips curved as they met his. Then they softened, and opened, and gave. He felt himself slide into her—a homecoming that was both sweet and exciting. The kiss heated even before she slipped her hands under his shirt, ran them up his back, then down again with nails scraping lightly.

"I want you," she murmured, moving sinuously against him. "Now, before we go—" she turned her head, nipped her teeth into his throat "—for luck."

His head swam as she reached between their bodies and found him. "I can always use a little extra luck."

She laughed, tugged him away from the car. They fell on the ground together and rolled over grass still damp with dew.

It was fast, and a little desperate. As the sun grew stronger, burning through the morning mist, they tugged at clothes, pawed each other.

"Let me…" He panted and dragged at denim. "I can't—"

"Here." Her hands fumbled with his, dragged material aside. "Hurry. God."

She rolled again, reared up and raced her mouth over his bare chest. She wanted to feast on him, needed to feast of those flavors, those textures. Sate herself with them. She would have sworn she felt the ground tremble as he turned her, hooked his teeth into her shoulder, one hand taking her breast, and the other…

"What are you… How can you…" Her head fell back as he ripped her viciously over the edge. Breath sobbing, she reached up, locked her arms around his neck and let the animal free.

She was with him, beat for beat, her body strong and agile. Her need was as greedy and as primal as his. Perhaps his hands bruised her in his rush, but hers were no less bold, no less rough. She turned her head, took his mouth with a wild avidity that tasted of the dark and the secret.

It was she who twisted, who dragged him down to her. "Now," she demanded, and her eyes gleamed like those of a cat on the hunt. "Right now." And wrapping herself around him, took him in.

He drove hard, burying himself in her. She met each

rough, wild stroke, those tilted cat's eyes wide and focused on his. The heat of her fueled him, and through that edgy violence of need he felt his heart simply shatter with an emotion just as brutal.

"I love you." His mouth clamped on hers, drank from it. "God, I love you."

"I know." And when he pressed his face into her hair, shuddering as he poured himself into her, she needed to know nothing else.

"Jack." She stroked his hair. The sun was in her eyes, his weight was on her, and the grass was damp against her back. She thought it one of the finest moments of her life. "Jack," she said again, and sighed.

He nearly had his wind back. "Maybe there's something to country living, after all." With a little groan, he propped up on his elbows. And felt his stomach sink. "What are you crying for? Are you trying to kill me?"

"I'm not. The sun's in my eyes." Then, feeling foolish, she flicked the single tear away. "It's not that kind of crying, anyway. Don't worry, I'm not going to blubber."

"Did I hurt you? Look, I'm sorry, I—"

"Jack." She heaved another sigh. "It's not that kind of crying, okay? And I'm done now, anyway."

Wary, he studied those gleaming eyes. "Are you sure?"

"Yes." Then she smiled. "You coward."

"Guilty." And he wasn't ashamed to admit it. He kissed her nose. "Now that we've got all this extra luck, we'd better get going."

"You're not going to try to pull a fast one, are you?"

He thought of the way she'd taken his face in her hands and told him she was sticking. There had never been anyone in his life who ever made him that one simple promise.

"No. I guess we're a team."

"Good guess."

M.J. waited until they were back on the highway, heading toward civilization, before she asked. "Okay, Jack, what's the plan?"

"Nothing fancy. Simplicity has fewer pitfalls. The way I see it, we've got to get to whoever's pulling the strings. Our only link with him, or her, is the guys in the van and maybe the Salvinis."

"So far, I'm with you."

"I need to have a little chat with them. To do that, I have to lure them out, maintain the advantage and convince them it's in their best interest to pass on some information."

"Okay, there are two guys with guns, one of whom is the approximate size of the Washington Monument. And you're going to convince them to chat with you." She beamed at him. "I admire your optimism."

"It's all a matter of leverage," he said, and explained how he planned to accomplish it.

Thunder was rumbling in a darkened sky when he pulled up in the lot at Salvini. It was a dignified building, separated from a strip mall by a large parking lot. And it was locked tight for the Monday holiday.

In the smaller, well-tended Salvini lot sat a lone Mercedes sedan.

"Know who owns that?"

"One of the creeps—Bailey's stepbrothers. Thomas,

I think. Bailey said they were closing down for an extended weekend. If he's inside, I don't know why."

"Let's poke around." Jack got out, wandered to the sedan. It was locked tight, its security light blinking. He checked the front doors of the building first, scanned the darkened showroom, saw no signs of life.

"Offices upstairs?" he asked M.J.

"Yeah. Bailey's, Thomas's, Timothy's." Her heart began to race. "Maybe she's in there, Jack. She rarely drives to work. We live so close."

"Uh-huh." And though it wasn't part of his plan, the worry in her voice had him going with impulse and pressing the buzzer beside the door. "Let's check the rear," he said a moment later.

"They could be holding her inside. She could be hurt. I should have thought of it before." Toward the west, lightning forked down like jagged blades. "She could be in there, hurt and—"

He turned. "Listen, if we're going to get through this, you've got to hold it together. We don't have time for a lot of hand-wringing and speculation."

Her head jerked back, then she squared her shoulders. "All right. Sorry."

After a short study of her face, he nodded, then continued to the back, where he took a long look at the steel security door. "Someone's been at the locks."

"What do you mean, 'at'?" She leaned over his shoulder as he crouched down. "Do you mean someone picked the locks?"

"Fairly recently, no rust, no dust in the scrapes. Wonder if he got in." He rose, examined the sides, the jambs. "He didn't try to jimmy it or hammer against it. I'd say he knew what he was doing. Under different circumstances, I'd say it was just your average break-in, but that's stretching it."

"Can you get in?"

That wasn't part of the immediate plan, either, but he considered. "Probably. Do you know what kind of alarm system they've got?"

"There's a box inside the door. It's coded. I don't know the code. You punch some numbers." She caught herself before she could indeed wring her hands. "Jack." She struggled to keep her voice calm. "She could be in there. She could be hurt. If we don't check, and something goes wrong..."

"Okay. But if I can't deal with the alarm, and fast, we're going to get busted." Still, he got his tools out of the trunk and went to work.

"Watch my back, will you?" he told her. "Make sure none of those holiday shoppers next door take an interest over here."

She turned, scanned the lot and the strip mall beyond. People came and went, obviously too involved in the bargains they'd bagged or those they were hunting to take notice of a man crouched at a security door of a locked building.

Thunder walked closer, and rain, long awaited, began to flood out of the sky. She didn't mind getting wet, considered the storm only a better cover. But she shuddered with relief when he gave her the all clear.

"Once I open this, I've probably got a minute to ninety seconds before the alarm. If I can't disengage it, we'll have to go, and fast."

"But—"

"No arguments here, M.J. If, by any chance, Bailey's in there, the cops'll be along in minutes, and they'll find her. We'll take our show on the road elsewhere. Agreed?"

What choice was there? "Agreed."

"Fine." He swiped dripping hair out of his eyes. "You stay right here. If I say go, you head for the car." Taking her silence for assent, he stepped inside. He saw the alarm box immediately, lifted a brow. "Interesting," he murmured, then signaled M.J. inside. "It's off."

"I don't understand that. It's always set."

"Just our lucky day." He winked, took her hand, then flipped on his flashlight with the other. "We'll try upstairs first, see if we get lucky again."

"Up these stairs," she told him. "Bailey's office is right down the hall."

"Nice digs," he commented, scanning the expensive carpeting, the tasteful colors, while keeping his ears tuned for any sound. There was nothing but drumming rain. He blocked M.J. with an outstretched arm, and swept the light into the office.

Quiet, organized, elegant and empty. He heard M.J. let out a rusty breath.

"No sign of struggle," he pointed out. "We'll check the rest of the floor, then downstairs before we go into phase one of plan A."

He moved down the hall and, a full yard before the next door, stopped. "Go back in her office, wait for me."

"Why? What is it?" Then she caught the heaviness in the air, recognized it for what it was. "Bailey! Oh, my God."

Jack rapped her back against the wall, pinned her until her struggles ceased. "You do what I tell you," he said between his teeth. "You stay here."

She closed her eyes, admitted there were some things she wasn't strong enough to face. Nodded.

Satisfied, he eased back. He moved down the hall quietly, eased the door open.

It was as bad as he'd ever seen, and death was rarely pretty. But this, he thought, trailing the light over the wreckage caused by a life-and-death struggle, had been madness.

Life had lost.

He turned away from it, went back to M.J. She was pale as wax, leaning against the wall. "It's not Bailey," he said immediately. "It's a man."

"Not Bailey?"

"No." He put a hand to her cheek, found it icy, but her eyes were losing their glazed look. "I'm going to check the other rooms. I don't want you to go in there, M.J."

She let out the breath that had been hot and trapped in her lungs. Not Bailey. "Was it like Ralph?"

"No." His voice was flat and hard. "It was a hell of a lot worse. Stay here."

He went through each room, checked corners and closets, careful not to touch anything or to wipe a surface when he had no choice but to touch. Saying nothing, he led M.J. downstairs and did a quick, thorough search of the lower level.

"Someone's been in here," he murmured, hunkering down to shine the light into a tiny alcove under the stairs. "The dust's disturbed." Considering, he stroked his chin. "I'd say if somebody was smart and needed a bolt-hole, this would be a good choice."

Her clothes were clinging wet against her skin. But that wasn't why she was shivering. "Bailey's smart."

He nodded, rose. "Keep that in mind. Let's do what we came for."

"Okay." She cast one last look over her shoulder, imagined Bailey hiding in the dark. From what? she wondered. From whom? And where was she now?

Outside, Jack secured the door, wiped the knob. "I figure if you need to, you can get over to that mall on those legs of yours in about thirty seconds at a sprint."

"I'm not running away."

"You will if I tell you." He pocketed the flashlight. "You're going to do exactly what I tell you. No questions, no arguments, no hesitation." His eyes flared into hers, made her shiver again. "Whoever did what I found upstairs is an animal. You remember that."

"I will." She clamped down ruthlessly on the next tremor. "And you remember we're in this together."

"The idea is for me to take these guys down, one at a time. If you can get to the van while I'm distracting them and disable it, fine. But don't take any chances."

"I've already told you I wouldn't."

"Once I have them secured," he continued, ignoring the impatience in her voice, "we can use their van. I can have a nice chat with them. I think I can get a name out of them." He examined his fist, then smiled craftily over it into her eyes. "Some basic information."

"Oooh…" She fluttered her wet lashes. "So macho."

"Shut up. Depending on the name and information we get, and the situation, we either go to the cops— which would be my second choice—or we follow the next lead."

"Agreed."

He opened the door of his car, waited until she slid

over the seat, then picked up her phone. "Make the call. Stretch it out for about a minute, just in case."

She dialed, then began to ramble to Grace's answering machine in Potomac. She kept her eyes on Jack's, and when he nodded, she pushed disconnect. "Phase two?" she said, struggling for calm.

"Now we wait."

Within fifteen minutes, the van turned into the lot at Salvini. The rain had slowed now, but continued to fall in a steady stream. In his position beside an aging station wagon, Jack hunched his shoulders against the wet and watched the routine.

The two men got out, separated and did a slow circle of the building.

The big one was his target.

Using parked cars as cover, Jack made his way over, watching as the man bent, picked up M.J.'s phone from the ground. It was a decent plant, Jack mused, gave him something to consider in that pea-size brain of his. As the big man pondered over the phone, Jack sprang and hit him at a dead run, bashing into his kidneys like a cannonball.

He took his quarry to his knees, and had the cuffs snapped over one steel-beam wrist before he was flicked off like a fly.

He felt the searing burn as his flesh scraped over wet, grainy asphalt, and rolled before a size-sixteen shoe could bash into his face. He made the grab, snagged the sledgehammer of a foot and heaved.

From her post, M.J. watched the struggle, wincing as Jack hit the ground, praying as he rolled. Hissing as fists crunched against bone. She started quietly toward the van, glancing back to see the progress of the bout.

He was outmatched, she thought desperately. Was going to get his neck broken, at the very least. Braced to spring to his aid, she saw the second man rounding the far corner of the building.

He'd be on them in moments, she thought. And Jack's plan to take them both quickly and separately was in tatters. She sucked in the breath to call out a warning, then narrowed her eyes. Maybe there was still a way to make it work.

She dashed out from behind cover, took a short run toward Salvini, away from Jack. She skidded to a halt when she saw the second man spot her, made her eyes widen with shock and fear. His hand went inside his jacket, but she held fast, waiting until he began closing in.

Then she ran, into the curtaining rain, drawing him away from Jack.

Both Jack and his sparring partner heard the shout. Both looked over instinctively and saw the woman with the bright cap of red hair racing away, and the man pursuing her.

Never listens, Jack thought with a bright spear of terror. Then he looked back, saw the big man grinning at him.

Jack grinned back, and his swollen left eye gleamed bright with malice. "Gotta take you down, and fast," he said conversationally as he rammed a fist into the man's mouth. "That's my woman your pal's chasing."

The giant swiped blood from his face. "You're meat."

"Yeah?" There wasn't any time to dally. Praying

M.J.'s legs and his neck would hold out, he lowered his head and charged like a mad bull. The force of the attack shot the man back, rapping his head smartly on the steel door. Bloodied, battered and exhausted, Jack drove his knee up, hard and high, and heard the satisfactory sound of air gushing out of a deflated blimp.

Blinking stinging sweat and warm rain out of his eyes, Jack wrenched the man's arms back, snapped on the second cuff.

"I'll be back for you," he promised, as he retrieved the phone and tore off in search of M.J.

Chapter 12

Jack had told her, if anything went wrong, to head for the shops, to lose herself in the crowds. Scream bloody murder if necessary.

With that on her mind, M.J. veered that way, her priority to lure the second gunman away from Jack and give him an even chance.

But as she raced toward the stores, with their bright On Sale signs, she saw couples, families, children being led by the hand, babies in strollers. And thought of the way the man chasing her had slipped a hand under his jacket.

She thought of what a gun fired at her in the midst of a crowd would do.

And she pivoted, changed direction on a dime and ran toward the far end of the lot.

Pumping her arms, she tossed a quick look over her

shoulder. She'd left her pursuer in the dust. He was still coming, but lagging now, overheated, she imagined, in his bagging suit coat and leather shoes. Slippery shoes on wet pavement. Just how far would he chase her, she wondered, before giving up and turning back to pick up his friend?

And stumble over Jack.

Deliberately she slowed her pace, let him close some of the distance, in order to keep his interest keen. Part of her worried that he would simply use that gun, slam a bullet into her leg. Or her back. With the image of that running riot in her head, she streaked into a line of parked cars.

She could hear her own breath whistling now. She'd run the equivalent of a fifty-yard touchdown dash in the blistering heat of a midsummer storm. Crouching behind a minivan, she swiped sweat from her eyes and tried to think.

Could she circle back, find a way to help Jack? Had the gorilla already pounded him into dust and set off to help his buddy? How long would her luck last before some innocent family of four, their bargain-hunting complete, ran through the downpour and into the line of fire?

Concentrating on silence more than speed, she duck-walked around the van, slid her way around a compact. She needed to catch her breath, needed to think. Needed to see what was happening behind the Salvini building.

Bracing herself, she put one trembling hand on the fender of the compact and risked a quick look.

He was closer than she'd anticipated. Four cars to the left, and taking his time. She ducked down fast, pressed her back into the bumper. If she stayed where she was, would he pass by, or would he spot her?

Better to die on the run, she thought, or with your fists raised, than to be picked off cowering behind an economy import.

She sucked in a breath, said another quick prayer for Jack, and headed for new ground. It was the ping on the asphalt beside her that stopped her heart. She felt the sharp edge of rock bounce off her jeans.

He was shooting at her. Her heart bounced from throat to stomach and back like a Ping-Pong ball, and she skidded around a parked car. Another inch, two at the most, and that bullet would have met flesh.

He'd tagged her, she realized. And now it would only be a matter of running her down, cornering her like a rabbit. Well, she would see about that.

Gritting her teeth, she bellied under the car, ignored the wet grit, the smell of gas and oil, and slid like a snake beneath the undercarriage, held her breath as she pulled herself through the narrow space and under the next vehicle.

She could hear him now. He was breathing hard, a wheeze on each inhale, a whistle on the exhale. She saw his shoes. Little feet, she thought irreverently, decked out in glossy black wing tips and argyle socks.

She closed her eyes for one brief moment, trying to get a picture of him planted in her mind. Five-eight, tops, maybe a hundred and sixty. Midthirties. Sharp eyes, a well-defined nose. Wiry but not buff. And out of breath.

Hell, she thought, going giddy. She could take him. She scooted another inch, was just preparing to make her move when she saw those shiny wing tips leave the ground.

There in front of her eyes were a pair of scuffed boots. Jack's boots. Jack's voice was muttering panting curses. Her vision blurred with relief and the terror as she heard the muffled thump that was the silenced gun firing again.

Skinning elbows and knees, she was out from under the car in time to see the gunman running for cover and Jack starting off in pursuit.

"Jack."

He skidded to a halt, whirled, sheer relief covering his battered face. And it was then that she saw the blood staining his shirt.

"Oh, God. Oh, God. You're shot." Her legs went weak, so that she stumbled toward him as he glanced down absently, pressing a hand to his side.

"Hell." The pain registered, but only dimly, as his arms filled with woman. "The car," he managed. "Get to the car. He's heading back."

His hand, wet with blood and rain, locked on hers.

Later, she would remember running. But none of it seemed real as it happened. Feet pounding on pavement, skidding, the jittery thud of her heart, the rising sense of fear and fury, the wide, shocked eyes of a woman carrying shopping bags who was nearly mowed down in their rush.

And Jack cursing her, steadily, for not doing as she was told.

The van screamed out of the lot as they skidded down the incline. "Damn it all to hell and back again." His lungs were burning, his side shot fire. Desperately he dug the keys out of his pocket. "In the car. Now!"

She all but dived through the window, barely maintaining her balance as he burned rubber in reverse. "You're hurt. Let me see—"

He batted her worried hands away and whipped the wheel around. "He got his three-ton friend, too. After all that trouble, they're not getting away." The car shimmied, fishtailed, then the tires bit the road as he swung into the chase. "Get the gun out of the glove box. Give it to me."

"Jack, you're bleeding. For God's sake."

"Didn't I tell you to run?" He punched the gas, screaming on the van's rear bumper as they rocketed toward the main drag. "I told you to head for people, to get lost. He could have killed you. Give me the damn gun."

"All right, all right." She beat a fist on the glove compartment until the sticky door popped open. "He's heading for the Beltway."

"I see where he's going."

"You're not going to shoot at him. You could hit some poor schmuck's car."

Jack snatched the gun out of her hand, swerved to make the exit, skidded on the damp roadway. "I hit what I aim at. Now strap in and be quiet. I'll deal with you later."

Her fear for him was such that she didn't blink an eye at his words. He zipped through traffic like a madman, hugging the bumper of the van like a lover. And when they hit ninety, a cold numbness settled over her, as if her system had been shot full of novocaine.

"You're going to kill someone," she said calmly. "It might not even be us."

"I can handle the car." That, at least, was perfect

truth. He threaded through traffic, staying on target like a heat-seeking missile, his fat new tires gripping true on the slick roadway. He was close enough that he could see the big man hunched in the passenger seat turn around and snarl.

"Yeah, I'm coming for you, you son of a bitch," Jack muttered. "You've got my spare cuffs."

"You're bleeding on the seat." M.J. heard herself speak, but the words seemed to come from outside her mind.

"I've got more." And with the gun on his lap, he whipped the wheel, gained inches on the side. He'd cut them off, he calculated, drive them to the shoulder. The big man was cuffed, and he could handle the other.

And then, they would see.

His eyes narrowed as he saw the driver of the van twist his head around, heard the wheels screech. The van shimmied, shuddered, then swerved wildly toward the oncoming exit.

"He can't make it." Jack pumped his brakes, fell back a foot and prepared to make the quick, sharp turn. "He can't make that turn. He'll lose it."

He swore when the van rocked, lost control on the rain-slicked road and hit the guardrail at eighty. The crash was huge, and sent the van flying up like a drunken high diver. It rolled once in the air. And amid the squeal of brakes of other horrified drivers, it landed twelve feet below, on the incline.

He had time to swing to the side, to push out of the car, before the explosion shoved him back like a huge, hot hand. M.J.'s hand gripped his shoulder as the flames spewed up. The air stank with gas.

"Not a chance," he murmured. "Lost them."

"Get in the car, Jack." It amazed her how cool, how composed, her voice sounded. Cars were emptying of drivers and passengers. People were rushing toward the wreck. "In the passenger side. I'm driving now."

"After all that," he said, dazed with smoke and pain. "Lost them, anyway."

"In the car." She led him around, ignoring the high, excited voices. Someone, surely, would have already called 911 on his car phone. There was nothing left to do. "We need to get out of here."

She drove on instinct back to her apartment. Safe or not, it was home, and he needed tending. Driving Jack's car was like manning a yacht, she thought, concentrating on her speed and direction as the rain petered out to a fine drizzle. A very old, very big boat. With a vague sense of surprise, she pulled in beside her MG.

Nothing much had changed, she realized. Her car was still there, the building still stood. A couple of kids who didn't mind getting wet were tossing a Frisbee in the side yard, as if it was an ordinary day in ordinary lives.

"Wait for me to come around." She dragged up her purse from the floor, found her keys. Of course, he didn't listen, and was standing on the sidewalk when she came around the hood. "You can lean on me," she murmured, sliding an arm around his waist. "Just lean on me, Jack."

"It should be all right to be here," he decided. "At least for a little while. We may have to move again soon." He realized he was limping, favoring an ache in his right leg that he hadn't noticed before.

Her heart had stopped stuttering and was numb. "We'll just get you cleaned up."

"Yeah. I could use a beer."

"I'll get you one," she promised as she led him inside. Though she habitually took the stairs, she steered him to the elevator. "Let's just get you inside." And then to a hospital, she thought. She had to see how bad it was first. Once she'd done what she could, she was dumping it all and going official. Cops, doctors, FBI, whatever it took.

She sent up a small prayer of thanksgiving when she saw that the corridor was empty. No nosy neighbors, she thought, ignoring the police tape and unlocking her door. No awkward questions.

She kicked a broken lamp out of her way, walked him around the overturned couch and into the bath. "Sit," she ordered, and flicked on the lights. "Let's have a look." And her trembling hands belied her steady voice as she gently lifted his bloody shirt over his head.

"God, Jack, that guy beat the hell out of you."

"I left him with his face in the dirt and his hands cuffed behind his back."

"Yeah." She made herself look away from the blooming purple bruises over his torso and wet a cloth. "Have you been shot before?"

"Once, in Abilene. Caught me in the leg. Slowed me down awhile."

Ridiculous as it was, it helped that this wasn't the first time. She pressed the cloth to his side, low along the ribs. Her eyes stung with hot tears that she wouldn't shed. "I know it hurts."

"You were going to get me a beer." Didn't she look

pretty, he thought, playing nurse, with her cheeks pale, her eyes dark, and her hands cool as silk.

"In a minute. Just be still now." She knelt beside him, steeling herself for the worst. Then sat back on her heels and hissed. "Damn it, Jack, it's only a scratch."

He grinned at her, feeling every bump and bruise as if in a personal carnival of pain. "That's supposed to be my line."

"I was ready for some big gaping hole in your side. It just grazed you."

He looked down, considered. "Bled pretty good, though." He took the cloth himself, pressed it against the long, shallow wound. "About that beer..."

"I'll get you a beer. I ought to hit you over the head with it."

"We'll talk about who conks who after I eat a bottle of aspirin." He got up, wincing, and pawed through the mirrored cabinet over the sink. "Maybe you could get me a shirt out of the car, sugar. I don't think I'm going to be wearing the other one again."

"You scared me." Anger, tears and desperate relief brewed a messy stew in her stomach. "Do you have any idea how much you scared me?"

He found the aspirin, closed the cabinet and met her eyes in the mirror. "I've got an idea, seeing how I felt when I saw you trying to draw that puss-for-brain's fire. You promised to head for the mall."

"Well, I didn't. Sue me." Out of patience, she shoved him down again, ignoring his muffled yelp of pain. "Oh, be quiet and let me finish up here. I must have some antiseptic here somewhere."

"Maybe just a leather strap to bite on while you pour salt in my wounds."

"Don't tempt me." She dampened another cloth, then knelt down and began to clean his face. "You've got a black eye blooming, your lip's swollen, and you've got a nice big knot right here." He yelped again when she pressed the cloth to his temple. "Baby."

"If you're going to play Nurse Nancy, at least give me some anesthesia first." Since she didn't seem inclined to give him any water, he swallowed the aspirin dry.

He continued to complain as she swabbed him with antiseptic, slapped on bandages. Out of patience, she pressed her lips to his, which caused him equal amounts of pain and pleasure. "Are you going to kiss everywhere it hurts?" he asked.

"You should be so lucky." Then she laid her head in his lap and let out a long, long sigh. "I don't care how mad you are. I didn't know what else to do. He was coming. He'd have had you. I only knew I had to draw him away from you."

He weakened, stroked her hair. "Okay, we'll get into all that later." He noticed for the first time the raw skin on her elbow. "Hey, you've got a few scrapes yourself."

"Burns some," she murmured.

"Aw. Come on, sugar, I'll be the doctor." He reversed their positions, grinned. "This may sting a little."

"You'd love that, wouldn't— Ouch! Damn it, Jack."

"Baby." But he kissed the abraded skin, then bandaged it gently. "You ever scare me like that again, and I'll keep you cuffed to the bed for a month."

"Promises, promises." She leaned forward, wrapped her arms around him. "They're dead, aren't they? They couldn't have lived through that."

"Chances are slim. I'm sorry, M.J., I never got anything out of them. Not a clue."

"*We* never got anything out of them," she corrected. "And we did our best." She struggled to bury the worry, straighten her shoulders. "There's still the creeps," she began, then went pale again, remembering. Odds were at least one of the Salvini brothers was dead.

But it hadn't been Bailey in there, she reminded herself, and took two deep breaths. "Well, at least now I can get myself some fresh clothes and some cash. And I'm calling into the pub." This was a dare. "I'll wait until we're ready to head out again, but I'm checking in, letting them know I'm okay, giving them the schedule for the rest of the week."

"Fine, be a businesswoman." He stood up, held her still. "We'll find your friends, M.J. I promise you that. And as much as it goes against the grain, it's time to call in the cops."

She let out a wavering sigh of relief. "Yeah. Three days of this is enough."

"There'll be a lot of questions."

"Then we'll give them the answers."

"I should tell you that a man in my line of work isn't real popular with straight cops. I've got a couple of contacts, but when you start moving up the ranks, the tolerance level shoots way down."

"We'll handle it. Should we call from here, or just go in?"

"Here. Cop shops make me itchy."

"I'm not giving them the stone." She planted her feet, prepared for an argument. "It's Bailey's—or it's her decision. I'm not turning it over to anyone but her."

"Okay," he said easily, and made her blink. "We'll

work around it. She and Grace come first, with both of us now."

Her smile spread. And the jangling ring made them both jolt. "What?" She stared down at her purse as if it had suddenly come alive and snapped at her. "It's my phone. My phone's ringing."

He touched a hand to his pocket, reassured when he felt the gun. "Answer it."

Barely breathing, she dug into the purse she'd dropped on the floor, hit the switch. "O'Leary." The tears simply rushed into her eyes as she sank down on the floor. "Bailey. Oh, my God, Bailey. Are you all right? Where are you? Are you hurt? What— What? Yes, yes, I'm fine. In my apartment, but where—"

Her hand reached up, gripped Jack's. "Bailey, stop asking me that and tell me where the hell you are. Yeah, I've got it. We'll be there in ten minutes. Stay."

She clicked off. "I'm sorry," she told Jack. "I've got to." Then burst into tears. "She's all right," she managed as he rolled his eyes and picked her up. "She's okay."

It was a quiet, established neighborhood with lovely old trees. M.J. gripped her hands together on her lap and scanned house numbers. "Twenty-two, twenty-four, twenty-six. There! That one." Even as Jack turned into the driveway of a tidy Federal-style home, she was reaching for the door handle. He merely hooked a hand in the waist of her jeans and hauled her back.

"Hold on, wait until I stop."

Even as he did, he saw the woman, a pretty blonde of fragile build, come racing out of the front door and across the wet grass. M.J. shoved herself out of the car and streaked into her arms.

It made a nice picture, Jack decided as he climbed out, gingerly. The two of them standing in the watery sunlight, holding on as if they could swallow each other whole. They swayed together on the lush grass, weeping, talking over each other and just clinging.

And as touching and attractive a scene as it was, there was nothing he wanted to avoid more than two sobbing women. He spotted the man standing just outside the door, noted the smile in his eyes, the fresh bandage on his arm. Without hesitation, Jack gave the women a wide berth and headed for the front door.

"Cade Parris."

Jack took the extended hand, measured his man. About six-two, trim, brown hair, eyes of a dreamier green than M.J.'s. A strong grip that Jack felt balanced out the glossy good looks.

"Jack Dakota."

Cade scanned the bruises, shook his head. "You look like a man who could use a drink."

Despite his sore mouth, Jack's lips spread in a grateful smile. "Brother, you just became my best friend."

"Come on in," Cade invited, with a last glance toward M.J. and Bailey. "They'll need some time, and we can fill each other in."

It took a while, but Jack was feeling considerably more relaxed, with his feet propped up on a coffee table, a beer in his hand.

"Amnesia," he murmured. "Must have been tough on her."

"She's had a rough few days. Seeing one slimy excuse for a stepbrother kill her other slimy excuse for a stepbrother, then come for her."

"We dropped in on Salvini's. I saw the results."

Cade nodded. "Then you know how bad it was. If she hadn't gotten away… Well, she did. She still doesn't remember all of it, but she'd already sent one of the diamonds to M.J. and one to Grace. I've been working the case since Friday morning, when she came to my office. You?"

"Saturday afternoon," Jack told him and cooled his throat with beer.

"It's been fast work all around." But Cade frowned as he looked toward the window. "Bailey was scared, confused, but she wanted answers and figured a private investigator could get them for her. We had a major breakthrough today."

Jack lifted a brow, gesturing toward the bandage. "That part of it?"

"The remaining Salvini," Cade said, his eyes level and cold. "He's dead."

Which meant one more dead end, Jack mused. "You figure they set the whole thing up?"

"No. They had a client. I haven't tracked him yet." Cade rose, wandered to the window. M.J. and Bailey were still standing in the yard, talking fast. "Cops are on it too, now. I've got a friend. Mick Marshall."

"Yeah, I know him. He's a rare one. A cop with a brain and a heart."

"That's Mick. Buchanan's over him, though. He doesn't much like P.I.'s."

"Buchanan doesn't much like anybody. But he's good."

"He's going to want to talk to you, and M.J."

The prospect had Jack sighing. "I think I could use another beer."

With a laugh, Cade turned from the window. "I'll get us both another. And you can tell me how you spent your weekend." His eyes roamed over Jack's face. "And how the other guy looks."

"Timothy," M.J. said with surprise. "I never liked him, but I never pictured him as a murderer."

"It was as if he'd lost his mind." Bailey kept her hand linked with M.J.'s, as if afraid her friend would vanish without the connection. "I blanked it all, just shut it out. Everything. Little pieces started to come back, but I couldn't get a grip on them. I wouldn't have made it through without Cade."

"I can't wait to meet him." She looked into Bailey's eyes, and her own narrowed in speculation. "It looks as though he works fast."

"It shows?" Bailey asked, and flushed.

"Like a big neon sign."

"Just days ago," Bailey said, half to herself. "It all happened fast. It doesn't seem like just a few days. It feels as if I've known him forever." Her lips curved, warmed her honey-brown eyes. "He loves me, M.J. Just like that. I know it sounds crazy."

"You'd be surprised what doesn't sound crazy to me these days. He makes you happy?" M.J. tucked Bailey's wave of hair behind her ear. "That's what counts."

"I couldn't remember you. Or Grace." A tear squeezed through as Bailey shut her eyes. "I know it was only a couple of days, but it was so lonely without you. Then, when I started to remember, it wasn't specifics, more just a feeling. A loss of something important. Then, when

I did remember, and we went to your apartment, you were gone. There'd been the break-in, and I couldn't find you. Everything happened so fast after that. It was only hours ago. Then I remembered that phone you cart around in your purse. I remembered and I called. And there you were."

"It was the best call I ever got."

"The best I ever made." Her lips trembled once. "M.J., I can't find Grace."

"I know." Drawing together, M.J. draped an arm around Bailey's shoulders. "We have to believe she's all right. Jack and I were just up at her country place this morning. She'd been there, Bailey. I could still smell her. And we found each other. We'll find her."

"Yes, we will." They walked toward the house together. "This Jack? Does he make you happy?"

"Yeah. When he's not ticking me off."

With a chuckle, Bailey opened the door. "Then I can't wait to meet him, either."

"I like your friend." Jack stood out on Cade's patio, contemplating after-the-rain in suburbia.

"She likes you, too."

"She's classy. And she's come through a rough time holding her own. Parris seems pretty sharp."

"He helped get her through, so he's aces with me."

"We filled in most of the blanks for each other. He's got a cool head, a quick mind. And he's crazy about your friend."

"I think I noticed that."

Jack took her hand, studied it. Not delicate like Bailey's, he mused, but narrow, competent. Strong. "He's got a lot to offer. Class again, money, fancy house. I guess you'd call it security."

Intrigued, she watched his face. "I guess you would."

He hadn't meant to get started on this, he realized. But however fast certain things could move, he'd decided life was too short to waste time.

"My old man was a bum," he said abruptly. "My mother served drinks to drunks when she felt like working. I worked my way through college hauling bricks and mixing mortar for a mason, which led me to a useless degree in English lit with a minor in anthropology. Don't ask me why, it seemed like the thing to do at the time. I've got a few thousand socked away for dry spells. You get dry spells in my line of work. I rent a couple of rooms by the month." He waited a beat, but she said nothing. "Not what you'd call security."

"Nope."

"Is that what you want? Security?"

She thought about it. "Nope."

He dragged his hand through his hair. "You know how those two stones looked when you and Bailey put them together? They looked spectacular, sure, all that fire and power in one spot. But mostly, they just looked right." He met her eyes, tried to see inside her. "Sometimes, it's just right."

"And when it is, you don't have to look for the reasons."

"Maybe not. I don't know what I'm doing here. I don't know why this is. I've lived my life alone, and liked it that way. Do you understand that?"

She enjoyed the irritation in his voice, and smirked. "Yeah, I understand that. The lone wolf. You want to howl at the moon tonight, or what?"

"Don't get smart with me when I'm trying to explain myself."

He took a quick circle around the patio. There was a hammock swinging between two big trees, and somewhere in those dripping green leaves a bird was singing its heart out.

His life, Jack mused, had never been that simple, that calm, or that pretty. He didn't have anything to offer but what he was, and what he had inside himself for her.

She'd have to decide if that was enough to build on.

"The point is, I don't want to keep living my life alone." His head snapped up, and his bruised eye glared out from under the arched, scarred brow. "Do you understand that?"

"Why wouldn't I?" Her smirk remained firmly in place. "You're sloppy in love with me, pal."

"Keep it up, just keep it up." He hissed out a breath, eased a hand onto his aching side. "My feelings aren't the issue, and maybe yours aren't, either. Things happen to people's emotions under intense circumstances."

"Now he's being philosophical again. Must be that minor in anthropology."

He closed his eyes, prayed for patience. "I'm trying to lay out my cards here. You come from a different place than I do, and maybe you don't want to head where I'm heading. Maybe you want to slow down some now, take it in more careful steps. More traditional."

Now she snorted. "Is that how I strike you? The traditional type?"

His frown only deepened. "Maybe not, but it doesn't change the fact that a week ago you were cruising along in your own lane just fine. You've got a right to ask questions, look for reasons. A couple of days with me—"

"I'm not asking questions or looking for reasons, Jack," she said, interrupting him. "I stopped cruising in my own lane the day I met you, and I'm glad of it."

Oh, hell, she thought, and braced. "It stands for Magdalen Juliette."

A cough of laughter escaped him. It was the last thing he'd expected. "You're kidding."

"It stands for Magdalen Juliette," she repeated between clenched teeth. "And the only people who know that are my family, Bailey and Grace. In other words, only people I love and trust, which now includes you."

"Magdalen Juliette," he repeated, rolling it around on his tongue. "Quite a handle, sugar."

"It's M.J. Legally M.J., because that's what I wanted. And if you ever call me any form of Magdalen Juliette other than M.J., I will personally and with great pleasure skin you alive."

She would, too, he thought with a quick, crooked grin. "If you don't want me using it, why did you tell me?"

She took a step toward him. "I told you that, and I'm telling you this, because my name is M. J. O'Leary, and I know what I want."

His eyes flared and burned away the grin. "You're sure of that?"

"The second stone's knowledge. And I know. Do you?"

"Yeah." His breathing took a hitch. "It's a big step."

"The biggest."

"Okay." His palms were sweaty in his pockets, so he pulled them free. "You go first."

Her grin flashed. "No, you."

"No way. I said it first last time. Fair's fair."

She supposed it was. Angling her head, she took a good long look at him. Yes, she thought. She knew. "Okay. Let's get married."

Relishing the swift kick of joy, he tucked his thumbs in his pockets. "Aren't you supposed to ask? You know, propose? A guy's entitled to a little romance at big moments."

"You're pushing your luck." Then she laughed and locked her arms around his neck. "But what the hell— will you marry me, Jack?"

"Sure, why not?"

And when she laughed again, he caught her against his sore and battered body.

Perfect fit.

* * * * *

SECRET STAR

To generous hearts

Chapter 1

The woman in the portrait had a face created to steal a man's breath and haunt his dreams. It was, perhaps, as close to perfection as nature would allow. Eyes of laser blue whispered of sex and smiled knowingly from beneath thick black lashes. The brows were perfectly arched, with a flirty little mole dotting the downward point of the left one. The skin was porcelain-pure, with a hint of warm rose beneath—just warm enough that a man could fantasize that heat was kindling only for him. The nose was straight and finely sculpted.

The mouth—and, oh, the mouth was hard to ignore—was curved invitingly, appeared pillow-soft, yet strong in shape. A bold red temptation that beckoned as clearly as a siren's call.

Framing that staggering face was a rich, wild tumble of ebony hair that streamed over creamy bare shoul-

ders. Glossy, gorgeous, generous. The kind of hair even
a strong man would lose himself in—fisting his hands
in all that black silk, while his mouth sank deep, and
deeper, into those soft, smiling lips.

Grace Fontaine, Seth thought, a study in the perfection of feminine beauty.

It was too damn bad she was dead.

He turned away from the portrait, annoyed that his
gaze and his mind kept drifting back to it. He'd wanted
some time alone at the crime scene, after the forensic
team finished, after the M.E. took possession of the
body. The outline remained, an ugly human-shaped
silhouette marring the glossy chestnut floor.

It was simple enough to determine how she'd died.
A nasty tumble from the floor above, right through the
circling railing, now splintered and sharp-edged, and
down, beautiful face first, into the lake-size glass table.

She'd lost her beauty in death, he thought, and that
was a damn shame, too.

It was also simple to determine that she'd been given
some help with that last dive.

It was, he mused, looking around, a terrific house.
The high ceilings offered space and half a dozen generous skylights gave light, rosy, hopeful beams from
the dying sun. Everything curved—the stairs, the door-
ways, the windows. Female again, he supposed. The
wood was glossy, the glass sparkling, the furniture all
obviously carefully selected antiques.

Someone was going to have a tough time getting the
bloodstains out of the dove-gray upholstery of the sofa.

He tried to imagine how it had all looked before whoever helped Grace Fontaine off the balcony
stormed through the rooms.

There wouldn't have been broken statuary or ripped cushions. Flowers would have been meticulously arranged in vases, rather than crushed into the intricate pattern of the Oriental rugs.

There certainly wouldn't have been blood, broken glass, or layers of fingerprint dust.

She'd lived well, he thought. But then, she had been able to afford to live well. She'd become an heiress when she turned twenty-one, the privileged, pampered orphan and the wild child of the Fontaine empire. An excellent education, a country-club darling, and the headache, he imagined, of the conservative and staunch Fontaines, of Fontaine Department Stores fame.

Rarely had a week gone by that Grace Fontaine didn't warrant a mention in the society pages of the *Washington Post*, or a paparazzi shot in one of the glossies. And it usually hadn't been due to a good deed.

The press would be screaming with this latest, and last, adventure in the life and times of Grace Fontaine, Seth knew, the moment the news leaked. And they would be certain to mention all of her escapades. Posing nude at nineteen for a centerfold spread, the steamy and very public affair with a very married English lord, the dalliance with a hot heartthrob from Hollywood.

There'd been other notches in her designer belt, Seth remembered. A United States senator, a bestselling author, the artist who had painted her portrait, the rock star who, rumor had it, had attempted to take his own life when she dumped him.

She'd packed a lot of men into a short life.

Grace Fontaine was dead at twenty-six.

It was his job to find out not only the how, but the who. And the why.

He had a line on the why already. The Three Stars of Mithra—a fortune in blue diamonds, the impulsive and desperate act of a friend, and greed.

Seth frowned as he walked through the empty house, cataloging the events that had brought him to this place, to this point. Since he had a personal interest in mythology, had since childhood, he knew something about the Three Stars. They were the stuff of legends, and had once been grouped in a gold triangle that had been held in the hands of a statue of the god Mithra.

One stone for love, he remembered, skimming through details as he climbed the curved stairs to the second level. One for knowledge, and the last for generosity. Mythologically speaking, whoever possessed the Stars gained the god's power. And immortality.

Which was, logically, a crock, of course. Wasn't it odd, though, he mused, that he'd been dreaming lately of flashing blue stones, a dark castle shrouded in mist, a room of glinting gold? And there was a man with eyes as pale as death, he thought, trying to clear the hazy details. And a woman with the face of a goddess.

And his own violent death.

Seth shook off the uneasy sensation that accompanied his recalling the snippets of dreams. What he required now were facts, basic, logical facts. And the fact was that three blue diamonds weighing something over a hundred carats apiece were worth six kings' ransoms. And someone wanted them, and didn't mind killing to gain possession.

He had bodies piling up like cordwood, he thought, dragging a hand through his dark hair. In order of death, the first had been Thomas Salvini, part owner of Salvini, gem experts who had been contracted by the Smithsonian Institution to verify and assess the three stones. Evidence pointed to the fact that verifying and assessing hadn't been quite enough for Thomas Salvini, or his twin, Timothy.

Over a million in cash indicated that they'd had other plans—and a client who wanted the Stars for himself.

Added to that was the statement from one Bailey James, the Salvinis' stepsister, and eyewitness to fratricide. A gemologist with an impeccable reputation, she claimed to have discovered her stepbrothers' plans to copy the stones, sell the originals and leave the country with the profits.

She'd gone in to see her brothers alone, he thought with a shake of his head. Without contacting the police. And she'd decided to face them down after she shipped two of the stones to her two closest friends, separating them to protect them. He gave a short sigh at the mysterious minds of civilians.

Well, she'd paid for her impulse, he thought. Walking in on a vicious murder, barely escaping with her life—and with her memory of the incident and everything before it blocked for days.

He stepped into Grace's bedroom, his heavy-lidded gold-toned eyes cooly scanning the brutally searched room.

And had Bailey James gone to the police even then? No, she'd chosen a P.I., right out of the phone book. Seth's mouth thinned in annoyance. He had very little respect and no admiration for private investigators. Through blind luck, she'd stumbled across a fairly decent one, he acknowledged. Cade Parris wasn't as bad

as most, and he'd managed—through more blind luck,
Seth was certain—to sniff out a trail.

And nearly gotten himself killed in the process.
Which brought Seth to death number two. Timothy
Salvini was now as dead as his brother. He couldn't
blame Parris overmuch for defending himself from a
man with a knife, but taking the second Salvini out
left a dead end.

And through the eventful Fourth of July weekend,
Bailey James's other friend had been on the run with
a bounty hunter. In a rare show of outward emotion,
Seth rubbed his eyes and leaned against the door jamb.

M. J. O'Leary. He'd be interviewing her soon, personally. And he'd be the one telling her, and Bailey
James, that their friend Grace was dead. Both tasks
fell under his concept of duty.

O'Leary had the second Star and had been underground with the skip tracer, Jack Dakota, since Saturday afternoon. Though it was only Monday evening
now, M.J. and her companion had managed to rack
up a number of points—including three more bodies.

Seth reflected on the foolish and unsavory bail
bondsman who'd not only set Dakota up with the
false job of bringing in M.J., but also moonlighted
with blackmail. The hired muscle who'd been after
M.J. had likely been part of some scam of his and had
killed him. Then they'd had some very bad luck on a
rain-slicked road.

And that left him with yet another dead end.

Grace Fontaine was likely to be third. He wasn't
certain what her empty house, her mangled possessions, would tell him. He would, however, go through
it all, inch by inch and step by step. That was his style.

He would be thorough, he would be careful, and he would find the answers. He believed in order, he believed in laws. He believed, unstintingly, in justice.

Seth Buchanan was a third-generation cop, and had worked his way up the rank to lieutenant due to an inherent skill for police work, an almost terrifying patience, and a hard-edged objectivity. The men under him respected him—some secretly feared him. He was well aware he was often referred to as the Machine, and took no offense. Emotion, temperament, the grief and the guilt civilians could indulge in, had no place in the job.

If he was considered aloof, even cold and controlled, he saw it as a compliment.

He stood a moment longer in the doorway, the mahogany-framed mirror across the wide room reflecting him. He was a tall, well-built man, muscles toned to iron under a dark suit jacket. He'd loosened his tie because he was alone, and his nightwing hair was slightly disordered by the rake of his fingers. It was full and thick, with a slight wave. He pushed it back from an unsmiling face that boasted a square jaw and tawny skin.

His nose had been broken years before, when he was in uniform, and it edged his face toward the rugged. His mouth was hard, firm, and rare to smile. His eyes, the dark gold of an old painting, remained cool under straight black brows.

On one wide-palmed hand he wore the ring that had been his father's. On either side of the heavy gold were the words *Serve* and *Protect*.

He took both duties seriously.

Bending, he picked up a pool of red silk that had

been tossed on the mountain of scattered clothing heaped on the Aubusson carpet. The callused tips of his fingers skimmed over it. The red silk gown matched the short robe the victim had been wearing, he thought.

He wanted to think of her only as the victim, not as the woman in the portrait, certainly not as the woman in those new and disturbing dreams that disrupted his sleep. And he was irritated that his mind kept swimming back to that stunning face—the woman behind it. That quality was—had been, he corrected—part of her power. That skill in drilling into a man's mind until he was obsessed with her.

She would have been irresistible, he mused, still holding the wisp of silk. Unforgettable. Dangerous.

Had she slipped into that little swirl of silk for a man? he wondered. Had she been expecting company— a private evening of passion?

And where was the third Star? Had her unexpected visitor found it, taken it? The safe in the library downstairs had been broken open, cleaned out. It seemed logical that she would have locked something that valuable away. Yet she'd taken the fall from up here.

Had she run? Had he chased her? Why had she let him in the house? The sturdy locks on the doors hadn't been tampered with. Had she been careless, reckless enough to open the door to a stranger while she wore nothing but a thin silk robe?

Or had she known him?

Perhaps she'd bragged about the diamond, even shown it off to him. Had greed taken the place of passion? An argument, then a fight. A struggle, a fall. Then the destruction of the house as cover.

It was an avenue, he decided. He had her thick address book downstairs, and would go through it name by name. Just as he, and the team he assigned, would go through the empty house in Potomac, Maryland, inch by inch.

But he had people to see now. Tragedy to spread and details to tie up. He would have to ask one of Grace Fontaine's friends, or a member of her family, to come in and officially identify the body.

He regretted, more than he wanted to, that anyone who had cared for her would have to look at that ruined face.

He let the silk gown drop, took one last look at the room, with its huge bed and trampled flowers, the scatter of lovely old antique bottles that gleamed like precious gems. He already knew that the scent here would haunt him, just as that perfect face painted beautifully in oils in the room downstairs would.

It was full dark when he returned. It wasn't unusual for him to put long, late hours into a case. Seth had no life to speak of outside of the job, had never sought to make one. The women he saw socially, or romantically, were carefully, even calculatingly, selected. Most tolerated the demands of his work poorly, and they rarely cemented a relationship. Because he knew how difficult and frustrating those demands of time, energy and heart were on those who waited, he expected complaints, sulking, even accusations, from the women who felt neglected.

So he never made promises. And he lived alone.

He knew there was little he could do here at the scene. He should have been at his desk—or at least, he thought, have gone home just to let his mind clear.

But he'd been pulled back to this house. No, to this woman, he admitted. It wasn't the two stories of wood and glass, however lovely, that dragged at him.

It was the face in the portrait.

He'd left his car at the top of the sweep of the drive, and walked to the house sheltered by grand old trees and well-trimmed shrubs green with summer. He'd let himself in, turned the switch that had the foyer chandelier blazing light.

His men had already started the tedious door-to-door of the neighborhood, hoping that someone, in another of the big, exquisite homes, would have heard something, seen anything.

The medical examiner was slow—understandably, Seth reminded himself. It was a holiday, and the staff was down to bare minimum. Official reports would take a bit longer.

But it wasn't the reports or lack of them that nagged at his mind as he wandered back, inevitably, to the portrait over the glazed-tile hearth.

Grace Fontaine had been loved. He'd underestimated the depth friendship could reach. But he'd seen that depth, and that shocked and racking grief in the faces of the two women he'd just left.

There had been a bond between Bailey James, M. J. O'Leary and Grace that was as strong as he'd ever seen. He regretted—and he rarely had regrets—that he'd had to tell them so bluntly.

I'm sorry for your loss.

Words cops said to euphemize the death they lived with—often violent, always unexpected. He had said the words, as he had too often in the past, and watched the fragile blonde and the cat-eyed redhead simply crumble. Clutching each other, they had simply crumbled.

He hadn't needed the two men who had ranged themselves as the women's champions to tell him to leave them alone with their grief. There would be no questions, no statements, no answers, that night. Nothing he could say or do would penetrate that thick curtain of grief.

Grace Fontaine had been loved, he thought again, looking into those spectacular blue eyes. Not simply desired by men, but loved by two women. What was behind those eyes, what was behind that face, that had deserved that kind of unquestioning emotion?

"Who the hell were you?" he murmured, and was answered by that bold, inviting smile. "Too beautiful to be real. Too aware of your own beauty to be soft." His deep voice, rough with fatigue, echoed in the empty house. He slipped his hands in his pockets, rocked back on his heels. "Too dead to care."

And though he turned from the portrait, he had the uneasy feeling that it was watching him. Measuring him.

He had yet to reach her next of kin, the aunt and uncle in Virginia who had raised her after the death of her parents. The aunt was summering in a villa in Italy and was, for tonight, out of touch.

Villas in Italy, he mused, blue diamonds, oil portraits over fireplaces of sapphire-blue tile. It was a world far removed from his firmly middle-class upbringing, and from the life he'd embraced through his career.

But he knew violence didn't play favorites.

He would eventually go home to his tiny little house

on its postage-stamp lot, crowded together with dozens of other tiny little houses. It would be empty, as he'd never found a woman who moved him to want to share even that small private space. But his home would be there for him.

And this house, for all its gleaming wood and acres of gleaming glass, its sloping lawn, sparkling pool and trimmed bushes, hadn't protected its mistress.

He walked around the stark outline on the floor and started up the stairs again. His mood was edgy—he could admit that. And the best thing to smooth it out again was work.

He thought perhaps a woman with as eventful a life as Grace Fontaine would have noted those events—and her personal feelings about them—in a diary.

He worked in silence, going through her bedroom carefully, knowing very well that he was trapped in that sultry scent she'd left behind.

He'd taken his tie off, tucked it in his pocket. The weight from his weapon, snug in his shoulder harness, was so much a part of him it went unnoticed.

He went through her drawers without a qualm, though they were largely empty now, as their contents were strewn around the room. He searched beneath them, behind them and under the mattress.

He thought, irrelevantly, that she'd owned enough clothing to outfit a good-size modeling troupe, and that she'd leaned toward soft materials. Silks, cashmeres, satins, thin brushed wools. Bold colors. Jewel colors, with a bent toward blues.

With those eyes, he thought as they crept back into his mind, why not?

He caught himself wondering how her voice had

sounded. Would it have fit that sultry face, been husky and low, another purr of temptation for a man? He imagined it that way, a voice as dark and sensual as the scent that hung on the air.

Her body had fit the face, fit the scent, he mused, stepping into her enormous walk-in closet. Of course, she'd helped nature along there. And he wondered why a woman would feel impelled to add silicone to her body to lure a man. And what kind of pea-brained man would prefer it to an honest shape.

He preferred honesty in women. Insisted on it. Which, he supposed, was one of the reasons he lived alone.

He scanned the clothes still hanging with a shake of his head. Even the killer had run out of patience here, it seemed. The hangers were swept back so that garments were crowded together, but he hadn't bothered to pull them all out.

Seth judged that the number of shoes totaled well over two hundred, and one wall of shelves had obviously been fashioned to hold handbags. These, in every imaginable shape and size and color, had been pulled out of their slots, ripped open and searched.

A cupboard had held more—sweaters, scarves. Costume jewelry. He imagined she'd had plenty of the real sparkles, as well. Some would have been in the now empty safe downstairs, he was sure. And she might have a lockbox at a bank.

That he would check on first thing in the morning.

She'd enjoyed music, he mused, scanning the wireless speakers. He'd seen speakers in every room of the house, and there had been CDs, tapes, even old albums, tossed around the living area downstairs. She'd had eclectic taste there. Everything from Bach to the B-52s.

Had she spent many evenings alone? he wondered. With music playing through the house? Had she ever curled up in front of that classy fireplace with one of the hundreds of books that lined the walls of her library?

Snuggled up on the couch, he thought, wearing that little red robe, with her million-dollar legs tucked up. A glass of brandy, the music on low, the starlight streaming through the roof windows.

He could see it too well. He could see her look up, skim that fall of hair back from that staggering face, curve those tempting lips as she caught him watching her. Set the book aside, reach out a hand in invitation, give that low, husky purr of a laugh as she drew him down beside her.

He could almost taste it.

Because he could, he swore under his breath, gave himself a moment to control the sudden upbeat of his heart rate.

Dead or alive, he decided, the woman was a witch. And the damn stones, preposterous or not, only seemed to add to her power.

And he was wasting his time. Completely wasting it, he told himself as he rose. He was covering ground best covered through rules and routine. He needed to go back, light a fire under the M.E., push for an estimated time of death. He needed to start calling the numbers in the victim's address book.

He needed to get out of this house that smelled of this woman. All but breathed of her. And stay out of it, he determined, until he was certain he could rein in his uncharacteristic imaginings.

Annoyed with himself, irked by his own deviation from strict routine, he walked back through the bedroom. He'd just started down the curve of the stairs when a movement caught his eye. His hand reached for his weapon. But it was already too late for that.

Very slowly, he dropped his hand, stood where he was and stared down. It wasn't the automatic pointed at his heart that stunned him motionless. It was the fact that it was held, steady as a rock, in the hand of a dead woman.

"Well," the dead woman said, stepping forward into the halo of light from the foyer chandelier. "You're certainly a messy thief, and a stupid one." Those shockingly blue eyes stared up at him. "Why don't you give me one good reason why I shouldn't put a hole in your head before I call the police?"

For a ghost, she met his earlier fantasy perfectly. The voice was a purr, hot and husky and stunningly alive. And for the recently departed, she had a very warm flush of temper in her cheeks. It wasn't often that Seth's mind clicked off. But it had. He saw a woman, runway-fresh in white silk, the glint of jewels at her ears and a shiny silver gun in her hand.

He pulled himself back roughly, though none of the shock or the effort showed as he met her demand with an unsmiling response. "I *am* the police."

Her lips curved, a generous bow of sarcasm. "Of course you are, handsome. Who else would be creeping around a locked house when no one's at home but an overworked cop on his beat?"

"I haven't been a beat cop for quite some time. I'm

Buchanan. Lieutenant Seth Buchanan. If you'd aim your weapon just a little to the left of my heart, I'll show you my badge."

"I'd just love to see it." Watching him, she slowly shifted the barrel of the gun. Her heart was thudding like a jackhammer with a combination of fear and anger, but she took another casual step forward as he reached two fingers into his pocket. The badge looked real enough, she mused. What she could see of the identification with the gold shield on the flap that he held up.

And she began to get a very bad feeling. A worse sinking in the stomach sensation than she'd experienced when she pulled up to the drive, saw the strange car and the lights blazing inside her empty house.

She flicked her eyes from the badge up to his again. Damned if he didn't look more like a cop than a crook, she decided. Very attractive, in a straight-edged, buttoned-down sort of fashion. The solid body, broad of shoulder and narrow of hip, appeared ruthlessly disciplined.

Eyes like that, cool and clear and golden brown, that seemed to see everything at once, belonged to either a cop or a criminal. Either way, she imagined, they belonged to a dangerous sort of man.

Dangerous men usually appealed to her. But at the moment, as she took in the oddity of the situation, her mood wasn't receptive.

"All right, Buchanan, Lieutenant Seth, why don't you tell me what you're doing in my house." She thought of what she carried in her purse—what Bailey had sent her only days before—and felt that unsettling sensation in her stomach deepen.

What kind of trouble are we in? she wondered. And just how do I slide out of it with a cop staring me down?

"Have you got a search warrant to go along with that badge?" she demanded.

"No, I don't." He'd have felt better, considerably better, if she'd put the gun down altogether. But she seemed content to hold it, aiming it lower now, no less steadily, but lower. Still, his composure had snapped back. Keeping his eyes on hers, he came down the rest of the stairs and stood in the lofty foyer, facing her. "You're Grace Fontaine."

She watched him tuck his badge back into his pocket, while those unreadable cop's eyes skimmed over her face. Memorizing features, she thought, irritated. Making mental note of any distinguishing marks. Just what the hell was going on?

"Yes, I'm Grace Fontaine. This is my property, my home. And as you're in it, without a proper warrant, you're trespassing. As calling a cop seems superfluous, maybe I'll just call my lawyer."

He angled his head, and unwillingly caught a whiff of that siren's scent of hers. Perhaps it was that, and feeling its instant and unwelcome effect on his system, that had him speaking without thought.

"Well, Ms. Fontaine, you look damn good for a dead woman."

Chapter 2

Her response was to narrow her eyes, arch a brow. "If that's some sort of cop humor, I'm afraid you'll have to translate."

It annoyed him that she'd jarred the remark out of him. It wasn't professional. Cautious, he brought a hand up slowly, tipped the barrel of the gun farther to the left. "Do you mind?" he said, then, quickly, before she could agree, he twisted it neatly out of her hand, pulled out the clip. It wasn't the time to ask if she had a license to carry, so he merely handed her back the empty gun and pocketed the clip.

"It's best to keep both hands on your weapon," he said easily, and with such sobriety that she suspected amusement lurked beneath. "And, if you want to keep it, not to get within reach."

"Thanks so much for the lesson in self-defense."

Obviously irritated, she opened her bag and dumped the gun inside. "But you still haven't answered my initial question, Lieutenant. Why are you in my house?"

"You've had an incident, Ms. Fontaine."

"An incident? More copspeak?" She blew out a breath. "Was there a break-in?" she asked, and for the first time took her attention off the man and glanced past him into the foyer. "A robbery?" she added, then caught sight of an overturned chair and some smashed crockery through the archway in the living area.

Swearing, she started to push past him. He curled a hand over her arm to stop her. "Ms. Fontaine—"

"Get your hand off me," she snapped, interrupting him. "This is my home."

He kept his grip firm. "I'm aware of that. Exactly when was the last time you were in it?"

"I'll give you a damn statement after I've seen what's missing." She managed another two steps and saw from the disorder in the living area that it hadn't been a neat or organized robbery. "Well, they did quite a job, didn't they? My cleaning service is going to be very unhappy."

She glanced down to where Seth's fingers were still curled around her arm. "Are you testing my biceps, Lieutenant? I do like to think they're firm."

"Your muscle tone's fine." From what he could see of her in the filmy ivory slacks, it appeared more than fine. "I'd like you to answer my question, Ms. Fontaine. When were you home last?"

"Here?" She sighed, shrugged one elegant shoulder. Her mind was flitting around the annoying details that were the backwash of a robbery. Calling her insurance agent, filing a claim, giving statements. "Wednesday

afternoon. I went out of town for a few days." She was
more shaken than she cared to admit that her house
had been robbed and ransacked in her absence. Her
things touched and taken by strangers. But she slid
him a smiling glance from under her lashes. "Aren't
you going to take notes?"

"As a matter of fact, I am. Shortly. Who was staying in the house in your absence?"

"No one. I don't care to have people in my home
when I'm away. Now if you'll excuse me…" She gave
her arm a quick, hard jerk and strode through the foyer
and under the arch. "Good God." The anger came first,
quick and intense. She wanted to kick something, no
matter that it was broken and ruined already. "Did they
have to break what they didn't cart out?" she muttered.
She glanced up, saw the splintered railing and swore
again. "And what the devil did they do up there? A lot
of good an alarm system does if anyone can just…"

She stopped her forward motion, her voice trailing
off, as she saw the outline on the gleaming chestnut
wood of the floor. As she stared at it, unable to tear
her eyes away, the blood drained out of her face, leaving it painfully cold and stiff.

Placing one hand on the back of the stained sofa for
balance, she stared down at the outline, the diamond
glitter of broken glass that had been her coffee table,
and the blood that had dried to a dark pool.

"Why don't we go into the dining room?" he said
quietly.

She jerked her shoulders back, though he hadn't
touched her. The pit of her stomach was cased in ice,
and the flashes of heat that lanced through her did

nothing to melt it. "Who was killed?" she demanded. "Who died here?"

"Up until a few minutes ago, it was assumed you did."

She closed her eyes, vaguely concerned that her vision was dimming at the edges. "Excuse me," she said, quite clearly, and walked across the room on numb legs. She picked up a bottle of brandy that lay on its side on the floor, fumbled open a display cabinet for a glass. And poured generously.

She took the first drink as medicine. He could see that in the way she tossed it back, shuddered twice, hard. It didn't bring the color back to her face, but he imagined it had shocked her system into functioning again.

"Ms. Fontaine, I think it would be better if we talked about this in another room."

"I'm all right." But her voice was raw. She drank again before turning to him. "Why did you think it was me?"

"The victim was in your house, dressed in a robe. She met your general description. Her face had been... damaged by the fall. She was your approximate height and weight, your age, your coloring."

Her coloring, Grace thought on a wave of staggering relief. Not Bailey or M.J., then. "I had no houseguest while I was gone." She took a deep breath, knowing the calm was there, if only she could reach it. "I have no idea who the woman was, unless it was one of the burglars. How did she—" Grace looked up again at the broken railing, the viciously sharp edges of wood. "She must have been pushed."

"That has yet to be determined."

"I'm sure it has. I can't help you as to who she was, Lieutenant. As I don't have a twin, I can only—" She broke off, her color draining a second time. Now her free hand fisted and pressed hard to her stomach. "Oh, no. Oh, God."

He understood, didn't hesitate. "Who was she?"

"I— It could have been... She's stayed here before while I was away. That's why I stopped leaving a spare key outside. She might have had it copied, though. She'd think nothing of that."

Turning her gaze away from the outline, she walked back through the debris, sat on the arm of the sofa. "A cousin." Grace sipped brandy again, slowly, letting it ease warmth back into her system. "Melissa Bennington— No, I think she took the Fontaine back a few months ago, after the divorce. I'm not sure." She pushed a hand through her hair. "I wasn't interested enough to be sure of a detail like that."

"She resembles you?"

She offered a weak, humorless smile. "It's Melissa's mission to *be* me. I went from finding it mildly flattering to mildly annoying. In the last few years I found it pathetic. There's a surface resemblance, I suppose. She's augmented it. She let her hair grow, dyed it my color. There was some difference in build, but she... augmented that, as well. She shops the same stores, uses the same salons. Chooses the same men. We grew up together, more or less. She always felt I got the better deal on all manner of levels."

She made herself look back, look down, and felt a wash of grief and pity. "Apparently I did, this time around."

"If someone didn't know you well, could they mistake you?"

"A passing glance, I suppose. Maybe a casual acquaintance. No one who—" She broke off again, got to her feet. "You think someone killed her believing her to be me? Mistaking her for me, as you did? That's absurd. It was a break-in, a burglary. A terrible accident."

"It's possible." He had indeed taken out his book to note down her cousin's name. Now he glanced up, met her eyes. "It's also more than possible that someone came here, mistook her for you, and assumed she had the third Star."

She was good, he decided. There was barely a flicker in her eyes before she lied. "I have no idea what you're talking about."

"Yes, you do. And if you haven't been home since Wednesday, you still have it." He glanced down at the bag she continued to hold.

"I don't generally carry stars in my purse." She sent him a smile that was shaky around the edges. "But it's a lovely, almost poetic, thought. Now, I'm very tired—"

"Ms. Fontaine." His voice was clipped and cool. "This victim is the sixth body I've dealt with today that traces back to those three blue diamonds."

Her hand shot out, gripped his arm. "M.J. and Bailey?"

"Your friends are fine." He felt her grip go limp. "They've had an eventful holiday weekend, all of which could have been avoided if they'd contacted and cooperated with the police. And it's cooperation I'll have from you now, one way or the other."

She tossed her hair back. "Where are they? What did you do, toss them in a cell? My lawyer will have them out and your butt in a sling before you can finish reciting the Miranda." She started toward the phone, saw it wasn't on the Queen Anne table.

"No, they're not in a cell." It goaded him, the way she snapped into gear, ready to buck the rules. "I imagine they're planning your funeral right about now."

"Planning my—" Her fabulous eyes went huge with distress. "Oh, my God, you told them I was dead? They think I'm dead? Where are they? Where's the damn phone? I have to call them."

She crouched to push through the rubble, shoving at him when he took her arm again. "They're not home, either of them."

"You said they weren't in jail."

"And they're not." He could see he'd get nothing out of her until she'd satisfied herself. "I'll take you to them. Then we're going to sort this out, Ms. Fontaine— I promise you."

Grace didn't speak as he drove her toward the tidy suburbs edging D.C. He'd assured her that Bailey and M.J. were fine, and her instincts told her that Lieutenant Seth Buchanan was saying nothing but the truth. Facts were his business, after all, she thought. But she still gripped her hands together until her knuckles ached.

She had to see them, touch them.

Guilt was already weighing on her, guilt that they should be grieving for her, when she'd spent the past few days indulging her need to be alone, to be away. To be somewhere else.

What had happened to them over the long weekend? Had they tried to contact her while she was out of reach? It was painfully obvious that the three blue diamonds Bailey had been assessing for the museum were at the bottom of it all.

As the afterimage of that stark outline on the chestnut floor flashed into her head, Grace shuddered once again.

Melissa. Poor, pathetic Melissa. But she couldn't think of that now. She couldn't think of anything but her friends.

"They're not hurt?" she managed to ask.

"No." Seth left it at that, drove through the wash of streetlights and headlights. Her scent was sliding silkily through his car, teasing his senses. Deliberately he opened his window and let the light, damp breeze chase it away. "Where have you been the last few days, Ms. Fontaine?"

"Away." Weary, she laid her head back, shut her eyes. "It's one of my favorite spots."

She jerked upright again when he turned down a tree-lined street, then swung into the drive of a brick house. She saw a shiny Jaguar, then an impossibly decrepit boat of a car. But no spiffy MG, no practical little compact.

"Their cars aren't here," she began, tossing him a look of distrust and accusation.

"But they are."

She climbed out and, ignoring him, hurried toward the front door. Her knock was brisk, businesslike, but her fist trembled. The door opened, and a man she'd never seen before stared down at her. His cool green eyes flickered with shock, then slowly warmed. His flash of a smile was blinding. Then he reached out, laid a hand gently on her cheek.

"You're Grace."

"Yes, I—"

"It's absolutely wonderful to see you." He gathered her into his arms, one of which was freshly bandaged, with such easy affection that she didn't have time to register surprise. "I'm Cade," he murmured, his gaze meeting Seth's over Grace's head. "Cade Parris. Come on in."

"Bailey. M.J."

"Just in here. They'll be fine as soon as they see you." He took her arm, felt the quick, hard tremors in it. But in the doorway of the living room, she stopped, laid a hand over his arm.

Inside, Bailey and M.J. stood, facing away, hands linked. Their voices were low, with tears wrenching through them. A man stood a short distance away, his hands thrust in his pockets and a look of helplessness on his bruised and battered face. When he saw her, his eyes, the gray of storm clouds, narrowed, flashed. Then smiled.

Grace took one shuddering breath, exhaled it slowly. "Well," she said in a clear, steady voice, "it's gratifying to know someone would weep copiously over me."

Both women whirled. For a moment, all three stared, three pair of eyes brimming over. To Seth's mind, they all moved as one, as a unit, so that their leaping rush across the room to each other held an uncanny and undeniably feminine grace. Then they were fused together, voices and tears mixing.

A triangle, he thought, frowning. With three points that made a whole. Like the golden triangle that held three priceless and powerful stones.

"I think they could use a little time," Cade said quietly, and gestured to the other man. "Lieutenant?" He motioned down the hall, lifting his brows when Seth hesitated. "I don't think they're going anywhere just now."

With a barely perceptible shrug, Seth stepped back. He could give them twenty minutes. "I need your phone."

"There's one in the kitchen. Want a beer, Jack?"

The third man grinned. "You're playing my song."

"Amnesia," Grace said a little time later. She and Bailey were huddled together on the sofa, with M.J. sitting on the floor at their feet. "Everything just blanked?"

"Everything." Bailey kept her hold on Grace's hand tight, afraid to break the link. "I woke up in this horrible little hotel room with no memory, over a million in cash, and the diamond. I picked Cade's name out of the phone book. Parris." She smiled a little. "Funny, isn't it?"

"I'm going to get you to France yet," Grace promised.

"He helped me through everything." The warmth in her tone had Grace sharing a quick look with M.J. This was something to be discussed in detail later. "I started to remember, piece by piece. You and M.J., just flashes. I could see your faces, even hear your voices, but nothing fit. He's the one who narrowed it down to Salvini, and when he took me there... He broke in."

"Shortly before we did," M.J. added. "Jack could tell the rear locks had been picked."

"We got inside," Bailey continued, and her tear-ravaged eyes went glassy. "And I remembered, I remembered it all then, how Thomas and Timothy were planning to steal the stones, copy them. How I'd shipped one off to each of you to keep it from happening. Stupid, so stupid."

"No, it wasn't." Grace slid an arm around Bailey's shoulders. "It makes perfect sense to me. You didn't have time for anything else."

"I should have called the police, but I was so sure I could turn things around. I was going into Thomas's office to have a showdown, tell them it was over. And I saw…" She trembled again. "The fight. Horrible. The lightning flashing through the windows, their faces. Then Timothy grabbed the letter opener, the knife. The power went out, but the lightning kept flashing, and I could see what he was doing…to Thomas. All the blood."

"Don't," M.J. murmured, rubbing a comforting hand on Bailey's knee. "Don't go back there."

"No." Bailey shook her head. "I have to. He saw me, Grace. He would have killed me. He came after me. I had grabbed the bag with their deposit money, and I ran through the dark. And I hid down under the stairs. In this little cave under the stairs. But I could see him hunting for me, blood all over his hands. I still don't remember how I got out, got to that room."

Grace couldn't bear to imagine it—her quiet, serious-minded friend, pursued by a murderer. "The important thing is that you did get away, and you're safe." Grace looked down at M.J. "We all are." She tried a bolstering grin. "And how did you spend your holiday?"

"On the run with a bounty hunter, handcuffed to a bed in a cheap motel, being shot at by a couple of creeps—with a little detour up to your place in the mountains."

Bounty hunter, Grace thought, trying to keep pace. The man named Jack, she supposed, with the bronze-tipped ponytail and the stormy gray eyes. And the killer grin. Handcuffs, cheap motels, and shootings. Pressing fingertips to her eyes, she latched on to the least disturbing detail.

"You were at my place? When?"

"It's a long story." M.J. gave a quick version of a handful of days from her first encounter with Jack, when he'd tried to take her in, believing her to be a bail jumper, to the two of them escaping that setup and working their way back to the core of the puzzle.

"We know someone's pulling the strings," M.J. concluded. "But we haven't gotten very far on figuring that out yet. The bail bondsman-cum-blackmailer who gave Jack the fake paperwork on me is dead, the two guys who came after us are dead, the Salvinis are dead."

"And Melissa," Grace murmured.

"It was Melissa?" Bailey turned to Grace. "In your house?"

"It must have been. When I got home, the cop was there. The place was torn up, and they'd assumed it was me." It took a moment, a carefully indrawn breath, a steady exhale, before she could finish. "She'd fallen off the balcony—or been pushed. I was miles away when it happened."

"Where did you go?" M.J. asked her. "When Jack and I got to your country place, it was locked up tight. I thought…I was sure you'd just been there. I could smell you."

"I left late yesterday morning. Got an itch to be

near the water, so I drove down the Eastern Shore, found a little B-and-B. I did some antiquing, rubbed elbows with tourists, watched a fireworks display. I didn't leave until late today. I nearly stayed over another night. But I called both of you from the B-and-B and got your machines. I started feeling uncomfortable about being out of contact, so I headed home."

She shut her eyes a moment. "Bailey, I hadn't been really thinking. Just before I left for the country, we lost one of the children."

"Oh, Grace, I'm sorry."

"It happens all the time. They're born with AIDS or a crack addiction or a hole in the heart. Some of them die. But I can't get used to it, and it was on my mind. So I wasn't really thinking. When I started back, I started to think. And I started to worry. Then the cop was there in my house. He asked about the stone. I didn't know what you wanted me to tell him."

"We've told the police everything now." Bailey sighed. "Neither Cade nor Jack seem to like this Buchanan very much, but they respect his abilities. The two stones are safe now, as we are."

"I'm sorry for what you went through, both of you. I'm sorry I wasn't here."

"It wouldn't have made any difference," M.J. declared. "We were scattered all over—one stone apiece. Maybe we were meant to be."

"Now we're together." Grace took each of their hands in hers. "What happens next?"

"Ladies." Seth stepped into the room, skimmed his cool gaze over them, then focused on Grace. "Ms. Fontaine. The diamond?"

She rose, picked up the purse she'd tossed carelessly

on the end of the couch. Opening it, she took out a velvet pouch, slid the stone out into her palm. "Magnificent, isn't it?" she murmured, studying the flash of bold blue light. "Diamonds are supposed to be cold to the touch, aren't they, Bailey? Yet this has…heat." She lifted her eyes to Seth's as she crossed to him. "Still, how many lives is it worth?"

She held her open palm out. When his fingers closed around the stone, she felt the jolt—his fingers on her skin, the shimmering blue diamond between their hands.

Something clicked, almost audibly.

She wondered if he'd felt it, heard it. Why else did those enigmatic eyes narrow, or his hand linger? The breath caught in her throat.

"Impressive, isn't it?" she managed, then felt the odd wave of emotion and recognition ebb when he took the stone from her hand.

He didn't care for the shock that had run up his arm, and he spoke bitingly. "I imagine this one's out of even your price range, Ms. Fontaine."

She merely smiled. No, she told herself, he couldn't have felt anything—and neither had she. Just imagination and stress. "I prefer to decorate my body in something less…obvious."

Bailey rose. "The Stars are my responsibility, unless and until the Smithsonian indicates otherwise." She looked over at Cade, who remained in the doorway. "We'll put them in the safe. All of them. And I'll speak with Dr. Linstrum in the morning."

Seth turned the stone over in his hand. He imagined he could confiscate it, and its mates. They were, after all, evidence in several homicides. But he didn't relish driving back to the station with a large fortune in his car.

Parris was an irritant, he reflected. But he was an honest one. And, technically, the stones were in Bailey James's keeping until the Smithsonian relieved her of them. He wondered just what the powers at the museum would have to say about the recent travels of the Three Stars.

But that wasn't his problem.

"Lock it up," he said, passing the stone off to Cade. "And I'll be talking with Dr. Linstrum in the morning, as well, Ms. James."

Cade took one quick, threatening step forward. "Look, Buchanan—"

"No." Quietly, Bailey stepped between them, a cool breeze between two building storms. "Lieutenant Buchanan's right, Cade. It's his business now."

"That doesn't stop it from being mine." He gave Seth one last, warning look. "Watch your step," he said, then walked away with the stone.

"Thank you for bringing Grace by so quickly, Lieutenant."

Seth looked down at the extended, and obviously dismissing, hand Bailey offered him. Here's your hat, he thought, what's your hurry. "I'm sorry you were disturbed, Ms. James." His gaze flicked over to M.J. "Ms. O'Leary. You'll keep available."

"We're not going anywhere." M.J.'s chin angled, a cocky gesture as Jack crossed to her. "Drive carefully, Lieutenant."

He acknowledged the second dismissal with a slight nod. "Ms. Fontaine? I'll drive you back."

"She's not leaving." M.J. jumped in front of Grace

like a tiger defending her cub. "She's not going back to that house tonight. She's staying here, with us."

"You may not care to go back home, Ms. Fontaine," Seth said coolly. "You may find it more comfortable to answer questions in my office."

"You can't be serious—"

He cut Bailey's protest off with a look. "I have a body in the morgue. I take it very seriously."

"You're a class act, Buchanan," Jack drawled, but the sound was low and threatening. "Why don't you and I go in the other room and…talk about our options?"

"It's all right." Grace stepped forward, working up a believable smile. "It's Jack, isn't it?"

"That's right." He took his attention from Buchanan long enough to smile at her. "Jack Dakota. Pleased to meet you…Miss April."

"Oh, my misspent youth survives." With a little laugh, she kissed his bruised cheek. "I appreciate the offer to beat up the lieutenant for me, Jack, but you look like you've already gone several rounds."

Grinning now, he stroked a thumb over his bruised jaw. "I've got a few more rounds in me."

"I don't doubt it. But, sad to say, the cop's right." She pushed her hair to her back and turned that smile, several degrees cooler now, on Seth. "Tactless, but right. He needs some answers. I need to go back."

"You're not going back to your house alone," Bailey insisted. "Not tonight, Grace."

"I'll be fine. But if it's all right with your Cade, I'll deal with this, pick up a few things and come back." She glanced over at Cade as he came back into the room. "Got a spare bed, darling?"

"You bet. Why don't I go with you, help you pick up your things and bring you back?"

"You stay here with Bailey." She kissed him, as well—a casual and already affectionate brush of lips. "I'm sure Lieutenant Buchanan and I will manage." She picked up her purse, turned and embraced both M.J. and Bailey again. "Don't worry about me. After all, I'm in the arms of the law."

She eased back, shot Seth one of those full candle-power smiles. "Isn't that right, Lieutenant?"

"In a manner of speaking." He stepped back and waited for her to walk to the door ahead of him.

She waited until they were in his car and pulling out of the drive. "I need to see the body." She didn't look at him, but lifted a hand to the four people crowded at the front door, watching them drive away. "You need— She'll have to be identified, won't she?"

It surprised him that she'd take the duty on. "Yes."

"Then let's get it over with. After—afterwards, I'll answer your questions. I'd prefer we handle that in your office," she added, using that smile again. "My house isn't ready for company."

"Fine."

She'd known it would be hard. She'd known it would be horrible. Grace had prepared herself for it—or she'd thought she had. Nothing, she realized as she stared down at what remained of the woman in the morgue, could have prepared her.

It was hardly surprising that they'd mistaken Melissa for her. The face Melissa had been so proud of was utterly ruined. Death had been cruel here, and, through her involvement with the hospital, Grace had reason to know it often was.

"It's Melissa." Her voice echoed flatly in the chilly white room. "My cousin, Melissa Fontaine."

"You're sure?"

"Yes. We shared the same health club, among other things. I know her body as well as I know mine. She has a sickle-shaped birthmark at the small of her back, just left of center. And there's a scar on the bottom of her left foot, small, crescent-shaped, in the ball of her foot, where she stepped on a broken shell in the Hamptons when we were twelve."

Seth shifted, found the scar, then nodded to the M.E.'s assistant. "I'm sorry for your loss."

"Yes, I'm sure you are." With muscles that felt like glass, she turned, her dimming vision passing over him. "Excuse me."

She made it nearly to the door before she swayed. Swearing under his breath, Seth caught her, pulled her out into the corridor and put her in a chair. With one hand, he shoved her head between her knees.

"I'm not going to faint." She squeezed her eyes tightly shut, battling fiercely against the twin foes of dizziness and nausea.

"Could have fooled me."

"I'm much too sophisticated for something as maudlin as a swoon." But her voice broke, her shoulders sagged, and for a moment she kept her head down. "Oh, God, she's dead. And all because she hated me."

"What?"

"Doesn't matter. She's dead." Bracing herself, she sat up again, let her head rest against the cold white wall. Her cheeks were just as colorless. "I have to call my aunt. Her mother. I have to tell her what happened."

He gauged this woman, studying the face that was no less staggeringly lovely for being bone-white. "Give me the name. I'll take care of it."

"It's Helen Wilson Fontaine. I'll do it."

He didn't realize until her hand moved that he'd placed his own over it. He pulled back on every level, and rose. "I haven't been able to reach Helen Fontaine or her husband. She's in Europe."

"I know where she is." Grace shook back her hair, but didn't try to stand. Not yet. "I can find her." The thought of making that call, saying what had to be said, squeezed her throat. "Could I have some water, Lieutenant?"

His heels echoed on tile as he strode off. Then there was silence—a full, damning silence that whispered of what kind of business was done in such places. There were scents here that slid slyly under the potent odors of antiseptics and industrial cleaning solutions.

She was pitifully grateful when she heard his footsteps on the return journey.

She took the paper cup from him with both hands, drinking slowly, concentrating on the simple act of swallowing liquid.

"Why did she hate you?"

"What?"

"Your cousin. You said she hated you. Why?"

"Family trait," she said briefly. She handed him back the empty cup as she rose. "I'd like to go now."

He took her measure a second time. Her color had yet to return, her pupils were dilated, the electric-blue irises were glassy. He doubted she'd last another hour.

"I'll take you back to Parris's," he decided. "You can get your things in the morning, come in to my office to make your statement."

"I said I'd do it tonight."

"And I say you'll do it in the morning. You're no good to me now."

She tried a weak laugh. "Why, Lieutenant, I believe you're the first man who's ever said that to me. I'm crushed."

"Don't waste the routine on me." He took her arm, led her to the outside doors. "You haven't got the energy for it."

He was exactly right. She pulled her arm free as they stepped back into the thick night air. "I don't like you."

"You don't have to." He opened the car door, waited. "Any more than I have to like you."

She stepped to the door, and with it between them met his eyes. "But the difference is, if I had the energy—or the inclination—I could make you sit up and beg."

She got in, sliding those long, silky legs in.

Not likely, Seth told himself as he shut the door with a snap. But he wasn't entirely sure he believed it.

Chapter 3

She felt like a weakling, but she didn't go home. She'd needed friends, not that empty house, with the shadow of a body drawn on the floor.

Jack had gone over, fetched her bags out of her car and brought them to her. For a day, at least, she was content to make do with that.

Since she was driving in to meet with Seth, Grace had made do carefully. She'd dressed in a summer suit she'd just picked up on the Shore. The little short skirt and waist-length jacket in buttercup yellow weren't precisely professional—but she wasn't aiming for professional. She'd taken the time to catch her waterfall of hair back in a complicated French braid and made up her face with the concentration and determination of a general plotting a decisive battle.

Meeting with Seth again felt like a battle.

Her stomach was still raw from the call she'd made to her aunt, and the sickness that had overwhelmed her after it. She'd slept poorly, but she had slept, tucked into one of Cade's guest rooms, secure that those who meant most to her were close by.

She would deal with the relatives later, she thought, easing her convertible into the lot at the station house. It would be hard, but she would deal with them. For now, she had to deal with herself. And Seth Buchanan.

If anyone had been watching as she stepped from her car and started across the lot, he would have seen a transformation. Subtly, gradually, her eyes went from weary to sultry. Her gait loosened, eased into a lazy, hip-swinging walk designed to cross a man's eyes. Her mouth turned up slightly at the corners, into a secret, knowing female smile.

It wasn't really a mask, but another part of her. Innate and habitual, it was an image she could draw on at will. She willed it now, flashing a slow under-the-lashes smile at the uniform who stepped to the door as she did. He flushed, moved back and nearly bobbled the door in his hurry to open it for her.

"Why, thank you, Officer."

Heat rose up his neck, into his face, and made her smile widen. She was right on target. Seth Buchanan wouldn't see a pale, trembling woman this morning. He'd see Grace Fontaine, just hitting her stride.

She sauntered up to the sergeant on duty at the desk, skimmed a fingertip along the edge. "Excuse me?"

"Yes, ma'am." His Adam's apple bobbed three times as he swallowed.

"I wonder if you could help me? I'm looking for a Lieutenant Buchanan. Are you in charge?" She skimmed her gaze over him. "You must be in charge, Commander."

"Ah, yes. No. It's sergeant." He fumbled for the sign-in book, the passes. "I— He's— You'll find the lieutenant upstairs, detective division. To the left of the stairs."

"Oh." She took the pen he offered and signed her name boldly. "Thank you, Commander. I mean, Sergeant."

She heard his little expulsion of breath as she turned, and felt his gaze on her legs as she climbed the stairs.

She found the detective division easily enough. One sweeping glance took in the front-to-front desks, some manned, some not. The cops were in shirtsleeves in an oppressive heat that was barely touched by what had to be a faulty air-conditioning unit. A lot of guns, she thought, a lot of half-eaten meals and empty cups of coffee. Phones shrilling.

She picked her mark—a man with a loosened tie, feet on the desk, a report of some kind in one hand and a Danish in the other. As she started through the crowded room, several conversations stopped. Someone whistled softly—it was like a sigh. The man at the desk swept his feet to the floor, swallowed the Danish.

"Ma'am."

About thirty, she judged, though his hairline was receding rapidly. He wiped his crumb-dusted fingers on his shirt, rolled his eyes slightly to the left, where one of his associates was grinning and pounding a fist to his heart.

"I hope you can help me." She kept her eyes on his, and only his, until a muscle began to twitch in his jaw. "Detective?"

"Yeah, ah, Carter, Detective Carter. What can I do for you?"

"I hope I'm in the right place." For effect, she turned her head, swept her gaze over the room and its occupants. Several stomachs were ruthlessly sucked in. "I'm looking for Lieutenant Buchanan. I think he's expecting me." Gracefully she brushed a loose flutter of hair away from her face. "I'm afraid I just don't know the proper procedure."

"He's in his office. Back in his office." Without taking his eyes from her he jerked a thumb. "Belinski, tell the lieutenant he has a visitor. A Miss…"

"It's Grace." She slid a hip onto the corner of the desk, letting her skirt hike up a dangerous inch. "Grace Fontaine. Is it all right if I wait here, Detective Carter? Am I interrupting your work?"

"Yes— No. Sure."

"It's so exciting." She brought the temperature of the overheated room up ten more degrees with a dazzling smile. "Detective work. You must have so many interesting stories."

By the time Seth had finished the phone call he was on when he was notified of Grace's arrival, shrugged back into the jacket he'd removed as a concession to the heat and made his way into the bull pen, Carter's desk was completely surrounded. He heard a low, throaty female laugh rise out of the center of the crowd.

And saw a half a dozen of his best men panting like puppies over a meaty bone.

The woman, he decided, was going to be an enormous headache.

"I see all cases have been closed this morning, and miraculously crime has come to a halt."

His voice had the desired effect. Several men jerked straight. Those less easily intimidated grinned as they skulked back to their desks. Deserted, Carter flushed from his neck to his receding sandy hairline. "Ah, Grace—that is, Miss Fontaine to see you, Lieutenant. Sir."

"So I see. You finish that report, Detective?"

"Working on it." Carter grabbed the papers he'd tossed aside and buried his nose in them.

"Ms. Fontaine." Seth arched a brow, gestured toward his office.

"It was nice meeting you, Michael." Grace trailed a finger over Carter's shoulder as she passed.

He'd feel the heat of that skimming touch for hours.

"You can cut the power back now," Seth said dryly as he opened the door to his office. "You won't need it."

"You never know, do you?" She sauntered in, moving past him, close enough for them to brush bodies. She thought she felt him stiffen, just a little, but his eyes remained level, cool, and apparently unimpressed. Miffed, she studied his office.

The institutional beige of the walls blended depressingly into the dingy beige of the aging linoleum floor. An overburdened department-issue desk, gray file cabinets, computer, phone and one small window didn't add any spark to the no-nonsense room.

"So this is where the mighty rule," she murmured. It disappointed her that she found no personal touches. No photos, no sports trophies. Nothing she could hold on to, no sign of the man behind the badge.

As she had in the bull pen, she eased a hip onto the

corner of his desk. To say she resembled a sunbeam would have been a cliché. And it would have been incorrect, Seth decided. Sunbeams were tame—warm, welcoming. She was an explosive bolt of heat lightning— Hot. Fatal.

A blind man would have noticed those satiny legs in the snug yellow skirt. Seth merely walked around, sat, looked at her face.

"You'd be more comfortable in a chair."

"I'm fine here." Idly she picked up a pen, twirled it. "I don't suppose this is where you interrogate suspects."

"No, we have a dungeon downstairs for that."

Under other circumstances, she would have appreciated his dust-dry tone. "Am I a suspect?"

"I'll let you know." He angled his head. "You recover quickly, Ms. Fontaine."

"Yes, I do. You had questions, Lieutenant?"

"Yes, I do. Sit down. In a chair."

Her lips moved in what was nearly a pout. A luscious come-on-and-kiss-me pout. He felt the quick, helpless pull of lust, and damned her for it. She moved, sliding off the desk, settling into a chair, taking her time crossing those killer legs.

"Better?"

"Where were you Saturday, between the hours of midnight and 3:00 a.m.?"

So that was when it had happened, she thought, and ignored the ache in her stomach. "Aren't you going to read me my rights?"

"You're not charged, you don't need a lawyer. It's a simple question."

"I was in the country. I have a house in western

Maryland. I was alone. I don't have an alibi. Do I need a lawyer now?"

"Do you want to complicate this, Ms. Fontaine?"

"There's no way to simplify it, is there?" But she flicked a hand in dismissal. The thin diamond bracelet that circled her wrist shot fire. "All right, Lieutenant, as uncomplicated as possible. I don't want my lawyer—for the moment. Why don't I just give you a basic rundown? I left for the country on Wednesday. I wasn't expecting my cousin, or anyone, for that matter. I did have contact with a few people over the weekend. I bought a few supplies in the town nearby, shopped at the gardening stand. That would have been Friday afternoon. I picked up some mail on Saturday. It's a small town, the postmistress would remember. That was before noon, however, which would give me plenty of time to drive back. And, of course, there was the courier who delivered Bailey's package on Friday."

"And you didn't find that odd? Your friend sends you a blue diamond, and you just shrug it off and go shopping?"

"I called her. She wasn't in." She arched a brow. "But you probably know that. I did find it odd, but I had things on my mind."

"Such as?"

Her lips curved, but the smile wasn't reflected in her eyes. "I'm not required to tell you my thoughts. I did wonder about it and worried a little. I thought perhaps it was a copy, but I didn't really believe that. A copy couldn't have what that stone has. Bailey's instructions in the package were to keep it with me until she contacted me. So that's what I did."

"No questions?"

"I rarely question people I trust."

He tapped a pencil on the edge of the desk. "You stayed alone in the country until Monday, when you drove back to the city."

"No. I drove down to the Eastern Shore on Sunday. I had a whim." She smiled again. "I often do. I stayed at a bed-and-breakfast."

"You didn't like your cousin?"

"No, I didn't." She imagined that quick shift of topic was an interrogation technique. "She was difficult to like, and I rarely make the effort with difficult people. We were raised together after my parents were killed, but we weren't close. I intruded into her life, into her space. She compensated for it by being disagreeable. I was often disagreeable in return. As we got older, she had a less…successful talent with men than I. Apparently she thought by enhancing the similarities in our appearance, she'd have better success."

"And did she?"

"I suppose it depends on your point of view. Melissa enjoyed men." To combat the guilt coating her heart, Grace leaned back negligently in the chair. "She certainly enjoyed men—which is one of the reasons she was recently divorced. She preferred the species in quantity."

"And how did her husband feel about that?"

"Bobbie's a…" She trailed off, then relieved a great deal of her own tension with a quick, delighted and very appealing laugh. "If you're suggesting that Bobbie— her ex—tracked her down to my house, murdered her, trashed the place and walked off whistling, you couldn't be more wrong. He's a cream puff. And he is, I believe, in England, even as we speak. He enjoys tennis and never misses Wimbledon. You can check easily enough."

Which he would, Seth thought, noting it down. "Some people find murder distasteful on a personal level, but not at a distance. They just pay for a service."

This time she sighed. "We both know Melissa wasn't the target, Lieutenant. I was. She was in my house." Restless, she rose, a graceful and feline movement. Walking to the tiny window, she looked out on his dismal view. "She's made herself at home in my Potomac house twice before when I was away. The first time, I tolerated it. The second, she enjoyed the facilities a bit too enthusiastically for my taste. We had a spat about it. She left in a huff, and I removed the spare key. I should have thought to change the locks, but it never occurred to me she'd go to the trouble of having copies made."

"When was the last time you saw her or spoke with her?"

Grace sighed. Dates ran through her head, people, events, meaningless social forays. "About six weeks ago, maybe eight. At the health club. We ran into each other in the steam room, didn't have much conversation. We never had much to say to each other."

She was regretting that now, Seth realized. Going over in her head opportunities lost or wasted. And it would do no good. "Would she have opened the door to someone she didn't know?"

"If the someone was male and was marginally attractive, yes." Weary of the interview, she turned back. "Look, I don't know what else I can tell you, what help I can possibly be. She was a careless, often arrogant woman. She picked up strange men in bars when she felt the urge. She let someone in that night, and she died for it. Whatever she was, she didn't deserve to die for that."

She brushed at her hair absently, tried to clear her mind as Seth simply sat, waiting. "Maybe he demanded she give him the stone. She wouldn't have understood. She paid for her trespassing, for her carelessness and her ignorance. And the stone is back with Bailey, where it belongs. If you haven't spoken to Dr. Linstrum yet this morning, I can tell you that Bailey should be meeting with him right now. I don't know anything else to tell you."

He kicked back for a moment, his eyes cool and steady on her face. If he discounted the connection with the diamonds, it could play another way. Two women, at odds all their lives. One of them returns home unexpectedly to find the other in her home. An argument. Escalating into a fight. And one of them ends up taking a dive off a second-floor balcony into a pool of glass.

The first woman doesn't panic. She trashes her own home to cover herself, then drives away. Puts distance between herself and the scene.

Was she a skilled enough actress to fake that stark shock, the raw emotion he'd seen on her face the night before?

He thought she was.

But despite that, the scene just didn't click. There was the undeniable connection of the diamonds. And he was dead sure that if Grace Fontaine had caused her cousin's fall, she would have been just as capable of picking up the phone and coolly reporting an accident.

"All right, that's all for now."

"Well." Her breath was a huff of relief. "That wasn't so bad, all in all."

He stood up. "I'll have to ask you to stay available."

She switched on the charm again, a hot, rose-colored light. "I'm always available, handsome. Ask anyone." She picked up her purse, moved with him to the door. "How long before I can have my house dealt with? I'd like to put things back to order as quickly as possible."

"I'll let you know." He glanced at his watch. "When you're up to going through things and doing an inventory to see what's missing, I'd like you to contact me."

"I'm on my way over now to do just that."

His brow furrowed a moment as he juggled responsibilities. He could assign a man to go with her, but he preferred dealing with it himself. "I'll follow you over."

"Police protection?"

"If necessary."

"I'm touched. Why don't I give you a lift, handsome?"

"I'll follow you over," he repeated.

"Suit yourself," she began, and grazed a hand over his cheek. Her eyes widened slightly as his fingers clamped on her wrist. "Don't like to be petted?" She purred the words, surprised at how her heart had jumped and started to race. "Most animals do."

His face was very close to hers, their bodies were just touching, with the heat from the room and something even more sweltering between them. Something old, and almost familiar.

He drew her hand down slowly, kept his fingers on her wrist.

"Be careful what buttons you push."

Excitement, she realized with surprise. It was pure,

primal excitement that zipped through her. "Wasted advice," she said silkily, daring him. "I enjoy pushing new ones. And apparently you have a few interesting buttons just begging for attention." She skimmed her gaze deliberately down to his mouth. "Just begging."

He could imagine himself shoving her back against the door, moving fast into that heat, feeling her go molten. Because he was certain she was aware of just how perfectly a man would imagine it, he stepped back, released her and opened the door to the din of the bull pen.

"Be sure to turn in your visitor's badge at the desk," he said.

He was a cool one, Grace thought as she drove. An attractive, successful, unmarried—she'd slipped that bit of data out of an unsuspecting Detective Carter— and self-contained man.

A challenge.

And, she decided as she passed through the quiet, well-designed neighborhood, toward her home, a challenge was exactly what she needed to get through the emotional upheaval.

She'd have to face her aunt in a few hours, and the rest of the relatives soon after. There would be questions, demands, and, she knew, blame. She would be the recipient of all of it. That was the way her family worked, and that was what she'd come to expect from them.

Ask Grace, take from Grace, point the finger at Grace. She wondered how much of that she deserved, and how much had simply been inherited along with the money her parents left her.

It hardly mattered, she thought, since both were hers, like it or not.

She swung into her drive, her gaze sweeping over and up. The house was something she'd wanted. The clever and unique design of wood and glass, the gables, the cornices, the decks and the ruthlessly groomed grounds. She'd wanted the space, the elegance that lent itself to entertaining, the convenience to the city. The proximity to Bailey and M.J.

But the little house in the mountains was something she'd needed. And that was hers, and hers alone. The relatives didn't know it existed. No one could find her there unless she wanted to be found.

But here, she thought as she set the brakes, was the neat, expensive home of one Grace Fontaine. Heiress, socialite and party girl. The former centerfold, the Radcliffe graduate, the Washington hostess.

Could she continue to live here, she wondered, with death haunting the rooms? Time would tell.

For now, she was going to concentrate on solving the puzzle of Seth Buchanan, and finding a way under that seemingly impenetrable armor of his.

Just for the fun of it.

She heard him pull in and, in a deliberately provocative move, turned, tipped down her shaded glasses and studied him over the tops.

Oh, yes, she thought. He was very, very attractive. The way he controlled that lean and muscled body. Very economical. No wasted movements. He wouldn't waste them in bed, either. And she wondered just how long it would be before she could lure him there. She had a hunch—and she rarely doubted her hunches where men were concerned—that there was a volcano bubbling under that calm and somewhat austere surface.

She was going to enjoy poking at it until it erupted.

As he crossed to her, she handed him her keys. "Oh, but you have your own now, don't you?" She tipped her glasses back into place. "Well, use mine…this time."

"Who else has a set?"

She skimmed the tip of her tongue over her top lip, darkly pleased when she saw his gaze jerk down. Just for an instant, but it was progress. "Bailey and M.J. I don't give my keys to men. I'd rather open the door for them myself. Or close it."

"Fine." He dumped the keys back in her hand, looking amused when her brows drew together. "Open the door."

One step forward, two steps back, she mused, then stepped up on the flagstone portico and unlocked her home.

She'd braced for it, but it was still difficult. The foyer was as it had been, largely undisturbed. But her gaze was drawn up now, helplessly, to the shattered railing.

"It's a long way to fall," she murmured. "I wonder if you have time to think, to understand, on the way down."

"She wouldn't have."

"No." And that was better, somehow. "I suppose not." She stepped into the living area, forced herself to look at the chalk outline. "Well, where to begin?"

"He got to your safe down here. Emptied it. You'll want to list what was taken out."

"The library safe." She moved through, under an arch and into a wide room filled with light and books.

A great many of those books littered the floor now, and an art deco lamp in the shape of an elongated woman's body—a small thing she'd loved—was cracked in two. "He wasn't subtle, was he?"

"I say he was rushed. And pissed off."

"You'd know best." She walked to the safe, noting the open door and the empty interior. "I had some jewelry— quite a bit, actually. A few thousand in cash."

"Bonds, stock certificates?"

"No, they're in my safe-deposit box at the bank. One doesn't need to take out stock certificates and enjoy the way they sparkle. I bought a terrific pair of diamond earrings just last month." She sighed, shrugged. "Gone now. I have a complete list of my jewelry, and photographs of each piece, along with the insurance papers, in my safety box. Replacing them's just a matter of—"

She broke off, made a small, distressed sound and rushed from the room.

The woman could move when she wanted, Seth thought as he headed upstairs after her. And she didn't lose any of that feline grace with speed. He turned into her bedroom, then into her walk-in closet behind her.

"He wouldn't have found it. He couldn't have found it." She repeated the words like a prayer as she twisted a knob on the built-in cabinet. It swung out, revealing a safe in the wall behind.

Quickly, her fingers not quite steady, she spun the combination, wrenched open the door. Her breath expelled in a whoosh as she knelt and took out velvet boxes and bags.

More jewelry, he thought with a shake of his head. How many earrings could one woman wear? But she was opening each box carefully, examining the contents.

"These were my mother's," she murmured, with a catch of undiluted emotion in the words. "They matter. The sapphire pin my father gave her for their fifth anniversary, the necklace he gave her when I was born. The pearls. She wore these the day they married." She stroked the creamy white strand over her cheek as if it were a loved one's hand. "I had this built for them, didn't keep them with the others. Just in case."

She sat back on her heels, her lap filled with jewelry that meant so much more than gold and pretty stones. "Well," she managed as her throat closed. "Well, they're here. They're still here."

"Ms. Fontaine."

"Oh, call me Grace," she snapped. "You're as stuffy as my Uncle Niles." Then she pressed a hand to her forehead, trying to work away the beginnings of a tension headache. "I don't suppose you can make coffee."

"Yes, I can make coffee."

"Then why don't you go down and do that little thing, handsome, and give me a minute here?"

He surprised her, and himself, by crouching down first, laying a hand on her shoulder. "You could have lost the pearls, lost all of it. You still wouldn't have lost your memories."

Uneasy that he'd felt compelled to say it, he straightened and left her alone. He went directly to the kitchen, pushing through the mess to fill the coffeepot. He set it up to brew and switched the machine on. Stuck his hands in his pockets, then pulled them out.

What the hell was going on? he asked himself. He should be focused on the case, and the case alone. Instead, he felt himself being pulled, tugged at, by the woman upstairs—by the various faces of that woman. Bold, fragile, sexy, sensitive.

Just which was she? And why had he spent most of the night with her face lodged in his dreams?

He shouldn't even be here, he admitted. He had no official reason to be spending this time with her. It was true he felt the case warranted his personal attention. It was serious enough. But she was only one small part of the whole.

And he'd be lying to himself if he said he was here strictly on an investigation.

He found two undamaged cups. There were several broken ones lying around. Good Meissen china, he noted. His mother had a set she prized dearly. He was just pouring the coffee when he sensed her behind him.

"Black?"

"That's fine." She stepped in, and winced as she took a visual inventory of the kitchen. "He didn't miss much, did he? I suppose he thought I might stick a big blue diamond in my coffee canister or cookie jar."

"People put their valuables in a lot of odd places. I was involved in a burglary case once where the victim saved her in-house cash because she'd kept it in a sealed plastic bag in the bottom of the diaper pail. What self-respecting B-and-E man is going to paw through diapers?"

She chuckled, sipped her coffee. Whether or not it had been his purpose, his telling of the story had made her feel better. "It makes keeping things in a safe seem foolish. This one didn't take the silver, or any of the electronics. I suppose, as you said, he was in too much of a hurry, and just took what he could stuff in his pockets."

She walked to the kitchen window and looked out. "Melissa's clothes are upstairs. I didn't see her purse. He might have taken that, too, or it could just be buried under the mess."

"We'd have found it if it had been here."

She nodded. "I'd forgotten. You've already searched through my things." She turned back, leaned on the counter and eyed him over the rim of her cup. "Did you go through them personally, Lieutenant?"

He thought of the red silk gown. "Some of it. You have your own department store here."

"I'd come by that naturally, wouldn't I? I have a weakness for things. All manner of things. You make excellent coffee, Lieutenant. Isn't there anyone who brews it for you in the morning?"

"No. Not at the moment." He set his coffee aside. "That wasn't very subtle."

"It wasn't intended to be. It's not that I mind competition. I just like to know if I have any. I still don't think I like you, but that could change." She lifted a hand to finger the tail of her braid. "Why not be prepared?"

"I'm interested in closing a case, not in playing games with you…Grace."

It was such a cool delivery, so utterly dispassionate it kindled her spirit of competition. "I suppose you don't like aggressive women."

"Not particularly."

"Well, then." She smiled as she stepped closer to him. "You're just going to hate this."

In a slick and practiced move, she slid a hand up into his hair and brought his mouth to hers.

Chapter 4

The jolt, lightning wrapped in black velvet, stabbed through him in one powerful strike. His head spun with it, his blood churned, his belly ached. No part of his system was spared the rapid onslaught of that lush and knowing mouth.

Her taste, unexpected yet familiar, plunged into him like hot spiced wine that rushed immediately to his head, leaving him dazed and drunk and desperate.

His muscles bunched, as if poised to leap. And in leaping, he would possess what was somehow already his. It took a vicious twist of will to keep his arms locked at his sides, when they strained to reach out, take, relish. Her scent was as dark, as drugging, as her flavor. Even the low, persuasive hum that sounded in her throat as she moved that glorious fantasy of a body against his was a tantalizing hint of what could be.

For a slow count of five, he fisted his hands, then relaxed them and let the internal war rage while his lips remained passive, his body rigid in denial.

He wouldn't give her the satisfaction of response…

She knew it was a mistake. Even as she moved toward him, reached for him, she'd known it. She'd made mistakes before, and she tried never to regret what was done and couldn't be undone.

But she regretted this.

She deeply regretted that his taste was utterly unique and perfect for her palate. That the texture of his hair, the shape of his shoulders, the strong wall of his chest, all taunted her, when she'd only meant to taunt him, to show him what she could offer. If she chose.

Instead, swept into need, rushed into it by that mating of lips, she offered more than she'd intended. And he gave nothing back.

She caught his bottom lip between her teeth, one quick, sharp nip, then masked an outrageous rush of disappointment by stepping casually back and aiming an amused smile at him.

"My, my, you're a cool one, aren't you, Lieutenant?"

His blood burned with every heartbeat, but he merely inclined his head. "You're not used to being resistible, are you, Grace?"

"No." She rubbed a fingertip lightly over her lip in a movement that was both absent and provocative. The essence of him clung stubbornly there, insisting it belonged. "But then, most of the men I've kissed haven't had ice water in their veins. It's a shame." She took her finger from her own lip, tapped it on his. "Such a nice mouth. Such potential. Still, maybe you just don't care for…women."

The grin he flashed stunned her. His eyes glowed with it, in fascinating tones of gold. His mouth softened with a charm that had a wicked and unpredictable appeal. Suddenly he was approachable, nearly boyish, and it made her heart yearn.

"Maybe," he said, "you're just not my type."

She gave one short, humorless laugh. "Darling, I'm every man's type. Well, we'll just chalk it up to a failed experiment and move on." Telling herself it was foolish to be hurt, she stepped to him again, reached up to straighten the tie she'd loosened.

He didn't want her to touch him, not then, not when he was so precariously perched on the edge. "You've got a hell of an ego there."

"I suppose I do." With her hands still on his tie, she looked up, into his eyes. The hell with it, she thought, if they couldn't be lovers, maybe they could be cautious friends. The man who had looked at her and grinned would be a good, solid friend.

So she smiled at him with a sweetness that was without art or guile, lancing his heart with one clean blow. "But then, men are generally predictable. You're just the exception to the rule, Seth, the one that proves it."

She brushed her hands down, smoothing his jacket and said something more, but he didn't hear it over the roaring in his ears. His control broke; he felt the snap, like the twang of a sword violently broken over an armored knee. In a movement he was hardly aware of, he spun her around, pressed her back against the wall, and was ravaging her mouth.

Her heart kicked in her chest, drove the breath out of her body. She gripped his shoulders as much for balance as in response to the sudden, violent need that shot from him to her and fused them together.

She yielded, utterly, then locked her arms around his neck and poured herself back.

Here, was all her dazzled mind could think. Oh, here, at last.

His hands raced over her, molded and somehow recognized each curve. And the recognition seared through him, as hot and real as the surge of desire. He wanted that taste, had to have it inside him, to swallow it whole. He assaulted her mouth like a man feeding after a lifelong fast, filled himself with the flavors of her, all of them dark, ripe, succulent.

She was there for him, had always been there—impossibly there. And he knew that if he didn't pull back, he'd never be able to survive without her.

He slapped his hands on the wall on either side of her head to stop himself from touching, to stop himself from taking. Fighting to regain both his breath and his sanity, he eased out of the kiss, stepped away.

She continued to lean back against the wall, her eyes closed, her skin luminous with passion. By the time her lashes fluttered up and those slumberous blue eyes focused, he had his control snapped back ruthlessly in place.

"Unpredictable," she managed, barely resisting the urge to press both hands to her galloping heart. "Very."

"I warned you about pushing the wrong buttons." His voice was cool, edging toward cold, and had the effect of a backhand slap.

She flinched from it, might have reeled, if she hadn't been braced by the wall. His eyes narrowed fractionally at the reaction. Hurt? he wondered. No, that was ridiculous. She was a veteran game player and knew all the angles.

"Yes, you did." She straightened, pride stiffening her spine and forcing her lips to curve in a casual smile. "I'm just so resistant to warnings."

He thought she should be required by law to carry one—Danger! Woman!

"I've got work to do. I can give you another five minutes, if you want me to wait while you pack some things."

Oh, you bastard, she thought. How can you be so cool, so unaffected? "You toddle right along, handsome. I'll be fine."

"I'd prefer you weren't in the house alone for the moment. Go pack some things."

"It's my home."

"Right now, it's a crime scene. You're down to four and a half minutes."

Fury vibrated through her in hot, pulsing beats. "I don't need anything here." She turned, started out, whirling back when he took her arm. "What?"

"You need clothes," he said, patient now. "For a day or two."

"Do you really think I'd wear anything that bastard might have touched?"

"That's a foolish and a predictable reaction." His tone didn't soften in the least. "You're not a foolish or a predictable woman. Don't be a victim, Grace. Go pack your things."

He was right. She could have despised him for that alone. But the frustrated need still fisted inside her was a much better reason. She said nothing at all, simply turned again and walked away.

When he didn't hear the front door slam, he was satisfied that she'd gone upstairs to pack, as he'd told her to. Seth turned off the coffeemaker, rinsed the cups and set them in the sink, then went out to wait for her.

She was a fascinating woman, he thought. Full of temperament, energy and ego. And she was undoing him, knot by carefully tied knot. How she knew exactly what strings to pull to do so was just one more mystery.

He'd taken this case on, he reminded himself. Riding a desk and delegating were only part of the job. He needed to be involved, and he'd involved himself with this—and therefore with her. Grace's part of the whole was small, but he needed to treat her with the same objectivity that he treated every other piece of the case with.

He looked up, his gaze drawn to the portrait that smiled down so invitingly.

He'd have to be more machine than man to stay objective when it came to Grace Fontaine.

It was midafternoon before he could clear his desk enough to handle a follow-up interview. The diamonds were the key, and he wanted another look at them. He hadn't been surprised when his phone conversation with Dr. Linstrum at the Smithsonian resulted in a testimonial to Bailey James's integrity and skill. The diamonds she'd gone to such lengths to protect remained at Salvini, and in her care.

When Seth pulled into the parking lot of the elegant corner building just outside D.C. that housed Salvini, he nodded to the uniformed cop guarding the main door. And felt a faint tug of sympathy. The heat was brutal.

"Lieutenant." Despite a soggy uniform, the officer snapped to attention.

"Ms. James inside?"

"Yes, sir. The store's closed to the public for the next week." He indicated the darkened showroom through the thick glass doors with a jerk of the head. "We have a guard posted at every entrance, and Ms. James is on the lower level. It's easier access through the rear, Lieutenant."

"Fine. When's your relief, Officer?"

"I've got another hour." The cop didn't wipe his brow, but he wanted to. Seth Buchanan had a reputation for being a stickler. "Four-hour rotations, as per your orders, sir."

"Bring a bottle of water with you next time." Well aware that the uniform sagged the minute his back was turned, Seth rounded the building. After a brief conversation with the duty guard at the rear, he pressed the buzzer beside the reinforced steel door. "Lieutenant Buchanan," he said when Bailey answered through the intercom. "I'd like a few minutes."

It took her some time to get to the door. Seth visualized her coming out of the workroom on the lower level, winding down the short corridor, passing the stairs where she'd hidden from a killer only days before.

He'd been through the building himself twice, top to bottom. He knew that not everyone could have survived what she'd been through in there.

The locks clicked, the door opened. "Lieutenant." She smiled at the guard, silently apologizing for his miserable duty. "Please come in."

She looked neat and tidy, Seth thought, with her trim blouse and slacks, her blond hair scooped back. Only the faint shadows under her eyes spoke of the strain she'd been under.

"I spoke with Dr. Linstrum," Seth began.

"Yes, I expect you did. I'm very grateful for his understanding."

"The stones are back where they started."

She smiled a little. "Well, they're back where they were a few days ago. Who knows if they'll ever see Rome again. Can I get you something cold to drink?" She gestured toward a soft-drink machine standing brightly against a dark wall.

"I'll buy." He plugged in coins. "I'd like to see the diamonds, and have a few words with you."

"All right." She pressed the button for her choice, and retrieved the can that clunked down the shoot. "They're in the vault." She continued to speak as she led the way. "I've arranged to have the security and alarm system beefed up. We've had cameras in the showroom for a number of years, but I'll have them installed at the doors, as well, and for the upper and lower levels. All areas."

"That's wise." He concluded that there was a practical streak of common sense beneath the fragile exterior. "You'll run the business now?"

She opened a door, hesitated. "Yes. My stepfather left it to the three of us, with my stepbrothers sharing eighty percent between them. In the event any of us died without heirs, the shares go to the survivors." She drew in a breath. "I survived."

"That's something to be grateful for, Bailey, not guilty about."

"Yes, that's what Cade says. But you see, I once had

the illusion, at least, that they were family. Have a seat, I'll get the Stars."

He moved into the work area, glanced at the equipment, the long worktable. Intrigued, he stepped closer, examining the glitter of colored stones, the twists of gold. It was going to be a necklace, he realized, running a fingertip over the silky length of a closely linked chain. Something bold, almost pagan.

"I needed to get back to work," she said from behind him. "To do something…different, my own, I suppose, before I faced dealing with these again."

She set down a padded box that held the trio of diamonds.

"Your design?" he asked, gesturing to the piece on the worktable.

"Yes. I see the piece in my head. I can't draw worth a lick, but I can visualize. I wanted to make something for M.J. and for Grace to…" She sighed, sat on the high stool. "Well, let's say to celebrate survival."

"And this is the one for Grace."

"Yes." She smiled, pleased that he'd sensed it. "I see something more streamlined for M.J. But this is Grace." Carefully she set the unfinished work in a tray, slid the padded box containing the Three Stars between them. "They never lose their impact. Each time I see them, it stuns."

"How long before you're finished with them?"

"I'd just begun when—when I had to stop." She cleared her throat. "I've verified their authenticity. They are blue diamonds. Still, both the museum and the insurance carrier prefer more in-depth verification. I'll be running a number of other tests beyond what I've already started or completed. A metallurgist is testing the triangle, but that will be given to me for further study in a day or two. It shouldn't take more than a week altogether before the museum can take possession."

He lifted a stone from the bed, knew as soon as it was in his hand that it was the one Grace had carried with her. He told himself that was impossible. His untrained eye couldn't tell one stone from either of its mates.

Yet he felt her on it. In it.

"Will it be hard to part with them?"

"I should say no, after the past few days. But yes, it will."

Grace's eyes were this color, Seth realized. Not sapphire, but the blue of the rare, powerful diamond.

"Worth killing for," he said quietly, looking at the stone in his hand. "Dying for." Then, annoyed with himself, he set the stone down again. "Your stepbrothers had a client."

"Yes, they spoke of a client, argued about him. Thomas wanted to take the money, the initial deposit, and run."

The money was being checked now, but there wasn't much hope of tracing its source.

"Timothy told Thomas he was a fool, that he'd never be able to run far or fast enough. That he—the client— would find him. He's not even human. Timothy said that, or something like it. They were both afraid, terribly afraid, and terribly desperate."

"Over their heads."

"Yes, I think very much over their heads."

"It would have to be a collector. No one could move these stones for resale." He glanced at the gems sparkling in their trays like pretty stars. "You acquire, buy and sell to collectors of gems."

"Yes—certainly not on a scale like the Three Stars, but yes." She skimmed her fingers absently through her hair. "A client might come to us with a stone, or a request for one. We'd also acquire certain gems on spec, with a particular client in mind."

"You have a client list, then? Names, preferences?"

"Yes, and we have records of what a client had purchased, or sold." She gripped her hands together. "Thomas would have kept it, in his office. Timothy would have copies in his. I'll find them for you."

He touched her shoulder lightly before she could slide from the stool. "I'll get them."

She let out a breath of relief. She had yet to be able to face going upstairs, into the room where she'd seen murder. "Thank you."

He took out his notebook. "If I asked you to name the top gem collectors, your top clients, what names come to mind? Off the top of your head?"

"Oh." Concentrating, she gnawed on her lip. "Peter Morrison in London, Sylvia Smythe-Simmons of New York, Henry and Laura Muller here in D.C., Matthew Wolinski in California. And I suppose Charles Van Horn here in D.C., too, though he's new to it. We sold him three lovely stones over the last two years. One was a spectacular opal I coveted. I'm still hoping he'll let me set it for him. I have this design in my head…"

She shook herself, trailed off when she realized why he was asking. "Lieutenant, I know these people. I've dealt with them personally. The Mullers were friends of my stepfather's. Mrs. Smythe-Simmons is over eighty. None of them are thieves."

He didn't bother to glance up, but continued to write. "Then we'll be able to check them off the list. Taking anything or anyone at face value is a mistake in an investigation, Ms. James. We've had enough mistakes already."

"With mine standing out." Accepting that fact, she nudged her untouched soft drink over the table. "I should have gone to the police right away. I should have turned the information—at the very least, my suspicions—over to the authorities. Several people would still be alive if I had."

"It's possible, but it's not a given." Now he did glance up, noted the haunted look in those soft brown eyes. Compassion stirred. "Did you know your stepbrother was being blackmailed by a second-rate bail bondsman?"

"No," she murmured.

"Did you know that someone was pulling the strings, pulling them hard enough to turn your stepbrother into a killer?"

She shook her head, bit down hard on her lip. "The things I didn't know were the problem, weren't they? I put the two people I love most in terrible danger, then I forgot about them."

"Amnesia isn't a choice, it's a condition. And your friends handled themselves. They still are—in fact, I saw Ms. Fontaine just this morning. She doesn't look any the worse for wear to me."

Bailey caught the disdainful note and turned to face him. "You don't understand her. I would have thought a man who does what you do for a living would be able to see more clearly than that."

He thought he caught a faint hint of pity in her voice,

and resented it. "I've always thought of myself as clear-sighted."

"People are rarely clear-sighted when it comes to Grace. They only see what she lets them see—unless they care enough to look deeper. She has the most generous heart of any person I've ever known."

Bailey caught the quick flicker of amused disbelief in his eyes and felt her anger rising against it. Furious, she pushed off the stool. "You don't know anything about her, but you've already dismissed her. Can you conceive of what she's going through right now? Her cousin was murdered—and in her stead."

"She's hardly to blame for that."

"Easy to say. But she'll blame herself, and so will her family. It's easy to blame Grace."

"You don't."

"No, because I know her. And I know she's dealt with perceptions and opinions just like yours most of her life. And her way of dealing with it is to do as she chooses, because whatever she does, those perceptions and opinions rarely change. Right now, she's with her aunt, I imagine, and taking the usual emotional beating."

Her voice heated, became rushed, as emotions swarmed. "Tonight, there'll be a memorial service for Melissa, and the relatives will hammer at her, the way they always do."

"Why should they?"

"Because that's what they do best." Running out of steam she turned her head, looked down at the Three Stars. Love, knowledge, generosity, she thought. Why did it seem there was so little of it in the world? "Maybe you should take another look, Lieutenant Buchanan."

He'd already taken too many, he decided. And he was wasting time. "She certainly inspires loyalty in her friends," he commented. "I'm going to look for those lists."

"You know the way." Dismissing him, Bailey picked up the stones to carry them back to the vault.

Grace was dressed in black, and had never felt less like grieving. It was six in the evening, and a light rain was beginning to fall. It promised to turn the city into a massive steam room instead of cooling it off. The headache that had been slyly brewing for hours snarled at the aspirin she'd already taken and leaped into full, vicious life.

She had an hour before the wake, one she had arranged quickly and alone, because her aunt demanded it. Helen Fontaine was handling grief in her own way— as she did everything else. In this case, it was by meeting Grace with a cold, damning and dry eye. Cutting off any offer of support or sympathy. And demanding that services take place immediately, and at Grace's expense and instigation.

They would be coming from all points, Grace thought as she wandered the large, empty room, with its banks of flowers, thick red drapes, deep pile carpeting. Because such things were expected, such things were reported in the press. And the Fontaines would never give the public media a bone to pick.

Except, of course, for Grace herself.

It hadn't been difficult to arrange for the funeral home, the music, the flowers, the tasteful canapés. Only phone calls and the invocation of the Fontaine name were required. Helen had brought the photograph herself, the large color print in a shining silver frame that now decorated a polished mahogany table and was flanked with red roses in heavy silver vases that Melissa had favored.

There would be no body to view.

Grace had arranged for Melissa's body to be released from the morgue, had already written the check for the cremation and the urn her aunt had chosen.

There had been no thanks, no acknowledgment. None had been expected.

It had been the same from the moment Helen became her legal guardian. She'd been given the necessities of life—Fontaine-style. Gorgeous homes in several countries to live in, perfectly prepared food, tasteful clothing, an excellent education.

And she'd been told, endlessly, how to eat, how to dress, how to behave, who could be selected as a friend and who could not. Reminded, incessantly, of her good fortune—unearned—in having such a family behind her. Tormented, ruthlessly, by the cousin she was there tonight to mourn, for being orphaned, dependent.

For being Grace.

She'd rebelled against all of it, every aspect, every expectation and demand. She'd refused to be malleable, biddable, predictable. The ache for her parents had eventually dimmed, and with it the child's desperate need for love and acceptance.

She'd given the press plenty to report. Wild parties, unwise affairs, unrestricted spending.

When that didn't ease the hurt, she'd found something else. Something that made her feel decent and whole.

And she'd found Grace.

For tonight, she would be just what her family had come to expect. And she would get through the next endless hours without letting them touch her.

She sat heavily on a sofa with overstuffed velvet seats. Her head pounded, her stomach clutched. Closing her eyes, she willed herself to relax. She would spend this last hour alone, and prepare herself for the rest.

But she'd barely taken the second calming breath when she heard footsteps muffled on the thick patterned carpet. Her shoulders turned to rock, her spine snapped straight. She opened her eyes. And saw Bailey and M.J.

She let her eyes close again, on a pathetic rush of gratitude. "I told you not to come."

"Yeah, like we were going to listen to that." M.J. sat beside her, took her hand.

"Cade and Jack are parking the car." Bailey flanked her other side, took her other hand. "How are you holding up?"

"Better." Tears stung her eyes as she squeezed the hands clasped in hers. "A lot better now."

On a sprawling estate not so many miles from where Grace sat with those who loved her, a man stared out at the hissing rain.

Everyone had failed, he thought. Many had paid for their failures. But retribution was a poor substitute for the Three Stars.

A delay only, he comforted himself. The Stars were his, they were meant to be his. He had dreamed of them, had held them in his hands in those dreams. Sometimes the hands were human, sometimes not, but they were always his hands.

He sipped wine, watched the rain, and considered his options.

His plans had been delayed by three women. That was humiliating, and they would have to be made to pay for that humiliation.

The Salvinis were dead—Bailey James.

The fools he'd hired to retrieve the second Star were dead—M. J. O'Leary.

The man he'd sent with instructions to acquire the third Star at any cost was dead—Grace Fontaine.

And he smiled. That had been indiscreet, as he'd disposed of the lying fool himself. Telling him there'd been an accident, that the woman had fought him, run from him, and fallen to her death. Telling him he'd searched every corner of the house without finding the stone.

That failure had been irritating enough, but then to discover that the wrong woman had died and that the fool had stolen money and jewels without reporting them. Well, such disloyalty in a business associate could hardly be tolerated.

Smiling dreamily, he took a sparkling diamond earring out of his pocket. Grace Fontaine had worn this on her delectable lobe, he mused. He kept it now as a good-luck charm while he considered what steps to take next.

There were only days left before the Stars would be in the museum. Extracting them from those hallowed halls would take months, if not years, of planning. He didn't intend to wait.

Perhaps he had failed because he had been overcautious, had kept his distance from events. Perhaps the gods required a more personal risk. A more intimate involvement.

It was time, he decided, to step out of the shadows, to meet the women who had kept his property from him, face-to-face. He smiled again, excited by the thought, delighted with the possibilities.

When the knock sounded on the door, he answered with great cheer and good humor. "Enter."

The butler, in stern formal black, ventured no farther than the threshold. His voice held no inflection. "I beg your pardon, Ambassador. Your guests are arriving."

"Very well." He sipped the last of his wine, set the empty crystal flute on a table. "I'll be right down."

When the door closed, he moved to the mirror, examined his flawless tuxedo, the wink of diamond studs, the gleam of the thin gold watch at his wrist. Then he examined his face—the smooth contours, the pampered, pale gold skin, the aristocratic nose, the firm, if somewhat thin, mouth. He brushed a hand over the perfectly groomed mane of silver-threaded black hair.

Then, slowly, smilingly, met his own eyes. Pale, almost translucent blue smiled back. His guests would see what he did, a perfectly groomed man of fifty-two, erudite and educated, well mannered and suave. They wouldn't know what plans and plots he held in his heart. They would see no blood on his hands, though it had been only twenty-four short hours since he used them to kill.

He felt only pleasure in the memory, only delight in the knowledge that he would soon dine with the elite and the influential. And he could kill any one of them with a twist of his hands, with perfect immunity.

He chuckled to himself—a low, seductive sound with shuddering undertones. Tucking the earring back in his pocket, he walked from the room.

The ambassador was mad.

Chapter 5

Seth's first thought when he walked into the funeral parlor was that it seemed more like a tedious cocktail party than like a memorial service. People stood or sat in little cliques and groups, many of them nibbling on canapés or sipping wine. Beneath the strains of a muted Chopin étude, voices murmured. There was an occasional roll or tinkle of laughter.

He heard no tears.

Lights were respectfully dimmed, and set off the glitter and gleam of gems and gold. The fragrance of flowers mixed and merged with the scents worn by both men and women. He saw faces, both elegant and bored.

He saw no grief.

But he did see Grace. She stood looking up into the face of a tall, slim man whose golden tan set off his golden hair and bright blue eyes. He held one of her hands in his and smiled winningly. He appeared to be speaking quickly, persuasively. She shook her head once, laid a hand on his chest, then allowed herself to be drawn into an anteroom.

Seth's lip curled in automatic disdain. A funeral was a hell of a place for a flirtation.

"Buchanan." Jack Dakota wandered over. He scanned the room, stuck his hands in the pockets of the suit coat he wished fervently was still in his closet, instead of on his back. "Some party."

Seth watched two women air kiss. "Apparently."

"Doesn't seem like one a sane man would want to crash."

"I have business," he said briefly. Which could have waited until morning, he reminded himself. He should have let it wait. It annoyed him that he'd made the detour, that he'd been thinking of Grace—more, that he'd been unable to lock her out of his head.

He pulled a copy of a mug shot out of his pocket, handed it to Jack. "Recognize him?"

Jack scanned the picture, considered. Slick-looking dude, he thought. Vaguely European in looks, with the sleek black hair, dark eyes and refined features. "Nope. Looks like a poster boy for some wussy cologne."

"You didn't see him during your amazing weekend adventures?"

Jack took one last, harder look, handed the shot back. "Nope. What's his connection?"

"His prints were all over the house in Potomac."

Jack's interest rose. "He the one who killed the cousin?"

Seth met Jack's eyes coolly. "That has yet to be determined."

"Don't give me the cop stand, Buchanan. What'd the guy say? He stopped by to sell vacuum cleaners?"

"He didn't say anything. He was too busy floating facedown in the river."

With an oath, Jack's gaze whipped around the room again. He relaxed fractionally when he spotted M.J. huddled with Cade. "The morgue must be getting crowded. You got a name?"

Seth started to dismiss the question. He didn't care for professions that stood a step back from the police. But there was no denying that the bounty hunter and the private investigator were involved. And there was no avoiding the connection, he told himself.

"Carlo Monturri."

"Doesn't ring a bell either."

Seth hadn't expected it would, but the police—on several continents—knew the name. "He's out of your league, Dakota. His type keeps a fancy lawyer on retainer and doesn't use the local bail bondsman to get sprung."

As he spoke, Seth's eyes moved around the room as a cop's did, sweeping corner to corner, taking in details, body language, atmosphere. "Before he took his last swim, he was expensive hired muscle. He worked alone because he didn't like to share the fun."

"Connections in the area?"

"We're working on it."

Seth saw Grace come out of the anteroom. The man who was with her had his arm draped over her shoulders, pulled her close in an intimate embrace, kissed her. The flare of fury kindled in Seth's gut and bolted up to his heart.

"Excuse me."

Grace saw him the moment he started across the room. She murmured something to the man beside her, dislodged him, then dismissed him. Straightening her spine, she fixed on an easy smile.

"Lieutenant, we didn't expect you."

"I apologize for intruding in your—" he flicked a glance toward the golden boy, who was helping himself to a glass a wine "—grief."

The sarcasm slapped, but she didn't flinch. "I assume you have a reason for coming by."

"I'd like a moment of your time—in private."

"Of course." She turned to lead him out and came face-to-face with her aunt. "Aunt Helen."

"If you could tear yourself away from entertaining your suitors," Helen said coldly, "I want to speak to you."

"Excuse me," Grace said to Seth, and stepped into the anteroom again.

Seth debated moving off, giving them privacy. But he stayed where he was, two paces from the doorway. He told himself murder investigations didn't allow for sensitivity. Though they kept their voices low, he heard both women clearly enough.

"I assume you have Melissa's things at your home," Helen began.

"I don't know. I haven't been able to go through the house thoroughly yet."

Helen said nothing for a moment, simply studied her niece through cold blue eyes. Her face was smooth and showed no ravages of grief in the carefully applied makeup. Her hair was sleek, lightened to a tasteful ash blond. Her hands were freshly manicured and glittered with the diamond wedding band she continued to wear, though she'd shared little but her husband's name in over a decade, and a square-cut sapphire given to her by her latest lover.

"I sincerely doubt Melissa came to your home without a bag. I want her things, Grace. All of her things. You'll have nothing of hers."

"I never wanted anything of hers, Aunt Helen."

"Didn't you?" There was a crackle in the voice—a whip flicking. "Did you think she wouldn't tell me of your affair with her husband?"

Grace merely sighed. It was new ground, but sickeningly familiar. Melissa's marriage had failed, publicly. Therefore, it had to be someone else's fault. It had to be Grace's fault.

"I didn't have an affair with Bobbie. Before, during or after their marriage."

"And whom do you think I would believe? You, or my own daughter?"

Grace tilted her head, twisted a smile on her face. "Why, your own daughter, of course. As always."

"You've always been a liar and a sneak. You've always been ungrateful, a burden I took on out of family duty who never once gave anything back. You were spoiled and willful when I opened my door to you, and you never changed."

Grace's stomach roiled viciously. In defense, she smiled, shrugged. Deliberately careless, she smoothed a hand over the hair sleeked into a coiled twist at the nape of her neck. "No, I suppose I didn't. I'll just have to remain a disappointment to you, Aunt Helen."

"My daughter would be alive if not for you."

Grace willed her heart to go numb. But it ached, and it burned. "Yes, you're right."

"I warned her about you, told her time and again what you were. But you continually lured her back, playing on her affection."

"Affection, Aunt Helen?" With a half laugh, Grace pressed her fingers to the throb in her left temple. "Surely even you don't believe she ever had an ounce of affection for me. She took her cue from you, after all. And she took it well."

"How dare you speak of her in that tone, after you've killed her!" In the pampered face, Helen's eyes burned with loathing. "All of your life you've envied her, used your wiles to influence her. Now your unconscionable life-style has killed her. You've brought scandal and disgrace down on the family name once again."

Grace went stiff. This wasn't grief, she thought. Perhaps grief was there, buried deep, but what was on the surface was venom. And she was weary of being struck by it. "That's the bottom line, isn't it, Aunt Helen? The Fontaine name, the Fontaine reputation. And, of course, the Fontaine stock. Your child is dead, but it's the scandal that infuriates you."

She absorbed the slap without a wince, though the blow printed heat on her cheek, brought blood stinging to the surface. She took one long, deep breath. "That should end things appropriately between the two of us," she said evenly. "I'll have Melissa's things sent to you as soon as possible."

"I want you out of here." Helen's voice shook for the first time—whether in grief or in fury, Grace couldn't have said. "You have no place here."

"You're right again. I don't. I never did."

Grace stepped out of the alcove. The color that had drained out of her face rose slightly when she met Seth's eyes. She couldn't read them in that brief glance, and didn't want to. Without breaking stride, she continued past him and kept walking.

The drizzle that misted the air was a relief. She welcomed the heat after the overchilled, artificial air inside, and the heavy, stifling scent of funeral flowers. Her heels clicked on the wet pavement as she crossed the lot to her car. She was fumbling in her bag for her keys when Seth clamped a hand on her shoulder.

He said nothing at first, just turned her around, studied her face. It was white again—but for the red burn from the slap—the eyes a dark contrast and swimming with emotion. He could feel the tremors of that emotion under the palm of his hand.

"She was wrong."

Humiliation was one more blow to her overwrought system. She jerked her shoulder, but his hand remained in place. "Is that part of your investigative technique, Lieutenant? Eavesdropping on private conversations?"

Did she realize, he wondered, that her voice was raw, her eyes were devastated? He wanted badly to lift a hand to that mark on her face, cool it. Erase it. "She was wrong," he said again. "And she was cruel. You aren't responsible."

"Of course I am." She spun away, jabbing her key at the door lock. After three shaky attempts, she gave up, and they dropped with a jingling splash to the wet pavement as she turned into his arms. "Oh, God." Shuddering, she pressed her face into his chest. "Oh, God."

He didn't want to hold her, wanted to refuse the role

of comforter. But his arms came around her before he could stop them, and one hand reached up to brush the smooth twist of her hair. "You didn't deserve that, Grace. You did nothing to deserve that."

"It doesn't matter."

"Yes, it does." He found himself weakening, drawing her closer, trying to will her trembling away. "It always does."

"I'm just tired." She burrowed into him while the rain misted her hair. There was strength here, was all she could think. A haven here. An answer here. "I'm just tired."

Her head lifted, their mouths met, before either of them realized the need was there. The quiet sound in her throat was of relief and gratitude. She opened her battered heart to the kiss, locking her arms around him, urging him to take it.

She had been waiting for him, and, too dazed to question why, she offered herself to him. Surely comfort and pleasure and this all-consuming need were reason enough. His mouth was firm—the one she'd always wanted on hers. His body was hard and solid—a perfect match for hers.

Here he is, she thought with a ragged sigh of joy.

She trembled still, and he could feel his own muscles quiver in response. He wanted to gather her up, carry her out of the rain to someplace quiet and dark where it was only the two of them. To spend years where it would only be the two of them.

His heart pounded in his head, masking the slick sound of traffic over the rain-wet street beyond the lot. Its fast, demanding beat muffled the warning struggling to sound in the corner of his brain, telling him to step back, to break away.

He'd never wanted anything more in his life than to bury himself in her and forget the consequences.

Swamped with emotions and needs, she held him close. "Take me home," she murmured against his mouth. "Seth, take me home, make love with me. I need you to touch me. I want to be with you." Her mouth met his again, in a desperate plea she hadn't known herself capable of.

Every cell in his body burned for her. Every need he'd ever had coalesced into one, and it was only for her. The almost vicious focus of it left him vulnerable and shaky. And furious.

He put his hands on her shoulders, drew her away. "Sex isn't the answer for everyone."

His voice wasn't as cool as he'd wanted, but it was rigid enough to stop her from reaching for him again. Sex? she thought as she struggled to clear her dazzled mind. Did he really believe she'd been speaking about something as simple as sex? Then she focused on his face, the hard set of his mouth, the faint annoyance in his eyes, and realized he did.

Her pride might have been tattered, but she managed to hold on to a few threads. "Well, apparently it's not for you." Reaching up, she smoothed her hair, brushed away rain. "Or if it is, you're the type who insists on being the initiator."

She made her lips curve, though they felt cold now and stiff. "It would have been just fine and dandy if you'd made the move. But when I do, it makes me—what would the term be? Loose?"

"I don't believe it's a term I used."

"No, you're much too controlled for insults." She bent down, scooped up her wet keys, then stood jingling them in her hand while she studied him. "But you wanted me right back, Seth. You're not quite controlled enough to have masked that little detail."

"I don't believe in taking everything I want."

"Why the hell not?" She gave a short, mirthless laugh. "We're alive, aren't we? And you, of all people, should know how distressingly short life can be."

"I don't have to explain to you how I live my life."

"No, you don't. But it's obvious you're perfectly willing to question how I live mine." Her gaze skimmed past him, back toward the lights glinting in the funeral home. "I'm quite used to that. I do exactly what I choose, without regard for the consequences. I'm selfish and self-involved and careless."

She lifted a shoulder as she turned and unlocked her door. "As for feelings, why should I be entitled to them?"

She slipped into her car, flipped him one last look. Her mouth might have curved with seductive ease, but the sultry smile didn't reach her eyes, or mask the misery in them. "Well, maybe some other time, handsome."

He watched her drive off into the rain. There would be another time, he admitted, if for no other reason than that he hadn't shown her the picture. Hadn't, he thought, had the heart to add to her unhappiness that night.

Feelings, he mused as he headed to his own car. She had them, had plenty of them. He only wished he understood them. He got into his car, wrenched his door shut. He wished to God he understood his own.

For the first time in his life, a woman had reached in and clamped a hand on his heart. And she was squeezing.

Seth told himself he wasn't postponing meeting with Grace again. The morning after the memorial service had been hellish with work. And when he did carve out time to leave his office, he'd headed toward M.J.'s. It was true he could have assigned this follow-up to one of his men. Despite the fact that the chief of police had ordered him to head the investigation, and give every detail his personal attention, Mick Marshall—the detective who had taken the initial call on the case— could have done this next pass with M. J. O'Leary.

Seth was forced to admit that he wanted to talk to her personally and hoped to slide a few details out of her on Grace Fontaine.

M.J.'s was a cozy, inviting neighborhood pub that ran to dark woods, gleaming brass and thickly padded stools and booths. Business was slow but steady in midafternoon. A couple of men who looked to be college age were sharing a booth, a duet of foamy mugs and an intense game of chess. An older man sat at the bar working a crossword from the morning paper, and a trio of women with department store shopping bags crowding the floor around them huddled over drinks and laughter.

The bartender glanced at Seth's badge and told him he'd find the boss upstairs in her office. He heard her before he saw her.

"Look, pal, if I'd wanted candy mints, I'd have ordered candy mints. I ordered beer nuts. I want them here by six. Yeah, yeah. I know my customers. Get me the damn nuts, pronto."

She sat behind a crowded desk with a battered top. Her short cap of red hair stood up in spikes. Seth watched her rake her fingers through it again as she hung up the phone and pushed a pile of invoices aside. If that was her idea of filing, he thought, it suited the rest of the room.

It was barely big enough to turn around in, crowded with boxes, files, papers, and one ratty chair, on which sat an enormous and overflowing purse.

"Ms. O'Leary?"

She looked up, her brow still creased in annoyance. It didn't clear when she recognized her visitor. "Just what I needed to make my day perfect. A cop. Listen, Buchanan, I'm behind here. As you know, I lost a few days recently."

"Then I'll try to be quick." He stepped inside, pulled the picture out of his pocket and tossed it onto the desk under her nose. "Look familiar?"

She pursed her lips, gave the slickly handsome face a slow, careful study. "Is this the guy Jack told me about? The one who killed Melissa?"

"The Melissa Fontaine case is still open. This man is a possible suspect. Do you recognize him?"

She rolled her eyes, pushed the photo back in Seth's direction. "No. Looks like a creep. Did Grace recognize him?"

He angled his head slightly, his only outward sign of interest. "Does she know many men who look like creeps?"

"Too many," M.J. muttered. "Jack said you came

by the memorial service last night to show Grace this picture."

"She was…occupied."

"Yeah, it was a rough night for her." M.J. rubbed her eyes.

"Apparently, though she seemed to have been handling it well enough initially." He glanced down at the photo again, thought of the man he'd seen her kiss. "This looks like her type."

M.J.'s hand dropped, her eyes narrowed. "Meaning?"

"Just that." Seth tucked the photo away. "If one's going by type, this one doesn't appear, on the surface, too far a step from the one she was cozy with at the service."

"Cozy with?" The narrowed eyes went hot, angry green flares. "Grace wasn't cozy with anyone."

"About six-one, a hundred and seventy, blond hair, blue eyes, five-thousand-dollar Italian suit, lots of teeth."

It only took her a moment. At any other time, she would have laughed. But the cool disdain on Seth's face had her snarling. "You stupid son of a bitch, that was her cousin Julian, and he was hitting her up for money, just like he always does."

Seth frowned, backtracked, played the scene through his mind again. "Her cousin…and that would be the victim's…?"

"Stepbrother. Melissa's stepbrother—her father's son from a previous."

"And the deceased's stepbrother was asking Grace for money at his stepsister's memorial?"

This time she appreciated the coating of disgust over

his words. "Yeah. He's slime—why should the ambience stop him from shaking her down? Most of them squeeze her for a few bucks now and then." She rose, geared up. "And you've got a hell of a nerve coming in here with your attitude and your superior morals, ace. She wrote that pansy-faced jerk a check for a few thousand to get him off her back, just like she used to pass bucks to Melissa, and some of the others."

"I was under the impression the Fontaines were wealthy."

"Wealth's relative—especially if you live the high life and your allowance from your trust fund is overdrawn, or if you've played too deep in Monte Carlo. And Grace has more of the green stuff than most of them, because her parents didn't blow the bucks. That just burns the relatives," she muttered. "Who do you think paid for that wake last night? It wasn't the dearly departed's mama or papa. Grace's witch of an aunt put the arm on her, then put the blame on her. And she took it, because she thinks it's easier to take it and go her own way. You don't know anything about her."

He thought he did, but the details he was collecting bit by bit weren't adding up very neatly. "I know that she's not to blame for what happened to her cousin."

"Yeah, try telling her that. I know that when we realized she'd left and we got back to Cade's, she was in her room crying, and there was nothing any of us could do to help her. And all because those bastards she has the misfortune to be related to go out of their way to make her feel rotten."

Not just her relatives, he thought with a quick twinge of guilt. He'd had a part in that.

"It seems she's more fortunate in her friends than in her family."

"That's because we're not interested in her money, or her name. Because we don't judge her. We just love her. Now, if that's all, I've got work to do."

"I need to speak with Ms. Fontaine." Seth's voice was as stiff as M.J.'s had been passionate. "Would you know where I might find her?"

Her lips curled. She hesitated a moment, knowing Grace wouldn't appreciate the information being passed along. But the urge to see the cop's preconceptions slapped down was just too tempting. "Sure. Try Saint Agnes's Hospital. Pediatrics or maternity." Her phone rang, so she snatched it up. "You'll find her," she said. "Yeah, O'Leary," she barked into the phone, and turned her back on Seth.

He assumed she was visiting the child of a friend, but when he asked at the nurses' station for Grace Fontaine, faces lit up.

"I think she's in the intensive-care nursery." The nurse on duty checked her watch. "It's her usual time there. Do you know the way?"

Baffled, Seth shook his head. "No." He listened to the directions, while his mind turned over a dozen reasons why Grace Fontaine should have a usual time in a nursery. Since none of them slipped comfortably into a slot, he headed down corridors.

He could hear the high sound of babies crying behind a barrier of glass. And perhaps he stopped for just a moment outside the window of the regular nursery, and his eyes might have softened, just a little, as he scanned the infants in their clear-sided beds. Tiny faces, some slack in sleep, others screwed up into wrinkled balls of fury.

A couple stood beside him, the man with his arm over the woman's robed shoulders. "Ours is third from the left. Joshua Michael Delvecchio. Eight pounds, five ounces. He's one day old."

"He's a beaut," Seth said.

"Which one is yours?" the woman asked.

Seth shook his head, shot one more glance through the glass. "I'm just passing through. Congratulations on your son."

He continued on, resisting the urge to look back at the new parents lost in their own private miracle.

Two turns down the corridor away from the celebration was a smaller nursery. Here machines hummed, and nurses walked quietly. And behind the glass were six empty cribs.

Grace sat beside one, cuddling a tiny, crying baby. She brushed away tears from the pale little cheek, rested her own against the smooth head as she rocked.

It struck him to the core, the picture she made. Her hair was braided back from her face and she wore a shapeless green smock over her suit. Her face was soft as she soothed the restless infant. Her attention was totally focused on the eyes that stared tearfully into hers.

"Excuse me, sir." A nurse hurried up. "This is a restricted area."

Absently, his eyes still on Grace, Seth reached for his badge. "I'm here to speak with Ms. Fontaine."

"I see. I'll tell her you're here, Lieutenant."

"No, don't disturb her." He didn't want anything to spoil that picture. "I can wait. What's wrong with the baby she's holding?"

"Peter's an AIDS baby. Ms. Fontaine arranged for him to have care here."

"Ms. Fontaine?" He felt a fist lodge in his gut. "It's her child?"

"Biologically? No." The nurse's face softened slightly. "I think she considers them all hers. I honestly don't know what we'd do without her help. Not just the foundation, but her."

"The foundation?"

"The Falling Star Foundation. Ms. Fontaine set it up a few years ago to assist critically ill and terminal children and their families. But it's the hands-on that really matters." She gestured back toward the glass with a nod of her head. "No amount of financial generosity can buy a loving touch or sing a lullaby."

He watched the baby calm, drift slowly to sleep in Grace's arms. "She comes here often?"

"As often as she can. She's our angel. You'll have to excuse me, Lieutenant."

"Thank you." As she walked away, he stepped closer to the isolation glass. Grace started toward the crib. It was then that her eyes met his.

He saw the shock come into them first. Even she wasn't skilled enough to disguise the range of emotions that raced over her face. Surprise, embarrassment, annoyance. Then she smoothed the expressions out. Gently, she laid the baby back into the crib, brushed a hand over his cheek. She walked through a side door and disappeared.

It was several minutes before she came out into the corridor. The smock was gone. Now she was a confident woman in a flame-red suit, her mouth carefully tinted to match. "Well, Lieutenant, we meet in the oddest places."

Before she could complete the casual greeting she'd practiced while she tidied her makeup, he took her chin firmly in his hand. His eyes locked intently on hers, probed.

"You're a fake." He said it quietly, stepping closer. "You're a fraud. Who the hell are you?"

"Whatever I like." He unnerved her, that long, intense and all-too-personal study with those golden-brown eyes. "And I don't believe this is the place for an interrogation. I'd like you to let me go now," she said steadily. "I don't want any scenes here."

"I'm not going to cause a scene."

She lifted her brows. "I might." Deliberately she pushed his hand away and started down the corridor. "If you want to discuss the case with me, or have any questions regarding it, we'll do it outside. I won't have it brought in here."

"It was breaking your heart," he murmured. "Holding that baby was breaking your heart."

"It's my heart." Almost viciously, she punched a finger at the button for the elevator. "And it's a tough one, Seth. Ask anyone."

"Your lashes are still wet."

"This is none of your business." Her voice was low and vibrating with fury. "Absolutely none of your business."

She stepped into the crowded elevator, faced front. She wouldn't speak to him about this part of her life, she promised herself. Just the night before, she'd opened herself to him, only to be pushed away, refused. She wouldn't share her feelings again, and certainly not her feelings about something as vital to her as the children.

He was a cop, just a cop. Hadn't she spent several miserable hours the night before convincing herself that was all he was or could be to her? Whatever he stirred in her would have to be stopped—or, if not stopped, at least suppressed.

She would not share with him, she would not trust him, she would not give to him.

By the time she reached the lobby doors, she was steadier. Hoping to shake him quickly, she started toward the lot. Seth merely took her arm, steered her away.

"Over here," he said, and headed toward a grassy area with a pair of benches.

"I don't have time."

"Make time. You're too upset to drive, in any case."

"Don't tell me what I am."

"Apparently that's just what I've been doing. And apparently I've missed several steps. That's not usual for me, and I don't care for it. Sit down."

"I don't want—"

"Sit down, Grace," he repeated. "I apologize."

Annoyed, she sat on the bench, found her sunglasses in her bag and slipped them on. "For?"

He sat beside her, removed the shielding glasses and looked into her eyes. "For not letting myself look beneath the surface. For not wanting to look. And for blaming you because I don't seem able to stop wanting to do this."

He took her face in his hands and captured her mouth with his.

Chapter 6

She didn't move into him. Not this time. Her emotions were simply too raw to risk. Though her mouth yielded beneath his, she lifted a hand and laid it on his chest, as if to keep him at a safe distance.

And still her heart stumbled.

This time she was holding back. He sensed it, felt it in the press of her hand against him. Not refusing, but resisting. And with a knowledge that came from somewhere too deep to measure, he gentled the kiss, seeking not only to seduce, but also to soothe.

And still his heart staggered.

"Don't." It made her throat ache, her mind haze, her body yearn. And it was all too much. She pulled away from him and stood staring out across the little patch of grass until she thought she could breathe again.

"What is it with timing?" Seth wondered aloud. "That makes it so hard to get right?"

"I don't know." She turned then to look at him. He was an attractive man, she decided. The dark hair and hard face, the odd tint of gold in his eyes. But she'd known many attractive men. What was it about this one that changed everything and made her world tilt? "You bother me, Lieutenant Buchanan."

He gave her one of his rare smiles—slow and full and rich. "That's a mutual problem, Ms. Fontaine. You keep me up at night. Like a puzzle where the pieces are all there, but they change shape right before your eyes. And even when you put it all together—or think you have—it doesn't stay the same."

"I'm not a mystery, Seth."

"You are the most fascinating woman I've ever met." His lips curved again when she lifted her brows. "That isn't entirely a compliment. Along with fascination comes frustration." He stood, but didn't step toward her. "Why were you so upset that I found you here, saw you here?"

"It's private." Her tone was stiff again, dismissive. "I go to considerable trouble to keep it private."

"Why?"

"Because I prefer it that way."

"Your family doesn't know about your involvement here?"

The fury that seared through her eyes was burning-cold. "My family has *nothing* to do with this. Nothing. This isn't a Fontaine project, one of their charitable sops for good press and a tax deduction. It's mine."

"Yes, I can see that," he said calmly. Her family had hurt her even more than he'd guessed. And more, he thought, than she had acknowledged. "Why children, Grace?"

"Because they're the innocents." It was out before she realized she meant to say it. Then she closed her eyes and sighed. "Innocence is a precious and perishable commodity."

"Yes, it is. Falling Star? Your foundation. Is that how you see them, stars that burn out and fall too quickly?"

It was her heart he was touching simply by understanding, by seeing what was inside. "It has nothing to do with the case. Why are you pushing me on this?"

"Because I'm interested in you."

She sent him a smile—half inviting, half sarcastic. "Are you? You didn't seem to be when I asked you to bed. But you see me holding a sick baby and you change your tune." She walked toward him slowly, trailed a fingertip down his shirt. "Well, if it's the maternal type that turns you on, Lieutenant—"

"Don't do that to yourself." Again his voice was quiet, controlled. He took her hand, stopped her from backtracking the trail of her finger. "It's foolish. And it's irritating. You weren't playing games in there. You care."

"Yes, I do. I care enormously. And that doesn't make me a hero, and it doesn't make me any different than I was last night." She drew her hand away and stood her ground. "I want you. I want to go to bed with you. That irritates you, Seth. Not the sentiment, but the bluntness of the statement. Isn't it games you'd prefer? That I'd pretend reluctance and let you conquer?"

He only wished it was something just that ordinary. "Maybe I want to know who you are before we end up in bed. I spent a long time looking at your face—that portrait of you in your house. And, looking, I wondered about you. Now, I want you. But I also want all those pieces to fit."

"You might not like the finished product."

"No," he agreed. "I might not."

Then again, she thought… Considering, she angled her head. "I have a thing tonight. A cocktail party hosted by a major contributor to the hospital. I can't afford to skip it. Why don't you take me, then we'll see what happens next?"

He weighed the pros and cons, knew it was a step that would have ramifications he might not be able to handle smoothly. She wasn't simply a woman, and he wasn't simply a man. Whatever was between them had a long reach and a hard grip.

"Do you always think everything through so carefully?" she asked as she watched him.

"Yes." But in her case it didn't seem to matter, he realized. "I can't guarantee my evenings will be free until this case is closed." He shifted times and meetings and paperwork in his head. "But if I can manage it, I'll pick you up."

"Eight's soon enough. If you're not there by quarter after, I'll assume you were tied up."

No complaints, he thought, no demands. Most of the women he'd known shifted to automatic sulk mode when his work took priority. "I'll call if I can't make it."

"Whatever." She sat again, relaxed now. "I don't imagine you came by to see my secret life, or to make a tentative date for a cocktail party." She slipped her sunglasses back on, sat back. "Why are you here?"

He reached inside his jacket for the photo. Grace caught a brief glimpse of his shoulder holster, and the weapon snug inside it. And wondered if he'd ever had occasion to use it.

"I imagine your time is taken up mainly with administration duties." She took the picture from him, but continued to look at Seth's face. "You wouldn't participate in many, what—busts?"

She thought she caught a faint glint of humor in his eyes, but his mouth remained sober. "I like to keep my hand in."

"Yes," she murmured, easily able to imagine him whipping the weapon out. "I suppose you would."

She shifted her gaze, scanned the face in the photo. This time the humor was in her eyes. "Ah, Joe Cool. Or more likely Juan or Jean-Paul Cool."

"You know him?"

"Not personally, but certainly as a type. He likely speaks the right words in three languages, plays a steely game of baccarat, enjoys his brandy and wears black silk underwear. His Rolex, along with his monogrammed gold cufflinks and diamond pinkie ring, would have been gifts from admirers."

Intrigued, Seth sat beside her again. "And what are the right words?"

"You're the most beautiful woman in the room. I adore you. My heart sings when I look into your eyes. Your husband is a fool, and darling, you must stop buying me gifts."

"Been there?"

"With some variations. Only I've never been married and I don't buy trinkets for users. His eyes are cold," she added, "but a lot of women, lonely women, would only see the polish. That's all they want to see."

She took a quick, short breath. "This is the man who killed Melissa, isn't it?"

He started to give her the standard response, but she looked up then, and he was close enough to read her eyes through the amber tint of her glasses. "I think it is. His prints were all over the house. Some of the surfaces were wiped, but he missed a lot, which leads me to think he panicked. Either because she fell or because he wasn't able to find what he'd come for."

"And you're leaning toward the second choice, because this isn't the type of man to panic because he'd killed a woman."

"No, he isn't."

"She couldn't have given him what he'd come for. She wouldn't have known what he was talking about."

"No. That doesn't make you responsible. If you indulge yourself by thinking it does, you'd have to blame Bailey, too."

Grace opened her mouth, closed it again, breathed deep. "That's clever logic, Lieutenant," she said after a moment. "So I shed my sackcloth and ashes and blame this man. Have you found him?"

"He's dead." He took the photo back, tucked it away. "And my clever logic leads me to believe that whoever hired him decided to fire him, permanently."

"I see." She felt nothing, no satisfaction, no relief. "So, we're nowhere."

"The Three Stars are under twenty-four-hour guard. You, M.J. and Bailey are safe, and the museum will have its property in a matter of days."

"And a lot of people have died. Sacrifices to the god?"

"From what I've read about Mithra, it isn't blood he wants."

"Love, knowledge and generosity," she said quietly. "Powerful elements. The diamond I held, it has vitality. Maybe that's the same as power. Does he want them because they're beautiful, priceless, ancient, or because he truly believes in the legend? Does he believe that if he has all of them in their triangle, he'll possess the power of the god, and immortality?"

"People believe what they choose to believe. Whatever reason he wants them, he's killed for them." Staring out across the grass, he stepped over one of his own rules and shared his thoughts with her. "Money isn't the driving force. He's laid out more than a million already. He wants to own them, to hold them in his hands, whatever the cost. It's more than coveting," he said quietly, as a murky scene swam into his mind.

A marble altar, a golden triangle with three brilliantly blue points. A dark man with pale eyes and a bloody sword.

"And you don't think he'll stop now. You think he'll try again."

Baffled and uneasy with the image, he shook it off, turned back to logic and instinct. "Oh, yeah." Seth's eyes narrowed, went flat. "He'll try again."

Seth made it to Cade's at 8:14. His final meeting of the day, with the chief of police, had gone past seven, and that had barely given him time to get home, change and drive out again. He'd told himself half a dozen times that he'd be better off staying at home, putting the reports and files away and having a quiet evening to relax his mind.

The press conference set for nine sharp the next morning would be a trial by fire, and he needed to be sharp. Yet here he was, sitting in his car feeling ridiculously nervous and unsettled.

He'd tracked a homicidal junkie through a condemned tenement without breaking a sweat, with a steady pulse he'd interrogated cold, vicious killers—but now, as the white ball of the sun dipped low in the sky, he was as jittery as a schoolboy.

He hated cocktail parties. The inane conversations, the silly food, the buffed faces, all feigning enthusiasm or ennui, depending on their style.

But it wasn't the prospect of a few hours socializing with strangers that unnerved him. It was spending time with Grace without the buffer of the job between them.

He'd never had a woman affect him as she did. And he couldn't deny—at least to himself—that he had been deeply, uniquely affected, from the moment he saw her portrait.

It didn't help to tell himself she was shallow, spoiled, a woman used to men falling at her feet. It hadn't helped before he discovered she was much more than that, and it was certainly no good now.

He couldn't claim to understand her, but he was beginning to uncover all those layers and contrasts that made her who and what she was.

And he knew they would be lovers before the night was over.

He saw her step out of the house, a charge of electric blue from the short strapless dress molded to her body, the long, luxurious fall of ebony hair, the endless and perfect legs.

Did she shock every man's system, Seth wondered,

just the look of her? Or was he particularly, specifically vulnerable? He decided either answer would be hard to live with, and got out of his car.

Her head turned at the sound of his door, and that heart-stopping face bloomed with a smile. "I didn't think you were going to make it." She crossed to him, unhurried, and touched her mouth to his. "I'm glad you did."

"I'd said I'd call if I wouldn't be here."

"So you did." But she hadn't counted on it. She'd left the address of the party inside, just in case, but she'd resigned herself to spending the evening without him. She smiled again, smoothed a hand down the lapel of his suit. "I never wait by the phone. We're going to Georgetown. Shall we take my car, or yours?"

"I'll drive." Knowing she expected him to make some comment on her looks, he deliberately kept silent as he walked around the car to open her door.

She slipped in, her legs sliding silkily inside. He wanted his hands there, right there where the abbreviated hem of her dress kissed her thighs. Where the skin would be tender as a ripened peach and smooth as white satin.

He closed the door, walked back around the car and got behind the wheel. "Where in Georgetown?" was all he said.

It was a beautiful old house, with soaring ceilings, heavy antiques and deep, warm colors. The lights blazed down on important people, people of influence and wealth, who carried the scent of power under their perfumes and colognes.

She belonged, Seth thought. She'd melded with the

whole from the moment she stepped through the door to exchange sophisticated cheek brushes with the hostess.

Yet she stood apart. In the midst of all the sleek black, the fussy pastels, she was a bright blue flame daring anyone to touch and be burned.

Like the diamonds, he thought. Unique, potent... irresistible.

"Lieutenant Buchanan, isn't it?"

Seth shifted his gaze from Grace and looked at the short, balding man who was built like a boxer and dressed in Savile Row. "Yes. Mr. Rossi, counsel for the defense. If the defense has deep enough pockets."

Unoffended, Rossi chuckled. "I thought I recognized you. I've crossed you on the stand a few times. You're a tough nut. I've always believed I'd have gotten Tremaine off, or at least hung the jury, if I'd have been able to shake your testimony."

"He was guilty."

"As sin," Rossi agreed readily, "but I'd have hung that jury."

As Rossi started to rehash the trial, Seth resigned himself to talking shop.

Across the room, Grace took a glass from a passing waiter and listened to her hostess's gossip with half an ear. She knew when to chuckle, when to lift a brow, purse her lips, make some interesting comment. It was all routine.

She wanted to leave immediately. She wanted to get Seth out of that dark suit. She wanted her hands on him, all over him. Lust was creeping along her skin like a hot rash. Sips of champagne did nothing to cool her throat, and only added to the bubbling in her blood.

"My dear Sarah."

"Gregor, how lovely to see you."

Grace shifted, sipped, smiled at the sleek, dark man with the creamy voice who bent gallantly over their hostess's hand. Mediterranean, she judged, by the charm of the accent. Fiftyish, but fit.

"You're looking particularly wonderful tonight," he said, lingering over her hand. "And your hospitality, as always, is incomparable. And your guests." He turned smiling pale silvery-blue eyes on Grace. "Perfect."

"Gregor." Sarah simpered, fluttered, then turned to Grace. "I don't believe you've met Gregor, Grace. He's fatally charming, so be very careful. Ambassador De-Vane, I'd like to present Grace Fontaine, a dear friend."

"I am honored." He lifted Grace's hand, and his lips were warm and soft. "And enchanted."

"Ambassador?" Grace slipped easily into the role. "I thought ambassadors were old and stodgy. All the ones I've met have been. That is, up until now."

"I'll just leave you with Grace, Gregor. I see we have some late arrivals."

"I'm sure I'm in delightful hands." With obvious reluctance, he released Grace's fingers. "Are you perhaps a connection of Niles Fontaine?"

"He's an uncle, yes."

"Ah. I had the pleasure of meeting your uncle and his charming wife in Capri a few years ago. We have a mutual hobby, coins."

"Yes, Uncle Niles has quite a collection. He's mad for coins." Grace brushed her hair back, lifted it off her bare shoulder. "And where are you from, Ambassador DeVane?"

"Gregor, please, in such friendly surroundings. Then I might be permitted to call you Grace."

"Of course." Her smile warmed to suit the new intimacy.

"I doubt you would have heard of my tiny country. We are only a small dot in the sea, known chiefly for our olive oil and wine."

"Terresa?"

"Now I am flattered again that such a beautiful woman would know my humble country."

"It's a beautiful island. I was there briefly, two years ago, and very much enjoyed it. Terresa is a small jewel in the sea, dramatic cliffs to the west, lush vineyards in the east, and sandy beaches as fine as sugar."

He smiled at her, took her hand again. The connection was as unexpected as the woman, and he found himself compelled to touch. And to keep. "You must promise to return, to allow me to show you the country as it should be seen. I have a small villa in the west, and the view would almost be worthy of you."

"I'd love to see it. How difficult it must be to spend the summer in muggy Washington, when you could be enjoying the sea breezes of Terresa."

"Not at all difficult. Now." He skimmed a thumb over her knuckles. "I find the treasures of your country more and more appealing. Perhaps you would consider joining me one evening. Do you enjoy the opera?"

"Very much."

"Then you must allow me to escort you. Perhaps—" He broke off, a flicker of annoyance marring his smooth features as Seth stepped up to them.

"Ambassador Gregor DeVane of Terresa, allow me to introduce Lieutenant Seth Buchanan."

"You are military," DeVane said, offering a hand.

"Cop," Seth said shortly. He didn't like the ambassador's looks. Not one bit. When he saw DeVane with Grace, he'd had a fast, turbulent impulse to reach for his weapon. But, strangely, his instinctive movement hadn't been up, to his gun, but lower on the side. Where a man would carry a sword.

"Ah, the police." DeVane blinked in surprise, though he already had a full dossier on Seth Buchanan. "How fascinating. I hope you'll forgive me for saying it's my fondest wish never to require your services." Smoothly DeVane slipped a glass from a passing tray, handed it to Seth, then took one for himself. "But perhaps we should drink to crime. Without it, you'd be obsolete."

Seth eyed him levelly. There was recognition, inexplicable, and utterly adversarial, when their eyes locked, pale silver to dark gold. "I prefer drinking to justice."

"Of course. To the scales, shall we say, and their constant need for balancing?" Gregor drank, then inclined his head. "You'll excuse me, Lieutenant Buchanan, I've yet to greet my host. I was—" he turned to Grace and kissed her hand again "—beautifully distracted from my duty."

"It was a pleasure to meet you, Gregor."

"I hope to see you again." He looked deeply into her eyes, held the moment. "Very soon."

The moment he turned away, Grace shivered. There had been something almost possessive in that last, long stare. "What an odd and charming man," she murmured.

Energy was shooting through Seth, the need to do

battle. His system sparked with it. "Do you usually let odd and charming men drool over you in public?"

It was small of her, Grace supposed, but she enjoyed a kick of satisfaction at the annoyance in Seth's tone. "Of course. Since I so dislike them drooling over me in private." She turned into him, so that their bodies brushed lightly. Then slanted a look up from under that thick curtain of lashes. "You don't plan to drool, do you?"

He could have damned her for shooting his system from slow burn up to sizzle. "Finish your drink," he said abruptly, "and say your goodbyes. We're going."

Grace gave an exaggerated sigh. "Oh, I do love being dominated by a strong man."

"We're about to put that to the test." He took her half-finished drink, set it aside. "Let's go."

DeVane watched them leave, studied the way Seth pressed a hand to the small of Grace's back to steer her through the crowd. He would have to punish the cop for touching her.

Grace was his property now, DeVane thought as he gritted his teeth painfully tight to suppress the rage. She was meant for him. He'd known it from the moment he took her hand and looked into her eyes. She was perfect, flawless. It wasn't just the Three Stars that were fated for him, but the woman who had held one, perhaps caressed it, as well.

She would understand their power. She would add to it.

Along with the Three Stars of Mithra, DeVane vowed, Grace Fontaine would be the treasure of his collection.

She would bring the Stars to him. And then she would belong to him. Forever.

As she stepped outside, Grace felt another shudder sprint down her spine. She hunched her shoulder blades against it, looked back. Through the tall windows filled with light she could see the guests mingling.

And she saw DeVane, quite clearly. For a moment, she would have sworn their eyes met—but this time there was no charm. An irrational sense of fear lodged in her stomach, had her turning quickly away again.

When Seth pulled open the car door, she got in without complaint or comment. She wanted to go, to get away from those brilliantly lit windows and the man who seemed to watch her from beyond them. Briskly she rubbed the chill from her arms.

"You wouldn't be cold if you'd worn clothes." Seth stuck the key in the ignition.

The single remark, issued with cold and savage control, made her chuckle and chased the chill away. "Why, Lieutenant, and here I was wondering how long you would let me keep on what I am wearing."

"Not a hell of a lot longer," he promised, and pulled out into the street.

"Good." Determined to see that he kept that promise, she squirmed over and began to nibble his ear. "Let's break some laws," she whispered.

"I could already charge myself with intent."

She laughed again, quick, breathless, and had him hard as iron.

He wasn't sure how he managed to handle the car, much less drive it through traffic out of D.C. and back into Maryland. She worked his tie off, undid half the buttons of his shirt. Her hands were everywhere, and her mouth teased his ear, his neck, his jaw, while she murmured husky promises, suggestions.

The fantasies she wove with unerring skill had the blood beating painfully in his loins.

He pulled to a jerky stop in his driveway, then dragged her across the seat. She lost one shoe in the car and the other halfway up the walk as he half carried her. Her laughter, dark, wild, damning, roared in his head. He all but broke his own door down to get her inside. The instant they were, he pushed her back against the wall and savaged her mouth.

He wasn't thinking. Couldn't think. It was all primal, violent need. In the darkened hallway, he hiked up her skirt with impatient hands, found the thin, lacy barrier beneath and ripped it aside. He freed himself, then, gripping her hips, plunged into her where they stood.

She cried out, not in protest, not in shock at the almost brutal treatment. But in pure, overwhelming pleasure. She locked herself around him, let him drive her ruthlessly, crest after torrential crest. And met him thrust for greedy, desperate thrust.

It was mindless and hot and vicious. And it was all that mattered. Sheer animal need. Violent animal release.

Her body shattered, went limp, as she felt him pour into her.

He slapped his hand against the wall to keep his balance, struggled to slow his breathing, clear his fevered brain. They were no more than a step inside his door, he realized, and he'd mounted her like a rutting bull.

There was no point in apologies, he thought. They'd both wanted fast and urgent. No, *wanted* was too tame a word, he decided. They'd craved it, the way starving animals craved meat.

But he'd never treated a woman with less care, or so completely ignored the consequences.

"I meant to get you out of that dress," he managed, and was pleased when she laughed.

"We'll get around to it."

"There's something else I didn't get around to." He eased back, studied her face in the dim light. "Is that going to be a problem?"

She understood. "No." And though it was rash and foolish, she felt a twinge of regret that there would be no quickening of life inside her as a result of their carelessness. "I take care of myself."

"I didn't want this to happen." He took her chin in his hand. "I should have been able to keep my hands off you."

Her eyes glimmered in the dark—confident and amused. "I hope you don't expect me to be sorry you didn't. I want them on me again. I want mine on you."

"While they are." He lifted her chin a little higher. "No one else's are. I don't share."

Her lips curved slowly as she kept his gaze. "Neither do I."

He nodded, accepting. "Let's go upstairs," he said, and swept her into his arms.

Chapter 7

He switched on the light as he carried her into his room. This time he needed to see her, to know when her eyes clouded or darkened, to witness those flickers of pleasure or shock.

This time he would remember man's advantage over the animal, and that the mind and heart could play a part.

She got a sense of a room of average size, simple buff-colored curtains at the windows, clean-lined furniture without color, a large bed with a navy spread tucked in with precise, military tidiness.

There were paintings on the walls that she told herself she would study later, when her heart wasn't skipping. Scenes both urban and rural were depicted in misty, dreamy watercolors that made a personal contrast to the practical room.

But all thoughts of art and decor fled when he set her on her feet beside the bed. She reached out, undid the final buttons of his shirt, while he shrugged out of his jacket. Her brows lifted when she noted he wore his shoulder holster.

"Even to a cocktail party?"

"Habit," he said simply, and took it off, hung it over a chair. He caught the look in her eye. "Is it a problem?"

"No. I was just thinking how it suits you. And wondering if you look as sexy putting it on as you do taking it off." Then she turned, scooped her hair over her shoulder. "I could use some help."

He let his gaze wander over her back. Instead of reaching for the zipper, he drew her against him and lowered his mouth to her bare shoulder. She sighed, tipped her head back.

"That's even better."

"Round one took the edge off," he murmured, then slid his hands around her waist, and up, until they cupped her breasts. "I want you whimpering, wanting, weak."

His thumbs brushed the curves just above the bold blue silk. Focused on the sensation, she reached back, linked her arms around his neck. Her body began to move, timed to his strokes, but when she tried to turn, he held her in place.

She moaned, shifted restlessly, when his fingers curved under her bodice, the backs teasing her nipples, making them heat and ache. "I want to touch you."

"Whimpering," he repeated, and ran his hands down her dress to the hem, then beneath. "Wanting." And cupped her. "Weak." Pierced her.

The orgasm flooded her, one long, slow wave that

swamped the senses. The whimper he'd waited for shuddered through her lips.

He toed off his shoes, then lowered her zipper inch by inch. His fingers barely brushed her skin as he spread the parted material, eased it down her body until it pooled at her feet. He turned her, stepped back.

. She wore only a garter, in the same hot blue as the dress, with stockings so sheer they appeared to be little more than mist. Her body was a fantasy of generous curves, and satin skin. Her hair fell like wild black rain over her shoulders.

"Too many men have told you you're beautiful for it to matter that I say it."

"Just tell me you want me. That matters."

"I want you, Grace." He stepped to her again, took her into his arms, but instead of the greedy kiss she'd expected, he gave her one to slowly drown in. Her arms clutched around him, then went limp, at this new assault to the senses.

"Kiss me again," she murmured when his lips wandered to her throat. "Just like that. Again."

So his mouth met hers, let her sink a second time. With a dreamy hum of pleasure, she slipped his shirt away, let her hands explore. It was lovely to be savored, to be given the gift of a slow kindling flame, to feel the control slip out of her hands into his. And to trust.

He let himself learn her body inch by generous inch. Pleasured them both by possessing those full firm breasts, first with hands, then with mouth. He lowered his hands, flicked the hooks of her stockings free one by one—hearing her quick catch of breath each time. Then slid his hands under the filmy fabric to flesh.

Warm, smooth. He lowered her to the bed, felt her

body yield beneath his. Soft, willing. Her lips answered his. Eager, generous.

They watched each other in the light. Moved together. First a sigh, then a groan. She found muscle, the rough skin of an old scar, and the taste of man. Shifting, she drew his slacks down, feasted on his chest as she undressed him. When he took her breasts again, pulled her closer to suckle, her arms quivered and her hair drifted forward to curtain them both.

She felt the heat rising, sliding through her blood like a fever, until her breath was short and shallow. She could hear herself saying his name, over and over, as he patiently built her toward the edge.

Her eyes went cobalt, fascinating him. Her pillow-soft lips trembled, her glorious body quaked. Even as the need for release clawed at him, he continued to savor. Until he finally shifted her to her back and, with his eyes locked on hers, buried himself inside her.

She arched upward, her hands fisting in the sheets, her body stunned with pleasure. "Seth." Her breath expelled in a rush, burned her lungs. "It's never… Not like this. Seth—"

Before she could speak again, he closed her mouth with his and took her.

When sleep came, Grace dreamed she was in her garden in the mountains, with the woods, thick and green and cool, surrounding her. The hollyhocks loomed taller than her head and bloomed in deep, rich reds and clear, shimmering whites. A hummingbird, shimmering sapphire and emerald, drank from a trumpet flower. Cosmos and coneflowers, dahlias and zinnias made a cheerful wave of mixed colors.

Pansies turned their exotic little faces toward the sun and smiled.

Here she was happy, at peace with herself. Alone, but never lonely. Here there was no sound but the song of the breeze through the leaves, the hum of bees, the faint music of the creek bubbling over rocks.

She watched deer walk quietly out of the woods to drink from the slow-moving creek, their hooves lost in the low-lying mist that hugged the ground. The dawn light shimmered like silver, sparkled off the soft dew, caught rainbows in the mist.

Content, she walked through her flowers, fingers brushing blooms, scents rising up to please her senses. She saw the glint among the blossoms, the bright, beckoning blue, and, stooping, plucked the stone from the ground.

Power shimmered in her hand. It was a clean, flowing sensation, pure as water, potent as wine. For a moment, she stood very still, her hand open. The stone resting in her palm danced with the morning light.

Hers to guard, she thought. To protect. And to give.

When she heard the rustle in the woods, she turned, smiling. It would be him, she was certain. She'd waited for him all her life, wanted so desperately to welcome him, to walk into his arms and know they would wrap around her.

She stepped forward, the stone warming her palm, the faint vibrations from it traveling like music up her arm and toward her heart. She would give it to him, she thought. She would give him everything she had, everything she was. For love had no boundaries.

All at once, the light changed, hazed over. The air went cold and whipped with the wind. By the creek, the deer lifted their heads, alert, alarmed, then turned as one and fled into the sheltering trees. The hum of bees died into a rumble of thunder, and lightning snaked over the dingy sky.

There in the darkened wood, close, too close to where her flowers bloomed, something moved stealthily. Her fingers clutched reflexively, closing fast over the stone. And through the leaves she saw eyes, bright, greedy. And watching.

The shadows parted and opened the path to her.

"No." Frantic, Grace pushed at the hands that held her. "I won't give it to you. It's not for you."

"Easy." Seth pulled her up, stroked her hair. "Just a nightmare. Shake it off now."

"Watching me…" She moaned it, pressed her face into his strong, bare shoulder, drew in his scent and was soothed. "He's watching me. In the woods, watching me."

"No, you're here with me." Her heart was pounding hard enough to bring real concern. Seth tightened his grip, as if to slow it and block the tremors that shook her. "It's a dream. There's no one here but me. I've got you."

"Don't let him touch me. I'll die if he touches me."

"I won't." He tipped her face back. "I've got you," he repeated, and warmed her trembling lips with his.

"Seth." Relief shuddered through her as she clutched at him. "I was waiting for you. In the garden, waiting for you."

"Okay. I'm here now." To protect, he thought. And then to cherish. Shaken by the depth of that, he eased her backward, brushed the tumbled hair away from her face. "Must have been a bad one. Do you have a lot of nightmares?"

"What?" Disoriented, trapped between the dream and the present, she only stared at him.

"Do you want the light?" He didn't wait for an answer, but reached around her to switch on the bedside lamp. Grace turned her face away from the glare, pressed her fisted hand against her heart. "Relax now. Come on." He took her hand, started to open her fingers.

"No." She jerked it back. "He wants it."

"Wants what?"

"The Star. He's coming for it, and for me. He's coming."

"Who?"

"I don't...I don't know." Baffled now, she looked down at her hand, slowly opened it. "I was holding the stone." She could still feel the heat, the weight. "I had it. I found it."

"It was a dream. The diamonds are locked in a vault. They're safe." He tipped a finger under her chin until her eyes met his. "You're safe."

"It was a dream." Saying it aloud brought both relief and embarrassment. "I'm sorry."

"It's all right." He studied her, saw that her face was white, her eyes were fragile. Something moved inside him, shifted, urged his hand to reach out, stroke that pale cheek. "You've had a rough few days, haven't you?"

It was just that, the quiet understanding in his voice, that had her eyes filling. She closed them to will back the tears and took careful breaths. The pressure in her chest was unbearable. "I'm going to get some water."

He simply reached out and drew her in. She'd hidden all that fear and grief and weariness inside her very well, he realized. Until now. "Why don't you let it go?"

Her breath hitched, tore. "I just need to—"

"Let it go," he repeated, and settled her head on his shoulder.

She shuddered once, then clung. Then wept.

He offered no words. He just held her.

At eight the next morning, Seth dropped her off at Cade's. She'd protested the hour at which he shook her out of sleep, tried to curl herself into the mattress. He'd dealt with that by simply picking her up, carrying her into the shower and turning it on. Cold.

He'd given her exactly thirty minutes to pull herself together, then packed her into the car.

"The gestapo could have taken lessons from you," she commented as he pulled up behind M.J.'s car. "My hair's still wet."

"I didn't have the hour to spare it must take to dry all that."

"I didn't even have time to put my makeup on."

"You don't need it."

"I suppose that's your idea of a compliment."

"No, it's just a fact."

She turned to him, looking arousing, rumpled and erotic in the strapless dress. "You, on the other hand, look all pressed and tidy."

"I didn't take twenty minutes in the shower." She'd sung in the shower, he remembered. Unbelievably off-key. Thinking of it made him smile. "Go away. I've got work to do."

She pouted, then reached for her purse. "Well,

thanks for the lift, Lieutenant." Then laughed when he pushed her back against the seat and gave her the long, thorough kiss she'd been hoping for.

"That almost makes up for the one miserly cup of coffee you allowed me this morning." She caught his bottom lip between her teeth, and her eyes sparkled into his. "I want to see you tonight."

"I'll come by. If I can."

"I'll be here." She opened the door, shot him a look over her shoulder. "If I can."

Unable to resist, he watched her every sauntering step toward the house. The minute she closed the front door behind her, he shut his eyes.

My God, he thought, he was in love with her. And it was totally impossible.

Inside, Grace all but danced down the hall. She was in love. And it was glorious. It was new and fresh and the first. It was what she'd been waiting for her entire life. Her face glowed as she stepped into the kitchen and found Bailey and Cade at the table, sharing coffee.

"Good morning, troops." She all but sang it as she headed to the coffeepot.

"Good morning to you." Cade tucked his tongue in his cheek. "I like your pajamas."

Laughing, she carried her cup to the table, then leaned down and kissed him full on the mouth. "I just adore you. Bailey, I just adore this man. You'd better snap him up quick, before I get ideas."

Bailey smiled dreamily into her coffee, then looked up, eyes shining and damp. "We're getting married in two weeks."

"What?" Grace bobbled her mug, sloshed coffee

dangerously close to the rim. "What?" she repeated, and sat heavily.

"He won't wait."

"Why should I?" Reaching over the table, Cade took Bailey's hand. "I love you."

"Married." Grace looked down at their joined hands. A perfect match, she thought, and let out a shaky sigh. "That's wonderful. That's incredibly wonderful." Laying a hand over theirs, she stared into Cade's eyes. And saw exactly what she needed to see. "You'll be good to her." It wasn't a question, it was acceptance.

After giving his hand a quick squeeze, she sat back. "Well, a wedding to plan, and a whole two weeks to do it. That ought to make us all insane."

"It's just going to be a small ceremony," Bailey began. "Here at the house."

"I'm going to say one word." Cade put a plea in his voice. *"Elopement."*

"No." With a shake of her head, Bailey drew back, picked up her mug. "I'm not going to start our life together by insulting your family."

"They're not human. You can't insult the inhuman. Muffy will bring the beasts with her."

"Don't call your niece and nephew beasts."

"Wait a minute." Grace held up a hand. Her brows knit. "Muffy? Is that Muffy Parris Westlake? She's your sister?"

"Guilty."

Grace managed to suppress most of the snort of laughter. "That would make Doro Parris Lawrence your other sister." She rolled her eyes, picturing the two annoying and self-important Washington hostesses. "Bailey, run for your life. Go to Vegas. You and

Cade can get married by a nice Elvis-impersonator judge and have a delightful, quiet life in the desert. Change your names. Never come back."

"See?" Pleased, Cade slapped a hand on the table. "She knows them."

"Stop it, both of you." Bailey refused to laugh, though her voice trembled with it. "We'll have a small, dignified ceremony—with Cade's family." She smiled at Grace. "And mine."

"Keep working on her." Cade rose. "I've got a couple things to do before I go into the office."

Grace picked up her coffee again. "I don't know his family well," she told Bailey. "I've managed to avoid that little pleasure, but I can tell you from what I do know, you've got the cream of the crop."

"I love him so much, Grace. I know it's all happened quickly, but—"

"What does time have to do with it?" Because she knew they were both about to get teary, she leaned forward. "We have to discuss the important, the vital, aspects of this situation, Bailey." She took a deep breath. "When do we go shopping?"

M.J. staggered in to the sound of laughter, and scowled at both of them. "I hate cheerful people in the morning." She poured coffee, tried to inhale it, then turned to study Grace. "Well, well," she said dryly. "Apparently you and the cop got to know each other last night."

"Well enough that I know he's more than a badge and an attitude." Irritated, she pushed her mug aside. "What have you got against him?"

"Other than the fact he's cold and arrogant, superior and stiff, nothing at all. Jack says they call him the Machine. Small wonder."

"I always find it interesting," Grace said coolly, "when people only skim the surface, then judge another human being. All those traits you just listed describe a man you don't know."

"M.J., drink your coffee." Bailey rose to get the cream. "You know you're not fit to be around until you've had a half a gallon."

M.J. shook her head, fisted a hand on a hip covered with a tattered T-shirt and equally tattered shorts. "Just because you slept with him, doesn't mean you know him, either. You're usually a hell of a lot more careful than that, Grace. You might let other people assume you pop into bed with a new guy every other night, but we know better. What the hell were you thinking of?"

"I was thinking of *me*," she shot back. "I wanted him. I needed him. He's the first man who's ever really touched me. And I'm not going to let you stand there and make something beautiful into something cheap."

No one spoke for a moment. Bailey stood near the table, the creamer in one hand. M.J. slowly straightened from the counter, whistled out a breath. "You're falling for him." Staggered, she raked a hand through her hair. "You're really falling for him."

"I've already hit the ground with a splat. So what?"

"I'm sorry." M.J. struggled to adjust. She didn't have to like the man, she told herself. She just had to love Grace. "There must be something to him, if he got to you. Are you sure you're okay with it?"

"No, I'm not sure I'm okay with it." Temper drained, and doubt snuck in. "I don't know why it's happened or what to do about it. I just know it is. It wasn't just sex." She remembered how he had held her while she cried. How he'd left the light on for her without her having to ask. "I've been waiting for him all my life."

"I know what that means." Bailey set the creamer down, took Grace's hand. "Exactly."

"So do I." With a sigh, M.J. stepped forward. "What's happening to us? We're three sensible women, and suddenly we're guarding ancient mythical stones, running from bad guys and falling headlong into love with men we've just met. It's crazy."

"It's right," Bailey said quietly. "You know it feels right."

"Yeah." M.J. laid her hand over theirs. "I guess it does."

It wasn't easy for Grace to go back into her house. This time, though, she wasn't alone. M.J. and Jack flanked her like bookends.

"Man." Scanning the wreck of the living area, M.J. hissed out a breath. "I thought they did a number on my place. Of course, you've got a lot more toys to play with."

Then her gaze focused on the splintered railing. And the outline below. "You don't want to do this now, Grace."

"The police cleared the scene. I have to get started on it sometime."

M.J. shook her head. "Where?"

"I'll start in the bedroom." Grace managed a smile. "I'm about to make my dry cleaner a millionaire."

"I'll see what I can do with the railing," Jack told her. "Jury-rig something so it's safe until you have it rebuilt."

"I'd appreciate it."

"Go on up," M.J. suggested. "I'll get a broom. And a bulldozer." She waited until Grace was upstairs before she turned to Jack. "I'm going to do this down here. Get rid of...things." Her gaze wandered to the outline. "She shouldn't have to handle that."

He leaned down to kiss her forehead. "You're a stand-up pal, M.J."

"Yeah, that's me." She inhaled sharply. "Let's see if we can dig up the stereo or the TV out of this mess. I could use some racket in here."

It took most of the afternoon before Grace was satisfied that the house was cleared out enough to call in her cleaning service. She wanted every room scrubbed before she lived there again.

And she was determined to do just that. To live, to be at home, to face whatever ghosts remained. To prove to herself that she could, she separated from M.J. and Jack and went shopping for the first replacements. Then, because the entire day had left her feeling raw, she stopped by Salvini.

She needed to see Bailey.

And she needed to see the Stars.

Once she was buzzed in, she found Bailey up in her office on the phone. With a smile, Bailey gestured her in. "Yes, Dr. Linstrum, I'm faxing the report to you now, and I'll bring you the original personally before five. I can complete the final tests you've ordered tomorrow."

She listened a moment, ran a finger down the soapstone elephant on her desk. "No, I'm fine. I appreciate your concern, and your understanding. The Stars are my priority. I'll have full copies of all the reports for your insurance carrier by end of business day Friday. Yes, thank you. Goodbye."

"You're working very quickly," Grace commented.

"Despite all that happened, hardly any time was lost. And everyone will feel more comfortable when the stones are in the museum."

"I want to see them again, Bailey." She let out a little laugh. "It's silly, but I really need to. I had this dream last night—nightmare, really."

"What kind of dream?"

Grace sat on the edge of the desk and told her. Though her voice was steady, her fingers tapped with nerves.

"I had dreams, too," Bailey murmured. "I'm still having them. So is M.J."

Uneasy, Grace shifted. "Like mine?"

"Similar enough to be more than coincidence." She rose, held out a hand for Grace's. "Let's go take a look."

"You're not breaking any laws, are you?"

As they walked downstairs together, Bailey sent her an amused look. "I think after what I've already done, this is a minor infraction." She tried to block it, but a shudder escaped as they descended the last flight of steps, under which she'd once hidden from a killer.

"Are you going to be all right here?" Instinctively Grace hooked an arm around Bailey's shoulder. "I hate thinking of what happened, and now thinking of you working here, remembering it."

"It's getting better. Grace, I've had my stepbrothers cremated. Or rather, Cade took care of the arrangements. He wouldn't let me handle any of it."

"Good for him. You don't owe them anything, Bailey. You never did. We're your family. We always will be."

"I know."

She passed into the vault room and approached the massive reinforced-steel doors. The security system was complex and intricate, and even with the ease of long practice, it took Bailey three full minutes to disengage.

"Maybe I ought to have one of these installed in my house," Grace said lightly. "That bastard popped my library safe like it was a gumball machine. He must have fenced the jewelry fast. I hate losing the pieces you made for me."

"I'll make you more. In fact—" Bailey picked up a square velvet box "—let's start now."

Curious, Grace opened the box to a pair of heavy gold earrings. The smooth crescent-shaped gold was studded with stones in deep, dark hues of emerald, ruby and sapphire.

"Bailey, they're beautiful."

"I'd just finished them before…well, before. As soon as I had, I knew they were yours."

"It's not my birthday."

"I thought you were dead." Bailey's voice shook, then strengthened when Grace looked up. "I thought I would never see you again. So let's consider these a celebration of the rest of our lives."

Grace removed the simple studs in her ears, began to replace them with Bailey's gift. "When I'm not wearing them, I'll keep them with my mother's jewelry. The things that matter most."

"They look perfect on you. I knew they would." Bailey turned, took the heavy padded box from its shelf in the vault. Holding it between them, she opened it.

Grace let out a long, uneven sigh. "I honestly thought one would be gone. I would drive up to the mountains and find it in my garden, sitting on the ground beneath the flowers. It was so real, Bailey."

Reaching out, Grace took a stone. Her stone. "I felt it in my hand, just as I do now. It pulsed in my hand like a heart." She laughed a little, but the sound was hollow. "My heart. That's what it seemed like. I didn't realize that until now. It was like holding my own heart."

"There's a link." A little pale, Bailey took another stone from the box. "I don't understand it, but I know it. This is the Star I had. If M.J. was here, she'd have picked hers."

"I never thought I believed in this sort of thing." Grace turned the stone in her hand. "I was wrong. It's incredibly easy to believe it. To know it. Are we protecting them, Bailey, or are they protecting us?"

"I like to think it's both. They brought me Cade." Gently, she replaced her stone, touched a fingertip to the second Star in its hollow. "Brought M.J. Jack." Her face softened. "I opened up the showroom for them a little while ago," she told Grace. "Jack dragged her in and bought her a ring."

"A ring?" Grace lifted a hand to her heart as it swelled. "An engagement ring?"

"An engagement ring. She argued the whole time, kept telling him not to be a jerk. She didn't need any ring. He just ignored her and pointed to this lovely green tourmaline—square-cut, with diamond baguettes. I designed it a few months ago, thinking that it would make a wonderful, nontraditional engagement ring for the right woman. He knew she was the right woman."

"He's perfect for her." Grace brushed a tear from her lashes and beamed. "I knew it as soon as I saw them together."

"I wish you'd seen them today. There she is, grumbling, rolling her eyes, insisting all this fuss is a waste of time and effort. Then he put that ring on her finger. She got this big, sloppy grin on her face. You know the one."

"Yeah." And she could see it, perfectly. "I'm so happy for her, for you. It's like all that love was there, waiting, and the stones…" She looked down at them again. "They opened the door for it."

"And you, Grace? Have they opened the door for you?"

"I don't know if I'm ready for that." Nerves suddenly sprang to her fingertips. She laid the stone back in its bed. "Seth certainly wouldn't be. I don't think he'd believe in magic of any sort. And as for love… even if that door is wide open and the opportunity is there, he's not a man to fall easily."

"Easy or not—" Bailey closed the lid, replaced the box "—when you're meant to fall, you fall. He's yours, Grace. I saw that in your eyes this morning."

"Well." Grace swallowed the nerves. "I think I may wait awhile to let him in on that."

Chapter 8

There were flowers waiting for her when Grace returned to Cade's. A gorgeous crystal vase was filled with long spears of paper-white long-stemmed roses. Her heart thudded foolishly into her throat as she snatched up the card, tore open the envelope.

Then it deflated and sank.

Not from Seth, she noted. Of course, it had been silly of her to think that he'd have indulged in such a romantic and extravagant gesture. The card read simply:

Until we meet again,
Gregor

The ambassador with the oddly compelling eyes, she mused, and leaned forward to sniff at the tender, just-opening blooms. It had been sweet of him, she told herself. A bit over-the-top, as there were easily three dozen roses in the vase, but sweet.

And she was irritated to realize that if they had been from Seth, she would have mooned over them like a starstruck teenager, would likely have pressed one between the pages of a book, even shed a few tears. She berated herself for being six times a fool.

If these appalling highs and lows were side effects of being in love, Grace thought she could have waited quite a bit longer to experience the sensation. She was just about to toss the card on the table when the phone rang.

She hesitated, as both Cade's and Jack's cars were in the drive, but when the phone rang the third time, she picked it up. "Parris residence."

"Is Grace Fontaine available?" The crisp tones of a well-trained secretary sounded in her ear. "Ambassador DeVane calling."

"Yes, this is she."

"One moment, please, Ms. Fontaine."

Lips pursed thoughtfully, Grace flipped the edge of the card against her palm. The man certainly had had no trouble tracking her down, Grace mused. And just how was she going to handle him?

"Grace." His voice flowed through the phone. "How delightful to speak with you again."

"Gregor." She flipped her hair behind her shoulder, edged a hip onto the table. "How extravagant of you. I've just walked in to your roses." She tipped one down, sniffed again. "They're glorious."

"Merely a token. I was disappointed not to have more time with you last evening. You left so early."

She thought of the wild ride to Seth's, the wilder sex. "I had…a previous engagement."

"Perhaps we can make up for it tomorrow evening. I have a box at the theater. *Tosca*. It's such a beautiful tragedy. There's nothing I would enjoy more than sharing it with you, then a late supper, perhaps."

"It sounds lovely." She rolled her eyes toward the flowers. Oh, dear, she thought. This would never do. "I'm so terribly sorry, Gregor, but I'm not free." With no regret whatsoever, she set the card aside. "Actually, I'm involved with someone, quite seriously."

For me, in any case, she thought. Then she looked through the glass panels of the front door, and her face lit up with surprise and pleasure when she saw Seth's car pull in.

"I see." She was too busy trying to steady her abruptly dancing pulse to notice how his voice had chilled. "Your escort of last evening."

"Yes. I'm terribly flattered, Gregor, and if I were any less involved, I'd leap at the invitation. I hope you'll forgive me, and understand."

Struggling not to squirm with delight, she crooked her finger in invitation as Seth stepped up to the door.

"Of course. If your circumstances change, I hope you'll reconsider."

"I certainly will." With a sultry smile, she walked her fingers up Seth's chest. "And thank you again, Gregor, so much, for the flowers. They're divine."

"It was my pleasure," he said, and his hands balled into bone-white fists as he hung up the receiver.

Humiliated, he thought, snapping his teeth together, grinding them viciously. Rejected for a suitful of muscles and a badge.

She would pay, he promised himself, taking her photo from his file and gently tapping a well-manicured finger against it. She would pay dearly. And soon.

With the ambassador completely forgotten the moment the connection was broken, Grace tipped her face up to Seth's. "Hello, handsome."

He didn't kiss her, but looked at the flowers, then at the card she'd tossed carelessly beside them. "Another conquest?"

"Apparently." She heard the cold distance in his tone and wasn't certain whether to be flattered or annoyed. She opted for a different tack altogether, and purred. "The ambassador was interested in an evening at the opera and...whatever."

The spurt of jealousy infuriated him. It was a new experience, and one he detested. It left him helpless, made him want to drag her out to his car by the hair, cart her off, lock her up where only he could see and touch and taste.

But more, there was fear, for her. A bone-deep sense of danger.

"It seems the ambassador—and you—move quickly."

No, she realized, the temper was going to come. There was no stopping it. She eased off the table, her smile an icy dare. "I move however it suits me. You should know."

"Yes." He dipped his hands into his pockets to keep them off her. "I should. I do."

Crushed, she angled her chin, aimed those laser blue eyes. "Which am I now, Lieutenant? The whore or the goddess? The ivory princess atop the pedestal, or the tramp? I've been them all—it just depends on the man and how he chooses to look."

"I'm looking at you," he said calmly. "And I don't know what I see."

"Let me know when you make up your mind." She started to move around him, came up short when he took her arm. "Don't push me." She tossed her head so that her hair flew out, settled.

"I could say the same, Grace."

She drew in one hot, deep breath, shoved his hand aside. "If you're interested, I gave the ambassador my regrets and told him I was involved with someone." She flashed a frigid smile and swung toward the stairs. "That, apparently, was my mistake."

He scowled after her, considered striding up the stairs of a house that wasn't his own and finishing the confrontation—one way or the other. Appalled, he pinched the bridge of his nose between his thumb and forefinger and tried to squeeze off the bitter headache plaguing him.

His day had been grueling, and had ended ten long hours after it began, with him staring at the group of photos on his board. Photos of the dead who were waiting for him to find the connection.

And he was already furious with himself because he'd already begun to run a search for data on Gregor DeVane. He couldn't be sure if he had done so due to a basic cop's hunch, or a man's territorial instinct. Or the dreams. It was a question, and a conflict, he'd never had to face before.

But one answer was clear as glass. He'd been out of line with Grace. He was still standing by the foyer table, frowning at the steps and weighing his options, when Cade strolled in from the rear of the house.

"Buchanan." More than a little surprised to see the

homicide lieutenant standing in his foyer scowling, Cade stopped, scratched his jaw. "Ah, I didn't know you were here."

He had no business being there, Seth reminded himself. "Sorry. Grace let me in."

"Oh." After one beat, Cade pinpointed the source of the heat still flashing in the air. "Oh," he said again, and wisely controlled a grin. "Fine. Something I can do for you?"

"No. I'm just leaving."

"Have a spat?"

Seth turned his head, met Cade's obviously amused eyes blandly. "Excuse me?"

"Just a wild stab in the dark. What did you do to tick her off?" Though Seth didn't answer, Cade noted that his gaze shifted briefly to the roses. "Oh, yeah. Guess you didn't send them, huh? If some guy sent Bailey three dozen white roses, I'd probably have to stuff them down his throat, one at a time."

It was the gleam of appreciation that flashed briefly in Seth's eyes that made Cade decide to revise his stance. Maybe he could like Lieutenant Seth Buchanan after all.

"Want a beer?"

The casual and friendly invitation threw Seth off balance. "I— No, I was leaving."

"Come on out back. Jack and I already popped a couple of tops. We're going to fire up the grill and show the women how real men cook." Cade's grin spread charmingly. "Besides, oiling yourself with a couple of brews will make it easier for you to crawl. You're going to crawl anyway, so you might as well be comfortable."

Seth hissed out a breath. "Why the hell not?"

* * *

Grace stayed stubbornly in her room for an hour. She could hear laughter, music, and the silly whack of mallets striking balls as people played an enthusiastic game of croquet. She knew Seth's car was still in the drive, and had promised herself she wouldn't go back down until it was gone.

But she was feeling deprived, and hungry.

Since she'd already changed into shorts and a thin cotton shirt, she paused at the mirror only long enough to freshen her lipstick, spritz on some perfume. Just to make him suffer, she told herself, then sauntered downstairs and out onto the patio.

Steaks were smoking on the grill with Cade at the helm wielding an enormous barbecue fork. Bailey and Jack were arguing over the croquet match, and M.J. was sulking at a picnic table while she nibbled on potato chips.

"Jack knocked me out of the game," she complained, and gestured with her beer. "I still say he cheated."

"Any time you lose," Grace pointed out as she picked up a chip, "it's because someone cheated." Then she slid her gaze to Seth.

He'd taken off his tie, she noted, and his jacket. He still wore his holster. She imagined that was because he didn't feel comfortable hanging his gun over a tree branch. He, too, had a beer in his hand, and was watching the game with apparent interest.

"You still here?"

"Yeah." He'd had two beers, but didn't think crawling was going to be any more comfortable with the lubricant. "I've been invited to dinner."

"Isn't that cozy?" Grace spied what she recognized

as a pitcher of M.J.'s special margaritas and poured herself a glass. The taste was tart, icy, and perfect. In dismissal, she wandered over to the grill to kibitz.

"I know what I'm doing," Cade was saying, and shifted to guard his territory as Seth joined them. "I marinated these vegetable kabobs personally. Go away and leave this to a man."

"I was merely asking if you preferred your mushrooms blackened."

Cade sent her a withering look. "Get her off my back, Seth. An artist can't work with critics breathing down his neck and picking on his mushrooms."

"Let's go over here." Seth took her elbow, and was braced for her jerk. He kept his grip firm and hauled her away into the rose garden.

"I don't want to talk to you," Grace said furiously.

"You don't have to talk. I'll talk." But it took him a minute. Apologies didn't come easily to a man who made it a habit not to make mistakes. "I'm sorry. I overreacted."

She said nothing, simply folded her arms and waited.

"You want more?" He nodded, didn't bother to sigh. "I was jealous, an atypical reaction for me, and I handled it poorly. I apologize."

Grace shook her head. "That's the weakest excuse for an apology I've ever heard. Not the words, Seth, the delivery. But fine, I'll accept it in the same spirit it was offered."

"What do you want from me?" he demanded, frustrated enough to raise his voice and grab her arms. "What the hell do you want?"

"That." She tossed back her head. "Just that. A little emotion, a little passion. You can take your cardboard-stiff apology and stuff it, just like you can stuff the cold, deliberate and dispassionate routine you gave me over the flowers. That icy control doesn't cut it with me. If you feel something—whatever the hell it is— then let me know."

She sucked in her breath, stunned, when he yanked her against him, savaged her mouth with heat and anger and need. She twisted once and was hauled roughly back. Then was left weak and singed and shaken by the time he drew away.

"Is that enough for you?" He hauled her to her toes, his fingers digging in. His eyes weren't dispassionate now, weren't cool, but turbulent. Human. "Enough emotion, enough passion? I don't like to lose control. You can't afford to lose control on the job."

Her breath was heaving. And her heart was flying. "This isn't the job."

"No, but it was supposed to be." He willed his grip to loosen. "You were supposed to be. I can't get you out of my head. Damn it, Grace. I can't get you out."

She laid a hand on his cheek, felt the muscle twitch. "It's the same for me. Maybe the only difference right now is that I want it to be that way."

For how long? he wondered, but he didn't say it. "Come home with me."

"I'd love to." She smiled, stroked her fingers back, into his hair. "But I think we'd better stay for dinner, at least. Otherwise, we'd break Cade's heart."

"After dinner, then." It wasn't difficult at all, he discovered, to bring her hands to his lips, linger over them, then look into her eyes. "I am sorry. But, Grace—?"

"Yes?"

"If DeVane calls you again, or sends flowers?"

Her lips twitched. "Yes?"

"I'll have to kill him."

With a delighted laugh, she threw her arms around Seth's neck. "Now we're talking."

"That was nice." With a satisfied sigh, Grace sank down in the seat of Seth's car and watched the moon shimmer in the sky. "I like seeing the four of them together. But it's funny. It's as if I blinked, and everyone took this huge, giant step forward."

"Red light, green light."

Confused, Grace turned her head to look at him. "What?"

"The game—the kid's game? You know, the person who's it has to say, 'Green light,' turn his back. Everybody can go forward, but then he says, 'Red light' and spins around. If he sees anybody move, they have to go back to the start."

When she gave a baffled laugh, it was his turn to look. "Didn't you ever play games like that when you were a kid?"

"No. I was given the proper lessons, lectured on etiquette and was instructed to take brisk daily walks for exercise. Sometimes I ran," she said softly, remembering. "Fast, and hard, until my heart was bumping in my chest. But I guess I always had to go back to the start."

Annoyed with herself, she shook her shoulders. "My, doesn't that sound pathetic? It wasn't, really. It was just structured." She scooped back her hair, smiled at him. "So what other games did young Seth Buchanan play?"

"The usual." Didn't she know how heartbreaking it was to hear that wistfulness in her voice, then see that quick, careless shrug as she pushed it all aside? "Didn't you have friends?"

"Of course." Then she looked away. "No. It doesn't matter. I have them now. The best of friends."

"Do you know any one of the three of you can start a sentence and either of the other two can finish it?"

"We don't do that."

"Yes, you do. A dozen times tonight, at least. You don't even realize it. And you have this code," he continued. "Little quirks and gestures. M.J.'s half smirk or eye roll, Bailey's downsweep of the lashes or hair-around-the-finger twist. And you lift your left brow, just a fraction, or catch your tongue between your teeth. When you do, you let each other know the joke's your little secret."

She hummed in her throat, not at all sure she liked being deciphered so easily. "Aren't you observant…"

"That's my job." He pulled into his driveway, turned to her. "It shouldn't bother you."

"I haven't decided if it does or not. Did you become a cop because you're observant, or are you observant because you're a cop?"

"Hard to say. I was never really anything else."

"Not even when you were young Seth Buchanan?"

"It was always part of my life. My grandfather was a cop. And my father. My father's brother. Our house was filled with them."

"So it was expected of you?"

"It was understood," he corrected. "If I'd wanted to be a plumber or a mechanic, that would have been fine. But it was what I wanted."

"Why?"

"There's right and there's wrong."

"Just that simple?"

"It should be." He looked at the ring on his finger. "My father was a good cop. Straight. Fair. Solid. You can't ask for more than that."

She laid a hand over his. "You lost him."

"Line of duty. A long time ago." The hurt had passed a long time before, as well, and left room for pride. "He was a good cop, a good father, a good man. He always said there was a choice between doing the right thing or the wrong thing. Either one had a price. But you could pay up on the first and still look yourself in the eye every morning."

Grace leaned over, kissed him lightly. "He did the right thing by you."

"Always. My mother was a cop's wife, steady as a rock. Now she's a cop's mother, and she's still steady. Still there. When I got my gold shield, it meant as much to her as it did to me."

There was a bond, she realized. Deep and true and unquestioned. "But she worries about you."

"Some. But she accepts it. Has to," he added, with the ghost of a smile. "I've got a younger brother and sister. We're all cops."

"It runs through the blood," she murmured. "Are you close?"

"We're family," he said simply, then thought of hers and remembered that such things weren't simple. They were precious. "Yes, we're close."

He was the oldest, she mused. He would have taken his generational placement seriously, and, when his father died, his responsibilities as man of the house with equal weight.

It was hardly a wonder, then, that authority, responsibility, duty, sat so naturally on him. She thought of the weapon he wore, touched a fingertip to the leather strap.

"Have you ever…" She lifted her gaze to his. "Have you ever had to?"

"Yes. But I can still look myself in the eye in the morning."

She accepted that without question. But the next subject was more difficult. "You have a scar, just here." Her memory of it was perfect as she touched her finger just under his right shoulder now. "You were shot?"

"Five years ago. One of those things." There was no point in relaying the details. The bust gone wrong, the shouts and the electric buzz of terror. The insult of the bullet and the bright, stupefying pain. "Most police work is routine—paperwork, tedium, repetition."

"But not all."

"No, not all." He wanted to see her smile again, wanted to prolong what had evolved into a sweet and intimate interlude in a darkened car. Just conversation, without the sizzle of sex. "You've got a tattoo on your incredibly perfect bottom."

She laughed then, and tossed her hair back. "I didn't think you'd noticed."

"I noticed. Why do you have a tattoo of a winged horse on your butt, Grace?"

"It was an impulse, one of those wild-girl things I dragged M.J. and Bailey into."

"They have winged horses on their—"

"No, and what they do have is their little secret. I wanted the winged horse because it was free. You couldn't catch it unless it wanted to be caught." She lifted a hand to his face, changed the mood subtly. "I never wanted to be caught. Before."

He nearly believed her. Lowering his head, he met her lips with his, let the kiss spin out. It was quiet, without urgency. The slow meeting of tongues, the lazy change of angles and depths. Easy sips. Testing nibbles.

Her body shifted fluidly, her hands sliding up his chest to link at the nape of his neck. A purr sounded in her throat. "It's been a long time since I necked in the front seat of a car."

He nudged her hair aside so that his mouth could find that sweet, sensitive curve between neck and shoulder. "Want to try the back seat?"

Her laugh was low and delighted. "Absolutely."

The need had snuck up on him, crept into his bloodstream to stagger his heart. "We'll go inside."

Her breath was a bit unsteady as she leaned back, grinned at him in the shimmer of moonlight. "Chicken."

His eyes narrowed fractionally, making her grin widen. "There's a perfectly good bed in the house."

She made a soft clucking noise, then, chuckling, rubbed her lips over his. "Let's pretend," she whispered, pressing her body to his, sliding it against his. "We're on a dark, deserted road and you've told me the car's broken down."

He said her name, an exasperated sound against her tempting lips. It was only another challenge to her.

"I pretend I believe you, because I want to stay, I want you to...persuade me. You'll say you just want to touch me, and I'll pretend I believe that, too." She took his hand, laid it on her breast and felt the quick thrill when his fingers flexed. "Even though I know that's not all you want. It's not all you want, is it, Seth?"

What he wanted was that dark, slippery slide into her. His hands moved under her shirt, found flesh. "We're not going to make it into the back seat," he warned her.

She only laughed.

He wasn't sure if he felt smug or stunned by his own behavior when he finally unlocked his front door. Had he been this randy as a teenager? he wondered. That ridiculously reckless? Or was it only Grace who made such things as making desperate love in his own driveway one more adventure?

She stepped inside, lifted the hair off her neck, then let it fall in a gesture that simply stopped his heart. "My place should be ready by tomorrow, the next day at the latest. We'll have to go there. We can skinny-dip in my pool. It's so hot out now."

"You're so beautiful."

She turned, surprised at the mix of resentment and desire in his voice. He stood just inside the door, as if he might turn at any moment and leave her.

"It's a dangerous weapon. Lethal."

She tried to smile. "Arrest me."

"You don't like to be told." He let out a half laugh. "You don't like to be told you're beautiful."

"I didn't do anything to earn how I look."

She said it, he realized, as if beauty were more of a curse than a gift. And in that moment he felt a new level of understanding. He stepped forward, took her face gently in his hands, looked deep and long.

"Well, maybe your eyes are a little too close to-gether."

Her hitch of laughter was pure surprise. "They are not."

"And your mouth, I think it might be just a hair off center. Let me check." He measured it with his own, lingering over the kiss when her lips curved. "Yeah. Just a hair, but it does throw things off, now that I really look. And let's see…" He turned her head to each side, paused to consider. "Yep. The left profile's weak. Are you getting a double chin there?"

She slapped his hand away, torn between insult and laughter. "I certainly am not."

"I really should check that, too. I don't know if I want to take this whole thing any further if you're getting a double chin."

He grabbed her, tugging her head back gently by the hair so that he could nibble freely under her jaw. She giggled—a young, foolish sound—and squirmed. "Stop that, you idiot." She let out a shriek when he hauled her up into his arms.

"You're no lightweight, either, by the way."

Her eyes went to slits. "Okay, buster, that's all. I'm leaving."

It was a delight to watch him grin—that quick, boy-ish flash of humor. "I forgot to tell you," he said as he headed for the stairs. "My car's broken down. I'm out of gas. The cat ate my homework. I'm just going to touch you."

He'd made it up two steps when the phone rang. "Damn." He brushed his lips absently over her brow. "I have to get that."

"It's all right. I'll remember where you were."

Though he set her down, she didn't think her feet hit the floor. Love was a cushy buffer.

But her smile faded as she saw his eyes change. Suddenly they were flat again, unreadable. She knew as she walked across the room toward him that he'd shifted seamlessly from man to cop.

"Where?" His voice was cool again, controlled. "Is the scene secured?" He swore lightly, barely a whisper under the breath. "Get it secured. I'm on my way." As he hung up, his eyes skimmed over her, focused. "I'm sorry, Grace, I have to go."

She moistened her lips. "Is it bad?"

"I have to go," was all he'd say. "I'll call for a black-and-white to take you back to Cade's."

"Can't I wait here for you?"

"I don't know how long I'll be."

"It doesn't matter." She offered a hand, but wasn't sure she could reach him. "I'd like to wait. I want to wait for you."

No woman ever had. That thought passed quickly through his mind, distracting him. "If you get tired of waiting, call the precinct. I'll leave word there for a uniform to drive you home if you call in."

"All right." But she wouldn't call in. She would wait. "Seth." She moved into him, brushed her lips against his. "I'll see you when you get back."

Chapter 9

Alone, Grace switched on the television, settled on the sofa. Five minutes later, she was up and wandering the house.

He didn't go in for knickknacks, she mused. Probably thought of them as dustcatchers. No plants, no pets. The living room furniture was simple, masculine, and good quality. The sofa was comfortable, of generous size and a deep hunter green. She would have spruced it up with pillows. Burgundy, navy, copper. The coffee table was a square of heavy oak, highly polished and dust-free.

She decided he had a weekly housekeeper. She just couldn't picture Seth wielding a polishing rag. There was a bookcase under the side window and, crouching, she scanned the titles. It pleased her that they had read many of the same books. There was even a gardening book she'd studied herself.

That she could see, she decided. Yes, she could see Seth working out in the yard, turning the earth, planting something that would last.

There was art in this room, as well. She moved closer, certain the watercolor portraits grouped on the wall were the work of the same artist who had done the cityscape and rural scene in his bedroom. She searched for the signature first, and found Marilyn Buchanan looped in the lower corner.

Sister, mother, cousin? she wondered. Someone he loved, and who loved him. She shifted her gaze and studied the first painting.

Seth's father, Grace realized with a jolt. It had to be. The resemblance was there, in the eyes, clear, intense, tawny. The jaw, squared off, almost chiseled. The artist had seen strength, a touch of sadness, and honor. A whisper of humor around the mouth and an innate pride in the set of the head. All were evident in the three-quarter profile view that had the subject staring off at something only he could see.

The next portrait was a woman, perhaps in her forties. It was a pretty face, but the artist hadn't hidden the faint and telltale lines of age, the touches of gray in the dark, curling hair. The hazel eyes looked straight ahead, with humor and with patience. And there was Seth's mouth, Grace thought, smiling easily.

His mother, she concluded. How much strength was contained inside those quiet hazel eyes? Grace wondered. How much was required to stand and accept when everyone you loved faced danger daily?

Whatever the amount, this woman possessed it.

There was another man, young, twenty-something, with a cocky grin and daredevil eyes shades darker than Seth's. Attractive, sexy, with a dark shock of hair falling carelessly over his brow. His brother, certainly.

The last was of a young woman with a shoulder-length sweep of dark hair, the tawny eyes alert, the sculpted mouth just curved in the beginnings of a smile. Lovely, with more of Seth's seriousness about her than the young man. His sister.

She wondered if she would ever meet them, or if she would know them only through their portraits. Seth would take the woman he loved to them, she thought, and let the little slice of hurt pass through her. He would want to—need to—bring her into his mother's home, watch how she melded and mixed with his family.

It was a door he'd have to open on both sides in welcome. Not just because it was traditional, she realized, but because it would matter to him.

But a lover? No, she decided. It wasn't necessary to share a lover with family. He'd never take a woman with whom he shared only sex home to meet his mother.

Grace closed her eyes a moment. Stop feeling sorry for yourself, she ordered briskly. You can't have everything you want or need, so you make the best of what there is.

She opened her eyes again, once more scanned the portraits. Good faces, she thought. A good family.

But where, Grace wondered, was Seth's portrait? There had to be one. What had the artist seen? Had she painted him with that cool cop's stare, that surprisingly beautiful smile, the all-too-rare flash of that grin?

Determined to find out, she left the television blaring and went on the hunt. In the next twenty minutes, she discovered that Seth lived tidily, kept a phone and notepad in every room, used the second bedroom as a combination guest room and office, had turned the tiny third bedroom into a minigym and liked deep colors and comfortable chairs.

She found more watercolors, but no portrait of the man.

She circled the guest room, curious that here, and only here, he'd indulged in some whimsy. Recessed shelves held a collection of figures, some carved in wood, others in stone. Dragons, griffins, sorcerers, unicorns, centaurs. And a single winged horse of alabaster caught soaring in midflight.

Here the paintings reflected the magical—a misty landscape where a turreted castle rose silver into a pale rose-colored sky, a shadow-dappled lake where a single white deer drank.

There were books on Arthur, on Irish legends, the gods of Olympus, and those who had ruled Rome. And there, on the small cherrywood desk, was a globe of blue crystal and a book on Mithra, the god of light.

It made her tremble, clutch her arms. Had he picked up the book because of the case? Or had it already been here? She touched a hand to the slim volume and was certain it was the latter.

One more link between them, she realized, forged before they'd even met. It was so easy for her to accept that, even to be grateful. But she wondered if he felt the same.

She went downstairs, oddly at home after her self-guided tour. It made her smile to see their coffee cups from that morning still in the sink, a little touch of intimacy. She found a bottle of wine in the refrigerator, poured herself a glass and took it with her into the living room.

She went back to the bookcase, thinking of curling up on the couch with the TV for company and a book to pass the time. Then a chill washed over her, so quick, so intense, the wine shook in her hand. She found herself staring out the window, her breath coming short, her other hand clutched on the edge of the bookcase.

Someone watching. It pounded in her brain, a frightened, whispering voice that might have been her own. *Someone watching.*

But she saw nothing but the dark, the shimmer of moonlight, the quiet house across the street.

Stop it, she ordered herself. There's no one there. There's nothing there. But she straightened and quickly twitched the curtains closed. Her hands were shaking.

She sipped wine, tried to laugh at herself. The late-breaking bulletin on the television had her turning slowly. A family of four in nearby Bethesda. Murdered.

She knew where Seth had gone now. And could only imagine what he was dealing with.

She was alone. DeVane sat in his treasure room, stroking an ivory statue of the goddess Venus. He'd come to think of it as Grace. As his obsession festered and grew, he imagined Grace and himself together, immortal through time. She would be his most prized possession. His goddess. And the Three Stars would complete his collection of the priceless.

Of course, she would have to be punished first. He knew what had to be done, what would matter most to her. And the other two women were not blameless—

they had complicated his plans, caused him to fail. They would have to die, of course.

After he had the Stars, after he had Grace, they would die. And their deaths would be her punishment.

Now she was alone. It would be so easy to take her now. To bring her here. She'd be afraid, at first. He wanted her to be afraid. It was part of her punishment. Eventually he would woo her, win her. Own her. They would have, after all, several lifetimes to be together.

In one of them he would take her back to Terresa. He would make her a queen. A god could settle for no less than a queen.

Take her tonight. The voice that spoke louder and louder in his head every day taunted him. He couldn't trust it. DeVane steadied his breathing, shut his eyes. He would not be rushed. Every detail had to be in place.

Grace would come to him when he was prepared. And she would bring him the Stars.

Seth downed one last cup of sludgy coffee and rubbed at the ache at the back of his neck. His stomach was still raw from what he'd seen in that neat suburban home. He knew civilians and rookie cops believed the vets became immune to the results of violent death— the sights, the smells, the meaningless waste.

It was a lie.

No one could become used to seeing what he'd seen. If they could, they shouldn't wear a badge. The law needed to retain its sense of disgust, of horror, for murder.

What drove a man to take the lives of his own children, of the woman he'd made them with, and then his own? There'd been no one left in that neat suburban home to answer that question. He knew it would haunt him.

Seth scrubbed his hands over his face, felt the knots of tension and fatigue. He rolled his shoulders once, twice, then squared them before cutting through the bull pen, toward the locker room.

Mick Marshall was there, rubbing his sore feet. His wiry red hair stood up like a bush that needed trimming from a face lined with weariness. His eyes were shadowed, his mouth was grim.

"Lieutenant." He pulled his socks back on.

"You didn't have to come in on this, Detective."

"Hell, I heard the gunshots from my own living room." He picked up one of his shoes, but just rested his elbows on his knees. "Two blocks over. Jesus, my kids played with those kids. How the hell am I going to explain this?"

"How well did you know the father?"

"Didn't, really. It's just like they always say, Lieutenant. He was a quiet guy, polite, kept to himself." He gave a short, humorless laugh. "They always do."

"Mulrooney's taking the case. You can assist if you want. Now go home, get some sleep. Go in and kiss your kids."

"Yeah." Mick scraped his fingers through his hair. "Listen, Lieutenant, I got some data on that DeVane guy."

Seth's spine tingled. "Anything interesting?"

"Depends on what floats your boat. He's fifty-two, never married, inherited a big fat pile from his old man, including this big vineyard on that island, that Terresa. Grows olives, too, runs some cattle."

"The gentleman farmer?"

"Oh, he's got more going than that. Lots of interests, spread out all over hell and back. Shipping, communications, import-export. Lots of fingers in lots of pies generating lots of dough. He was made ambassador to the U.S. three years ago. Seems to like it here. He bought some nifty place on Foxhall Road, big mansion, likes to entertain. People don't like to talk about him, though. They get real nervous."

"Money and power make some people nervous."

"Yeah. I haven't gotten a lot of information yet. But there was a woman about five years ago. Opera singer. Pretty big deal, if you're into that sort of thing. Italian lady. Seems like they were pretty tight. Then she disappeared."

"Disappeared." Seth's waning interest snapped back. "How?"

"That's the thing. She just went poof. Italian police can't figure it. She had a place in Milan, left all her things—clothes, jewelry, the works. She was singing at that opera house there, in the middle of a run, you know? Didn't show for the evening performance. She went shopping on that afternoon, had a bunch of things sent back to her place. But she never went back."

"They figure kidnapping?"

"They did. But then there was no ransom call, no body, no sign of her in nearly five years. She was…" Mick screwed up his face in thought. "Thirty, supposed to be at the top of her form, and a hell of a looker. She left a big pile of lire in her accounts. It's still there."

"DeVane was questioned?"

"Yeah. Seems he was on his yacht in the Ionian Sea, soaking up rays and drinking ouzo, when it all went down. A half-dozen guests on board with him. The

Italian cop I talked to—big opera fan, by the way—he didn't think DeVane seemed shocked enough, or upset enough. He smelled something, but couldn't make anything stick. Still, the guy offered a reward, five million lire, for her safe return. No one ever collected."

"I'd say that was fairly interesting. Keep digging." And, Seth thought, he'd start doing some digging himself.

"One more thing." Mick cracked his neck from side to side. "And I thought this was interesting too—the guy's a collector. He has a little of everything—coins, stamps, jewelry, art, antiques, statuary. He does it all. But he's also reputed to have a unique and extensive gem collection—rivals the Smithsonian's."

"DeVane likes rocks."

"Oh, yeah. And get this. Two years ago, more or less, he paid three mil for an emerald. Big rock, sure, but its price spiked because it was supposed to be a magic rock." The very idea made Mick's lips curl. "Merlin was supposed to have, you know, conjured it up for Arthur. Seems to me a guy who'd buy into that would be pretty interested in three big blue rocks and all that god and immortality stuff that goes with them."

"I just bet he would." And wasn't it odd, Seth mused, that DeVane's name hadn't been on Bailey's list? A collector whose U.S. residence was only miles from Salvini, yet he'd never done business with them?

No, the lack was too odd to believe.

"Get me what you've got when you go on shift, Mick. I'd like to talk to that Italian cop personally. I appreciate the extra time you put into this."

Mick blinked. Seth never failed to thank his men for good work, but it was generally mechanical. There had been genuine warmth this time, on a personal level. "Sure, no sweat. But you know, Lieutenant, even if you can tie this guy to the case, he'll bounce. Diplomatic immunity. We can't touch him."

"Let's tie him first, then we'll see." Seth glanced over, distracted, when a locker slammed open nearby as a cop was coming on shift. "Get some sleep," he began, then broke off. There, taped to the back of the locker, was Grace, young, laughing and naked.

Her head was tossed back, and that teasing smile, that feminine confidence, that silky power, sparkled in her eyes. Her skin was like polished marble, her curves were generous, with only that rainfall of hair, artfully draped to drive a man insane, covering her.

Mick turned his head, saw the centerfold and winced. Cade had filled him in on the lieutenant's relationship with Grace, and all Mick could think was that someone—very likely the cop currently standing at his locker whistling moronically—was about to die.

"Ah, Lieutenant…" Mick began, with some brave thought of saving his associate's life.

Seth merely held up a hand, cut Mick off and walked to the locker. The cop changing his shirt glanced over. "Lieutenant."

"Bradley," Seth said, and continued to study the glossy photo.

"She's something else, isn't she? One of the guys on day shift said she'd been in and looked just as good in person."

"Did he?"

"You bet. I dug this out of a pile of magazines in my garage. None the worse for wear."

"Bradley." Mick whispered the name and buried his head in his hands. The guy was dead meat.

Seth took a long breath, resisted the urge to rip the photo down. "Female officers share this locker room, Bradley. This is inappropriate." Where was the tattoo? Seth thought hazily. What had she been when she posed for this? Nineteen, twenty? "Find somewhere else to hang your art."

"Yes, sir."

Seth turned away, then shot one last look over his shoulder. "And she's better in person. Much better."

"Bradley," Mick said as Seth strode out, "you just dodged one major bullet."

Dawn was breaking when Seth let himself into the house. He'd gone by the book on the case in Bethesda. It would close when the forensic and autopsy reports confirmed what he already knew. A man of thirty-six who made a comfortable living as a computer programmer had gotten up from his sofa, where he was watching television, loaded his revolver and ended four lives in the approximate space of ten minutes.

For this crime, Seth could offer no justice.

He could have headed home two hours earlier. But he'd made use of the time difference in Europe to make calls, ask questions, gather data. He was slowly putting together a picture of Gregor DeVane.

A man of wealth he had never sweated for. One who enjoyed prestige and power, who traveled in exalted circles, and had no family.

There was no crime in any of that, Seth thought as he closed his front door behind him.

There was no crime in sending white roses to a beautiful woman.

Or in once being involved with one who'd disappeared. But wasn't it interesting that DeVane had been involved with another woman? A Frenchwoman, a prima ballerina of great beauty who'd been considered the finest dancer of the decade. And who had been found dead of a drug overdose in her Paris home.

The verdict had been suicide, though those closest to her insisted she had never used drugs. She had been fiercely disciplined about her body. DeVane had been questioned in that matter, as well, but only as a matter of form. He had been dining at the White House at the very hour the young dancer slipped into a coma, and then into death.

Still, Seth and the Italian detective agreed it was quite a fascinating coincidence.

A collector, Seth mused, switching off lights automatically. An acquirer of beautiful things, and beautiful women. A man who would pay double the value of an emerald to possess a legend, as well.

He would see how many more threads he could tie, and he would, he decided, have an official chat with the ambassador.

He stepped into the living room, started to hit the next switch, and saw Grace curled upon the couch.

He'd assumed she'd gone home. But there she was, curled into a tight, protective ball on his couch, sleeping. What the hell was she doing here? he wondered.

Waiting for you. Just as she said she would. As no woman had waited before. As he'd wanted no woman to wait.

Emotion thudded into his chest, flooded into his

heart. It undid him, he realized, this irrational love. His heart wasn't safe here, wasn't even his own any longer. He wanted it back, wanted desperately to be able to turn away, leave her and go back to his life.

It terrified him that he wouldn't. Couldn't.

She was bound to get bored before too much longer, to lose interest in a relationship he imagined was fueled by impulse and sex on her part. Would she just drift away, he wondered, or end it cleanly? It would be clean, he decided. That would be her way. She wasn't, as he'd once wanted to believe, callous or cold or calculating. She had a very giving heart, but he thought it was also a restless one.

Moving over, he crouched in front of her, studied her face. There was a faint line between her brows. She didn't sleep easily, he realized. What dreams chased her? he asked himself. What worries nagged her?

Poor little rich girl, he thought. Still running until you're out of breath and there's nothing to do but go back to the start.

He stroked a thumb over her brow to smooth it, then slid his arms under her. "Come on, baby," he murmured, "time for bed."

"No." She pushed at him, struggled. "Don't."

More nightmares? Concerned, he gathered her close. "It's Seth. It's all right. I've got you."

"Watching me." She turned her face into his shoulder. "Outside. Everywhere. Watching me."

"Shhh… No one's here." He carried her toward the steps, realizing now why every light in the house had been blazing. She'd been afraid to be alone in the dark. Yet she'd stayed. "No one's going to hurt you, Grace. I promise."

"Seth." She surfaced to the sound of his voice, and her heavy eyes opened and focused on his face. "Seth," she said again. She touched a hand to his cheek, then her lips. "You look so tired."

"We can switch. You can carry me."

She slid her arms around him, pressed her cheek, warm to his. "I heard, on the news. The family in Bethesda."

"You didn't have to wait."

"Seth." She eased back, met his eyes.

"I won't talk about it," he said flatly. "Don't ask."

"You won't talk about it because it troubles you to talk about it, or because you won't share those troubles with me?"

He set her down beside the bed, turned away and peeled off his shirt. "I'm tired, Grace. I have to be back in a few hours. I need to sleep."

"All right." She rubbed the heel of her hand over her heart, where it hurt the most. "I've already had some sleep. I'll go downstairs and call a cab."

He hung his shirt over the back of a chair, sat to take off his shoes. "If that's what you want."

"It's not what I want, but it seems it's what you want." She barely lifted a brow when he heaved his shoe across the room. Then he stared at it as if it had leaped there on its own.

"I don't do things like that," he said between his teeth. "I never do things like that."

"Why not? It always makes me feel better." And because he looked so exhausted, and so baffled by himself, she relented. Walking to him, she stepped in close to where he sat and began to knead the stiff muscles of his shoulders. "You know what you need around here,

Lieutenant?" She dipped her head to kiss the top of his. "Besides me, of course. You need to get yourself a bubble tub, something you can sink down into that'll beat all these knots out of you. But for now we'll see what I can do about them."

Her hands felt like glory, smoothing out the knotted muscles in his shoulders. "Why?"

"That's one of your favorite questions, isn't it? Come on, lie down, let me work on this rock you call a back."

"I just need to sleep."

"Um-hmm." Taking charge, she nudged him back, climbed onto the bed to kneel beside him. "Roll over, handsome."

"I like this view better." He managed a half smile, toyed with the ends of her hair. "Why don't you come here? I'm too tired to fight you off."

"I'll keep that in mind." She gave him a push. "Roll over, big boy."

With a grunt, he rolled over on his stomach, then let out a second grunt when she straddled him and those wonderful hands began to press and stroke and knead.

"You, being you, would consider a regular massage an indulgence. But that's where you're wrong." She pressed down with the heels of her hands, worked forward to knead with her fingertips. "You give your body relief, it works better for you. I get one every week at the club. Stefan could do wonders for you."

"Stefan." He closed his eyes and tried not to think about another man with his hands all over her. "Figures."

"He's a professional," she said dryly. "And his wife is a pediatric therapist. She's wonderful with the children at the hospital."

He thought of the children, and that was what weakened him. That, and her soothing hands, her quiet voice. Sunlight filtered, a warm red, through his closed lids, but he could still see.

"The kids were in bed."

Her hands froze for a moment. Then, with a long, quiet breath, she moved them again, up and down his spine, over his shoulder blades, up to the tight length of his neck. And she waited.

"The youngest girl had a doll—one of those Raggedy Anns. An old one. She was still holding it. There were Disney posters all over the walls. All those fairy tales and happy endings. The way it's supposed to be when you're a kid. The older girl had one of those teen magazines beside the bed—the kind ten-year-olds read because they can't wait to be sixteen. They never woke up. Never knew neither one of them would get to be sixteen."

She said nothing. There was nothing that could be said. But, leaning down, she touched her lips to the back of his shoulder and felt him let loose a long, ragged breath.

"It twists you when it's kids. I don't know a cop who can deal with it without having it twist his guts. The mother was on the stairs. Looks like she heard the shots, starting running up to her kids. After, he went back to the living room, sat down on the sofa and finished it."

She curled herself into him, hugged herself to his back and just held on. "Try to sleep," she murmured.

"Stay. Please."

"I will." She closed her eyes, listened to his breathing deepen. "I'll stay."

* * *

But he woke alone. As sleep was clearing, he wondered if he'd dreamed the meeting at dawn. Yet he could smell her—on the air, on his own skin where she'd curled close. He was still stretched crosswise over the bed, and he tilted his wrist to check the watch he'd neglected to take off.

Whatever else was going on inside him, his internal clock was still in working order.

He gave himself an extra two minutes under the shower to beat back fatigue, and when shaving promised himself to do nothing more than vegetate on his next personal day. He pretended it wasn't going to be another hot, humid, hazy day while he knotted his tie.

Then he swore, scooped fingers though his just-combed hair, remembering he'd neglected to set the timer on his coffeemaker. The minutes it would take to brew it would not only set his teeth on edge, they would eat into his schedule.

But the one thing he categorically refused to do was start the day with the poison that simmered at the cop shop.

His mind was so focused on coffee that when the scent of it wafted like a siren's call as he came down the stairs, he thought it was an illusion.

Not only was the pot full of gloriously rich black liquid, Grace was sitting at his kitchen table, reading the morning paper and nibbling on a bagel. Her hair was scooped back from her face, and she appeared to be wearing nothing more than one of his shirts.

"Good morning." She smiled up at him, then shook her head. "Are you human? How can you look so official and intimidating on less than three hours' sleep?"

"Practice. I thought you'd gone."

"I told you I'd stay. Coffee's hot. I hope you don't mind that I helped myself."

"No." He stood exactly where he was. "I don't mind."

"If it's all right with you, I'll just loiter over coffee awhile before I get dressed. I'll get myself back to Cade's and change. I want to drop by the hospital later this morning, then I'm going home. It's time I did. The cleaning crew should be finished by this afternoon, so I thought…" She trailed off as he just continued to stare at her.

"What is it?" She gave an uncertain smile and rubbed at her nose.

Keeping his eyes on hers, he took the phone from the wall and punched in a number on memory. "This is Buchanan," he said. "I won't be in for a couple hours. I'm taking personal time." He hung up, held out a hand. "Come back to bed. Please."

She rose, and put her hand in his.

When clothes were scattered carelessly on the floor, the sheets turned back, the shades pulled to filter the beat of the sun, he covered her.

He needed to hold, to touch, to indulge himself for one hour with the flow of emotion she caused in him. Only an hour, yet he didn't hurry. Instead, he lingered over slow, deep, drugging kisses that lasted eons, loitered over long, smooth, soft caresses that stretched into forever.

She was there for him. Simply there. Open, giving, offering a seemingly endless supply of warmth.

She sighed, shakily, as he stroked her to helpless response, moving over her tenderly, his patience infinite. Each time their mouths met, with that slow slide of tongue, her heart shuddered in her breast.

There were the soft, slippery sounds of intimacy, the quiet murmurs of lovers, drifting into sighs and moans. Both of them were lost, mired in thick layers of sensation, the air around them like syrup, causing movement to slow and pleasure to last.

Her breath sighed out as he trailed lazily down her body with hands and mouth, as her own hands stroked over his back, then his shoulders. She opened for him, arching up in welcome, then shuddering as his tongue brought on a long, rolling climax.

And because he needed it as much as she, she let her hands fall limply, let him take her wherever he chose. Her blood beat hot and the heat brought a dew of roused passion to her skin. His hands slicked over her skin like silk.

"Tell me you want me." He trailed slow, open-mouthed kisses up her torso.

"Yes." She gripped his hips, urged him. "I want you."

"Tell me you need me." His tongue slid over her nipple.

"Yes." She moaned again when he suckled gently. "I need you."

Tell me you love me. But that he demanded only in his mind as he brought his mouth to hers again, sank into that wet, willing promise.

"Now." He kept his eyes open and on hers.

"Yes." She rose to meet him. "Now."

He glided inside her, filling her so slowly, so achingly, that they both trembled. He saw her eyes swim with tears and found the urge for tenderness stronger than any other. He kissed her again, softly, moved inside her one slow beat at a time.

The sweetness of it had a tear spilling over, trailing down her glowing cheek. Her lips trembled, and he felt her muscles contract and clutch him. "Don't close your eyes." He whispered it, sipped the tear from her cheek. "I want to see your eyes when I take you over."

She couldn't stop it. The tenderness stripped her. Her vision blurred with tears, and the blue of her eyes deepened to midnight. She said his name, then murmured it again against his lips. And her body quivered as the next long, undulating wave swamped her.

"I can't—"

"Let me have you." He was falling, falling, falling, and he buried his face in her hair. "Let me have all of you."

Chapter 10

In the nursery, Grace was rocking an infant. The baby girl was barely big enough to fill the crook of her arm from elbow to wrist, but the tiny infant watched her steadily with the deeply blue eyes of a newborn.

The hole in her heart had been repaired, and her prognosis was good.

"You're going to be fine, Carrie. Your mama and papa are so worried about you, but you're going to be just fine." She stroked the baby's cheek and thought—hoped—Carrie smiled a little.

Grace was tempted to sing her to sleep, but knew the nursing staff rolled their eyes and snickered whenever she tried a lullaby. Still, the babies were rarely critical of her admittedly poor singing voice, so she half sang, half murmured, until Carrie's baby owl's eyes grew heavy.

Even when she slept, Grace continued to rock. It was self-serving now, she knew. Anyone who had ever rocked a baby understood that it soothed the adult, as well as the child. And here, with an infant dozing in her arms, and her own eyes heavy, she could admit her deepest secret.

She pined for children of her own. She longed to carry them inside her, to feel the weight, the movement within, to push them into life with that last sharp pang of childbirth, to hold them to her breast and feel them drink from her.

She wanted to walk the floor with them when they were fretful, to watch them sleep. To raise them and watch them grow, she thought, closing her eyes as she rocked. To care for them, to comfort them in the night, even to watch them take that first wrenching step away from her.

Motherhood was her greatest wish and her most secret desire.

When she first involved herself with the pediatric wing, she'd worried that she was doing so to assuage that gnawing ache inside her. But she knew it wasn't true. The first time she held a sick child in her arms and gave comfort, she'd understood that her commitment encompassed so much more.

She had so much to give, such an abundance of love that needed to be offered. And here it could be accepted without question, without judgment. Here, at least, she could do something worthwhile, something that mattered.

"Carrie matters," she murmured, kissing the top of the sleeping baby's head before she rose to settle her in her crib. "And one day soon you'll go home, strong and healthy. You won't remember that I once rocked you to sleep when your mama couldn't be here. But I will."

She smiled at the nurse who came in, stepped back. "She seems so much better."

"She's a tough little fighter. You've got a wonderful touch with the babies, Ms. Fontaine." The nurse picked up charts, began to make notes.

"I'll try to give you an hour or so in a couple of days. And you'll be able to reach me at home again, if you need to."

"Oh?" The nurse looked up, peered over the top of wire-framed glasses. The murder at Grace's home, and the ensuing investigation, were hot topics at the hospital. "Are you sure you'll be… comfortable at home?"

"I'm going to make sure I'm comfortable." Grace gave Carrie a final look, then stepped out into the hall.

She just had time, she decided, to stop by the pediatric ward and visit the older children. Then she could call Seth's office and see if he was interested in a little dinner for two at her place.

She turned and nearly walked into DeVane.

"Gregor?" She fixed a smile on her face to mask the sudden odd bumping of her heart. "What a surprise. Is someone ill?"

He stared at her, unblinking. "Ill?"

What was wrong with his eyes? she wondered, that they seemed so pale and unfocused. "We are in the hospital," she said, keeping the smile on her face, and, vaguely concerned, she laid a hand on his arm. "Are you all right?"

He snapped back, appalled. For a moment, his mind seemed to have switched off. He'd only been able to see her, to smell her. "Quite well," he assured her. "Momentarily distracted. I didn't expect to see you, either."

Of course, that was a lie, he'd planned the meeting meticulously. He took her hand, bowed over it, kissed her fingers.

"It is, of course, a pleasure to see you anywhere. I've come by here as our mutual friends interested me in the care children receive here. Children and their welfare are a particular interest of mine."

"Really?" Her smile warmed immediately. "Mine, too. Would you like a quick tour?"

"With you as my guide, how could I not?" He turned, signaled to two men who stood stiffly several paces back. "Bodyguards," he told Grace, tucking her hand into the crook of his arm and patting it. "Distressingly necessary in today's climate. Tell me, why am I so fortunate as to find you here today?"

As she usually did, she covered the truth and kept her privacy. "The Fontaines donated significantly to this particular wing. I like to stop in from time to time to see what the hospital's doing with it." She flashed a twinkling look. "And you just never know when you might run into a handsome doctor—or ambassador."

She strolled along, explaining various sections and wondering how much she might, with a little time and charm, wheedle out of him for the children. "General pediatrics is on the floor above. Since this section houses maternity, they wouldn't want kids zooming down the corridors while mothers are in labor or resting."

"Yes, children can be quite boisterous." He detested them. "It's one of my deepest regrets that I have none of my own. But having never found the right woman..."

He gestured with his free hand. "As I grow older, I'm resigned to having no one to carry on my name."

"Gregor, you're in your prime. A strong, vital man who can have as many children as he likes for years yet."

"Ah." He looked into her eyes again. "But there is still the right woman to be found."

She felt a shiver of discomfort at his pointed statement and intense gaze. "I'm sure you'll find her. We have some preemies here." She stepped closer to the glass. "So tiny," she said softly. "So defenseless."

"It's a pity when they're flawed."

She frowned at his choice of words. "Some of them need more time under controlled conditions and medical care to fully develop. But I wouldn't call them flawed."

Another error, he thought with an inner sense of irritation. He could not seem to keep his mind sharp with her scent invading his senses. "Ah, my English is sometimes awkward. You must forgive me."

She smiled again, wanting to ease his obvious discomfort. "Your English is wonderful."

"Is it clever enough to convince you to share a quiet lunch with me? As friends," he said, lacing his smile with regret. "With similar interests."

She glanced, as he did, at the babies. It was tempting, she admitted. He was a charming man—a wealthy and influential one. She might, with careful campaigning, persuade him to assist her in setting up an international branch of Falling Star, an ambition that had been growing in her lately.

"I would love to, Gregor, but right now I'm simply swamped. I was just on my way home when I ran into you. I have to check on some…repairs." That seemed the simplest way to explain it. "But I'd love to have a rain check. One I'd hope to cash in very soon. There's something concerning our similar interests that I'd love to have your advice on, and your input."

"I would love to be of any service whatsoever." He kissed her hand again. Tonight, he thought. He would have her tonight, and there would be no more need for this charade.

"That's so kind of you." Because she felt guilty for her disinterest and coolness in the face of his interest, she kissed his cheek. "I really must run. Do call me about that rain check. Next week, perhaps, for lunch." With a final, flashing smile, she dashed off.

As he watched her, his fisted fingers dug crescents into his palms. Fighting for control, he nodded to one of the silent men who waited for him. "Follow her only," he ordered. "And wait for instructions."

Cade didn't think of himself as a whiner—and, considering how well he tolerated his own family, he believed himself one of the most patient, most amiable, of men. But he was certain that if Grace had him shift one more piece of furniture from one end of her enormous living area to the other, he would break down and weep.

"It looks great."

"Hmm…" She stood, one hand on her hip, the fingers of the other tapping against her lip.

The gleam in her eye was enough to strike terror in Cade's heart and had his already aching muscles crying out in protest. "Really, fabulous. A hundred percent. Get the camera. I see a cover of *House and Garden* here."

"You're wheedling, Cade," she said absently. "Maybe the conversation pit did look better facing the other way." His moan was pitiful, and only made her lips twitch. "Of course, that would mean the coffee table and those two accent pieces would have to shift. And the palm tree—isn't it a beauty?—would have to go there."

The beauty weighed fifty pounds if it weighed an ounce. Cade abandoned pride and whined. "I still have stitches," he reminded her.

"Ah, what's a few stitches to a big, strong man like you?" She fluttered at him, patted his cheek and watched his ego war with his sore back. Giving in, she let loose a long, rolling laugh. "Gotcha. It's fine, darling, absolutely fine. You don't have to carry another cushion."

"You mean it?" His eyes went puppylike with hope. "It's done?"

"Not only is it done, but you're going to sit down, put up your feet, while I go get you an icy beer that I stocked in my fridge just for tall, handsome private investigators."

"You're a goddess."

"So I've been told. Make yourself at home. I'll be right back."

When Grace came back bearing a tray, she saw that Cade had taken her invitation to heart. He sat back on the thick cobalt-blue cushions of her new U-shaped sofa arrangement, his feet propped on the mirror-bright surface of the ebony coffee table, his eyes shut.

"I really did wear you out, didn't I?"

He grunted, opened one eye. Then both popped open in appreciation when she set the loaded tray on the table. "Food," he said, and sprang for it.

She had to laugh as he dived into her offer of glossy green grapes, Brie and crackers, the heap of caviar on ice with toast points. "It's the least I can do for such an attractive moving man." Settling beside him, she picked up the glass of wine she'd poured for herself. "I owe you, Cade."

With his mouth half-full, he scanned the living room, nodded. "Damn straight."

"I don't just mean the manual labor. You gave me a safe haven when I needed one. And most of all, I owe you for Bailey."

"You don't owe me for Bailey. I love her."

"I know. So do I. I've never seen her happier. She was just waiting for you." Leaning over, Grace kissed his cheek. "I always wanted a brother. Now, with you and Jack, I have two. Instant family. They fit, too, don't they?" she commented. "M.J. and Jack. As if they've always been a team."

"They keep each other on their toes. It's fun to watch."

"It is. And speaking of Jack, I thought he was going to give you a hand with our little redecorating project."

Cade scooped caviar onto a piece of toast. "He had a skip to trace."

"A what?"

"A bail jumper to bring in. He didn't think it was going to take him long." Cade swallowed, sighed. "He doesn't know what he's missing."

"I'll give him the chance to find out." She smiled. "I still have plans for a couple of the rooms upstairs."

It gave Cade his opening. "You know, Grace, I wonder if you're rushing this a little. It's going to take some time to put a house this size back in shape. Bailey and I would like you to stay at our place for a while."

Their place, Grace mused. Already it was their place. "It's more than livable here, Cade. M.J. and I talked about it," she continued. "She and Jack are going to her apartment. It's time we all got back to our routines."

But M.J. wasn't going to be alone, Cade thought, and thoughtfully sipped his beer. "There's still somebody pulling the strings out there. Somebody who wants the Three Stars."

"I don't have them," Grace reminded him. "I can't get them. There's no reason to bother with me at this point."

"I don't know how much reason has to do with it, Grace. I don't like you being here alone."

"Just like a brother." Delighted with him, she gave his arm a squeeze. "Listen, Cade, I've got a new alarm system, and I'm considering buying a big, mean, ugly dog." She started to mention the pistol she had in her nightstand, and the fact that she knew how to use it, but thought that would only worry him more. "I'll be fine."

"What does Buchanan think?"

"I haven't asked him. He's going to come by later—so I won't really be alone."

Satisfied with that, Cade handed her a grape. "You've got him worried."

Her lips curved as she popped the grape into her mouth. "Do I?"

"I don't know him well—I don't think anyone does. He's…I guess *self-contained* would be the word. Doesn't let a lot show on the surface. But when

I walked in yesterday, after you'd gone upstairs, he was just standing there, looking up after you." Now Cade grinned. "There was plenty on the surface then. It was pretty illuminating. Seth Buchanan, human being." Then he winced, tipped back his beer. "Sorry, I didn't mean to—"

"It's all right. I know exactly what you mean. He's got an almost terrifying self control, and that impenetrable aura of authority."

"It seems to me that you've managed to dent the armor. In my opinion, that's just what he needed. You're just what he needed."

"I hope he thinks so. It turns out he's just what I needed. I'm in love with him." With a half laugh, she shook her head and sipped her wine. "I can't believe I told you that. I rarely tell men my secrets."

"Brothers are different."

She smiled at him. "Yes, they are."

"I hope Seth appreciates just how lucky he is."

"I don't think Seth believes in luck."

She suspected Seth didn't believe in the Three Stars of Mithra, either. And she had discovered that she did. In a very short time, she'd simply opened her mind, stretched her imagination and accepted. They had magic, and they had power. She had been touched by both—as had Bailey and M.J. and the men who were linked to them.

Grace had no doubt that whoever wanted that magic, that power, would stop at nothing to gain them. It wouldn't matter when they were in the museum. He would still crave them, still plot to possess them.

But he could no longer reach the stones through her.

That part of her connection, she thought with relief, was over. She was safe in her own home, and would learn to live there again. Starting now.

She dressed carefully in a long white dress of thin watered silk that left her shoulders bare and flirted with her ankles. Beneath the flowing silk she wore only skin, creamed and scented.

She left her hair loose, scooped back at the sides with silver combs, her mother's sapphire drops at her ears, gleaming like twin stars. On impulse, she'd clasped a thick silver bracelet high on her forearm—a touch of pagan.

When she looked into the mirror after dressing, she'd felt an odd jolt—as if she could see herself in the glass, with the faint ghost of someone else merged with her.

But she'd laughed it off, chalked it up to nerves and anticipation, and busied herself completing her preparations.

She filled the rooms she'd redone with candles and flowers, pleased with the welcome they offered. On the table by the window facing her side garden she arranged the china and crystal for her meticulously plotted dinner for two.

The champagne was iced, the music was on low and the lights were romantically dimmed. All she needed was the man.

Seth saw the candles in the windows when he pulled up in the drive. Fatigue layered over frustration and had him, in the dim light of the car, rubbing gritty eyes.

And there were candles in the windows.

He was forced to admit that for the first time in his

adult life he didn't have a handle on himself, or on the world around him. He certainly didn't have a handle on the woman who had lit those candles, and who was waiting in that soft, flickering light.

He'd moved on DeVane on pure instinct—and part of that instinct, he knew, was territorial. Nothing could have been more out of character for him. Perhaps that was why he was feeling slightly…out of himself. Out of control. Grace had become a center, a focal point.

Or was it an obsession?

Hadn't he come here because he couldn't keep away? Just as he had dug into DeVane's background because the man roused some primal defense mechanism.

Maybe that was how it started, Seth admitted, but his cop's instincts were still honed. DeVane was dirty. And with a little more time, a little more digging, he would link the man with the deaths surrounding the diamonds.

Without the diplomatic block, Seth thought, he had enough already to bring the man in for questioning. DeVane liked to collect—and he collected the rare, the precious, and frequently those items that held some whiff of magic.

And Gregor DeVane had financed an expedition the year before to search for the legendary Stars. A rival archaeologist had found them first, and the Washington museum had acquired them.

DeVane had lost more than two million dollars on the hunt and the Stars had slipped through his fingers.

And the rival archaeologist had met with a tragic and fatal accident three months after the find, in the jungles of Costa Rica.

Seth didn't believe in coincidence. The man who

had kept DeVane from possessing the diamonds was dead. And so, Seth had discovered, was the head of the expedition DeVane had put together.

No, he didn't believe in coincidence.

DeVane had been a resident of D.C. for nearly two years, on and off, without ever meeting Grace. Now, directly after Grace's connection with the Stars, the man was not only at the same social function, but happened to make a play for her?

Life simply wasn't that tidy.

A little more time, Seth promised himself, rubbing his temples to clear the headache. He'd find the solid connection—link DeVane to the Salvinis, to the bail bondsman, to the men who had died in a crashed van, to Carlo Monturri. He needed only one link, and then the rest of the chain would fall into place.

But at the moment, he needed to get out of the stuffy car, go inside and face what was happening to his personal life.

With a short laugh, Seth climbed out of the car. A personal life. Wasn't that part of the problem? He'd never had one, hadn't allowed himself one. Now, a matter of days after he'd met Grace, it was threatening to swallow him.

He needed time there, too, he told himself. Time to step back, gain some distance for a more objective look. He'd allowed things to move too fast, to get out of control. That would have to be fixed. A man who fell in love overnight couldn't trust himself. It was time to reassert some logic.

They were dynamically different—in backgrounds, in life-styles and in goals. Physical attraction was bound to fade, or certainly stabilize. He could al-

ready foresee her easing back once the initial excitement peaked. She'd grow restless, certainly annoyed
with the demands on his work. He would be neither
willing nor able to spin her through the social whirl
that was such an intricate part of her life.

She was bound to look toward someone else who
would. A beautiful woman, vital, sought-after, flattered
at every turn, wouldn't be content to light a candle in
the window for many nights.

He'd be doing them both a favor by slowing down,
stepping back. As he lifted a hand to the gleaming
brass knocker, he refused to hear the mocking voice
inside his head that called him a liar—and a coward.

She answered the knock quickly, as if she'd only
been waiting for it. She stood in the doorway, soft light
filtering through the long flow of white silk. The power
of her, pure and pagan, stopped his breath.

Though he kept his arms at his sides, she moved into
him, and ripped at his heart with a welcoming kiss.

"It's good to see you." Grace skimmed her fingers along his cheekbones, under his shadowed eyes.
"You've had a long one, Lieutenant. Come in and
relax."

"I haven't got a lot of time. I've got work." He
waited, saw the flicker of disappointment in her eyes.
It helped justify what he was determined to do. But
then she smiled, took his hand.

"Well, let's not waste what time you've got standing
in the foyer. You haven't eaten, have you?"

Why didn't she ask him why he couldn't stay? he
wondered, irrationally irritated. Why wasn't she com-
plaining? "No."

"Good. Sit down and have a drink. Can you have

a drink, or are you officially on duty?" She walked
into the living area as she spoke, then drew the chilling champagne from its silver bucket. "I don't suppose one glass would matter, in any case. And I won't
tell." She released the cork with an expert's twist and
a muffled, celebratory pop. "I've just put the canapés
out, so help yourself."

She gestured toward the silver tray on the coffee
table before moving off with a quiet, slippery rustle
of silk to pour two flutes.

"Tell me what you think. I worked poor Cade to
death pushing things around in here, but I wanted to
get at least the living space in order again quickly."

It looked as if it had been clipped from a glossy
magazine on perfect living. Nothing was out of place,
everything was gleaming and lovely. Bold colors mixed
with whites and blacks, tasteful knickknacks, and artwork that appeared to have been selected with incredible care over a long period of time.

Yet she'd done it in days—or hours. That, Seth supposed, was the power of wealth and breeding.

Yet the room didn't look calculated or cold. It looked
generous and welcoming. Soft surfaces, soft edges,
with touches that were so Grace everywhere. Antique
bottles in jewel tones, a china cat curled up for a nap,
a lush, thriving fern in a copper pot.

And flowers, candlelight.

He looked up, noted the unbroken gleam of wood
circling the balcony. "I see you've had it repaired."

Something's wrong, was all she could think as she
stepped forward and handed him his glass. "Yes, I
wanted that done as soon as possible. That, and the
new security system. I think you'll approve."

"I'll take a look at it, if you like."

"I'd like it better if you'd relax while you can. Why don't I bring dinner in?"

"You cooked?"

Now she laughed. "I wouldn't do that to you, but I'm an expert at ordering in—and at presentation. Try to unwind. I'll be right back."

As she glided out, he looked down at the tray. A silver bowl of glossy black caviar, little fancy bites of elegant finger foods. He turned his back on them and, carrying his glass, walked over to study her portrait.

When she came back, wheeling an antique cart, he continued to look at her painted face. "He was in love with you, wasn't he? The artist?"

Grace drew a careful breath at that cool tone. "Yes, he was. He knew I didn't love him. I often wished I could have. Charles is one of the kindest, gentlest men I know."

"Did you sleep with him?"

A chill snaked up her spine, but she kept her hands steady as she set plates on the candle-and-flower-decked table. "No. It wouldn't have been fair, and I care about him too much."

"You'd rather sleep with men you don't care about."

She hadn't seen it coming, Grace realized. How foolish of her not to have seen this coming. "No, but I won't sleep with men who I could hurt like that. I would have hurt Charles by being his lover, so I stayed his friend."

"And the wives?" He did turn now, eyes narrowed as he studied the woman instead of the portrait. "Like the woman who was married to that earl you were mixed up with? Didn't you worry about hurting her?"

Grace picked up her wine again, quite deliberately cocked her head. She had never slept with the earl he'd mentioned, or with any other married man. But she had never bothered to argue with public perception. Nor would she bother to deny it now.

"Why would I? I wasn't married to her."

"And the guy who tried to kill himself after you broke your engagement?"

She touched the glass to her lips, swallowed frothy wine that burned like shards of glass in her throat. "Overly dramatic of him, wasn't it? I don't think you're in the mood for Caesar salad and steak Diane, are you, Lieutenant? Rich food doesn't set well during interrogations."

"No one's interrogating you, Grace."

"Oh, yes, you are. But you neglected to read me my rights."

Her frigid anger helped justify his own. It wasn't the men—he knew it wasn't the men he'd very deliberately tossed in her face that scraped at him. It was the fact that they didn't matter to him, that somehow nothing seemed to matter but her.

"It's odd you're so sensitive about answering questions about men, Grace. You hadn't troubled to hide your…track record."

"I expected better from you." She said it softly, so he barely heard, then shook her head, smiled coolly. "Foolish of me. No, I've never troubled to hide anything— unless it mattered. The men didn't matter, for the most part. Do you want me to tell you that you're different? Would you believe me if I did?"

He was afraid he would. Terrified he would. "It isn't

necessary. We've moved too fast, Grace. I'm not comfortable with it."

"I see." She thought she did now, perfectly. "You'd like to slow things down." She set her glass aside, knowing her hand would start to shake. "It appears you've taken a couple of those giant steps while I've had my back turned. I really should have played that game as a child, so I'd be more alert for sudden moves."

"This isn't a game."

"No, I suppose it isn't." She had her pride, but she also had her heart. And she had to know. "How could you have made love with me like that this morning, Seth, and do this tonight? How could you have touched me the way you have—the way no one ever has—and hurt me like this?"

It was because of what had swamped him that morning, he realized. The helplessness of his need. "I'm not trying to hurt you."

"No, that only makes it worse. You're doing both of us a favor, aren't you? Isn't that how you've worked it out? Break things off before they get too messy? Too late." Her voice broke, but she managed to shore it up again. "It's already messy."

"Damn it." He took a step toward her, then stopped dead when her head whipped up, and those hot blue eyes scorched him.

"Don't even think about touching me now, when those thoughts are still in your head. You go your tidy way, Lieutenant, and I'll go mine. I don't believe in slowing down. You either go forward, or you stop."

Furious with herself, she lifted a hand and flicked a tear off her cheek. "Apparently, we've stopped."

Chapter 11

He stood there wondering what in the hell he was doing. Here was the woman he loved, who—by some wild twist of fate—might actually love him. Here was a chance for that life he'd never allowed himself, the family, the home, the woman. He was pushing them all away, with both hands, and couldn't seem to stop.

"Grace...I want to give us both time to consider what we're doing, where this is going."

"No, you don't." She tossed back her hair with one angry jerk of her head. "Do you think because I've only known you a matter of days that I don't understand how your head works? I've been more intimate with you than I've been with anyone in my life. I *know* you." She managed a deep, ragged breath. "What you want is to get that wheel back under your hands, that control button back under your thumb. This whole thing has run away from you, and you just can't let that happen."

"That may be true." Was true, he realized. Was absolutely, mortifyingly true. "But it doesn't change the point. I'm in the middle of an investigation, and I'm not as objective as I need to be, because I'm involved with you. After it's done—"

"After it's done, what?" she demanded. "We pick up where you left off? I don't think so, Lieutenant. What happens when you're in the middle of the next investigation? And the next? Do I strike you as someone who's going to wait around until you have the time, and the room, to continue an on-again, off-again relationship with me?"

"No." His spine stiffened. "I'm a cop, and my work takes priority."

"I don't believe I've ever asked you to change that. In fact, I found your dedication to your work admirable, attractive. Even heroic." Her smile was thin and brief. "But that's irrelevant, and so is this conversation." She turned away, picked up her wine again. "You know the way out."

No, she'd never asked him to change anything. Never questioned his work. What the hell had he done? "This needs to be discussed."

"That's your style, not mine. Do you actually think you can stand here, in my home…" Her voice began to hitch and jerk. "In my home, and break my heart, dump me and expect a civilized conversation? I want you *out*." She slammed her glass down, snapping the fragile stem of the glass, splattering wine. "Right now."

Where had the panic come from? he wondered. His

beeper went off and was ignored. "We're not leaving it this way."

"Exactly this way," she corrected. "Do you think I'm stupid? Do you think I don't see that you walked in here tonight looking to pick a fight so that it would end exactly this way? Do you think I don't know now that no matter how much I gave you, you'd hold back from me, question, analyze, dissect everything? Well, analyze this. I was willing to give more, whatever you wanted to take. Now you can spend the rest of your life wondering just what you lost here tonight."

As his beeper sounded again, she swept by him, wrenched open the front door. "You'll have to answer that call of duty elsewhere, Lieutenant."

He stepped to her, but, though his arms ached, he resisted the need to reach out. "When I'm done with this, I'm coming back."

"You won't be welcome."

He could feel himself step up to a line he'd never crossed. "That isn't going to matter. I'm coming back."

She said nothing at all, simply shut the door in his face and turned the lock with a hard, audible click.

She leaned back against the door, her breath shallow now, and hot, as pain swept through her. It was worse now that the door was closed, now that she had shut him out. And the candles still flickered, the flowers still bloomed.

She saw that every step she'd taken that day, and the day before, all they way back to the moment she'd walked into her own home and seen him coming down the stairs toward her, had been leading to this moment of blind grief and loss.

She'd been powerless to stop it, she thought, to

change what she was, what had come before or what would come after. It was only fools who believed they controlled their own destiny as she'd once believed she controlled hers.

And she'd been a fool to indulge in those pathetic fantasies, dreams where they had belonged together, where they'd made a life together, a home and children together. Where she'd believed she was only waiting for him to finally make all those longings that had always, always, been one handspan out of her reach, come true.

The mythical power of the stones, she thought with a half laugh. Love, knowledge and generosity. Their magic had been cruel to her, giving her that tantalizing glimpse of her every desire, then wrenching it away again and leaving her alone.

The knock on the door had her closing her eyes. How dare he come back, she thought. How dare he, after he'd smashed all her dreams, her hopes, her needs. And how dare she still love him in spite of it.

Well, he wouldn't see her cry, she promised herself, and straightened to scrub her hands over her damp cheeks. He wouldn't see her crawl. He wouldn't see her at all, because she wouldn't let him in.

Resolutely she headed for the phone. He wouldn't be pleased when she called 911 and reported an intruder, she mused. But it would make her point. She picked up the receiver just as the sound of shattering glass had her whirling toward her terrace doors.

She had time to see the man burst through them, time to hear her alarm scream in warning. She even had time to struggle as thick arms grabbed her. Then the cloth was over her face, smelling sickeningly of chloroform.

And she had time only to think of Seth before her world spun and went black.

Seth was barely three miles away when the next call came through. He jerked up his phone, snarled into it. "Buchanan."

"Lieutenant, Detective Marshall again. I just heard an automatic come through on dispatch. Suspected break-in, 2918 East Lark Lane, Potomac."

"What?" For one stunning moment, his mind went blank. "Grace?"

"I recognized the address from the homicide. Her alarm system's been triggered, she didn't answer the check-in call."

"I'm five minutes from there." He was already swinging around in a fast, tire-squealing turn. "Get the two closest black-and-whites on the scene. Now."

"I'm already on it. Lieutenant—"

But Seth had already tossed the phone aside.

It was a new system, Seth told himself, fighting for calm and logic. New systems often had glitches.

She was upset, not answering her phone, ignoring the confusion. It would be just like her. She was even now defiantly pouring herself another glass of champagne, cursing him.

Maybe she'd even set off the alarm herself, just so he'd come streaking back with his stomach encased in ice and his heart paralyzed. It would be just like her.

And that was one more lie, he thought as he careened around a corner. It was nothing like her at all.

The candles were still burning in her windows. He

tried to be relieved by that as he stood on the brakes in her driveway and bolted out of his car. Dinner would still be warm, the music would still be playing, and Grace would be there, standing under her portrait, furious with him.

He beat on the door foolishly, wildly, before he snapped himself back. She wouldn't answer. She was too angry to answer. When the first patrol car pulled up, he turned, flashed his badge.

"Check the east side," he ordered. "I'll take the west."

He turned on his heel, started around the side. He caught the glimmer of the blue water in her pool in the moonlight, and the thought slid in and out of his mind that they'd never used it together, never slipped into that cool water naked.

Then he saw the broken glass. His heart simply stopped. His weapon was in his hand and he was through the shattered door, with no thought to procedure. Someone was shouting her name, racing from room to room in blind panic. It couldn't be him, yet he found himself on the stairs, short of breath, ice cold, dizzy with fear and watching a uniformed cop bend to pick up a scrap of cloth.

"Smells like chloroform, Lieutenant." The officer hesitated, took a step toward the man clinging to the banister. "Lieutenant?"

He couldn't speak. His voice was gone, and every sweaty hour of training with it. Seth's dulled gaze shifted, focused on the face, the portrait. Slowly, and with great effort, he widened his vision again, pulled on the mask of control.

"Search the house. Every inch of it." His eyes locked

on the second uniform. "Call in for backup. Now. Then make a sweep of the grounds. Move."

Grace came to slowly, with a roll of nausea and a blinding headache. A nightmare, still black at the edges, circled dully, like a vulture patiently waiting to drop. She squeezed her eyes tighter, rolled her head on the pillow, then cautiously opened them.

Where? The thought was dull, foolish. Not my room, she realized, and struggled to fight off the clinging mists that clouded her brain.

It was satin beneath her cheek. She knew the cool, slippery feel of satin against the skin. White satin, like a bride's dress. Baffled, she skimmed her hand over the thick, luxurious spread of the huge canopied bed.

She could smell jasmine, and roses, and vanilla. All white scents, cool white scents. The walls of the room were ivory and had a sheen like silk. For a moment, she thought she was in a coffin, a huge, elaborate coffin, and her heart beat thick and fast.

She made herself sit up, almost afraid that her head would hit the lid and she would find herself screaming and clawing for freedom as she smothered. But there was nothing, only that fragrant air, and she took a long, unsteady breath of it.

She remembered now—the crash of glass, the big man in black with thick arms. She wanted to panic and forced herself to take another of those jerky breaths. Carefully, hampered by her spinning head, she slid her legs over the edge of the bed until her feet sank into thick, virginal white carpet. She swayed, nearly retched, then forced her feet over that sea of white to the door.

She went slippery with panic when the knob resisted her. Her breath came in ragged gulps as she fought and tugged on the knob of faceted crystal. Then she turned her back, leaned against it and made herself survey what she understood now was her prison.

White on white on white, blinding to the eye. A dainty Queen Anne chair brocaded in white, filmy lace curtains hung like ghosts, heaps of white pillows on a curved white chaise. There were edges of gold that only enhanced the avalanche of white, elegant furniture in pale wood smothered in that snowfall.

She went to the windows first, shuddered when she found them barred, the slices of night beyond them silvered by the moon. She saw nothing familiar—a long roll of lawn, meticulously planted flowers and shrubs, tall, shielding trees.

Wheeling, she saw another door, bolted for it, nearly wept when the knob turned easily. But beyond was a lustrous bath, white-tiled, the frosted-glass windows barred, the angled skylight a soaring ten feet above the floor.

And on the long gleaming counter were jars, bottles, creams, powders. All her own preferences, her scents, her lotions. Her stomach knotted greasily.

Ransom, she told herself. It was a kidnapping, someone who believed her family could be forced to pay for her safe return.

But she knew that was a lie.

The Stars. She leaned weakly against the jamb, pressed her lips together to keep the whimper silent. She'd been taken because of the Three Stars. They would be her ransom.

Her knees trembled as she turned away, ordered herself to calm down, to think clearly. There had to be a way out. There always was.

Her alarm had gone off, she remembered. Seth couldn't have been far away. Would he have gotten the report, come back? It didn't matter. He would have gotten it soon enough. Whatever had happened between them, he would do everything in his power to find her. From duty, if nothing else.

In the meantime, she was on her own. But that didn't mean she was defenseless.

She took two stumbling steps back when the lock on her door clicked, then forced herself to stop, straighten. The door opened, and two men stepped inside. One she recognized quickly enough as her abductor. The other was smaller, wiry, dressed in formal black, with a face as giving as rock.

"Ms. Fontaine," he said in a voice both British and cultured. "If you'd come with me, please."

A butler, she realized, and had to swallow a bubble of hysteria. She knew the type too well, and she assumed an amused and annoyed expression. "Why?"

"He's ready to see you now."

When she made no move to obey, the bigger man stepped in, towering over her, then jerked a thumb toward the doorway.

"Charming," she said dryly. She took a step forward, calculating how quickly she would have to move. The butler inclined his head impassively.

"You're on the third floor," he told her. "Even if you could somehow reach the main level on your own, there are guards. They are under order not to harm you, unless it's unavoidable. If you'll pardon me, I would advise against risking it."

She would risk it, she thought, and a great deal more. But not until she had at least an even chance of success. Without so much as a flick of a glance at the man beside her, she followed the butler out of the room and down a gently lit corridor.

The house was old, she calculated, but beautifully restored. At least three stories, so it was large. A glimpse at her watch told her it had been less than two hours since she was drugged. Time enough to drive some distance, she imagined.

But the view through the bars hadn't been countryside. She'd seen lights—city lights, houses through the trees. A neighborhood, she decided. Exclusive, wealthy, but a neighborhood.

Where there were houses, there were people. And where there were people, there was help.

She was led down a wide, curving staircase of gleaming oak. And saw the guard at the landing, his gun holstered but visible.

Down another hallway. Antiques, paintings, artwork. Her eye was expert enough to recognize the Monet on the wall, the porcelain vase from the Han dynasty on a pedestal, the Nok terra-cotta head from Nigeria.

Her host, she thought, had excellent and eclectic taste. The treasures she saw, small and large, spanned continents and centuries.

A collector, she realized with a chill. Now he had her, and was hoping to trade her for the Three Stars of Mithra.

With what Grace considered absurd formality, under the circumstances, the butler approached tall double doors, opened them, and with seamless expertise bowed slightly from the waist.

"Miss Grace Fontaine."

Seeing no immediate alternative, she stepped through the open doors into an enormous dining room with a frescoed ceiling and a dazzling trio of chandeliers. She scanned the long mahogany table, the Georgian candelabra gaily lit and spaced at precise intervals down its length, and focused on the man who rose and smiled charmingly.

Her worlds overlapped—reality and fear. "Gregor."

"Grace." Elegant in his tux, diamonds winking, he crossed to her, took her numb hand in his. "How delightful to see you." He tucked her arm through his, patted it affectionately. "I don't believe you've dined."

He knew where she was. Seth had no doubt of it, but his first fiery urge to rush to the elegant estate in D.C. and tear it apart single-handedly had to be suppressed.

He could get her killed.

He was certain Ambassador Gregor DeVane had killed before.

The call that interrupted his scene with Grace had been confirmation of yet another woman who had once been linked to the ambassador, a beautiful German scientist who had been found murdered in her home in Berlin, the apparent victim of a bungled burglary.

The dead woman had been an anthropologist who had a keen interest in Mithraism. For six months during the previous year, she had been romantically linked with Gregor DeVane. Then she was dead, and none of her research notes on the Three Stars of Mithra had been recovered.

He knew DeVane was responsible, just as he knew DeVane had Grace. But he couldn't prove it, and he didn't have probable cause to sway any judge to issue a search warrant into the home of a foreign ambassador.

Once more he stood in Grace's living room. Once more he stared up at her portrait and imagined her dead. But this time, he wasn't thinking like a cop.

He turned as Mick Marshall stepped beside him. "We won't find anything here to link him. In twelve hours, the diamonds will be turned over to the museum. He's going to use her to see that doesn't happen. I'm going to stop him."

Mick looked up at the portrait. "What do you need?"

"No. No cops."

"Lieutenant...Seth, if you're right, and he's got her, you're not going to get her out alone. You need to put together a team. You need a hostage negotiator."

"There's no time. We both know that." His eyes weren't flat and cool now, weren't cop's eyes. They were full of storms and passions. "He'll kill her."

His heart was coated with a sheet of ice, but it beat with fiery heat inside the casing. "She's smart. She'll play whatever game she needs to in order to stay alive, but if she makes the wrong move he'll kill her. I don't need a psychiatric profile to see into his head. He's a sociopath with a god complex and an obsession. He wants those diamonds and what he believes they represent. Right now he wants Grace, but if she doesn't serve his purpose, she'll end up like the others. That's not going to happen, Mick."

He reached into his pocket, took out his badge and held it out. This time he wouldn't go by the book, couldn't afford to play by the rules. "You take this for me, hang on to it. I may want it back."

"You're going to need help," Mick insisted. "You're going to need men."

"No cops," Seth repeated, and pushed his badge into Mick's reluctant hand. "Not this time."

"You can't go in solo. It's suicide, professional and literal."

Seth cast one last glance at the portrait. "I won't be alone."

She wouldn't tremble, Grace promised herself. She wouldn't show him how frightened she was. Instead, she brushed her hair from her shoulder with a careless hand.

"Do you always have your dinner companions abducted from their homes and drugged, Ambassador?"

"You must forgive the clumsiness." Considerately he drew out a chair for her. "It was necessary to be quick. I trust you're suffering no ill effects."

"Other than great annoyance, no." She sat, skimmed her gaze over the dish of marinated mushrooms a silent servant placed before her. They reminded her, painfully, of the noise-filled cookout at Cade's. "And a loss of appetite."

"Oh, you must at least sample the food." He sat at the head of the table, picked up his fork. It was gold and heavy and had once slipped between the lips of an emperor. "I've gone to considerable trouble to have your favorites prepared." His smile remained genial, but his eyes went cold. "Eat, Grace. I detest waste."

"Since you've gone to such lengths." She forced

down a bite, ordered her hand not to shake, her stomach not to revolt.

"I hope your room is comfortable. I had to have it prepared for you rather quickly. You'll find appropriate clothing in the armoire and bureau. You've only to ask if there's something else you wish."

"I prefer windows without bars, and doors without locks."

"Temporary precautions, I promise you. Once you're at home here..." his hand covered hers, the grip tightening cruelly when she attempted to pull away "...and I do very much want you to be at home here, such measures won't be necessary."

She didn't wince as the bones in her hand ground together. When she stopped the resistance, his fingers relaxed, stroked once, then slid away.

"And just how long do you intend to keep me here?"

He smiled, picked up her wineglass, held it out to her. "Eternity. You and I, Grace, are destined to share eternity."

Under the table, her aching hand shook and went clammy. "That's quite some time." She started to set her wine down, untouched, then caught the hard glint in his eye and sipped. "I'm flattered, but confused."

"It's pointless to pretend you don't understand. You held the Star in your hand. You survived death, and you came to me. I've seen your face in my dreams."

"Yes." She could feel her blood drain slowly, as if leeched out of her veins. Looking into his eyes she remembered the nightmares—the shadow in the woods. Watching. "I've seen you in mine."

"You'll bring me the Stars, Grace, and the power. I understand why I failed now. Every step was simply another on the path that brought us here. Together we'll possess the Stars. And I will possess you. Don't worry," he said when she flinched. "You'll come to me a willing bride. But my patience has limits. Beauty is my weakness," he continued, and skimmed a fingertip down her bare arm, toyed idly with the thick silver bracelet she wore. "And perfection my greatest delight. You, my dear, have both. Understand, you'll have no choice should my patience run out. My household staff is…well trained."

Fear was a bright, icy flash, but her voice was steady with disgust. "And would turn a deaf ear and blind eye to rape?"

"I don't enjoy that word during dinner." He gave a sulky little shrug and signaled for the next course. "A woman of your appetites will grow hungry soon enough. And one of your intelligence will undoubtedly see the wisdom of an amiable partnership."

"It's not sex you want, Gregor." She couldn't bear to look down at the tender pink salmon on her plate. "It's subjugation. I'm so poor at subjugation."

"You misunderstand me." He forked up fish and ate with enjoyment. "I intend to make you a goddess, and subject to no one. And I will have everything. No mortal man will come between us." He smiled again. "Certainly not Lieutenant Buchanan. The man is becoming a nuisance. He's probing into my affairs, where he has no business probing. I've seen him…"

DeVane's voice trailed off to a whisper, and there was a hint of fear in it. "In the night. In my dreams. He comes back. He always comes back. No matter how often I kill him." Then his eyes cleared, and he sipped wine the color of melted gold. "Now he's stirring up old business and looking for new."

She could feel the alarming beat of her pulse in her throat, at her wrists, in her temples. "He'll be looking for me, very soon now."

"Possibly. I'll deal with him, when and if the time comes. That could have been tonight, had he not left you so abruptly. Oh, I have considered just what will be done about the lieutenant. But I prefer to wait until I have the Stars. It's possible…" Thoughtfully DeVane picked up his napkin, dabbed at his lips. "I may spare him once I have what belongs to me. If you wish it. I can be magnanimous…under the right circumstances."

Her heart was in her throat now, filling it, blocking it. "If I do what you want, you'll leave him alone?"

"It's possible. We'll discuss it. But I'm afraid I developed an immediate dislike for the man. And I am still annoyed with you, dear Grace, for rejecting my own invitation for such an ordinary man."

She didn't hesitate, couldn't afford to, while her mind whirled with fear for Seth. She made her lips curve silkily. "Gregor, surely you forgive me for that. I was so…crushed when you didn't press your case. A woman, after all, enjoys a more determined pursuit."

"I don't pursue. I take."

"Obviously." She pouted. "It was horrid of you to have manhandled me that way, and frightened me half to death. I may not forgive you for it."

"Be careful how deep you play the game." His voice was low with warning and, she thought, with interest. "I'm not green."

"No." She skimmed a hand over his cheek before she rose. "But maturity has so many advantages."

Her legs were watery, but she roamed the cavernous room, her gaze traveling quickly toward windows, exits. Escape. "You have such a beautiful home. So many treasures." She angled her head, hoped the challenge she issued was worth the risk. "I do love…things. But I warn you, Gregor, I won't be any man's pretty toy."

She walked to him slowly, skimming a fingertip down her throat, between her breasts, while the silk she wore whispered around her. "And when I'm backed into a corner…I scratch."

Seductively she laid a hand on the table, leaned toward him. "You want me?" she breathed it, purred it, watching his eyes darken, sliding her fingers toward the knife beside his plate. "To touch me? To have me?" Her fingers closed over the handle, gripped hard.

"Not in a hundred lifetimes," she said as she struck.

She was fast, and she was desperate. But he'd shifted to draw her to him, and the knife struck his shoulder instead of his heart. As he cried out in shock and rage, she whirled. Grabbing one of the heavy chairs, she smashed the long window and sent glass raining out. But when she leaped forward, strong arms grabbed her from behind.

She fought viciously, her breath panting out. The fragile silk she wore ripped. Then she froze when the knife she had used was pressed against her throat. She didn't bother to struggle against the arms that held her as DeVane leaned his face close to hers. His eyes were mad with fury.

"I could kill you for that. But it would be too little and too quick. I would have made you my equal.

I would have shared that with you. Now I'll just take what I choose from you. Until I tire of you."

"You'll never get the Stars," she said steadily. "And you'll never get Seth."

"I'll have exactly what I choose. And you'll help me."

She started to shake her head, flinched as the blade nicked. "I'll do nothing to help you."

"But you will. If you don't do exactly as I tell you, I will pick up the phone. With one single word from me, Bailey James and M. J. O'Leary will die tonight. It will only take a word."

He saw the wild fear come into her eyes, the helpless terror that hadn't been there for her own life. "I have men waiting for that word. If I give it, there will be a terrible and tragic explosion in the night at Cade Parris's home. Another at a small neighborhood pub, just before closing. And as one last twist, a third explosion will destroy the home, and the single occupant, of a certain Lieutenant Buchanan's residence. Their fate is in your hands, Grace. And the choice is yours."

She wanted to call his bluff, but, staring into his eyes, she understood that he wouldn't hesitate to do as he threatened. No, he longed to do it. Their lives meant nothing to him. And everything to her.

"What do you want me to do?"

Bailey was fighting against panic when the phone rang. She stared at it as if it were a snake that had rattled into life. With a silent prayer, she lifted the receiver. "Hello?"

"Bailey."

"Grace." Her fingers went white-knuckled as she

whirled. Seth shook his head, held up a hand in caution. "Are you all right?"

"For the moment. Listen very carefully, Bailey, my life depends on it. Do you understand?"

"No. Yes." Stall, she knew she'd been ordered to stall. "Grace, I'm so frightened for you. What happened? Where are you?"

"I can't go into that now. You have to be calm, Bailey. You have to be strong. You were always the calm one. Like when we took that art history exam in college and I was so intimidated by Professor Greenbalm, and you were so cool. You have to be cool now, Bailey, and you have to follow my instructions."

"I will. I'll try." She looked helplessly at Seth as he signaled her to stretch it out. "Just tell me if you're hurt."

"Not yet. But he will hurt me. He'll kill me, Bailey, if you don't do what he wants. Get him what he wants. I know I'm asking a great deal. He wants the stones. You have to go get them. You can't take Cade. You can't call…the police."

String it out, Bailey reminded herself. Keep Grace talking. "You don't want me to call Seth?"

"No. He isn't important. He's just another cop. You know he doesn't matter. You're to wait until 1:30 exactly, then you're to leave the house. Go to Salvini, Bailey. You've got to go to Salvini. Leave M.J. out of it, just like we used to. Understand?"

Bailey nodded, kept her eyes on Seth's. "Yes, I understand."

"Once you get to Salvini, put the stones in a briefcase. Wait there. You'll get a call with the next set of instructions. You'll be all right. You know how you used to like to sneak out of the dorm at night and go out driving alone after curfew? Just think of it that way. Exactly that way, Bailey, and you'll be fine. If you don't, he'll take everything away from me. Do you understand?"

"Yes. Grace—"

"I love you," she managed before the phone went dead.

"Nothing," Cade said tightly as he stared down at the tracing equipment. "He's got it jammed. The signal's all over the board. It wouldn't home in."

"She wants me to go to Salvini," Bailey said quietly.

"You're not going anywhere," Cade said, interrupting her, but Bailey laid a hand on his arm, looked toward M.J.

"No, she meant that part. You understood?"

"Yeah." M.J. pressed her fingers to her eyes, tried to think past the terror. "She was pumping in as much as she could. Bailey and Grace never left me out of anything, so she wanted me along. She wants us out of here, but she was stringing him about the stones. Bailey never jumped curfew."

"She was giving you signals," Jack said. "Trying to punch in what she could manage."

"She knew we'd understand. He must have told her something would happen to us if she didn't cooperate." Bailey reached out for M.J.'s hand. "She wanted us to contact Seth. That's why she said you didn't matter—because we know you do."

Seth dragged a hand through his hair—a rare wasted motion. He had no choice but to trust their instincts. No choice but to trust Grace's sense of survival. "All right. She wants me to know what's happening, and wants you out of the house."

"Yes. She wants us out of the house, thinks we'll be safer at Salvini."

"You'll be safer at the precinct," Seth told her. "And that's where both of you are going."

"No." Bailey's voice remained calm. "She wants us at Salvini. She made a point of it."

Seth studied her, and gauged his options. He could have them taken into protective custody. That was the logical step. Or he could let the game play out. That was a risk. But it was the risk that fit.

"Salvini, then. But Detective Marshall will arrange for guards. You'll stay put until you hear differently."

M.J. bristled. "You expect us to just sit around and wait while Grace is in trouble?"

"That's exactly what you're going to do," Seth said coolly. "She's risking her life to see that you're safe. I'm not going to disappoint her."

"He's right, M.J." Jack lifted a brow as she snarled at him. "Go ahead and fume. But you're outnumbered here. You and Bailey follow instructions."

Seth noted with some surprise that M.J. closed her mouth, gave one brisk nod in assent. "What was the business about the art history exam, Bailey?"

Bailey sucked in air. "Professor Greenbalm's first name was Gregory."

"Gregory." *Gregor.* "Close enough." Seth looked at the two men he needed. "We don't have a lot of time."

Chapter 12

Grace doubted very much that she would live through the night. There were so many things she hadn't done. She had never shown Bailey and M.J. Paris, as they had always planned. She would never see the willow she'd planted on her country hillside grow tall and bend gracefully over her tiny pond. She had never had a child.

The unfairness clawed at her, along with the fear. She was only twenty-six years old, and she was going to die.

She'd seen her sentence in DeVane's eyes. And she knew he intended to kill those she loved, as well. He wouldn't be satisfied with anything less than erasing all the lives that had touched what his obsessed mind considered his.

All she could hang on to now was the hope that Bailey had understood her.

"I'm going to show you what you could have had." His arm bandaged, a fresh tuxedo covering the damage, DeVane led her through a concealed panel, and down a well-lit set of stone stairs that were polished like ebony. He'd taken a painkiller. His eyes were glassy with it, and vicious.

They were the eyes that had stared out of the woods in her nightmares. And as he walked down the curve of those glossy black stairs, she felt the tug of some deep memory.

By torchlight then, she thought hazily. Down and down, with the torches flickering and the Stars glittering in their home of gold, on a white stone. And death waiting.

The harsh breathing of the man beside her. DeVane's? Someone else's? It was a hot, secret sound that chilled the skin. A room, she thought, struggling to grip the slippery chain of memories. A secret room of white and gold. And she had been locked in it for eternity.

She stopped at the last curve, not so much in fear as in shock. Not here, she thought frantically, but somewhere else. Not her, but part of her. Not him, but someone like him.

DeVane's fingers dug into her arm, but she barely felt the pain. Seth—the man with Seth's eyes, dressed as a warrior, coated with dust and the dents of battle. He'd come for her, and for the Stars.

And died for it.

"No." The stairway spun, and she gripped the cool wall for balance. "Not again. Not this time."

"There's little choice." DeVane jerked her forward, pulled her down the remaining steps. He stopped at a thick door, gestured impatiently for his guard to step back. Holding Grace's arm in a bruising grip, he drew out a heavy key, fit it in an old lock that for reasons Grace couldn't fathom made her think of Alice's rabbit hole.

"I want you to see what could have been yours. What I would have shared with you."

At his rough shove, she stumbled inside and stood blinking in shock.

No, not the rabbit hole, she realized, her dazzled eyes wide and stunned. Ali Baba's cave. Gold gleamed in mountains, jewels winked in rivers. Paintings she recognized as works of the masters crowded together on the walls. Statues and sculpture, some as small as the Fabergé eggs perched on gold stands, others soaring to the ceiling, were jammed inside.

Furs and sweeps of silk, ropes of pearls, carvings and crowns, were jammed into every available space. Mozart played brilliantly on hidden speakers.

It was, she realized, not a fairy-tale cave at all. It was merely a spoiled boy's elaborate and greedy clubhouse. Here he could hide his possessions from the world, keep them all to himself and chortle over them, she imagined.

And how many of these toys had he stolen? she wondered. How many had he killed for?

She wouldn't die here, she promised herself. And neither would Seth. If this was indeed history overlapping, she wouldn't allow it to repeat itself. She would fight with whatever weapons she had.

"You have quite a collection, Gregor, but your presentation could use some work." The first weapon was mild disdain, laced with amusement. "Even the precious loses impact when crammed together in such a disorganized manner."

"It's mine. All of it. A lifetime's work. Here." Like that spoiled boy, he snatched up a goblet of gold, thrust it out to her for admiration. "Queen Guinevere sipped from this before she cuckolded Arthur. He should have cut out her heart for that."

Grace turned the cup in her hand and felt nothing. It was empty not only of wine, she mused, but of magic.

"And here." He grabbed a pair of ornate diamond earrings, thrust them into Grace's face. "Another queen—Marie Antoinette—wore these while her country plotted her death. You might have worn them."

"While you plotted mine." With deliberate scorn, she dismissed the offering and turned away. "No, thank you."

"I have an arrow the goddess Diana hunted with. The girdle worn by Juno."

Her heart thrummed like a harp, but she only chuckled. "Do you really believe that?"

"They're mine." Furious with her reaction, he pushed his way through his collection, laid a hand over the cold marble slab he'd had built. "I'll have the Stars soon. They will be the apex of my collection. I'll set them here, with my own hands. And I'll have everything."

"They won't help you. They won't change you." She didn't know where the words came from, or the knowledge behind them, but she saw his eyes flicker in surprise. "Your fate's already sealed. They'll never be yours. It's not meant, not this time. They're for the light, and for the good. You'll never see them here in the dark."

His stomach jittered. There was power in her words, in her eyes, when she should have been cowed and frightened. It unnerved him. "By sunrise I'll have them here. I'll show them to you." His breath was short and shallow as he approached her. "And I'll have you. I'll keep you as long as I wish. Do with you what I wish."

The hand against her cheek was cold, made her think wildly of a snake, but she didn't cringe away. "You'll never have the Stars, and you'll never have me. Even if you hold us, you'll never have us. That was true before, but it's only more true now. And that will eat away at you, day after day, until there's nothing left of you but madness."

He struck her, hard enough to knock her back against the wall, to have pain spinning in her head. "Your friends will die tonight." He smiled at her, as if he were discussing a small mutual interest. "You've already sent them to oblivion. I'm going to let you live a long time knowing that."

He took her by the arm and, pulling open the door, dragged her from the room.

"He'll have surveillance cameras," Seth said as they prepared to scale the wall at the rear of DeVane's D.C. estate. "He's bound to have guards patrolling the grounds."

"So we'll be careful." Jack checked the point of his knife, stuck it in his boot, then examined the pistol he'd tucked in his belt. "And we'll be quiet."

"We stick together until we reach the house." Cade

went over the plan in his head. "I find security, dis-arm it."

"Failing that, set the whole damn business off. We could get lucky in the confusion. It'll bring the cops. If things don't go well, you could be dealing with a lot more than a bust for a B-and-E."

Jack issued a pithy one-word opinion on that. "Let's go get her out." He shot Seth one quick grin as he boosted himself up. "Man, I hope he doesn't have dogs. I really hate when they have dogs."

They landed on the soft grass on the other side. It was possible their presence was detected from that moment. It was a risk they were willing to take. Like shadows, they moved through the starstruck night, slip-ping through the heavy dark amid the sheltering trees.

Before, on his quest for the Stars and the woman, he'd come alone, and perhaps that arrogance had been his defeat. Baffled by the sudden thought, the quick spurt of what some might have called vision, Seth pushed the feeling aside.

He could see the house through the trees, the glim-mer of lights in windows. Which room was she in? How badly was she frightened? Was she hurt? Had he touched her?

Baring his teeth, he bit off the thoughts. He had to focus only on getting inside, finding her. For the first time in years, he felt the weight of his weapon at his side. Knew he intended to use it.

He gave no thought to rules, to his career, to the life he'd built step by deliberate step.

He saw the guard pass by, only a yard beyond the verge of the grove. When Jack tapped his shoulder and signaled, Seth met his eyes, nodded.

Seconds later, Jack sprang at the man from behind, and with a quick twist, rammed his head into the trunk of an oak and then dragged the unconscious body into the shadows.

"One down," he breathed and tucked his newly acquired weapon away.

"They'll have regular check-in," Cade murmured. "We can't know how soon they'll miss his contact."

"Then let's move." Seth signaled Jack to the north, Cade to the south. Staying low, they rushed those gleaming lights.

The guard who escorted Grace back to her room was silent. At least two hundred and fifty pounds of muscle, she calculated. But she'd seen his eyes flicker down over her bodice, scan the ripped silk that exposed flesh at her side.

She knew how to use her looks as a weapon. Deliberately she tipped her face up to his, let her eyes fill helplessly. "I'm so frightened. So alone." She risked touching a hand to his arm. "You won't hurt me, will you? Please don't hurt me. I'll do anything you want."

He said nothing, but his eyes were keen on her face when she moistened her lips with the tip of her tongue, keeping the movement slow and provocative. "Anything," she repeated, her voice husky, intimate. "You're so strong, so...in charge." Did he even speak English? she wondered. What did it matter? The communication was clear enough.

At the door to her prison, she turned, flashed a smoldering look, sighed deeply. "Don't leave me alone," she murmured. "I'm so afraid of being alone. I need... someone." Taking a chance, she lifted a fingertip, rubbed it over his lips. "He doesn't have to know," she whispered. "No one has to know. It's our secret."

Though it revolted her, she took his hand, placed it on her breast. The flex of his fingers chilled her skin, but she made herself smile invitingly as he lowered his head and crushed her mouth.

Don't think of it, don't think, she warned herself as his hands roamed her. It's not you. He's not touching you.

"Inside." She hoped he interpreted her quick shudder as desire. "Come inside with me. We'll be alone."

He opened the door, his eyes still hungry on her face, on her body. She would either win here, she thought, or lose everything. She let out a teasing laugh as he grabbed for her the moment the door was locked behind him.

"Oh, there's no hurry now, handsome." She tossed her hair back, glided out of his reach. "No need to rush such a lovely friendship. I want to freshen up for you."

Still he said nothing, but his eyes were narrowing with impatience, suspicion. Still smiling, she reached for the heavy cut-crystal atomizer on the bureau. A woman's weapon, she thought coldly as she gently spritzed her skin, the air. "I prefer using all of my senses." Her fingers tightened convulsively on the bottle as she swayed toward him.

She jerked the bottle up and sprayed perfume directly into his leering eyes. He hissed in shock, grabbed instinctively for his stinging eyes. Putting all her strength behind it, she smashed the crystal into his face, and her knee into his groin.

He staggered, but didn't go down. There was blood on his face, and beneath it, his skin had gone a pasty shade of white. He was fumbling for his gun and, frantic, she kicked out, aiming low again. This time he went to his knees, but his hands were still reaching for the gun snapped to his side.

Sobbing now, she heaved up a footstool, upholstered in white, tasseled in gold. She rammed it into his already bleeding face, then, lifting it high, crashed it onto his head. Desperately she scrabbled to unstrap his gun, her clammy hands slipping off leather and steel. When she held it in two shaking hands, prepared to do whatever was necessary, she saw that he was unconscious.

Her breath tore out of her lungs in a wild laugh. "I guess I'm just not that kind of girl." Too frightened for caution, she yanked the keys free of his clip, stabbed one after the other at the lock until it gave. And raced like a deer fleeing wolves, down the corridor, through the golden light.

A shadow moved at the head of the stairs, and with a low, keening moan, she lifted the gun.

"That's the second time you've pointed a weapon in my direction."

Her vision grayed at the sound of Seth's voice. Clamping down hard on her lip, she cleared it as he stepped out of the shadows and into the light. "You. You came."

It wasn't armor he wore, she thought dizzily. But black—shirt, slacks, shoes. It wasn't a sword he carried, but a gun.

It wasn't a memory. It was real.

Her dress was torn, bloody. Her face was bruised, her eyes were glassy with shock. He'd killed two men to get this far. And seeing her this way, he thought it hadn't been enough. Not nearly enough.

"It's all right now." He resisted the urge to rush to her, grab her close. She looked as though she might shatter at a touch. "We're going to get you out. No one's going to hurt you."

"He's going to kill them." She forced air in and out of her lungs. "He's going to kill them no matter what I do. He's insane. They're not safe from him. We're none of us safe from him. He killed you before," she ended on a whisper. "He'll try again."

He took her arm to steady her, gently slipped the gun from her hand. "Where is he, Grace?"

"There's a room, through a panel in the library, down the stairs. Just like before…lifetimes ago. Do you remember?" Spinning between images, she pressed a hand to her head. "He's there with his toys, all the glittering toys. I stabbed him with a dinner knife."

"Good girl." How much of the blood was hers? He could detect no wound other than the bruises on her face and arms. "Come on now, come with me."

He led her down the stairs. There was the guard she'd seen before. But he wasn't standing now. Averting her eyes, she stepped around him, gestured. She was steadier now. The past didn't always run in a loop, she knew. Sometimes it changed. People made it change.

"It's back there, the third door down on the left." She cringed when she caught a movement. But it was Jack, melting out of a doorway.

"It's clear," he said to Seth.

"Take her out." His eyes said everything as he nudged her into Jack's arms. *Take care of her. I'm trusting you.*

Jack hitched her against his side to keep his weapon hand free. "You're okay, honey."

"No." She shook her head. "He's going to kill them. He has explosives, something, at the house, at the pub. You have to stop him. The panel. I'll show you."

She wrenched away from Jack, staggered like a drunk toward the library. "Here." She turned a rosette in the carving of the chair rail. "I watched him." The panel slid smoothly open.

"Jack, get her out. Call in a 911. I'll deal with him."

She was floating, just under the surface of thick, warm water. "He'll have to kill him," she said faintly as Seth disappeared into the opening. "This time he can't fail."

"He knows what he has to do."

"Yes, he always does." And the room spun once, wildly. "Jack, I'm sorry," she managed before she spun with it.

He hadn't locked the door, Seth noted. Arrogant bastard, so sure no one would trespass on his sacred ground. With his weapon lifted, Seth eased the heavy door open, blinked once at the bright gleam of gold.

He stepped inside, focused on the man sitting in a thronelike chair in the center of all the glory. "It's done, DeVane."

DeVane wasn't surprised. He'd known the man would come. "You risk a great deal." His smile was cold as a snake's, his eyes mad as a hatter's. "You did before. You remember, don't you? Dreamed of it, didn't you? You came to steal from me before, to take the Stars and the woman. You had a sword then, heavy and unjeweled."

Something vague and quick passed through Seth's mind. A stone castle, a stormy sky, a room of great wealth. A woman beloved. On an altar, a triangle wrenched from the hands of the god, adorned with diamonds as blue as stars.

"I killed you." DeVane laughed softly. "Left your body for the crows."

"That was then." Seth stepped forward. "This is now."

DeVane's smile spread. "I am beyond you." He lifted his hand, and the gun he held in it.

Two shots were fired, so close together they sounded as one. The room shook, echoed, settled, and went back to gleaming. Slowly Seth stepped closer, looked down at the man who lay facedown on a hill of gold.

"Now you are," Seth murmured. "You're beyond me now."

She heard the shots. For one unspeakable moment everything inside her stopped. Heart, mind, breath, blood. Then it started again, a tidal wave of feeling that had her springing off the bench where Jack had put her, the air heaving in and out of her lungs.

And she knew, because she felt, because her heart could beat, that it hadn't been Seth who'd met the bullet. If he had died, she would have known. Some piece of her heart would have broken off from the whole and shattered.

Still, she waited, her eyes on the house, because she had to see.

The stars wheeled overhead, the moon shot light through the trees. Somewhere in the distance, a night bird began to call out, with hope and joy.

Then he walked out of the house. Whole. Tears clogged her throat and were swallowed. They stung her eyes and were willed away. She had to see him clearly, the man she had accepted that she loved, and couldn't have.

He walked to her, his eyes dark and cool, his gait steady.

He'd already regained control, she realized. Already tucked whatever he'd had to do away in some compartment where it wouldn't interfere with what had to be done next.

She wrapped her arms around herself, hands clamped tight on her forearms. She'd never know that one gesture, that turning into herself and not him, was what stopped him from reaching for her.

So he stood, with an armspan of distance between them and looked at the woman he accepted that he loved, and had pushed away.

She was pale, and even now he could see the quick trembles that ripped through her. But he wouldn't have said she was fragile. Even now, with death shimmering between them, she wasn't fragile.

Her voice was strong and steady. "It's over?"

"Yeah, it's over."

"He was going to kill them."

"That's over, too." His need to touch her, to hold on, was overwhelming. He felt that his knees were about to give way. But she turned, shifted her body away, and looked out into the dark.

"I need to see them. Bailey and M.J."

"I know."

"You need my statement."

God. His control wavered enough for him to press his fingers against burning eyes. "It can wait."

"Why? I want it over. I need to put it behind me." She steadied herself again, then turned slowly. And when she faced him, his hands were at his sides and his eyes clear. "I need to put it all behind me."

Her meaning was clear enough, Seth thought. He was part of that all.

"Grace, you're hurt and you're in shock. An ambulance is on the way."

"I don't need an ambulance."

"Don't tell me what the hell you need." Fury swarmed through him, buzzed in his head like a nest of mad hornets. "I said the damn statement can wait. You're shaking. For God's sake, sit down."

When he reached out to take her arm, she jerked back, her chin snapping up, her shoulders hunching. "Don't touch me. Just…don't." If he touched her, she might break. If she broke she would weep. And weeping, she would beg.

The words were a knife in the gut, the deep and desperate blue of her eyes a blow to the face. Because he felt his fingers tremble, he stuffed them into his pockets, took a step back. "All right. Sit down. Please."

Had he thought she wasn't fragile? She looked as if she would shatter into pieces with one hard thought. She was sheet pale, her eyes enormous. Blood and bruises marked her face.

And there was nothing he could do. Nothing she would let him do.

He heard the distant wail of sirens, and footsteps from behind him. Cade, his face grim, walked to Grace, tucked a blanket he'd brought from the house over her shoulders.

Seth watched as she turned into him, how her body seemed to go fluid and flow into the arms Cade offered her. He heard the fractured sob even as she muffled it against Cade's shoulder.

"Get her out of here." His fingers burned to reach out, stroke her hair, to take something away with him. "Get her the hell out of here."

He walked back into the house to do what needed to be done.

The birds sang their morning song as Grace stepped out into her garden. The woods were quiet and green. And safe. She'd needed to come here, to her country escape. To come alone. To be alone.

Bailey and M.J. had understood. In a few days, she thought, she would go into town, call, see if they'd like to come up, bring Jack and Cade. She would need to see them soon. But she couldn't bear to go back yet. Not yet.

She could still hear the shots, the quick jolt of them shuddering through her as Jack had taken her outside. She'd known it was DeVane and not Seth who had met the bullet. She'd simply known.

She hadn't seen Seth again that night. It had been easy to avoid him in the confusion that followed. She'd answered all the questions the local police had asked, made statements to the government officials. She'd stood up to it, then quietly demanded that Cade or Jack take her to Salvini, take her to Bailey and M.J.

And the Three Stars.

Stepping down onto her blooming terraces, she brought it back into her head, and her heart. The three of them standing in the near dark of a near-empty room, she with her torn and bloody dress.

Each of them had taken a point of the triangle, had

felt the sing of power, seen the flicker of impossible light. And had known it was done.

"It's as if we've done this before," Bailey had murmured. "But it wasn't enough then. It was lost, and so were we."

"It's enough now." M.J. had looked up, met each of their eyes in turn. "Like a cycle, complete. A chain, with the links forged. It's weird, but it's right."

"A museum instead of a temple this time." Regret and relief had mixed within Grace as they set the Stars down again. "A promise kept, and, I suppose, destinies fulfilled."

She'd turned to both of them, embraced them. Another triangle. "I've always loved you both, needed you both. Can we go somewhere? The three of us." The tears had come then, flooding. "I need to talk."

She'd told them everything, poured out heart and soul, hurt and terror, until she was empty. And she supposed, because it was them, she'd healed a little.

Now she would heal on her own.

She could do it here, Grace knew, and, closing her eyes, she just breathed. Then, because it always soothed, she set down her gardening basket, and began to tend her blooms.

She heard the car coming, the rumble of wheels on gravel, and her brow creased in mild irritation. Her neighbors were few and far between and rarely intruded. She wanted no company but her plants, and she stood, her flowers flowing at her feet, determined to politely and firmly send the visitor away again.

Her heart kicked once, hard, when she saw that the car was Seth's. She watched in silence as it stopped in the middle of her lane and he got out and started toward her.

She looked like something out of a misty legend herself, he thought. Her hair blowing in the breeze, the long, loose skirt of her dress fluttering, and flowers in a sea around her. His nerves jangled.

And his stomach clutched when he saw the bruise marring her cheek.

"You're a long way from home, Seth." She spoke without expression as he stopped two steps beneath her.

"You're a hard woman to find, Grace."

"That's the way I prefer it. I don't care for company here."

"Obviously." Both to give himself time to settle and because he was curious, he scanned the land, the house perched on the hill, the deep secrets of the woods. "It's a beautiful spot."

"Yes."

"Remote." His gaze shifted back to hers so quickly, so intensely, he nearly made her jolt. "Peaceful. You've earned some peace."

"That's why I'm here." She lifted a brow. "And why are you here?"

"I needed to talk to you. Grace—"

"I intended to see you when I came back," she said quickly. "We didn't talk much that night. I suppose I was more shaken up than I realized. I never even thanked you."

It was worse, he realized, that cool, polite voice was worse than a shouted curse. "You don't have anything to thank me for."

"You saved my life and, I believe, the lives of the

people I love. I know you broke rules, even the law, to find me, to get me away from him. I'm grateful."

The palms of his hands went clammy. She was making him see it again, feel it again. All that rage and terror. "I'd have done anything to get you away from him."

"Yes, I think I know that." She had to look away. It hurt too much to look into his eyes. She'd promised herself, sworn to herself she wouldn't be hurt again. "And I wonder if any of us had a choice in what happened over that short, intense period of time. Or," she added with a ghost of a smile, "if you choose to believe what happened, over centuries. I hope you haven't— that your career won't suffer because of what you did for me."

His eyes went dark, flat. "The job's secure, Grace."

"I'm glad." He had to leave, she thought. He had to leave now, before she crumbled. "I still intend to write a letter to your superiors. And you might know I have an uncle in the Senate. I wouldn't be surprised, when the smoke clears, if you got a promotion out of it."

His throat was raw. He couldn't clear it. "Look at me, damn it." When her gaze shot back to his face, he curled his hands into fists to keep from touching her. "Do you think that matters?"

"Yes, I do. It matters, Seth, certainly to me. But for now, I'm taking a few days, so if you'll excuse me, I want to get to my gardening before the heat of the day."

"Do you think this ends it?"

She leaned over, took up her clippers and snipped off wilted blooms. They faded all too quickly, she thought. And that left an ache in the heart. "I think you already ended it."

"Don't turn away from me." He took her arm, hauled

her toward him, as panic and fury spiraled through him. "You can't just turn away. I can't—" He broke off, his hand lifting to lie on the bruise on her cheek. "Oh, God, Grace. He hurt you."

"It's nothing." She stepped back quickly, nearly flinching, and his hand fell heavily to his side. "Bruises fade. And he's gone. You saw to that. He's gone, and it's over. The Three Stars are where they belong, and everything's back in its place. Everything's as it was meant to be."

"Is it?" He didn't step to her, couldn't bear to see her shrink back from him again. "I hurt you, and you won't forgive me for it."

"Not entirely," she agreed, fighting to keep it light. "But saving my life goes a long way to—"

"Stop it," he said in a voice both ragged and quiet. "Just stop it." Undone, he whirled away, pacing, nearly trampling her bedding plants. He hadn't known he could suffer like this—the ice in the belly, the heat in the brain.

He spoke, looking out into her woods, into shadows and cool green shade. "Do you know what it did to me, knowing he had you? Knowing it. Hearing your voice on the phone, the fear in it?"

"I don't want to think about it. I don't want to think about any of that."

"I can't do anything but think of it. And see you— every time I close my eyes, I see you the way you stood there in that hallway, blood on your dress, marks on your skin. Not knowing—not knowing what he'd done to you. And remembering—half remembering some other time when I couldn't stop him."

"It's over," she said again, because her legs were turning to water. "Leave it alone."

"You might have gotten away without me," he continued. "You took out a guard twice your size. You might have pulled it off without any help from me. You might not have needed me at all. And I realized that was part of my problem all along. Believing, being certain, I needed you so much more than you could possibly need me. Being afraid of that. Stupid to be afraid of that," he said as he came up the steps again. "Once you understand real fear, the fear of knowing you could lose the most important thing in your life in one single heartbeat, nothing else can touch you."

He gathered her to him, too desperate to heed her resistance. And, with a shuddering gulp of air, buried his face in her hair. "Don't push me away, don't send me away."

"This isn't any good." It hurt to be held by him, yet she wished she could go on being held just like this, with the sun warm on her skin and his face pressed into her hair.

"I need you. I need you," he repeated, and turned his urgent mouth to hers.

The hammer blow of emotion struck and she buckled. It swirled from one of them to the other in an unbridled storm, left her heart shaken and weak. She closed her eyes, slid her arms around him. Need would be enough, she promised herself. She would make it enough for both of them. There was too much inside her that she ached to give for her to turn him away.

"I won't send you away." Her hands stroked over his back, soothed the tension. "I'm glad you're here.

I want you here." She drew back, brought his hand to her cheek. "Come inside, Seth. Come to bed."

His fingers tightened on hers. Then gently lifted her head up. It made him ache to realize she believed there was only that he wanted from her. That he'd let her think it.

"Grace, I didn't come here to take you to bed. I didn't come here to start where we left off."

Why had he been so resistant to seeing what was in her eyes? he wondered. Why had he refused to believe what was so blatantly real, so generously offered to him.

"I came here to beg. The third Star is generosity," he said, almost to himself. "You didn't make me beg. I didn't come here for sex, Grace. Or for gratitude."

Confused, she shook her head. "What do you want, Seth? Why did you come?"

He wasn't sure he'd fully realized why until just now. "To hear you tell me what you want. What you need."

"Peace." She gestured. "I have that here. Friendship. I have that, too."

"And that's it? That's enough?"

"It's been enough all my life."

He caught her face in his hands before she could step away. "If you could have more? What do you want, Grace?"

"Wanting what you can't have only makes you unhappy."

"Tell me." He kept his eyes focussed on hers. "Straight out, for once. Just say what you want."

"Family. Children. I want children and a man who loves me—who wants to make that family with me."

Her lips curved slowly, but the smile didn't reach her eyes. "Surprised I'd want to spoil my figure? Spend a few years of my life changing diapers?"

"No." He slid his hands down to her shoulders, firming his grip. She was poised to move, he noted. To run. "No, I'm not surprised."

"Really? Well." She moved her shoulders as if to shrug off the weight of his touch. "If you're going to stay, let's go inside. I'm thirsty."

"Grace, I love you." He watched her smile slide away from her face, felt her body go absolutely still.

"What? What did you say to me?"

"I love you." Saying it, he realized, was power. True power. "I fell in love with you before I'd seen you. Fell in love with an image, a memory, a wish. I can't be sure which it is, or if it was all of them. I don't know if it was fate, or choice, or luck. But it was so fast, so hard, so deep, I wouldn't let myself believe, and I wouldn't let myself trust. And I turned you away because you let yourself do both. I came here to tell you that." His hands slid down her arms and clasped hers.

"Grace, I'm asking you to believe in us again, to trust in us again. And to marry me."

"You—" She had to take a step back, had to press a hand to her heart. "You want to marry me."

"I'm asking you to come back with me today. I know it's old-fashioned, but I want you to meet my family."

The pressure in her chest all but burst her heart. "You want me to meet your family."

"I want them to meet the woman I love, the woman I want to have a life with. The life I've been waiting to start—waiting for her to start." He brought her hand to his cheek, held it there while his eyes looked deep into hers. "The woman I want to make children with."

"Oh." The weight on her chest released in a flood, poured out of her...until her heart was in her swimming eyes.

"Don't cry." It seemed he would beg after all. "Grace, please, don't. Don't tell me I left it too late." Awkwardly he brushed at her tears with his thumbs. "Don't tell me I ruined it."

"I love you so much." She closed her fingers around his wrists, watched the emotion leap into his eyes. "I've been so unhappy waiting for you. I was so sure I'd missed you. Again. Somehow."

"Not this time." He kept his hands on her face, kissed her gently. "Not ever again."

"No, not ever again," she murmured against his lips.

"Say yes," he asked her. "I want to hear you say yes."

"Yes. To everything."

She held him close in the flower-scented morning where the stars slept behind the sky. And felt the last link of an endless chain fall into place.

"Seth."

He kept his eyes shut, his cheek on her hair. And his smile bloomed slow and easy. "Grace."

"We're where we're supposed to be. Can you feel it?" She drew a deep breath. "All of us are where we belong now."

She lifted her face, found his mouth waiting. "And now," he said quietly, "it begins."

* * * * *

HARLEQUIN
PLUS

Announcing a **BRAND-NEW** multimedia subscription service for romance fans like you!

Read, Watch and Play.

Experience the easiest way to get the romance content you crave.

Start your **FREE 7 DAY TRIAL** at <u>www.harlequinplus.com/freetrial</u>.